# THE SILENT WAR

*Also by Victor Pemberton*

Our Family
Our Street
Our Rose

# THE SILENT WAR

Victor Pemberton

HEADLINE

Copyright © 1996 Victor Pemberton

The right of Victor Pemberton to be identified as the Author
of the Work has been asserted by him in accordance with the
Copyright, Designs and Patents Act 1988.

First published in 1996
by HEADLINE BOOK PUBLISHING

10 9 8 7 6 5 4 3

All rights reserved. No part of this publication may be
reproduced, stored in a retrieval system, or transmitted,
in any form or by any means without the prior written
permission of the publisher, nor be otherwise circulated
in any form of binding or cover other than that in which
it is published and without a similar condition being
imposed on the subsequent purchaser.

All characters in this publication are fictitious
and any resemblance to real persons, living or dead,
is purely coincidental.

British Library Cataloguing in Publication Data

Pemberton, Victor
The silent war
1.English fiction – 20th century
I.Title
823.9′14 [F]

ISBN 0 7472 1682 7

Typeset by Palimpsest Book Production Limited,
Polmont, Stirlingshire
Printed and bound in Great Britain by
Mackays of Chatham PLC, Chatham, Kent

HEADLINE BOOK PUBLISHING
A division of Hodder Headline PLC
338 Euston Road
London NW1 3BH

For Beryl,

a dear friend, with love,

and dedicated to all those
who lived through their own
'Silent War'

# *Chapter 1*

Sunday hated her name. For as long as she could remember she had always resented being named after a day of the week instead of being called something nice and ordinary, like Gladys or Lilian or Mary. Of course, she blamed it all on her mum and dad, not her real mum and dad, but the ones who adopted her when, as a newborn baby, she was found one Sunday evening, abandoned in a brown paper carrier bag on the steps of the Salvation Army Hall near Highbury Corner in Islington, North London. She got so fed up with the endless jibes from the girls she worked with down the Bagwash. At closing time on Saturday afternoons it was always the same old parting yells of 'See yer Monday – Sunday!' as they all streamed out into the yard outside, screeching with laughter at their same old worn-out gags.

It was way back in 1930 when old Ma Briggs first opened her Bagwash premises in a grubby back-street mews just off the Holloway Road. Once used as an old brewer's stable-yard, it was a place where, for a few coppers, customers could bring their dirty washing wrapped up in a bed-sheet, and get it boiled and scrubbed clean in one of three stone tubs. It was then squeezed out through the rollers of a huge iron mangle until it was drained of water, wrapped up neatly in a bundle, and tied up again in the bed-sheet ready for collection. Briggs Bagwash was a real hell-hole of a place to work in, especially for a seventeen-year-old like Sunday Collins. It was stiflingly hot both in summer and winter, with hot steam constantly curling up from the boiling water in the three huge tubs, which were heated by the cheapest coke available. Even worse was the pungent smell of soap suds, washing soda, and carbolic soap, which at times was so powerful that one or two of the younger 'Baggies' (as the girls were known locally) had just fainted away for lack of fresh air. But this was May 1944, and with the war now in its fifth year, young girls were lucky to have a paid job at all.

'Collins!'

To Sunday, the high-pitched squeal of Ma Briggs's voice was like a hot knife through butter. 'Yes, Mrs Briggs?' she called, turning from the mangle where she was struggling to guide a large folded bed-sheet through the rollers.

With arms crossed and a Capstan fag dangling from her lips, the boss-lady picked her way past the other girls towards Sunday. 'You was ten minutes late again this mornin'. That's the fird time in two weeks. Wot d'yer fink you're playin' at?'

'Sorry about that Mrs Briggs.' Sunday had to shout to be heard, for she had to compete with Charles Shadwell and his BBC Radio Orchestra on *Music While You Work* booming out from a tannoy on the wall just above her. 'Mum forgot to wake me up.'

The boss-lady glared back at the girl, unaware that she had let her ash fall on to a newly mangled pile of bagwash. Ma Briggs had a bony face with a pinched, upturned nose, which perfectly matched her hunched-up shoulders and painfully skinny middle-aged body. She had once sacked a girl who'd likened her to the Wicked Witch of the West in *The Wizard of Oz*. 'Wos up wiv you, Collins? Why d'yer 'ave to rely on yer old gel ter wake yer up? Can't yer buy yerself an alarm clock or somefin'?'

Sunday was dying to snap back, 'Not on the wages *you* pay me, you old bitch!' But, even though she was impulsive enough actually to say it, she bit her tongue firmly to resist the temptation. 'It won't happen again, Mrs Briggs.'

'Too true it won't!' The boss-lady unfolded her arms and finally pulled the fag stub from her lips. 'Let me tell yer somefin', Miss Clever Arse!' she said, smoke filtering out through her brown-stained teeth as she spoke. 'Your hours are eight 'til five. Next time yer get 'ere past the hour, I'll bolt the bleedin' door on yer!'

Sunday didn't answer. She couldn't. She knew only too well that if she raised her eyes and looked straight into Ma Briggs's face, she would say something she'd be bound to regret. Relishing the power she held over her girls, the boss-lady tossed the remains of her fag to the floor and stubbed it out with the sole of her foot. As if consolidating her victory over someone who she knew would not dare to argue with her, she attempted to straighten her hunched shoulders and stretch herself to a height above her normal five feet four inches.

'Oh, an' just one more fing, *Miss* big shot Collins,' she sniped, leaning so close to Sunday that the smell of Capstan fags on her breath practically overpowered the girl. 'I saw yer showin' off yer arse to them sailor boys on the dance floor down the Athenaeum the uvver night. Fink you're really somefin', don't yer, *duckie*? Wonder wot your old woman'd say if she knew 'alf wot you get up to?' And lowering her voice, she added, 'Bet she wouldn't like 'er mates up the Salvation Army to 'ear such fings.'

Chuckling to herself, Ma Briggs brushed some fag ash from her white cotton blouse and black skirt, adjusted her turban, and made her way back to her room at the rear of the Bagwash.

Sunday watched her go. As soon as the boss-lady had closed her door, the other 'Baggies' stopped what they were doing and waited for Sunday's reaction. But Sunday did not react. She merely carried on where she had left off, turning the wheel of the huge mangle with one hand and easing the wet sheet through the rollers with the other. Whatever her thoughts were, she was keeping them to herself.

*Music While You Work* had now come to an end, and as it was 11 o'clock in the morning, Sandy MacPherson at the BBC organ was on the air, with his regular programme of listeners' requests.

'Take no notice, Sun,' called one of the 'Baggies' who was at the tub closest to Sunday. 'Briggs is all mouf an' no trousers!'

Sunday turned back to look at her best mate, Pearl Simpson, a dumpy little thing with jet-black hair, large emerald-coloured eyes and a lovely moon-shaped face with a small mole on her left cheek.

'I'm not fussed,' said Sunday, coldly. '*Mrs* Briggs doesn't mean a damned thing to me. Her trouble is, she's frustrated. Ever since her old man went down at Dunkirk, she's been grateful for every bit of hard she can get her hands on.'

'Yer can say that again!' Pearl left the tub where she was stirring clothes in boiling water, and after making sure that the other girls could not overhear her, she joined Sunday at the mangle. 'Did yer know she's been bangin' it away wiv Tommy Leeson,' she said, doing her best to compete with Sandy MacPherson's organ-playing.

Sunday abruptly stopped turning the mangle wheel. 'Tommy Leeson! That one behind the bar down the Nag's Head? She can't be. She's old enough to be his grandmother!'

'Tommy ain't fussy,' sniffed Pearl, with a huge grin on her face. ''E likes ter lay old hens. Reckons they're always better at it than spring lambs!'

Both girls burst into laughter. Their workmates turned to glare at them, disliking the fact that they were not privy to the joke. And when Ernie Mancroft turned up with another pile of washing for

Sunday to put through the mangle, he shrunk at the sound of the two girls' laughter. Being one of only two young blokes working in the Bagwash who had not yet been called up, he was sure that, as usual, he was the reason for another of their piss-taking jokes. And, as usual, Sunday and Pearl never gave him cause to think otherwise, containing their laughter only long enough for him to dump the washing and leave. But Ernie never responded to their jibes. He fancied Sunday far too much to stir up trouble. Every time he even caught a glimpse of her, he was determined that one day she'd find out what he was made of.

On the stroke of five that evening, like every evening five days a week, it took no more than a minute for the Bagwash to empty. Eight hours was long enough to expect any human being to endure, cooped up in the stifling atmosphere of steaming hot tubs. As usual, Ma Briggs was at the main doors waiting to lock up. It was the time of day she hated most, watching her 'Baggies' filter into the mews outside, and rushing off in an excitable gaggle of laughter towards the Holloway Road. Once she was alone, she felt all the power drained from her. After the last girl had gone, the boss-lady slammed the door behind her and padlocked it grudgingly. To make things worse, it was Saturday evening. No more power now until Monday morning.

In the road outside, Sunday and Pearl breathed in the fresh May air, and sighed with relief. Sunday ran her fingers through her shoulder-length strawberry-blonde hair, then ruffled it up to restore some life to it. From in front and behind them, there were the usual calls from the other 'Baggies' of 'See yer Monday, Sunday!' The same old gag. And, to gales of laughter, 'Save us a bit er trousers at the dance ternight!' As usual, Sunday ignored them all. Apart from Pearl, she considered herself a cut above the other 'Baggies'. To her they were really just a bunch of knuckle-heads, who'd never really taken to her because she didn't speak their lingo.

Holloway Road had an end-of-the-week feel about it. There were plenty of people around, most of them hurrying home after shopping in the busy Seven Sisters Road, others already joining the queues outside the Gaumont Cinema and the local fish and chips shops, and others just strolling idly in the last hours of the day's warm sunshine. In fact, it had been the first really warm day of the year, and Sunday loved to see people walking around without a topcoat for the first time since the end of summer the previous year. It was a sure sign that in half an hour or so the pubs would be open, for there were plenty of blokes already hanging around in small groups chatting to each other about the end of the football season, or which pub Darts Team was playing that evening. But it was the smell that Sunday loved most of all. The sweet, fresh smell of spring, a smell that quickly made her forget that the Bagwash even existed, a smell that helped to erase the memory of those savage early years of the war, when so many of the surrounding streets had been bombed during the Blitz. As she and Pearl strode off at a brisk pace along the Holloway Road towards the Nag's Head, Sunday felt good to be alive – no bombs, no bagwash to mangle, no Ma Briggs, and Saturday night out at the Athenaeum Dance Hall to look forward to.

'I've promised ter see Lennie Jackson at the dance ternight,' said Pearl, as she and Sunday waited for a tram to pass before they crossed the road outside the Royal Northern Hospital. ''E says 'e's goin' ter teach me how ter dance the samba.'

'The samba? You!'

Pearl was immediately stung by Sunday's implied remark. Looking hurt and depressed, she said, 'See yer then,' and moved off towards her bus stop outside the Foresters' Hall.

'No, Pearl – wait!' Sunday immediately hurried to catch up with her pal. She could have bitten off her tongue for being so insensitive. 'I didn't mean – I didn't mean what you thought I meant.'

'I can't 'elp the way I look, Sun,' said Pearl, eyes looking aimlessly towards the boarded-up Holloway Empire, where dozens of pigeons were fluttering on and off the rooftop in a spectacular display of home ownership. 'I'm not fat 'cos I eat too much.'

Sunday was cringing inside. 'Of course you don't eat too much, Pearl. How could you on the bits of food we get on the ration. You're not fat, honest you're not. That's not what I was saying.'

The two girls came to a halt at the bus stop.

'I'm in love wiv 'im, Sun,' Pearl said, quite suddenly. 'Me an' Lennie. 'E feels the same way.'

Sunday couldn't believe what Pearl had just told her. As she looked at her best mate, she thought that despite her chubby appearance, she was really quite beautiful, with her black hair cut into a fringe across her forehead, and long eyelashes that accentuated her sparkling green eyes. 'You mean, you're going steady?' were the only words Sunday managed to get out.

Pearl lowered her eyes and blushed before she answered. 'Sort of.'

'But Lennie Jackson's in the Army.'

'Not for much longer,' said Pearl, quickly. 'Everyone says the war'll be over next year. My dad says that once the invasion starts, it's only a matter of time before Jerry 'as ter give in.'

For a moment there was silence between them, and both girls turned to look along the Holloway Road waiting for a sight of Pearl's trolleybus. Quite suddenly, a cool breeze came up, and immediately deprived the spring sunshine of its true heat. At the edge of the pavement, a tall elm tree, which had survived bomb-blast during the fierce aerial bombardments of the Battle of Britain, had succumbed to the breeze, for its newly formed leaves were shimmering and clinging on to their mother branches with grim determination.

Sunday didn't know what to say to Pearl. It had never occurred to her that anyone could possibly fancy her best friend, could fancy anyone who wasn't slim and sexy.

'Lennie says 'e likes the way I look,' said Pearl, as if she knew only too well what Sunday was thinking. 'He says he prefers fat girls – more meat on 'em.' She attempted a chuckle, but somehow just couldn't manage it. 'But I'm goin' ter lose weight, Sunday. I've made up me mind.'

Before Sunday had a chance to answer, to say something reassuring, the number 609 trolleybus arrived. Although Pearl's legs were quite trim, they were rather short, and she had to use some effort to climb aboard the bus platform. 'See yer ternight!' she called, before making her way to a seat on the lower deck.

Sunday waved to Pearl as the bus pulled away. And then she turned, and slowly made her way home down Holloway Road, stopping only briefly to look at the posters for the week's film outside the imposing Gaumont Cinema. All the way to the Nag's Head she couldn't get Pearl off her mind, but didn't know why. Was it because she felt protective of her mate, or was it because she was jealous of her? Had Pearl 'done it' with Lennie Jackson, she wondered? Was it possible? Was it really possible? But why shouldn't a good-looking bloke fancy someone like Pearl, she asked herself? After all, fat girls must be just as sexy as – well, someone like Sunday herself. Quite unconsciously, she was shaking her head; Pearl had certainly given her a lot to think about.

By the time she reached the Nag's Head, where Holloway Road crossed between Parkhurst and Seven Sisters Road, Sunday found herself hoping that the war would soon be over, and that Pearl would be able to get Lennie home safe and sound again. Whilst waiting at the traffic lights to cross the busy Parkhurst Road, she casually glanced up at the puffs of small white clouds that seemed to be sprinting across the blue early-evening sky. And she sighed with relief, relief that it had now been quite some time since out of that very same sky Hitler's bombers had brought so much death and destruction to the streets of Holloway and the rest of poor old London. Yes, Pearl was right, Sunday said to herself. It's all over bar the shouting. Nothing to fear now. The war's over. Now's the time to have some fun.

The traffic lights changed and Sunday crossed the road. As she did so, she trod on the previous day's copy of the *Daily Sketch* with its bold headline: HITLER'S SECRET WEAPON. The breeze grabbed hold of the heavily soiled newspaper, lifted it, and tossed it up into the mild evening air.

Peacock Buildings wasn't quite such a grim place as some of the other Borough Council residential blocks in Islington, and like a lot of similar dwellings built before the Second World War they were at least cheap and functional. Situated on the main road, between the Nag's Head and Holloway Road Tube Station, 'the Buildings', as they were known locally, were constructed of red bricks and concrete and laid out on six floors, which could only be reached by climbing endless flights of well-worn stone steps. Most residents in the surrounding streets were divided in their opinions concerning the look of 'the Buildings': some thought they were an eyesore; others thought they added something to the Holloway Road, though as to exactly what nobody was too certain. Luckily, 'the Buildings' had escaped the worst of the air-raids during the war, except for endless broken windows and fallen ceilings from bomb-blast in the neighbouring streets.

As usual, Madge Collins was anxiously peering out through her bedroom window at the rear of 'the Buildings', waiting for the first sight of her daughter as she entered the courtyard below. Sunday always hated her mum doing this, for it meant that by the time she had climbed the steps to their flat on the top floor, her tea would be already waiting for her on the parlour table. If there was one thing Sunday hated more than anything else, it was daily routine. Some evenings when she got home, she just felt like sitting down for a while, kicking off her shoes, and listening to some big band music on the wireless. But her mum would have none of it. As soon as the girl came through the front door, tea was on the table, and within minutes the scrambled dried eggs on toast, or sausage and mash, or spam and bubble and squeak was steaming hot beside it. It was a ritual.

The noise in the yard that evening was deafening. Clearly it was to do with the fine, warm weather, for it had brought out hordes of kids, all yelling and laughing their heads off as they either played hopscotch with a couple of stones, or relentlessly kicked a football against the back wall of one of the blocks. That was the trouble with living in a communal block, no privacy, no peace and quiet for longer than a few minutes at a time. If it wasn't kids running riot, it was the sound of someone's wireless set turned up to full volume. Sunday loved music, but not when it was so loud that it practically burst her eardrums. She had always found it peculiar that after all the horrors of the Blitz, when each night the air was fractured with the sound of falling bombs and anti-aircraft fire, people just didn't seem to relish the opportunity to live a quiet and peaceful life.

The first thing Sunday noticed as she entered 'the Buildings' through the rear door, was the smell of carbolic. When she had left in the morning, a stray dog had clearly found its way on to the second-floor landing and done its big job there. But there was no smell of it now; both the landing and the stairs leading up to it were cleaner than a new pin. And Sunday didn't have to guess very hard who was responsible for that.

''Ow many times do I 'ave ter tell these people ter keep that bleedin' door shut downstairs! Every cat an' dog treats this place like their own personal bog!'

Jack Popwell was at the door of his flat, polishing the brass letterbox, something he did with regular monotony seven days a week.

'I don't know what we'd do without you, Mr Popwell,' said Sunday, as she reached the landing. Despite the fact that she always regarded her neighbour to be a bit of a prissy old maid, Sunday was really quite fond of him. He made her laugh, and to her way of thinking anyone who could do that was worth something. And she admired the poor man for the way he'd managed to pull himself together after his missus was killed in an air-raid up near Finsbury Park at the beginning of the war.

Jack was positively glowing with the compliment Sunday had just paid him. 'By the way,' he beamed, adjusting with one finger the small quiff of hair he used to disguise his practically bare pate, 'I 'aven't fergotten that jam sponge I promised yer last week. I'm just waiting on me god-daughter ter get me some more saccharin tablets. I've got no more coupons left on me sugar ration.'

'No rush, Mr Popwell,' said Sunday, her eyes constantly flicking up to that quiff. 'It'll taste all the better by the time we get it.'

For a brief moment, Jack Popwell's smile faded. 'Tell that to yer Aunt Louie,' he sniffed, indignantly. 'Every time she catches sight of me, she goes on about people who don't keep their promises.'

The mention of her Aunt Louie's name suddenly reminded Sunday why she rarely looked forward to coming home from work in the evening. Her mum's sister. Aunt Louie. Oh God! The thought of seeing that woman again! 'I wouldn't take too much notice of *her*, Mr Popwell,' replied Sunday reassuringly. 'Aunt Louie can't even boil a kettle of water!'

'Sunday? Is that you, luvvie?'

Madge Collins's voice echoed down the stone staircase, reminding Sunday that her scrambled dried egg on toast was waiting for her on the parlour table.

As it turned out, however, dried eggs were not on the menu this evening. As soon as Sunday entered the tiny flat she could already smell the grilled bloaters, which her mum usually got from the fish man who always called with his barrow at 'the Buildings' on a Saturday.

Sunday wasn't surprised to see that the tea table had been laid with only two places instead of the usual three; clearly, Aunt Louie had decided to eat on her own after the row she and Sunday had had over breakfast that morning. Sunday couldn't care less. It wasn't the first time she'd fallen out with her tempestuous aunt, and it certainly wouldn't be the last. Despite that, the table itself looked a picture, with a clean white tablecloth, a posy of small spring flowers in a glass tumbler, and a huge brown teapot full to the brim. Each plate contained a pair of sizzling-hot bloaters, and several slices of bread had been sliced from the farmhouse loaf which Madge had bought from Millers the baker earlier in the day. Sadly, there was very little margarine to go with the bread, for the week's butter coupons had already been used up. Sunday barely had enough time to go to the lavatory, because her mum was already seated at the table waiting to eat with her.

'Wonderful news, luvvie!' Madge said, excitedly. She was clearly bursting to tell Sunday what she'd had to bottle up all day.

Sunday looked up from the tiny bones she was trying to separate from the bloaters on her plate. She always loved the look on her mum's face when she was excited about something. It was a sweet look, full of childish enthusiasm.

'The Army's on the move!' Although Madge was already holding her knife and fork, she hadn't yet started on her bloaters. 'Every Sunday for the next four weeks. The band's touring all over

Islington – Highbury Corner, the Angel, Essex Road, Hornsey Rise, Highgate. We're starting off outside the Marlborough Cinema tomorrow afternoon. Colonel Faraday's coming down from Headquarters to give the address.'

For a brief moment, Sunday watched her mum with deep affection. To her it was weird enough that Madge always referred to the Salvation Army as 'the Army', especially in wartime, but to get so excited about the band playing hymns outside pubs up and down the borough seemed so trivial. Nonetheless, if that's what made her mum happy, then Sunday was happy too. After all, her adopted mum had brought her up and cared for her – and taught her how to speak properly, not in a Cockney slang like her mates at work. 'That's lovely, Mum,' was all Sunday could say, as she chewed a piece of dry bread to help down the bloater.

Madge beamed, and leaned across towards her daughter. '*You* could come along too if you want,' she said hopefully. 'Everyone keeps saying how much they'd love to see you at one of the meetings.'

Sunday put down her knife and fork and looked across the table at her mum. 'Now don't let's go through all that again – *please*, Mum,' she said, trying hard not to upset Madge. 'You know I don't like getting involved in all that kind of stuff.'

Madge's sweet smile faded immediately, and her once cherubic face, now heavily lined, crumpled up in disappointment. 'You used to – when you were little.'

Sunday always dreaded this type of exchange with her mum, mainly because the poor woman was so vulnerable. She knew only too well that Madge had to deal not only with her sister Louie's endless tantrums, but also with a daughter who refused to embrace her own passion for religion. 'It was different when I was little, Mum,' she said, biting her lip anxiously. Then she stretched one hand across the table and placed it affectionately on to her mum's hand. 'Things were different when I was little, Mum,' she said softly. 'I'm grown up now. I have to do things for myself – my own things.'

'But I'm only asking you to come and listen to the band. You love music. You always have.'

'Of course I love music, Mum.' Sunday felt herself tensing. 'But not *your* kind of music. I like to dance to Glenn Miller, or Harry Roy, or Ivy Benson.'

Madge sat straight in her chair. As she was barely five feet tall and only slightly built, the tea table still seemed to dwarf her. 'I've always told you, Sunday,' she said, a touch imperiously, 'dance halls are no substitute for God's work.'

Suddenly, Sunday had no appetite for her bloaters. For the next few minutes, she sat back in her chair and listened to another of her mum's dissertations on how wonderful it was to be one of God's 'soldiers'. To Madge, the Salvation Army was the very essence of good itself, always caring for those in need, in peace and war. Unfortunately, Sunday knew that everything her mum was saying was true. The 'Army' really were a magnanimous lot, and during the height of the Blitz they had provided food and comfort to everyone who had to endure the nightly aerial bombardments. But, although Sunday certainly shared their beliefs, it was not the way she wanted to live her own life. But it *was* difficult, oh so difficult. Living in a tiny two-bedroomed council flat with a loving mum who was constantly trying to get her into a bonnet and uniform, and a bullying aunt who was determined to get her way about everything, there were times when Sunday felt as though she was a prisoner in her own home. Oh if only she had known her dad. If only he hadn't died when Sunday was a tiny child. Things would have been so different. Or would they?

Sunday's only escape at times like this was to shut out the sound of her mum's voice and scan the room. By now she knew the entire pattern of the wallpaper, the same badly hung wallpaper that had remained unchanged since before the war. The pink roses were gradually fading, but the brown woodwork around the windows and wainscoting was still remarkably fresh, with very few chips, and the fawn-coloured tiles around the minute fireplace with its built-in gas fire were virtually glistening in the early-evening sunshine. Although it was a small parlour room, Madge kept it immaculately clean. At home and at work, Sunday often despaired that her whole world seemed to be dominated by the pervading smell of carbolic. She'd loved the time when the whole place had had to be treated with DDT, for Aunt Louie had screamed the place down after finding a cockroach squatting comfortably in the middle of the eiderdown on her bed.

Sunday's eyes had now scanned the entire room, from floor to ceiling, kitchen door to passage door and lavatory beyond, and her own bedroom door, and the neat lace curtains from the North London Drapery Stores in Seven Sisters Road, which only partly disguised the anti-bomb-blast tape protecting the glass panes of the two small windows. Finally, her eyes came to rest on the door of the bedroom which her mum shared with Aunt Louie. Until this moment, she hadn't noticed that the door was slightly ajar. Oh yes! So the old bag's having a good listen.

'What about Aunt Louie?'

Sunday knew she was being mischievous, because her voice was raised. But at least it stopped her mum in her tracks.

'Auntie?' replied Madge, puzzled by the sudden, unexpected question. 'What about her?'

'Is *she* coming to hear your band playing tomorrow?'

The question immediately prompted Madge to swing a nervous glance over her shoulder towards the bedroom door. 'I don't know,' she said, so obviously keeping her voice low. 'Auntie likes to have her sleep on Sunday afternoons.'

'Wouldn't do her any harm to give up her precious afternoon sleep just for once,' quipped Sunday, making quite sure her voice carried across to the bedroom door. 'She's got nothing else to do all day!'

Madge immediately panicked, got up from the table, hurried across to her bedroom door, and closed it.

'You mustn't be unkind to your auntie,' said Madge, lowering her voice almost to a whisper. 'You *know* she's got a weak heart.'

'Oh come off it, Mum!' snapped Sunday, getting up from her place at the table, and collecting the plate containing her half-finished bloater. 'You wait on her hand and foot. She does nothing to help you round here – absolutely nothing! That's why I blew up at her this morning. I hate the way she just lives off you. It's time she found a place of her own!'

Madge was getting more and more flustered. She quickly followed her daughter into the tiny kitchen whilst nervously checking over her shoulder to see if her bedroom door was still closed.

'You mustn't talk about your auntie like that, Sunday,' Madge whispered, her carpet-slippers quietly padding on the bare lino floor. 'I don't expect her to do things for me. She's my sister, Sunday, my own flesh and blood. If she left, I – I don't know what I'd do. Don't you understand? I love her.'

'Well *I* don't!' Sunday's response was emphatic.

Madge looked horrified. 'Sunday! How can you say such a thing?'

Sunday remained defiant. 'It's true, Mum! You know it is!' And she meant it. She turned to look out through the kitchen window. In the yard way down below, she could see some of the kids from 'the Buildings', shouting their heads off as they kicked their football against the bare brick wall. For as long as Sunday could remember her Aunt Louie had been a total pain in the neck, always rabbiting on at her every time she did anything that the old bag didn't approve of. Sunday knew only too well that ever since her precious aunt had come to live in the flat all those years ago, she had used her sister as a meal ticket. She was sick to death at the way her mum always took Aunt Louie's part, going on about how sad she was and how the poor woman had never had any love in her life. Surely it was plain as a pikestaff to see why no bloke in his right mind would want even to touch a cold fish like her. Dear Aunt Louie was nothing but a lazy, interfering old bag, whose influence over Sunday's mum had caused more trouble in their lives than anything or anyone else.

'You shouldn't've talked to her the way you did this morning, Sunday.'

Sunday swung round to her mum, and was about to answer her, but Madge spoke first.

'When you have a row with her like that, it's not Auntie you hurt. It's me.'

As much as she loved her, this was one of those moments when Sunday wished that she had a robust mum who was twenty years younger, instead of this meek and mild silver-haired woman who had adopted her over seventeen years before.

Madge stood with her back to the white enamel sink. Close to tears, she seemed a lot older than her seventy-two years. 'I took Auntie in, because – because when your dad died, I needed someone to talk to – to look after. You were only a little girl. It seemed the right thing to do.'

Sunday felt awful. She had allowed her hatred of Auntie Louie to overshadow her own mum's feelings. In the yard below, the kids were shouting louder than ever, and they were beginning to get on Sunday's nerves. Leaning out of the window, she yelled out, 'Shut up, will you – you lousy little buggers!'

The kids briefly stopped kicking their football, to look up at the window of the flat on the top floor. When they saw who was shouting at them, they all raised two fingers at her and yelled insults back.

Sunday did not bother to exchange banter with them. She merely slammed the window, and turned to face her mum again. With a deep sigh, she went across and put her arms around her. 'I'm sorry, Mum,' she said quietly. 'I'll try and behave myself.'

Madge quickly wiped her eyes with her pinny, and looked up at her daughter eagerly. 'Will you, Sunday? Will you really?'

Sunday nodded, and kissed her mum on the cheek. 'Promise.'

'Then will you go and make it up with her?'

Sunday felt her inside collapse. 'Mum!'

There was a begging look in Madge's eyes.

Sunday sighed deeply. There was no use pursuing the subject, for she had been through this time and time again.

A few minutes later, she was back in the parlour, heading towards her mum's bedroom. For a moment or so, she just stood in front of the door, trying hard to calm herself before going in to face the onslaught, just hoping the old bag hadn't heard too much of the conversation she'd just had with her mum. Finally, she plucked up enough courage to tap on the door.

'Auntie,' she called, 'can I come in?'

The voice that boomed out from inside sounded more like that of a hefty-voiced man than an elderly woman.

'Go away!' she called. 'I'm in the middle of packing. I hope you're satisfied!'

# Chapter 2

Saturday night at the Athenaeum Dance Hall was like a magnet to young people. They flocked there from not only the Parkhurst Road area, which had the dubious distinction of sharing the neighbourhood with the castellated façade of Holloway Women's Prison on the opposite side of Camden Road, but from places as far apart as Highgate, Muswell Hill, Finsbury Park, Highbury, and the Angel Islington. Its only real rival was the Arcade at the Nag's Head, but that was usually more busy on a Friday pay night, and was mainly a meeting place for the local Irish 'Paddys'. The dance floor at the Athenaeum itself wasn't a particularly large area, more the size of a small church hall, so that when a lot of dancers were crammed together it became more of a shuffle than a waltz or a foxtrot. On most nights, the music was provided by gramophone records of some of the favourite bands of the day, such as Tommy Dorsey, Kay Keyser, Harry Roy, Geraldo, and of course, Glenn Miller, but occasionally there was 'live' music such as piano, saxophone, and drums.

By the time Sunday and Pearl arrived, the place was 'jumpin'. A small queue had formed at the entrance, and it was all of twenty minutes before they could get inside. Once they had powdered their noses in the cloakroom, they gradually managed to edge their way into the hall itself, where the hordes of dancers were doing their best to find enough space to quickstep to a gramophone record of Jack Hylton and his orchestra playing 'I'll See You In My Dreams'. As usual, there were more girls hanging around in groups on one side of the floor, for so many boys were now serving in the forces. But the young boys that did remain had a pretty good choice of dancing partners to choose from, and took their time before they were quite sure who they wanted to go for.

Within just a few minutes of her arrival with Pearl, two different boys asked Sunday to dance. It was easy to see why, for she looked dazzling in her new blue cotton dress which she had recently bought from Damants Ladies Shop in the Seven Sisters Road with her own ration coupons and a few more donated by her mum. The colour set off beautifully her strawberry-blonde hair, which had been pinned back behind her ears to show off her clear pale complexion and slightly rouged cheeks. Her mum, of course, had disapproved of the alterations Sunday had made to the dress, which she had cut low at the neck to reveal as much of her cleavage as she dared, and also the hemline, which was tacked up to at least an inch above her knees, to reveal her new silk stockings bought on the black market for four shillings. But, like a lot of the other girls who were dancing with each other, Sunday decided to decline the two boys' offers, and partner Pearl in a slow waltz. However, this didn't last very long.

'May I have this dance, please, miss?'

Right in the middle of the crowded dance floor, Pearl turned with a start to find a young soldier boy grabbing her around the waist from behind.

'Lennie! Where yer been? I been lookin' all over for yer.'

'Didn't look 'ard enuff, did yer?' The young soldier spun her round to face him. 'I was over by the bar.'

'Wot a surprise!' Pearl had to shout to be heard above the sound of Jack Hylton's orchestra. 'The last place I'd ever expect ter find *you*, Lennie Jackson!'

To Sunday's intense irritation, Pearl had her arms wrapped around Lennie's neck while he kissed her full on the lips. The other dancers were pretty aggravated too, for they pushed and shoved the couple so that they had to move on.

'Sorry about this, Sun!' Pearl called, as Lennie whisked her off to join the throng of dancers trying to make some sense of the quickstep.

'See yer later, Sun!' called Lennie. 'Don't worry about 'er. I'll make sure she don't be'ave 'erself!'

Left stranded in the middle of the dance floor, Sunday tried to convince herself that she was happy for Pearl. But she wasn't. She strode off the floor, practically pushing the other dancers out of the way as she went. Making her way straight to the narrow, floor-side bar, she ordered herself a glass of lemonade, the only drink she was used to. Just as well, for, with the exception of rather weak beer, there was currently a very severe shortage of alcohol.

For several minutes, Sunday stood with her back to the bar counter, surveying the dancers all crushed together and whirling around the floor in what seemed to be one huge mass of bodies. She was particularly sniffy around those girls who, unable like her to afford stockings on the black market, had chosen to cover their legs with make-up. The place was airless, for a thick pall of fag smoke had turned the atmosphere into a dense blue-grey fog. But no one seemed to mind, for even at the bar itself practically every girl and her feller was lighting up yet another cheap fag.

For several minutes, Sunday sipped her lemonade and tapped her foot in time to another current hit song, 'Chattanooga Choo-Choo', which had sent the dancers into a frenzy of train engine catcalls, as they cut up the hard-used parquet floor with another quickstep. She tried hard not to look envious as some of her 'Baggie' mates swept by with their partners, some of them showing off like mad with elaborate steps clearly designed to upset her. But Sunday couldn't care a toss about their fancy steps. At this moment, the only people she really cared about were Pearl and Lennie, who were clutched so tightly together on the dance floor that there could hardly have been breathing space between them. Every so often Pearl would wave to Sunday as she caught sight of her above the mass of bodies. Sunday waved back, but only half-heartedly, then tried to give the impression that she couldn't really see them. The fact was, she was as jealous as hell of Pearl, more than she ever thought she could be. Ever since she left school when she was fifteen, she had fancied Lennie Jackson herself, fancied him like mad. His slim body and coarse good looks were everything she had ever wanted in a feller, and with his short, dark hair, bushy eyebrows, and rough Cockney slang, she would have killed to get her hands on him. But she knew only too well that Lennie would never be for her. He had shown her so several times, when he had totally ignored her in favour of any bit of skirt that happened to be around at the time. But why Pearl? It was a question she had asked herself over and over again. How could a real bloke like that go for a girl who was so fat that at this very moment sweat was running down her blood-red face as she danced. Yes, Sunday was jealous all right. If it wasn't for the fact that Pearl was her best friend, she'd go all out to get Lennie bloody Jackson for herself.

''As anyone told you, yer've got the best tits round 'ere?'

Sunday had already noticed the boy in RAF uniform who had made his way towards her from the other end of the bar. If she didn't like his style then it was her own fault, for she had seen him eyeing her, and quite deliberately egged him on.

'Bit of an expert, are you?' Sunday replied, rather tartly.

'I know the best when I see it.' The boy's eyes were flicking back and forward from Sunday's eyes to her breasts. 'Fag?'

Sunday was about to shake her head, when over the RAF boy's shoulder she caught sight of Pearl waving to her. 'Ta,' she replied, taking out a Gold Flake from the packet the RAF boy was holding out for her. Only when the boy had lit the fag, and she drew in the first puff of smoke, did she realise what a daft thing she was doing. However, despite the fact that Sunday had never smoked before, she was quite determined to put on as big an act as she could, and make quite sure that both Pearl and Lennie could see her.

'M'name's 'Arry. 'Arry Smike.' The boy was looking all over Sunday with the most come-to-bed eyes she had seen in a long time.

'Sunday.'

Harry looked puzzled. 'Say that again.'

'My name's Sunday,' she answered, raising her voice to compete with the 'Chattanooga Choo-Choo' catcalls. 'It's too long a story to tell why.'

Harry asked no more. He just grinned at her, puffed at his fag and swallowed as much of the nicotine as he could. He liked this girl. He liked her a lot. She had a good tongue. She had a good body. This one he was not going to let go.

'What's the propeller for?' asked Sunday, nodding towards the small flash on the sleeve of Harry's blue uniform tunic.

'LAC. Leading Aircraftman.'

'Is that important?'

'Well, at least it's one up from AC plonk.'

That was good enough for Sunday. Her eyes darted momentarily across to Lennie Jackson, who was bending the dumpy figure of Pearl backwards in some showy exhibition of his quickstep dancing talents. There was certainly no flash of any kind on *his* plain army tunic.

For a moment or so, Harry watched this sexy bird sipping from her glass of lemonade, taking in minimal puffs of smoke from the fag he had given her. 'Wouldn't yer like somefin' stronger than that stuff?' he asked, his lips practically pressed against her ear.

'I don't drink,' she said, without turning to look at him.

'Wot *do* yer do?'

Harry's predictable question didn't worry Sunday one little bit. She merely turned to face him, and with their lips almost touching each other's replied, 'I dance.'

As she spoke, the lights in the hall came up full, and over the tannoy system came the voice of the dance MC: 'Ladies an' gentlemen. Boys an' girls. Take your partners for – the jitterbug!'

To the accompaniment of a loud cheer from all the dancers, the floor cleared instantly, leaving behind only a small group of younger people, mainly teenagers. From the loudspeaker now came the sound of Kay Keyser and his band with a frantic version of 'Gotta Gal Named Sal', which was the cue for the few remaining couples to burst into an energetic display of the latest dance craze – the jitterbug.

Without warning, Harry suddenly grabbed hold of Sunday's hand. 'OK,' he said. 'You wanna dance? Let's dance!'

Pearl and Lennie watched in astonishment as Sunday was dragged by her RAF boyfriend through the crowd of dancers lining the floor, and straight into the small group of jitterbug fanatics who were already twisting and turning and throwing themselves into a wild display of acrobatic dancing.

With music blaring out from the loudspeaker, and the crowd of onlookers clapping their hands and thumping their feet in time, Sunday, Harry, and the rest of the jitterbug gang leapt at each other, the boys with legs wide apart and knees bent, swaying back and forth to the fast and furious beat, and the girls twisting their heels into the parquet floor, skirts and dresses swirling, holding on to their partners with one hand, and the other hand waving to and fro with the beat. One boy was even bold enough to do a somersault, only to land in a split on the floor. This brought an uproarious cheer from the crowd, which immediately prompted the other members of the jitterbug gang to venture even more daring exploits. After a while, however, the frenetic pace gradually took its toll on the small energetic group, and they were eliminated couple by couple, finally leaving only Sunday and Harry to slog it out.

At this point, Sunday seemed unstoppable. Her whole body twisted and turned in time to the jitterbug beat, sending shockwaves of lust through every red-blooded young bloke in the hall. As the perspiration ran down her body, her cherished blue dress clung to her so tightly that it accentuated every sensuous curve she possessed. Sunday loved the feeling of total abandonment. She literally gave herself to the throbbing sounds coming out of the loudspeaker on the tiny platform, she embraced them as though they were telling her to go on and on. Although she knew her fresh home-perm would be an early casualty, she recklessly ran her fingers through her strawberry-blonde hair, yelling out a scream of ecstasy at the overpowering musical beat which dominated the room. She was the centre of attention, and she loved it. They were all out there, Pearl and Lennie and the other 'Baggies' – all watching, admiring, envying her. Sunday had even caught a glimpse of Ma Briggs, togged up in a tight-fitting black dress, with that same large chunky rolled-gold bracelet that she wore every day of her life. Yes, the old witch was there all right, clinging on to her young piece of trousers from the Nag's Head pub, and hating every moment of what she was watching on the dance floor.

Sunday was by now in a state of delirium. She was passionate about music at the best of times, but the sounds she was now hearing were sending her wild. It was much the same with Harry, for the Brylcreem from his hair was now running into the sweat that was streaming down his face. In fact, he was on such a high that he didn't think twice about taking Sunday to the ultimate goal of the jitterbug. Grabbing hold of her hand, he dragged her to the floor, slid her entire body beneath his legs, and lifted her in one perilous movement up on to his shoulders. This inevitably brought cheers and applause from the crowd, and Sunday, arms outstretched in unrestrained triumph, lapped up all the admiration. But that triumph was to be shortlived. An alien sound had suddenly pierced the roars of excitement from the dance-hall crowd.

'Air-raid!'

The MC's shock announcement through the loudspeaker was soon drowned by the wail of the air-raid siren.

The atmosphere immediately changed to astonishment, for as there had been no air-raids for some time, people had begun to take it for granted that the war was all but over. Whilst the lights in the hall were being quickly extinguished, there was a sudden rush towards every available exit door. Harry quickly lowered Sunday down from his shoulders, took her hand, and tried to lead her through the crowd. But before they could even reach the door, they were separated by the desperate efforts of the dancers to reach the nearest air-raid shelters.

In the road outside, hordes of people were streaming out of the dance hall. The colourful dresses and elaborate hairdos were quickly forgotten in the mad rush to get away from the place, and by the time Sunday managed to ease herself out of the hall, there were so many people around her that it was impossible to find Harry. Not that she intended to try too hard. The RAF boy wasn't a bad bit of trousers, but he wasn't anything to write home about. Anyway, he had served his purpose.

Sunday decided to make her way home via Hillmarton Road. It was a bit out of the way, but as there was a public shelter in Caledonian Road, she thought it was probably the safer route.

By the time she had gone halfway down the quiet back road, the sound of anxious people rushing out of the dance hall behind her was gradually fading. There was a slight breeze, and as it was still only May, there was a cold nip in the night air. As she hurried along, Sunday could hear the clip-clop of her own high heels on the pavement, but it wasn't too easy to see where she was going, for, despite the spring moon that was popping in and out of dark night clouds, the blackout was preventing any light from filtering through the windows of the tall, terraced Edwardian houses on each side of the road. After a moment or so, she quickened her pace as she began to hear the distant rumble of ack-ack fire, and was only too relieved to see that the sky was still dotted with the ominous dark shapes of silent, brooding barrage balloons, just waiting to deal with any intruder aircraft that might break through the outer London defences.

Just before she reached the Caledonian Road, Sunday heard the first sound of approaching aircraft. There weren't many of them, possibly only a couple, but it was enough to set off the ack-ack guns in nearby Finsbury Park. The sudden blast unnerved her, and her hurried walk quickly became a run. But by the time she had reached the stone walls of the old churchyard, the sky seemed to open up, and all hell was let loose. As she ran, Sunday covered her head with her hands, and would have panicked if someone had not suddenly grabbed hold of her around the waist, and dragged her into the cover of the church portico.

'Wot's a respectable girl like you doin' out on a night like this?'

Although it was pitch-dark, Sunday recognised the voice at once. It was Ernie Mancroft, the boy who worked with her down the Bagwash.

'What's this all about?' asked Sunday, shivering with the cold. 'We haven't had a raid for months. I thought this rotten war was supposed to be over.'

'Not yet it ain't.' Even though Ernie's voice was low, it echoed in the arch of the portico. 'But it will be after Ike and Monty start the Second Front.'

'Second Front! Second Front! That's all people ever talk about.' Sunday was not only cold, but irritable. 'It's about time the Allies stopped yakking, and got on with it.'

'Well, all I 'ope is they get on wiv it before I get called up. I don't fancy catchin' a packet at my age.'

Sunday didn't bother to answer him. Ernie Mancroft had always let it be known that, in his opinion, only suckers wanted to fight for their country. When she thought of all the good blokes from 'the Buildings' who'd gone off to fight in the war, she despised him, and hoped it wouldn't be long before he got his call-up papers.

As they stood there in the dark, the sound of the two approaching aircraft drew closer and closer, and Sunday began to feel utterly vulnerable. It was the first time she had been caught outside in an air-raid, and she was nervous. Every so often a flash of gunfire lit up the sky, and each time it did so she caught a momentary glimpse of Ernie's face, staring at her. She didn't like it, not because he was bad-looking; in fact, he had quite a masculine face for a boy his age, despite his pathetic attempts to grow a pencil-thin moustache. Her main concern was that Ernie fancied her. He had always fancied her, and she knew it. Ever since the first day he set eyes on her when he came to work at the Bagwash, she had caught him staring, leering at her. On one occasion, when she had to squeeze past him in a narrow passage to get to the women's toilet, she had felt him deliberately press his body against her. But then, in her heart of hearts, she knew that there were times when she had led him on, so if he tried anything she only had herself to blame.

High above them, searchlights were scanning the sky for the two intruder aircraft, who were dodging in and out of the killer wires of the barrage balloons.

'Must be a couple of strays,' Ernie said, watching the dark outline of Sunday's silhouette as he spoke. ''Itler's last fling before it's all over.'

Ernie was now standing so close to Sunday that she could smell the beer on his breath. 'We ought to get to the shelter, Ernie,' she said. 'It's not safe out here.'

'Wouldn't go out there just yet,' said Ernie immediately. 'If them guns open up again, there'll be shrapnel comin' down all over the place.'

'If you don't mind,' insisted Sunday, easing her way past him, 'I'll take my chances.'

As she spoke, the Finsbury Park guns fired a deafening salvo of shells up into the sky. Sunday literally fell back against the church door as the building vibrated from top to bottom.

Ernie immediately grabbed his opportunity and leapt forward to protect Sunday with his own body, pinning her back against the church door. 'See wot I mean!' he yelled, above the cacophony of gunfire. And leaning his body as close as he could against hers, his head buried into her shoulder, he croaked breathlessly, 'Nuffin' ter worry about, Sun. You're safe wiv me. I won't let no 'arm come to yer. Not now. Not never.'

With pieces of shrapnel from the anti-aircraft shells now scattering down on to the road outside and the gravestones in the churchyard, and Ernie pinning her against the church door, Sunday felt trapped. By now she could feel that Ernie was aroused. The thin cotton trousers he was wearing were bursting at his flies, and she now realised that if she didn't get out of there fast it would be too late. And yet, although she didn't quite know why, something inside told her that she didn't particularly want to get out of there. Maybe it had something to do with the danger she was in, danger from the air-raid, danger from Ernie Mancroft. The dilemma she was facing was exciting her, and as she felt Ernie's body pressing hard against her own, and his hands starting to explore her breasts, she felt an urge to go along with whatever he wanted to do. For some reason she wasn't frightened by the prospect. But then, why should she be? After all she'd done it before with a couple of other blokes, so why not Ernie? After all, he *was* a bloke, and young blokes were hard to find during wartime.

At that moment, another gigantic salvo lit up the sky, and in that split second, Sunday not only felt this boy's body pressing hard against her, but she could also see him. Suddenly reality took over from fantasy. 'No, Ernie,' she said, trying to push him away. 'No more. I want to get home.'

'Wot's the rush?' Ernie asked, as he held her tight and refused to let her go. 'You're safe I tell yer. Come on, Sun. Yer know 'ow I feel about yer. Yer know yer want me – *really*.'

'No, Ernie! Get away from me!' Sunday was now struggling, but Ernie was very muscular, and much too strong for her.

He tried to kiss her, but she turned her head away. He pulled her face back again, and when he did press his lips against hers, she pushed him off, and wiped her own lips with the back of her hand. Then she felt his hands clawing at her dress, trying to pull it up to her waist.

'No, Ernie!' she snapped. 'If you don't cut it out, I'll yell the place down.'

Ernie was now tugging at her panties. 'Stop 'avin' me on, Sun! You're always 'avin' me on. You're mine, Sun. Yor'll always be mine!'

Sunday was so shocked to hear Ernie talk like this, that when the next salvo of shells burst with a deafening crack overhead, she somehow found the strength to push him off and make a quick dash for the road.

To her surprise, Sunday found that she was able to outpace Ernie, for once she was in the Caledonian Road, a quick glance over her shoulder showed that he had turned back towards the church portico.

The Caledonian Road itself was completely deserted, for the audience had left the nearby Mayfair Cinema over an hour before, and clearly no one was taking the chance of being caught out in the first air-raid for months.

Once she was certain that she was no longer being followed, Sunday made her way straight towards one of the small public shelters on the road itself. Although the two intruder aircraft had now passed over, the ack-ack barrage was still in full swing, and pieces of jagged shrapnel were tinkling down on to the rooftops all around her. As she hurried along, she had to cover her ears against the deafening gunfire, which seemed so different to the claps of thunder that so excited her whenever there was a thunderstorm.

Sunday finally managed to reach the public shelter unharmed. She had always thought these brick and concrete constructions to be nothing more than a sitting target should they receive a direct hit, but at least she would be protected from the falling shrapnel, and there would be people there with whom she could slog it out.

'Come on in gel – quick as yer can!'

To Sunday's great relief, an air-raid warden was waiting at the door to let her in, and as she entered, she was met by a thick pall of fag smoke. The place was jam-packed, mainly with young people from the dance hall. Needless to say, none of the boys offered to give her their seat, so an old bloke who was smoking a pipe of stale baccy immediately got up and gave her his. Sunday was about to take up his offer when she heard someone calling to her.

'Sunday! Over 'ere – Sun!'

It was Pearl, at the far end of the shelter. Lennie Jackson was with her, but he had his back turned towards Sunday, and she could only just see Pearl's face peering out over his shoulder. They were clearly snogging against the back wall in full view of everyone.

A cold chill went up Sunday's spine, and she suddenly decided not to sit down.

'Sunday! Wot yer doin'? Come over 'ere! There's room!'

Lennie turned only reluctantly to look across at Sunday. Then after a smile that was more a smirk, he turned back to Pearl again, and smooched her on the neck.

Sunday felt quite sick. All she could do was to turn, make her way back to the entrance again, and leave.

The old bloke who had offered her his seat shook his head in bewilderment. Then he sat down again, and continued to puff away at his pipe.

Once in the street outside, Sunday started to run. She was only a short distance from 'the Buildings', and despite the tinkling of shrapnel which now sounded to her like a mad song being played on a strange musical instrument, she was more prepared to take her chances in the street than sit in a stuffy old air-raid shelter with Pearl and Lennie.

Pearl may have been her best friend, but tonight she could have bloody well strangled her.

# Chapter 3

Louie Clipstone hated men. Well, that's what most people assumed, for every time a member of the opposite sex was mentioned in her presence, her chiselled features swelled up in indignation, and her dark grey eyes turned bloodshot. No one could ever make out why she felt the way she did, for she always refused to discuss the matter. To avoid embarrassment, her younger sister Madge usually excused Louie's odd behaviour by telling how the poor woman had once had an 'unfortunate association' with a gentleman friend – when she was much younger, of course. The strange thing was, to most of her neighbours in 'the Buildings', Louie herself looked more like a man than a seventy-four-year-old woman. With her short, cropped hair, bullish neck, and baggy trousers, her very appearance seemed intimidating, and she gave the impression that she could be a match for the World Champion himself, Joe Louis, in the boxing ring.

Unlike Sunday's mum, who not only kept the flat clean and tidy, but also did the cooking, ironing, and washing-up, Aunt Louie never seemed to do a stroke of work, but spent most days studying the racing papers. She had no income, for in the early part of her life she had been in and out of jobs like a dose of salts. That's why, when Madge's husband Reg died of cancer when Sunday was only three years old, Louie had moved in with her. It meant a roof over her head, food in her stomach, and a life of Riley.

That Sunday morning, Sunday had a bit of a lie-in. The night before had been quite an experience, what with dancing the jitterbug with an RAF Lance-Corporal, and nearly being raped by Ernie Mancroft in a church portico. It was amazing that she had survived to tell the tale, if she ever decided to do such a thing. Luckily, the surprise air-raid had passed over in a very short time, and Sunday had been able to get home without being hit by any pieces of shrapnel. She woke up at about nine o'clock, and for about half an hour just lay there gazing aimlessly around the walls at the cut-out magazine photos of some of her favourite crooners, like Bing Crosby and Sam Browne, and bandleaders such as Joe Loss, and her number-one favourite, Glenn Miller. In fact, there were so many photos plastered all over the walls of the tiny room that it was difficult to see what remained of the faded flower-patterned wallpaper.

When Sunday eventually surfaced, the first thing that hit her was the smell of Aunt Louie's hand-rolled fags. She recognised it at once for it was a sour, pungent smell, which totally obliterated the fresh odour of Madge Collins's carbolic. Sunday had often seen her aunt buying her usual two ounces of cheap tobacco. Usually she went to the kiosk at Holloway Road Tube Station for there she could argue with the assistant that she was being overcharged by a penny for the tobacco, and that if she didn't get it at the proper retail price, she'd write a letter of complaint to the tobacco company. Aunt Louie always won. In fact, she always won at everything she did.

'Your mother's left you a bacon sandwich for your breakfast,' growled Aunt Louie, as Sunday came out of her bedroom. 'I've no doubt she's given up her own week's ration – as usual,' she added acidly.

Sunday refused to rise to the bait. It had already stuck in her gullet that she'd had to apologise to her aunt the previous evening for all the things she had said about her, and she knew only too well that if she started another row now, Aunt Louie would again threaten to pack her things and move out. Of course, Sunday knew that the old battle-axe would never do any such thing, despite the fact that she had made repeated threats over the years. But it was the distress those threats caused to Sunday's mum that prevented her from telling her aunt a few home truths.

Sunday sat opposite her aunt at the parlour table, where her mum had laid a place for her before leaving for Sunday morning church parade at the Highbury Salvation Army Mission Hall. She tucked into the bacon sandwich, then felt the teapot beneath the cosy and found that the tea was still warm, so she poured herself a cup. During all this, Aunt Louie remained hidden behind the *Sunday Pictorial*, which she always read starting from the sports pages at the back. Sunday herself only half-heartedly glanced at the front-page story which was being held up in front of her, with its reports of the dramatic capture by British and Polish soldiers of the First German Parachute Division's bastion in the monastery at Cassino in Italy.

'Things would be very different round here if your father was still alive.'

Aunt Louie's voice behind the newspaper took Sunday by surprise.

'If he'd had *his* way, you'd have been in bed by ten o'clock every night.' Louie suddenly peered at Sunday over the top of her newspaper. 'And I do mean *every* night,' she said, emphatically. 'Including Saturdays.'

Sunday ignored her aunt, and carried on eating her bacon sandwich.

'Your father was a pig of a man,' Louie said, refusing to be ignored. 'Did you know that?'

Sunday's eyes flicked up momentarily. 'I wish you wouldn't talk about Dad like that,' she said, trying hard not to be intimidated.

'Why not?' Louie was determined to have her say. 'What do *you* care? You never knew him.'

'Even more reason,' Sunday said, lowering her eyes, and eating her sandwich again.

Aunt Louie put down her newspaper. 'There are things I could tell you about your father that would make your hair curl.'

It was a typically stupid remark for Louie to make, knowing full well that even without her home-made perm, Sunday had a head of naturally curly blonde hair.

'He never wanted to keep you, you know. Oh no.' Louie was determined to maintain the aggravation. 'When your mother brought you home after finding you on that doorstep up the Salvation Army, he blew his top.' She took hold of her fag roller, and started packing it as tight as she could with tobacco which she kept in a small, flat tin. 'He told her that if he couldn't have kids of his own, then he didn't want other people's.' She flicked her eyes up for a brief moment, and fixed Sunday with a tiger-like glare. 'That wasn't the real reason, of course. Oh no.'

Although she had no sugar in her cup, Sunday was unconsciously stirring her tea, whilst trying hard not to show that she was listening to anything Aunt Louie was saying.

'He was jealous of her,' rasped Louie, inserting the fag paper into her roller. 'Oh it wasn't just you. It wasn't just a small baby no bigger than a puppy. No. He was jealous of anyone who came near her.' She carefully lifted the ready-made fag out of the roller, licked the edges of the paper, and sealed it. 'You know something?' she continued, relentlessly. 'When your mother and I were kids together back home in Edmonton, we were the best of friends. Couldn't keep us apart.' Having finished the completed fag, she placed it between her lips. 'Soon as *he* came along, it all changed.'

Clasping the cup of tea firmly in both hands, Sunday leaned back in her chair in an attempt to keep clear of the tobacco smoke that

Aunt Louie was deliberately puffing out across the table from her newly lit fag.

'And I'll tell you something else.'

'Aunt Louie, I'm not interested.' Sunday was getting irritated.

'He used to beat her.' Louie was leaning across the table again. 'Oh yes. He thought I didn't know. But I did. During all the time he was alive, I never once came to this place. Oh no. But Madge came over to me. She came lots of times. And when she did, there was always a bruise on her cheek, or a cut from his wedding ring where he'd whacked her across the face with the back of his hand. She never told me – but I knew.'

Sunday suddenly saw red. 'I don't know why you're telling me all this, Aunt Louie. It's all in the past. It's got nothing to do with me.'

Louie stood up from the table. 'That's where you're wrong. It concerns you all right. Oh yes. It concerns you a great deal, young madam. And d'you know why?'

This time, Sunday just had to look up at her aunt, who was standing with her two hands leaning on the table, and a fag stuck firmly between her lips.

'Because if you think *I'm* so bad to live with, I'd like to know how you think you'll get on with a new *daddy*?'

Sunday's eyes widened. She was too shocked to answer.

Despite the weather forecast on the wireless that it was going to be a hot and sunny afternoon, thick grey rain-clouds were rolling past high above the Holloway Road, giving the impression that this was not a pleasant Sunday afternoon in May but a chilly, autumnal day in late October. In fact, by the time Madge and her fellow Salvation Army officers had set up their musical instruments and bandstands in the forecourt of the Marlborough Cinema, the first raindrops were already tip-tapping their way down on to the bandparts. Within just a few minutes, the pavements were shimmering with wet reflections of the sulky sky above, and a thin trickle of water gradually snaked its way along the gutters to disappear into the sewers below.

However, the men and women of the Highbury Division Salvation Army Brass Band were made of stern stuff, and so, wrapped up in their uniforms and black and red bonnets and caps, they launched straight into their own stirring version of 'John Brown's Body'.

The moment she came out of 'the Buildings', Sunday could hear the distant sound of tambourines clattering, the beating of the big bass drum, a trumpet blasting, cymbals clashing, and the whine of the harmonium. Huddled beneath her leaking brolly, she quickly made her way along the Holloway Road, where she soon found the Sunday afternoon band service in full swing. Much to her astonishment, there was a sizeable crowd gathered round. Some of them were regular followers, but the rest were just killing time before the doors opened at the Marlborough Cinema for the Sunday afternoon performance of *The Man in Grey*. But despite the driving rain, the atmosphere was joyful and exhilarating, with the worshippers singing out loud, clapping their hands and stamping their feet in time to 'Glory! Glory, Hallelujah! His soul goes marching on!'

Madge Collins's face lit up when she saw Sunday standing at the back of the crowd. Madge was, of course, an active member of the band, but the huge euphonium she was playing seemed to be almost as tall as herself, and as she blew through the mouthpiece, her chubby cheeks puffed out in time to the music, the effort of which had turned her face a startling blood-red.

The rain was now a downpour, and the sound of raindrops pelting down on top of Sunday's brolly made a curious, ethereal accompaniment to the robust chorus of human voices, tambourines, euphonium, cymbals, harmonium, and, of course, the dominant big bass drum. Even a small bunch of snotty-nosed kids were thoroughly enjoying themselves by marching up and down in the rain and mimicking the musicians. However, Sunday was only half-heartedly joining in the chorus, for her attention was focused on scanning the faces of the members of the band and their small choir of Salvationist officers grouped around them in a semicircle. Needless to say, over the years she had got to know most of them, for, each week when she was a little girl, her mum had taken her up to the Salvation Army Hall at Highbury to listen to endless band practices and Bible readings. There were so many 'aunties' and 'uncles' that she couldn't keep up with them. Her particular favourite was 'Auntie' Elsie, who worked in Lavalls' Sweet Shop in Seven Sisters Road, and who regularly brought her jelly babies until the war came along and they were rationed. She also quite liked 'Auntie' Vera, except that every time she spoke to Sunday she kept quoting bits of the Bible at her, and telling her that 'God always looks after little children – but only if they behave themselves.' 'Uncle' Sid was a funny man, for he was always telling Sunday jokes. The only trouble was, he always laughed louder than anyone else at them and never stopped poking her in the ribs as he did so.

Yes, there were lots of 'aunties' and 'uncles', and quite a few of them were here today. But there was one particular 'uncle' she was interested in. Unfortunately, she didn't yet know which one, for Aunt Louie had refused to put a name to the 'uncle' who might one day become her new 'dad'.

Once the soul of 'John Brown's Body' had gone marching on, a tall, gangly man stepped forward to address the crowd. Despite the weather, there was a radiant glow on his face, and although his red and black Salvation Army cap and uniform were soaking wet, they fitted him perfectly.

'Brothers and sisters – welcome!'

Sunday hadn't seen the officer before, so she imagined he was the bigwig from Headquarters her mum had been so excited about.

'God has brought us here together to this place today,' proclaimed Colonel Faraday. 'Let us rejoice in His work! Let us rejoice in the Family of Man!'

Sunday wasn't really in the mood for rejoicing, not even for the Good Lord Himself. As for the Family of Man, she let that pass. Man? Why not Family of Woman, or Family of 'Aunties' and 'Uncles'? No, she was more interested in all those Salvation Army faces spread out before her. And especially the 'uncles'. If she was to believe the venom her aunt Louie had tried to pour into her over breakfast that morning, that her mum was getting 'more than friendly with a gentleman friend up at the Hall', then she had to know which one.

Madge caught a brief glimpse of Sunday beneath her brolly, and gave her a broad smile. But when Colonel Faraday asked everyone to pray, she had to close her eyes like everyone else.

Sunday, however, did not close her eyes. Not because she didn't approve, but because she just had to study those faces. She knew very well how much her mum had missed her dad over the years, but was she really capable of having a 'friendship' with another man? Sunday stared hard along the rows of glistening, rain-soaked faces. Which one? Which one?

'Close yer eyes, yer naughty gel.'

Sunday didn't have to turn around to know who was standing just behind her. It was Bess Butler.

'You'll never go ter 'Eaven if yer don't listen ter wot the man says.' Bess kept her voice low as she spoke into Sunday's ear from behind.

Sunday couldn't resist stepping backwards out of the crowd to join Bess. 'Oh, it's so good to see you, Bess,' she said, holding her brolly over both of them. 'I've had just about enough of all this for one day.'

Bess grinned. 'Feel like a cuppa?'

Sunday didn't have to be asked twice.

When Madge Collins opened her eyes again, her heart sank as she discovered that Sunday had left the crowd. And her cherubic face soon crumpled up in disdain when she saw in the distance her daughter making her way back along the Holloway Road with their neighbour, Bess Butler.

It never failed to surprise Sunday how different Bess's flat in 'the Buildings' was to the one she lived in with her mum and Aunt Louie. Not that number 7 was any cleaner or tidier than number 84 – quite the reverse in fact – but that Bess and her husband, Alf, had managed to create a home rather than just somewhere to exist. Number 7 was a corner flat on the third floor, overlooking Holloway Road on one side and Camden Road on the other. Despite the fact that Alf was a keen do-it-yourself fanatic, none of the rooms had seen a new coat of paint since before the war, but only because home decoration materials of any kind had been hard to come by. However, Bess had managed to give the place a stylish look, for in the parlour she had frilled and looped the lace curtains, hung framed copies of old paintings which she had bought from second-hand junk shops, and placed the parlour table by the Camden Road window so that she and Alf could watch passers-by down below. All the furniture was utility-made, which meant that it was very plain, simple, but functional.

'Never expected to see you spending your Sunday afternoon listening to a Salvation Army Band,' said Sunday, who sat in the most comfortable of the utility armchairs. 'Weren't you bored out of your mind?'

Bess, who had kicked off her shoes and had her legs curled up on the sparse utility sofa, replied, 'Let me tell yer somefin', Sun. I don't believe in knockin' the old Glory Brigade. At least they're good an' 'onest – they care about people. Which is more than yer can say about some of the shit in these "Buildin's".' She picked up an already open packet of American cigarettes from the floor beside her, and offered one to Sunday. 'Fag? Oh no, I fergot – yer don't, do yer?'

To Bess's surprise, Sunday stretched across and helped herself to a cigarette.

Bess shook the pack until she was able to take out one of

the cigarettes with her lips. 'I remember 'ow they looked after everyone durin' the Blitz. Bloody saints they was, servin' up tea to firemen and injured people wiv bombs droppin' all 'round 'em, sayin' prayers over dead people, singing hymns to cheer people up. No, mate. Bess Butler don't knock people like that.'

The more Sunday knew Bess, the more she liked her. Most important of all, she respected her. Although Bess was over twenty years older than herself, she felt a great affinity with her. When she was in her company she felt relaxed, and able to talk about the things that worried her. Bess also had the knack of making her feel that she wasn't just a seventeen-year-old kid, but a young woman with a mind and feelings of her own.

'Your mum's like that, yer know. A good person – right down to 'er bones.'

Bess leaned across to light Sunday's fag, but smiled a bit when the smoke made the girl cough. ''Ow's the old gel gettin' on?' she asked.

Sunday shrugged her shoulders, and quickly tried to inhale another mouthful of smoke.

'Wos up?'

Sunday, unsuccessful in her attempts to inhale the smoke into her lungs, looked across at Bess. 'Nothing,' she replied.

'Come on, Sun. I weren't born yesterday, yer know.'

From the floor at her side, Sunday picked up the cup of tea that Bess had made. There was no saucer. Bess didn't believe in such etiquette.

'Bess,' said Sunday, leaning back in her chair, her eyes staring aimlessly up at the ceiling. 'D'you think my mum's too old to have a boyfriend?'

Now it was Bess's turn to cough out some fag smoke. 'Say that again.'

Sunday swung back to look at her friend. 'I'm not joking, Bess.'

Bess took her legs off the sofa, and turned to face Sunday. 'Is yer mum too old ter 'ave a boyfriend?' she repeated in a high-pitched voice. 'Who told yer *that*, may I ask?'

'Aunt Louie.'

Bess suddenly let rip with a fag-filled chesty laugh that was loud enough to wake up a dead man, let alone all the neighbours. 'Good old Louie!' she bellowed. 'Never fails ter come up wiv somefin' new!'

For a moment, Sunday just watched her friend as she rocked to and fro with laughter. She liked Bess too much to care whether she was taking the piss out of her. Besides, she admired this woman *so* much. For her age, she was such a good-looking woman, and even though she wore too much make-up, she had a wonderful milk-white complexion, blue eyes, and a full bust that needed very little help from a bra. Sunday knew, of course, that Bess's hair was dyed dark brown, but as she had never seen the original colour, she had no idea what it actually was.

Bess gradually stopped laughing, and fixed her young friend with an affectionate smile. ''Ow old are yer now, Sun?'

Sunday hesitated for a moment before answering. 'Seventeen.'

'Seventeen! God – are yer really? It don't seem possible.'

Bess picked up her own cup of tea from the floor, got up from the sofa, and walked across the room to the window. As soon as she got there, she swung around to look at Sunday. 'Don't be a nark, Sun,' she said, firmly. 'If yer mum *'as* got a boyfriend, then good luck to 'er. Every woman should 'ave a boyfriend, no matter *'ow* old she is, no matter if she's married or not. Why should fellers 'ave all the fun? Women 'ave a lot ter offer, Sun. Don't you ever ferget that.'

For one brief moment, Sunday felt embarrassed, and she had to lower her eyes. What Bess had said was obviously what Bess herself had always felt. The fact was, Bess was a woman with – a reputation. She loved her husband – yes, that was without doubt. But everyone in 'the Buildings' knew about her other life, the life she led down 'the Dilly', Piccadilly Circus in the West End, where she had been seen night after night 'on the game' outside the Stage Door Canteen, where she was available for any well-paid American serviceman who wanted a good night out. Bess had never confided in Sunday as to why she had to do such a thing, and Sunday had never asked. But the only person who didn't seem to know what was going on was Bess's old man, Alf, who was now prematurely retired on account of ill health, and who had always been under the impression that the bread his missus was earning came from all-night work as a receptionist at a posh West End hotel.

Bess was soon aware of Sunday's discomfort. She crossed to the parlour table, stubbed out her half-finished fag, took out another one from the packet, and quickly lit it. 'Tell me somefin', Sun,' she said, briskly, fag in lips, one elbow resting on her hand. 'Are yer still a virgin?'

Sunday looked up with a start. If it had been anyone else asking her that sort of question – anyone, even her own mum – she would have exploded. But because it was Bess, she had no hesitation at all in answering. 'No,' she said calmly. 'As a matter of fact, I'm not.'

Bess paused a moment before continuing. 'Does that worry yer?'

Sunday looked surprised. 'No. Why should it?'

'No reason. Oh, don't worry, I 'ad my first session when I was a good bit younger than you. It's all right if yer enjoy it, if yor careful.' Without realising what she was doing, she went back to the ash-tray and stubbed out her newly lit fag. 'The only fing is, it's not worf takin' chances, Sun. If yer take chances, well—' For her own reasons, Bess made a point of avoiding Sunday's look. 'I don't 'ave ter tell yer, do I?'

After an odd, brief silence between them, Bess went across to Sunday, and crouched down on the floor beside her. 'This lot 'round 'ere reckon yor a bit of a wild'un. Wot d'yer reckon, Sun?'

Sunday grinned. 'If that's what they think, let them think it.'

Now Bess grinned too. 'Good fer you, gel,' she said, taking hold of Sunday's hands, and clasping them into her own. 'But look, wot I've said to yer before still goes. If yer ever want ter talk ter me about anyfin' – anyfin' at all – yer will do so, won't yer?'

Sunday's grin broadened at once into a beaming smile. She nodded a very definite yes.

Bess squeezed Sunday's hands, and also smiled. ''Ave a fag,' she said, taking the packet and offering her one. 'No. Take the packet,' she added, with a twinkle in her eyes. 'Don't worry. There's plenty more where *they* came from.'

# Chapter 4

Sunday liked to have a good time. That was something she had never denied. It was true what Bess Butler had told her, how a lot of people in 'the Buildings' had thought of her as a bit of a 'wild'un'. But in Sunday's opinion, it wasn't her fault. Apart from the fact that she had been brought up by two elderly women instead of her own mum and dad, the war had prevented her from having the freedom to do all the things a girl of her age would like to do. Everything was hard to get – decent clothes, make-up, nice food, lots of little luxuries like eau de cologne, paper and envelopes, even empty milk bottles had to be handed back because there was a shortage of glass, and she was not even allowed to leave the wireless set switched on for too long in case it wasted the valves. Yes, life for a teenager during wartime was not only hard, it was unnatural. Unnatural because she was forced to act and think like an adult, and thinking things out for herself was something Sunday was always reluctant to do. It was like being asked to make a decision. Why should someone of her age be expected to do things like that. Surely decisions were the responsibility of old people, like her mum. She couldn't bear being told by people to 'grow up, and stop behaving like a child'. If making decisions was being 'grown-up', then Sunday wanted no part of it. Anyway, the war had deprived her of her childhood, a fact which she deeply resented. Most times she was at war with the world, and that included her own friends.

Oddly enough, however, Sunday did occasionally feel remorse, and after two weeks of almost totally ignoring Pearl, she tried – and failed – to find a way of making it up with her. Not that Pearl was even remotely responsible for any bad feeling between them. After all it had been Sunday who had taken umbrage when Lennie Jackson had turned up at the Athenaeum that Saturday night. The reasons for Sunday's jealousy were plain and obvious: Sunday wanted Lennie; Lennie wanted Pearl. That's all there was to it. Of course, deep down inside, Sunday knew who was to blame, but she would never have the strength to admit it. And so, as always happened when she went quiet on someone who had upset her, it was left to Pearl to make the first move.

''Arry Smike was askin' after you, Sun.'

At first, Sunday pretended that she hadn't heard Pearl talking to her. 'Oh – sorry. Did you say something?'

It was the morning teabreak at Briggs Bagwash, and most of the 'Baggies' were outside in the stable-yard, taking the opportunity of a few minutes' fresh air in the warm sunshine.

Pearl tried again. ''Arry Smike. Yer know – that Air Force boy down the Afenaeum that night. The jitterbug – remember?'

Sunday paused a moment, as though that evening was no more than a distant memory. 'Oh – *him*,' she replied, grandly. 'Where d'you see him then?'

'Turns out he lives in the next street ter me. Lives wiv 'is mum and dad and 'is two bruvvers.' With only a few minutes left to spare before Ma Briggs terminated the teabreak, Pearl blew at the tea in her chipped white mug to cool it. 'Sounds like 'e really fancies yer,' she said, peering at Sunday over the cup as she sipped the tea.

'Oh yes.' Sunday was determined to show indifference.

''E wants us ter go out wiv 'im. You an' me. An' I can bring Lennie.'

Sunday froze.

'Apparently 'e's got an aunt who works as a part-time usherette up the Finsbury Park Empire. 'E says 'e can get us some tickets for Tuesday week.'

Sunday sipped her tea. 'What's so special about Tuesday week?'

Pearl looked up with a surprised start. 'Yer mean yer don't know? It's the broadcast. It's comin' live from the featre.'

'What broadcast?' asked Sunday. 'What are you talking about?'

'*'Enry 'All's Guest Night*!' Pearl looked at Sunday as though her friend had been living on another planet all her life. 'Didn't yer read about it? It's been in all the papers – well, the *Islington Gazette* anyway.'

Sunday was suddenly interested. Henry Hall at the Finsbury Park Empire! A chance to see not only a real band on the stage, but to be present at a broadcast performance of one of the most famous programmes on the wireless. 'How much are the tickets?' she asked, trying not to sound too eager.

'Fer free!' said Pearl. ''E says 'e can get us seats downstairs in the stalls. Just fink of it, Sun. I've only ever bin upstairs in the gods. I've never been down in the posh seats.'

And neither had Sunday. By the time Ma Briggs appeared at the back door, she had agreed to make up the foursome with Pearl and Harry.

The one flea in the ointment was Lennie Jackson.

Doll and Joe Mooney hardly ever went shopping together. Joe hated trailing his wife with a bunch of kids in tow, and then having to stand outside Sainsbury's whilst she gabbed with one of the assistants on the cheese counter. But this was a special occasion, for within the next few days their youngest, Josie, was having her third birthday. Luckily, they soon found a toy car for the birthday girl. It came from the Children's Department in the North London Drapery Stores in Seven Sisters Road, although a bit on the expensive side at two shillings and sixpence. A toy car was an unusual choice, but Josie much preferred the presents her brothers got to the dolls and toy kitchen sets that were supposed to be so beloved by little girls.

Sunday and her mum bumped into the Mooneys as the family were making their way along Hornsey Road on their way back to 'the Buildings'. The Mooneys lived in the same block as the Collinses, but on the floor below. They had the reputation of being like rabbits because they had already bred four kids, and as good Catholics, chances were they had every intention of completing a football team.

'Looks like it's all over bar the shouting,' bleated Doll Mooney, who, with all her hair pinned on top of her head, was only as tall as her husband. 'Did you hear it on the eight o'clock news this morning? They reckon the invasion's comin' any minute.'

Sunday could have screamed. She was sick to death of hearing about the invasion. Yes, she had heard it on the wireless that morning, and she couldn't care less. In fact, she was far more interested in what the Radio Doctor had to say about gall bladders than whether and when the Allies were going to land in France.

'I shall pray for them every night,' sighed Madge anxiously. 'When I think of what our boys went through at Dunkirk, it sends a chill up my spine.'

Two of the Mooneys' older kids started laughing and playing tag with each other. Sunday wanted to laugh with them, but even she thought it was hardly the moment to do so.

'Cut it out you two!' snarled Joe Mooney, in his rich Irish brogue. It was his only contribution to the idle pavement gossip, for he had a wandering eye for any bit of skirt that happened to pass within a hundred yards or so.

'The fing I'm really worried about though are these secret weapons they keep talkin' about.' As Josie was beginning to grizzle, Dolly had to pick her up out of her pushchair and hold her in her arms. 'They're sayin' if it's true, this time 'Itler could blow up the 'ole of London.'

''Itler's got no secret weapons,' growled Joe. 'It's all bluff.'

'I don't know, Joe,' said Madge. 'The papers are full of it.'

'Planes wivout pilots. That's wot I read.' Doll was doing her best to keep little Josie's fingers from prodding her in the eye.

'Planes without pilots! Come off it Doll!' Joe pushed his flat cap to the back of his head, and retrieved a dog-end from behind his ear. 'Next t'ing yer'll be tellin' me is that they're fillin' up bombs with horse shit!'

'Joe!' snapped Doll. 'Don't be so coarse!'

This time Sunday did laugh. All in all, she liked the Mooneys; they were always good for a laugh, despite Doll's doom-laden forecasts of death and destruction. However, despite her efforts to dismiss all thoughts of the war from her mind, Sunday was also concerned about the possibility of a renewed aerial bombardment by the *Luftwaffe*, this time from pilotless bomber planes. It was true what her mum had said. The newspapers were full of speculation about Hitler's last-ditch stand, and how his new retaliatory secret weapon had been designed to turn the tide of the war in his favour. Sunday still had painful memories of those dark days during the Blitz, when life and death for everyone was balanced on a knife's edge. She remembered how her poor mum had come home during the early hours of every morning, tired out after a night of trying to help and comfort the victims of endless aerial bombardment. To Sunday, her mum was a saint, and so were all her mum's Salvation Army pals who always did so much for everyone in return for nothing. And as she stood there on the corner of Hornsey and Tollington Roads, staring up at the quiet dignity of the surrounding houses and shops, their windows still covered with the criss-cross patterns of protective sticky tape, in her mind's eye she could still see all the carnage and havoc that covered the streets after a night's bombing, and the sounds of children crying, people calling out for help, and the incessant drone of enemy planes as they passed over on their way to the next point of destruction. Could it really happen again, she asked herself?

'We have to be going now, Doll,' Madge said. 'We've got to get the shopping done for the weekend. We're going to get Sunday a new pair of shoes.' She suddenly realised that Sunday's attention was miles away. 'Are you ready, dear?'

For a moment Sunday didn't respond. She was busily exchanging smiles with little Barry, the Mooneys' six-year-old, who was Sunday's favourite because he always seemed to be deep in thought.

Madge had to repeat herself. 'Sunday? Shall we go, dear?'

'Pardon?' said Sunday, turning back to her mum. 'Oh – yes. Righto.'

'We've got to be off too,' said Dolly, putting little Josie back into her pushchair. 'If Joe's late for the Arsenal, there'll be all 'ell ter pay!'

Joe didn't bother to answer his wife. He merely grabbed hold of two of his younger children, and started to move off down Tollington Road.

'See yer later then, Madge,' called Doll, as she took hold of another child's hand, and hurriedly pushed Josie's pushchair off behind the rest of her family. 'Oh, by the way,' she called, over her shoulder. 'Your friend sent 'is love. You know, that nice Mr Billings. We saw 'im just going in ter The Eaglet ter 'ave a drink wiv Jack Popwell. 'E said 'e'll see yer at the service termorrow mornin'.'

Madge tried not to look uneasy, so she smiled back at Doll, waved at her, and walked on in the opposite direction with Sunday.

Madge and her daughter reached the back gates of Pakeman Street School before they said a word to each other. Finally, Sunday couldn't resist asking the question: 'Who's Mr Billings?'

Madge quickened her pace as she made her way along the road. 'Oh, just one of the helpers up at Highbury,' she said quite matter-of-factly. 'He's a nice man.'

As they crossed Mayton Street and finally reached the traffic lights at Seven Sisters Road, Madge didn't mention another word about Mr Billings. And as much as she was dying to know about Madge's new 'friend', Sunday loved her mum too much to ask. For the time being at any rate.

'Hallo, everyone. This *is* Henry Hall speaking – and tonight is my Guest Night.'

Whilst Sunday was waiting for the light bulb at the side of the microphone to turn from green to red, her heart was thumping so loud she thought it would be heard all over the country. So by the time Henry Hall himself spoke into the microphone, and then turned around to conduct his BBC Dance Orchestra in his opening signature tune, she thought she would die from excitement.

The first house evening performance at the Finsbury Park Empire was stuffed to capacity. Every seat in the place was taken from gods to stalls, for *Henry Hall's Guest Night* was one of the most famous programmes on the wireless. For half an hour, the whole country would be tuned in to what was happening on the stage of that very same music hall where, during the war years, Sunday had seen and heard some of her favourite dance bands. And for the first time in her life, she was seeing it from the posh seats – to be precise, from the centre of the third row, front stalls. And what a night to be there, after the announcement earlier in the day that the Allies had launched their eagerly awaited invasion of mainland Europe!

It was also only the second time she had met Harry Smike, and she really quite liked him. He wasn't, of course, as sexy and good-looking as Lennie Jackson, but she did have to admit that he had a smile that was quite titillating. The two boys were sitting on either side of the girls, so that during the show after the broadcast, Sunday and Pearl could exchange intimate chitchat about their boyfriends without being overheard.

Henry Hall himself clearly warmed to the heady atmosphere his show always generated, and his tall, gangly figure, immaculate in black tie and dinner suit, blended beautifully with the red plush, gold-tasselled stage curtains, which tastefully matched the stall and dress-circle seats, and the ornate gold-leaf stuccos around the stage boxes. Although he seemed to Sunday to be a shy man, when Henry Hall raised his baton, the sounds coming from his talented band of musicians sent Sunday into a state of total ecstasy. And the moment he made a reference to 'our gallant boys who are now fighting the Nazis on French soil', the place rocked with thunderous cheers. Sunday also clapped hard and long with the rest of the audience as each 'guest' appeared, especially those who sang, but she even laughed at the special guest, Jeanne de Casalis, whose 'on the telephone' act as the dithery 'Mrs Feather' was a great favourite with everyone.

During the broadcast, Sunday had been so carried away by the excitement of the occasion that she hadn't realised that Harry Smike was not only holding her hand, but squeezing it. On one occasion, whilst a marvellous young singer called Dorothy Squires was singing 'You'll Never Know' with her husband Billy Reid at the piano, Harry even leaned across and kissed Sunday on her ear. By the time the half-hour broadcast had come to an end with Henry

Hall's familiar fade-out song, 'Here's To The Next Time', Harry had snaked his arm around Sunday's shoulders.

After the end of the first house show, Sunday and Harry came out of the theatre with Pearl and Lennie, and they all went to have a drink at the pub by the railway bridge just near the Tube Station. Considering it was a weekday, the place was absolutely crowded, and the two girls had to wait on the pavement outside whilst the two fellers fought their way through to the counter.

'Listen, Sun,' yelled Pearl, trying to be heard above the rowdy singsong coming from inside the pub. 'I've bin wantin' ter say 'ow sorry I am – about wot 'appened down the Afenaeum the uvver Saturday night.'

All of a sudden, Sunday felt awful. She was the one who should be apologising, not Pearl. It happened every time. If ever she, Sunday, was in the wrong, she could never bring herself to say so. And even now, as she looked at Pearl's dumpy little face all racked with unnecessary guilt, she couldn't actually put into words what she really wanted to say. So she made do with, 'Forget it, Pearl! It doesn't matter.' She had to shout really loud, for the singsong inside had been replaced by loud, boozy cheers.

Pearl waited for the row to calm down before speaking again. 'It *does* matter, Sun,' she said. 'Lennie 'ad no right ter take me off an' leave you on yer own. It was – 'orrible. I told Lennie.'

'Stop apologising, Pearl,' Sunday said brusquely. 'You're always apologising. I've forgotten all about it.'

'Well, *I* 'aven't, Sun. I 'ate it when you an' me fall out. You're the best friend a gel could ever 'ave. An' that's the 'onest troof.'

Sunday felt as though she wanted to curl up and die. Just for once why couldn't she say that she was the one to blame, not Pearl? Why couldn't she say that she was the one who walked out in a huff that night, because she was jealous – jealous that Lennie Jackson fancied Pearl and not her? How could she treat her best friend with such disdain? Pearl was more like her sister, she trusted her, she loved her. In fact, after her own mum, she probably loved Pearl more than anyone else in the whole world.

'Don't drink it too fast, gels,' said Lennie, calling from the pub door. 'You ain't gettin' anuvver one 'til turnin'-out time!'

The two fellers, hot and sweaty after their battle to squeeze past the crowd of drunks inside the pub, finally reached Sunday and Pearl with their drinks held high over their heads.

Harry smiled at Sunday, and gave her the glass of lemonade she'd asked for. 'I wish you'd 'ave somefin' stronger than that,' he said, standing as close to her as he possibly could. 'Makes yer relax,' he added, with a cool smirk on his face.

'I know,' replied Sunday. 'That's what I'm afraid of.'

All four laughed, including Lennie, who had his drink in one hand and his other arm around Pearl's waist. 'Yer know, I really enjoyed that ternight,' he said. 'Old 'Enry puts on a pretty good show, don't 'e?'

'Well don't sound so surprised,' Pearl said, scoldingly. 'Some people'd give their right arm to get in ter see that show. Fanks ever so much, 'Arry. It was a real treat.'

'Any time,' replied Harry, who, not to be outdone by Lennie, now had his arm around Sunday's shoulders. 'Fank my Aunt Lil, not me.' Sunday turned her face away when he tried to kiss her on the side of her lips, but when she saw Lennie doing the same thing to Pearl, she turned back again, and virtually forced Harry's lips against her own.

Although there was now a crowd on the pavement outside the pub, nobody took any notice of the two servicemen snogging with their girls. Across the road, the audience was just flowing out of the majestic Astoria Cinema, and almost immediately bus queues had formed on either side of the Seven Sisters Road, whilst hordes of people hurried across to catch late-evening trains from Finsbury Park Tube Station.

Once Lennie had pulled away from Pearl he used the back of his hand to wipe her dark red lipstick from his lips, allowing them both to take a swig of their drinks. Harry took a little longer to pull away from Sunday. Although she knew he would make a meal of it, she did nothing to discourage him, as long as she could be quite sure that Lennie could see everything she was doing. What she didn't notice, however, was that someone else was also interested. In fact, that same person had been watching her every movement from inside the pub ever since she had arrived.

It was Ernie Mancroft.

'Last orders please, ladies and gents!'

The landlord's voice was used to yelling above the din of his rowdy customers, so it easily reached the pavement outside.

Lennie quickly downed the last dregs of bitter from his pint glass. 'Feel like a fill-up, 'Arry? One fer the road?'

'No fanks, mate,' replied Harry, after draining his own glass. 'Don't fink I could cope wiv gettin' back to that counter.'

'Come on!' Lennie was already collecting the girls' empty glasses. 'I've got ter make the best of me last night.'

Sunday swung a startled glance at him. 'Last night?'
'Yeh. I'm on postin' termorrer.'
Sunday immediately switched her glance to Pearl.
'I'm tryin' 'ard not ter fink about it,' sighed Pearl, who looked thoroughly miserable.
'Does that mean . . .' Sunday asked, tentatively. 'Is it the invasion?'
'You don't ask questions like that,' replied Lennie, half scoldingly.
'Why not?'
''Cos I can't answer them.'
Harry put one arm around Sunday's waist, and leaned his head on her shoulder. 'Yer know wot they say, Sun. Careless talk costs lives.'
'There's too many lives been lost in this war already!' snapped Sunday. 'It's time it was all over!'
'Well there's no chance of that,' snorted Lennie, with a wry chuckle. 'Not 'til we do somefin' about it.'
Sunday's outburst had turned a few heads, but she was much too upset to care about what any of them were thinking. Ironically enough, it was Harry who latched on. Several times during the evening he had noticed the way Sunday had been taking sly looks at Lennie, and her outburst had confirmed to him that the guy she fancied most of all was Private Lennie smartarse Jackson. But Harry made up his mind that he was not going to let Sunday spoil Pearl's last evening alone with Lennie, so he quickly suggested that the two couples split up and go their separate ways.
Sunday's farewell handshake with Lennie may have seemed convincing to her, but inside she felt like bawling her head off.

The night air smelt as sweet as perfume. Everything was so fresh, so bursting with life, and now that the pubs had closed, the stench of beer was gradually losing its battle against the smell of freshly cut grass in the nearby park, and the distant approach of another glorious early summer's day.
June was Sunday's favourite month, for the days were long and the nights were short, and that meant not having to go to bed early like a good little girl. Sunday didn't want to be a good little girl. In fact, it was the last thing in the world she ever wanted to be, despite the fact that her mum couldn't get to sleep whenever Sunday was out even a minute after ten o'clock at night. So she didn't feel a moment's guilt when, after leaving

Pearl and Lennie, she had readily accepted Harry's invitation to go for a stroll.

By eleven o'clock, the streets became deserted very quickly. Here and there a drunk was being helped home by his mates, or a van would turn up to collect the day's fill of pig-swill bins from some of the back streets. And as they made their way along Seven Sisters Road towards Manor House, Sunday and Harry were suddenly startled by an unseen figure shouting, 'Put yer light out missus! Don't yer know there's a war on!' Although the offending light was quickly extinguished, the disturbance set a dog barking, who in turn provoked a network of panicked messages to practically every dog in the neighbourhood.

Although Harry strolled along with his arm around Sunday's waist, her thoughts were miles away. They were with Lennie Jackson, who, she imagined, was probably at that very minute snogging with Pearl in some back alley, and doing things which Sunday would much prefer he did to her. A whole range of emotions flashed through her mind, from bitterness to rage, and to the dread that if Lennie were to be killed taking part in the invasion, she would never see him again.

As they dawdled idly along the main road, Sunday and Harry could hear distant laughter coming from the RAF and Army crews in the adjacent Finsbury Park who were keeping a constant watch on the barrage of crafty silver balloons which floated silently on the ends of their steel cables in the skies above, acting as a stockade against any hostile aerial attack. On such a still night, the laughter seemed a strange sound, for it seemed to have no reason, no logic, no place in time.

Sunday suddenly felt the urge to go into the park, but as the gates were always closed to the public at sunset, there was no way in. But Harry, excited by the thought of getting Sunday all to himself in there, told her that if she would be prepared to walk with him to the other side of the park, he knew a gap in the wooden fence that had replaced the old iron railings, which had been taken away at the beginning of the war to be used for scrap metal. Sunday agreed without hesitation, and once they had passed Manor House Tube Station and made their way down Green Lanes opposite Harringay Stadium, they soon found Harry's gap in the fence along Endymion Road.

It was pitch-dark down by the park lake, and the chorus of tetchy ducks trying to get some sleep on the island in the middle was a sure sign that they had not taken too kindly to the approach of night intruders. As she and Harry made their way towards the tea pavilion, Sunday was acutely aware of the sounds their feet were making on the narrow gravelled paths. Although it was too dark for them to see the vegetable allotments that before the war had been beautiful flower-beds, Sunday could smell the early spring onions planted there amongst the potatoes, cabbages, carrots and all the other necessary vegetables that were so vital in keeping people fed during the 'Dig for Victory' campaign.

As they walked, Harry kept his arm firmly around Sunday's waist, as if making sure that she wouldn't change her mind and try to get away. After a while, he ventured to lean across and kiss her on the cheek, but when he kissed her full on the lips, he was only too aware that her response was pretty half-hearted. 'Sorry it's not the Army, eh Sun?' he whispered mockingly.

Sunday abruptly pulled her mouth away from him. 'What's that supposed to mean?'

'Come off it, Sun. I wasn't born yesterday, yer know. If Lennie Jackson was 'ere now, yer'd be feelin' a bit different, wouldn't yer?'

Sunday pulled loose from him brusquely. They had come to a halt in a small clearing just behind the tea pavilion. 'You know your trouble, don't you, Harry?' she snapped, a raw nerve clearly exposed. 'You've got an inferiority complex!'

Harry wasn't at all put out by Sunday's anger. In fact, it amused him. 'I watched yer down that pub. Couldn't keep yer eyes off 'im, could yer?' He moved closer to her. Although it was far too dark for him to see anything more than the outline of her figure, he knew that she was standing with her back to the timber planks lining the pavilion walls. 'Tell me somefin', Sun,' he said in a low, mischievous voice. 'Wot's Private Jackson got wot I 'aven't?'

To Harry's astonishment, Sunday suddenly threw her arms around his neck, and kissed him full on the lips. It didn't matter to him that she was doing it as an act of defiance, for the passion with which her mouth was pressed against his own was overwhelming, far more than he had ever thought her capable of. All he knew was that whatever she was trying to prove to him was exciting.

When Sunday finally pulled away, they were both breathless.

'Is that 'ow yer'd like ter do it ter Lennie?' he asked in a low but taunting voice.

Sunday, immediately enraged, tried to push him away. But Harry, prepared for her reaction, grabbed hold of her wrists and twisted them above her head. Then, in one swift movement, he pinned her back against the timber pavilion wall, leaned his body against her, and fought for her lips. Eventually, her anger gave way to passion, for she was now just as aroused as he was.

'I want you, Sun,' he whispered in her ear as their lips parted. His voice then became a plea. '*Please*.'

There was a moment's silence between them, and now that Duck Island had calmed down, the night was curiously still. Without saying a word, Sunday raised her skirt and removed her panties. Instinctively, Harry started to unbutton first his uniform tunic, and then his trousers.

Sunday was the first to speak. 'Have you got something? I don't want babies.'

Harry's voice was only just audible. 'You're jokin'. Neiver do I!'

Sunday leaned her back against the pavilion wall, and waited for Harry to come to her. In the dark she could hear him opening a packet of something; she knew only too well that most servicemen carried French letters, because she had often peered through barber shop windows and seen men buying them. It was several moments before she felt him pressing against her. Although she hated the feel of his blue uniform serge, which was prickly and anything but sensuous, she was now too excited to care about anything except the thrill of what was about to happen to her.

Harry lowered his trousers and underpants, took hold of Sunday's hands and arms and curled them around his neck, and then positioned himself. 'You're fantastic, Sun,' he whispered, his breath and body now burning-hot. 'This'll be much better than Lennie Jackson.'

At this sudden mention of Lennie's name again, Sunday felt the urge to pull away. But gradually, the idea excited her, and for a moment, whilst Harry was probing her body with his fingers, her imagination visualised Lennie with his arms around her, Lennie's bare abdomen pressing against her own, and Lennie . . .

But at that crucial moment when Sunday's fantasy was about to take full flight, a voice suddenly yelled out from the dark. 'Yer dirty bastard!'

Sunday was horrified, for she had recognised the voice immediately. 'Ernie!' she shouted.

Ernie Mancroft sprang up from nowhere, and leapt at Harry, tackling him straight to the ground.

Sunday quickly stepped out of the way, but could only hear the desperate fight that was going on at her feet. There were shouts of '*Bastard!*' and '*Yer sod!*' and the thudding sounds of fists as they struck home at face and body. Although she couldn't see the two men tearing at each other, the sounds of pain coming from Harry were enough to convince Sunday that the young RAF boy was getting the worst of it.

'Stop it, Ernie!' Sunday yelled, over and over again. 'Get out of here! It's nothing to do with you!'

The fact that Ernie wouldn't respond meant that he was determined to go on with his brutal attack.

'Ernie . . . !'

Sunday's desperate shout echoed across the park, sending the inhabitants of Duck Island into a frenzied chorus of panic. Simultaneously, Harry let out an agonised gasp before falling silent. Ernie had clearly laid him out for the count.

'Harry!' yelled Sunday, totally disoriented in the pitch-dark.

Sunday's yells provoked another sound, this time coming from a distant part of the park. It was a long blast on a police whistle.

Sunday fell to her knees, desperately trying to feel around for Harry on the ground. With her outstretched hands, she finally located him. 'Harry!' she cried, trying to lift his head. 'Harry! Talk to me!' As her fingers followed the outline of his face, she felt the blood trickling down his chin from his nose and from his mouth. 'Oh Christ, Ernie!' she said, trying hard to see him in the dark. 'What have you done to him, you sod!'

Ernie's voice came from an unexpected direction. 'I told yer, Sun.' He was standing directly behind her. 'Din't I tell yer? You're mine, Sun. Yer'll always be mine. No poncy little bastard like this is goin' ter take you away from me.'

'You're mad, Ernie!' she called back. 'You're stark, raving mad!' Whilst she was yelling at him, she was cradling Harry's battered head in her lap. 'I wouldn't touch a mad sod like you with fifty thousand bargepoles!'

At that moment, the police whistle echoed out again. The sound was getting closer.

'Over here!' Sunday bellowed. 'Over here!'

She had to raise her voice as loud as she could, because the ducks were flapping in and out of the water in panic on their island, making it difficult for Sunday to hear which way Ernie was running off to get away from the rapidly approaching police whistle.

'Ernie! Come back – you bloody coward! Come back . . . !'

Her shouts, however, were smothered by yet another sound. It was some way off, but its impact sent a chill down Sunday's spine.

It sounded like an aircraft, with an engine that seemed to chug rather than hum. And as she looked up at the dark night sky, in the far distance beyond the park, she could see a bright flame burning. Then the chugging sound stopped, and the flame extinguished. The silence that followed was climaxed by the most devastating explosion, which terrified Sunday so much that she threw herself right across Harry's lifeless body.

The extraordinary sounds Sunday had just heard were a chilling reminder that the war was not yet over.

In fact, it was about to begin all over again.

# *Chapter 5*

Overnight, elation turned to anxiety and fear. Whatever it was that had dropped out of the sky during the night of Tuesday, 13 June, everyone was now convinced that the first of Hitler's retaliatory secret weapons had arrived. Despite the fact that the explosion had occurred somewhere on the outskirts of London, most people in 'the Buildings' had heard it, and some, like Sunday, swore that they had actually seen that mysterious flame lighting up the dark night sky somewhere over the East End of London. Although the newspapers were very cagey about giving any details of the secret weapon, Doll Mooney was taking no chances, and from the first moment she heard that explosion she made all her four kids wear their gas masks in bed at night. The only hope now for a quick end to the war was the Allied invasion in France, now at the end of its second week, and gaining momentum.

Sunday, however, had other problems. The incident in Finsbury Park two nights previously had not only got her into trouble with the police, but it had also left Harry Smike with a fractured jaw and two broken front teeth. Worse still, Ernie Mancroft appeared to be getting off scot-free, having denied any part in the savage and unprovoked attack on the young airman. Sunday had always disliked Ernie but now she hated him. Sometimes she felt as though he was obsessed with her; all this talk about her belonging to him frightened her. She might have taunted him a little but she had never given him any reason to think about her like that. In fact, even though she had to work with him at the Bagwash each day, she had done everything in her power to ignore him. The way he had set upon poor Harry Smike had terrified her. Ernie came from a family of 'bruisers', a pig of a father and five sons who all went around as though they owned the place. If anyone ever dared say one word out of place they would give them a hiding they'd never forget. Ernie took after his dad and brothers all right. He was tough, strong, and very muscular, and he used that strength with horrifying brutality. Sunday's only hope was that once he was called up, the Army would knock the living daylights out of him.

'Yer know somefin', Sun,' said Pearl, sweat pouring down her face as she and Sunday worked the Bagwash tubs, 'We din't oughta be workin' durin' an air-raid. That siren went nearly two hours ago. It's dangerous up 'ere. We all oughta be down in the cellars.'

'Some hopes,' replied Sunday, who was at the scrubbing board trying hard to remove dirt from a shirt collar. 'If we lost five minutes' work that bloody woman'd stop it from our wages!'

'You're absolutely right, Collins.'

Both Sunday and Pearl turned with a start to find Ma Briggs, hands on hips, fag in mouth, standing just behind them.

'An' I'll tell yer anuvver fing, Miss Clever Arse,' she said, taking the fag from her lips and pointing it straight at Sunday, 'one more word out of you, and you're out!'

Sunday suddenly lost her cool. 'You've got no right to keep us up here during an air-raid,' she snapped. 'Those flying bombs come over without warning. We could all get killed.'

'There 'asn't bin an air-raid for munfs,' bawled Ma Briggs, furious that the girl had answered her back. 'If you fink I'm goin' ter stop work every time the bleedin' siren goes, yer've got anuvver fink comin'!'

'*You* don't stop work, Mrs Briggs – because *you* never start it!' At this point, Sunday had abandoned any idea of caution. 'We're the ones who do the work round here, not you!'

Pearl gasped, and dropped the washing soap she was using into the tub. Around her 'Baggies' everywhere stopped what they were doing, and were staring at Sunday and Ma Briggs in astonishment.

Ma Briggs was seething. She tossed her newly lit fag to the stone floor and twisted her shoe on to it furiously as though it was Sunday's face. 'You!' she snarled, calmly, as though trying to show the others who was boss. 'In my office – now!' She turned, and moved off.

Sunday did not follow her. 'You have no right to endanger our lives!' she called out, defiantly. 'You're a wicked old sow!'

There was a gasp from the 'Baggies', and a smirk from Ernie Mancroft, who was enjoying the exchange from the backyard door.

Ma Briggs stopped in her tracks, and turned. 'What did you say?' she demanded, face white with anger.

'She din't mean nuffin', Mrs Briggs,' Pearl said anxiously, going to Sunday and squeezing her arm. 'It's just that – well, we're all scared about these new flyin' bomb fings. They're not like wot we've 'ad before. We're scared, that's all. Sun din't mean nuffin' – honest she din't.' She turned to Sunday with pleading eyes. 'Did yer, Sun?'

'Oh yes, I did!' replied Sunday, quite fearlessly. 'I'm sick to death of this woman putting our lives at risk.' She tossed her bar of washing soap into the tub, sending up a splash of water straight into Ma Briggs's face. 'And I'm sick to death of being exploited!' she snapped, coming down from the tub step to confront the boss-lady. 'Sick to death of working in this place for a pittance! You don't want employees,' she said, glaring, voice restrained but angry, 'you want bloody slaves!'

Ma Briggs paused a moment, then walked off to the backyard door, pushed Ernie Mancroft out of the way, and opened it. Then turning back to Sunday, she yelled, 'Out!'

'No, Sunday!' pleaded a distraught Pearl. 'Please!'

Sunday shrugged her arm away from Pearl, took off her white working apron, and threw it into the hot tub of boiling water she had been working at. Then she marched off to the door where Ma Briggs was waiting for her. 'I wouldn't stay in this pigsty if you gave me a hundred pounds a week!' she snarled. 'Not for the likes of you I wouldn't.' And with that she took off her work-turban, and thrust it straight at the boss-lady. To her disgust, Ernie Mancroft was waiting by the door to hand her her own hat. Sunday snatched it from him, turned, and started to leave.

Ma Briggs immediately stepped in front of the door, and for a brief moment refused to let her pass. 'I'll say just one thing ter you, miss,' she growled, teeth clenched. 'You fink you're really somefin', don't yer? Well let me tell yer somefin' – you ain't. Your sort are a dime a dozen. 'Ere terday – gone termorrer!' She turned briefly from Sunday to address all the other 'Baggies'. 'An' that goes fer the rest of yer!'

The Bagwash was now at a standstill, for every girl had stopped work to listen to Ma Briggs. It was a strange sight, with small groups of anxious sweat-streaked faces peering through the hot steam that was curling up remorselessly from the three huge stone washing tubs. Even the 'Baggies'' cat, Moggie, was cowering behind one of the large mangles, with condensation trickling down on to his coal-black fur from the bleak white plaster walls.

'Yer know the trouble wiv you lot, don't yer?' yelled Ma Briggs, clearly out to instil the fear of God into her 'gels'. 'Yer've got it wiv jam on! OK! So I don't pay yer as much as I'd like. But at least yer get a week's pay and food in yer stomachs, which is more than yer can say fer some of them poor sods who've bin bombed out and lost everyfin' they ever 'ad!' Hands defiantly on hips, she raised her voice above the sound of boiling water bubbling away in the three washing tubs. 'But in case yer 'aven't 'eard – there's a war goin' on! An' it's up ter the likes of you an' me ter keep the 'ome front goin' 'til the blokes get back. An' make no mistake about it, they *are* comin' back! This bloody war's nearly over – over, d'yer 'ear! At this very moment our boys are bashin' the daylights out of 'Itler in France. In a couple er weeks they'll be in Berlin – an' it'll all be over!' She deliberately caught Pearl in her eyeline. 'So stop gettin' worked up about flyin' bombs – or whatever they call 'em. We've 'ad everythin' but the kitchen sink thrown at us before – an' we survived!'

Now Ma Briggs returned her attention to Sunday. 'An' as fer *exploitin'* my gels,' she said disdainfully, wagging a heavily nail-varnished finger straight at Sunday's face. 'Just let me tell yer somefin', *Miss* Collins.'

Sunday made a move to push past Briggs, but again found her exit barred.

'In this world, no one gets anyfin' fer nuffin'! All me life I've 'ad ter work me arse off doin' the fings I 'ate most. I pay wot I can afford. There's no crime in that!'

Sunday wasn't really listening to her. Stony-faced, she gazed at the chunky rolled-gold bracelet that forever dangled on the boss-lady's wrist.

Over by the largest of the three washing tubs, Pearl also wasn't listening. Subconsciously, she was looking up towards the ceiling.

'You're a troublemaker. Yer know that, don't yer, Collins.'

Sunday raised her eyes to look at Briggs. For one split second she felt sorry for this woman who had made her life such a misery. For one brief moment she felt pity. Briggs wasn't all bad. Her only problem was that she just wasn't young any more.

'From now on, there's only one way fer you ter go, mate. And that's down.' She stood back to allow Sunday to pass. 'Now piss off!'

'Shut up!'

Briggs stopped dead in her tracks. But it wasn't Sunday who had yelled at her. It was Pearl.

'Wot did you say?' growled Briggs, striding across to Pearl.

'Shut up, will yer!'

The other 'Baggies' stared on in shocked disbelief.

'Right!' rasped Briggs. As she spoke, she grabbed hold of Pearl's wrist, dragged her away from the washing tub, and virtually threw her across the workshop. 'Go on! Get back to yer mate! Out!'

Sunday immediately rushed to Pearl's aid. But Pearl, sprawled out on the stone floor, didn't attempt to get up. 'Listen!' she gasped, a look of terror on her face. Her eyes were transfixed on the ceiling. 'Can't yer 'ear it?'

All eyes immediately lifted upwards. For a moment, the only sounds that could be heard came from the bubbling hot water in the three washtubs. But gradually, cutting through this, was a very different sound.

The droning of a plane engine. A very different type of engine, throbbing, pulsating, menacing. And then came the barrage of ack-ack gunfire. Some of the 'Baggies' started to scream.

'Shut up all of yer!' yelled Briggs above the mayhem. 'Stay where yer are! Keep calm!'

Terrified out of their lives, the girls did as they were told.

Although the ack-ack fire became more frenzied, the determined droning sound rose above it. Whatever the approaching menace in the sky was, it seemed to be getting closer and closer.

Suddenly, the droning sound overhead cut out, followed by the ack-ack fire.

All was silent, save the bubbling of the boiling water in the washtubs.

A sea of frightened, anxious faces turned towards the ceiling. Someone was crying. Another was breathing hard. Another had her hands clasped together in silent prayer. Pearl, eyes closed, bit her lip. Sunday's entire body was tense and as hard as nails. 'Please God, don't let it fall here.' Her plea was silent, but desperate.

The next sound was like an approaching gush of air.

At that very moment, Sunday felt herself rugby-tackled by Ernie Mancroft, who had leapt across the workshop, grabbed hold of her, and quite literally propelled the two of them outside into the courtyard. Simultaneously, the gush of air descended on to the roof of the workshop, and the deafening explosion that followed was interspersed with screams.

Spread-eagled on the flagstone floor of the courtyard, Sunday, trying to protect her ears with her hands, found herself covered by the powerful weight and frame of Ernie Mancroft's body. With the entire workshop collapsing like a pack of cards behind them, they were instantly buried beneath a massive pile of falling debris.

In those few moments that seemed like hours, a stifling cloud of dust twisted up into the clear blue sky of a hot summer's afternoon.

The only sounds that remained now came from beneath the wreckage of what was once Briggs Bagwash.

Sobs and groans and pleading cries for help.

Madge Collins slapped her sister's face. In fact, she slapped it really hard. She had never done such a thing before, and it clearly hurt her more than Louie herself. But the explosion had sent Louie into hysterics, and it was the only way to snap her out of it.

'I told you we should have gone down to the shelter,' sobbed Louie, who for all her outward bravado was nothing but a bag of nerves. 'That air-raid warning's been on all day. We should have taken cover until the all-clear.'

'Everything's all right now, dear,' said Madge, trying to calm her sister with a tot of brandy from a bottle she had kept since before the war. 'Just take deep breaths and drink that down.'

'That's the trouble with people,' persisted Louie. 'Everyone's so stupid. Just because there's been a lull in the bombing, they carry on as though the war's over. Of course it's not over! It'll never be over while Jerry's using those – those terrible things against us.' And with that, she burst into tears.

Madge refused to wallow in her sister's hysteria. She had more pressing anxieties of her own. 'It wasn't very far away, that's for sure,' she said, struggling to open the parlour window on which two panes of glass had been literally blown out of the frame. 'Thank God we were in the bedroom when it happened.'

When she finally managed to get the window open and lean out, Madge could see a scene of utter confusion in the backyard of 'the Buildings'. People were running in and out of their flats, children crying, the ground covered with shattered glass and broken roof tiles, and the air was echoing to the sound of ambulance, police, and fire engine bells. In the middle of it all, Madge caught a glimpse of Doll Mooney helping some of the other residents to sweep up the broken glass. 'Doll!' she shouted at the top of her voice. 'Up here, Doll!'

Doll stopped briefly to look up. Some of her neighbours did likewise.

'Where is it, Doll?' called Madge, cupping her hands over her mouth in an attempt to be heard above the pandemonium in the yard below. 'Where is it?'

Doll couldn't hear a thing. All she could do was shrug her shoulders and wave back.

Luckily, Jack Popwell had heard Madge's voice, so he quickly came out on to the small balcony below, just in front of his kitchen. 'Wot is it Mrs Collins?' he called, craning his neck up to see her.

Madge leaned out as far as she dared on to her windowsill and called back down to him. 'Where did it come down, Jack?'

'Don't know exactly. Did yer see it? *I* did. Ruddy 'orrible fing! Looked like a plane wiv its arse on fire – if yer'll pardon the expression! Did yer 'ear its engine cut out?'

'Yes, I did,' replied Madge, her stomach twisting with anxiety.

'I reckon it come down 'round the Nag's 'Ead somewhere. It was pretty close I tell yer!'

'Thanks, Jack.'

Madge left the window. As she did so, the all-clear siren wailed out across the rooftops.

'About time too!' complained Louie, who had finished her brandy, and was clearly hoping for a quick refill.

Madge didn't respond. She was already on her way out of the flat.

In the backyard downstairs, the cleaning-up operation was in full swing. By the time Madge came out from the flats, small groups of neighbours were busily swapping stories about the flying bomb that had passed right above 'the Buildings' on its way to its point of destruction.

'Does anyone know where it's come down?' she asked nervously.

'It's down 'Olloway Road somewhere, Madge,' said Doll, who was secretly enjoying all the drama. Even so, she was only too aware of the reason for Madge's anxiety. 'Don't worry, dear. I'm sure it's nowhere near the Bagwash.'

Although Madge always contained her real feelings, inside she was going out of her mind with worry.

At this point, Lily Armstrong, another of Madge's neighbours, came into the yard from the main road outside. She was a large woman, and was ashen after the ordeal of being caught out whilst shopping when the flying bomb came down. 'I thought this bleedin' war was supposed ter be over,' she said breathlessly. 'I don't wanna go fru nuffin' like that again as long as I live.'

One of the women rushed forward and helped her with her shopping bag. 'Oh Lil!' she said. 'Where were yer, gel?'

'Down the Seven Sisters Road. I just got as far as Liptons, when all the windows blew out and Gord knows what. I tell yer, I'm lucky ter be 'ere terday!'

'Where'd it come down, Lil?' asked another woman, who was almost too scared to hear the answer.

'Just up past the 'ospital,' replied Lil. 'They say the Bagwash caught a packet.' The moment she caught sight of Madge, she could have bit her tongue off.

Shocked and grim-faced, the entire group of women turned to look at Madge.

A few minutes later, Madge was halfway along the Holloway Road, and passing the Nag's Head. Her legs felt like jelly, and she felt sure they would give way beneath her at any moment.

As she crossed the main road, she hardly noticed that the traffic lights had been blown out by the bomb-blast, and what little traffic there was had become stranded in the aftermath of the explosion. Hardly one shop window had survived the blast, and she was walking on broken glass, fallen chimney pots and masonry everywhere. On the other side of the main road, the staff of the imposing Gaumont Cinema building were busily sweeping up their own broken glass and fallen wall tiles. Even patrons from the matinée performance were helping out, and despite the interruption, the familiar wartime 'BUSINESS AS USUAL' placard was already on display.

As she drew closer to the Bagwash, Madge's heart was thumping hard, for in the distance she could see the fleet of emergency services lined up along the main road, which had been completely blocked off by the full force of the explosion. As she passed the Royal Northern Hospital, doctors, nurses, and a team of volunteers were out on the pavement clearing up bomb-blast damage. Others were guiding stretcher-bearers towards the site of the explosion further along the road.

Only when Madge arrived there herself did she realise the horror of what had happened. She came to an abrupt halt at a police cordon set up by special constables who had sealed off the area with rope and ahead of her was a scene of absolute carnage.

Madge's blood turned to ice as she stared at the huge pile of wreckage that was once Briggs Bagwash. The dust from the building's collapse had still not settled, and it was partially obscuring the vast team of rescue workers, dogs, and volunteers who were frantically trying to dig out any survivors. Madge was too stunned to cry. Her first action was to pull up the rope and make her way straight to the pile of wreckage.

'Can't come back 'ere, missus.'

Madge found herself being held back by a special constable.

'Please,' Madge begged. 'My daughter's in there.'

The constable put his arm around Madge's shoulders. 'It won't do any good, darlin',' he said, holding her to him as sympathetically as he could. 'There's nuffin' left of the place.'

'Isn't anyone alive?' Madge asked, her eyes pleading for just one word of hope. 'Anyone at all?'

The constable tried a weak, comforting smile. 'Too early ter say yet, darlin'. Just say yer prayers.'

As the constable spoke, two stretcher-bearers brought out a victim, covered over completely with a red hospital blanket.

Madge didn't know what to say, or to think. The only thing the lifelong Salvationist could do was what she had done every day of her life. Dropping to her knees, she closed her eyes and clasped her hands together.

'Oh God,' she said, in a voice only barely audible. 'Oh dear, dear God. Please don't forsake me. Not now. Not now.'

On the far side of the wreckage a young hospital nurse picked something out of the debris.

It was a chunky rolled-gold bracelet.

# *Chapter 6*

It was a beautiful day, sun streaking through the branches of the big oak trees, their heavily veined rich green leaves shimmering in the bright sunshine. Ducks preening themselves along the sides of the lake. Greedy seagulls swooping down for the bits of bread that Sunday was casting into the water. Her mum was there too, kneeling on the grass, knitting Sunday a thick woolly jumper. Unfortunately, Aunt Louie was also there, lying flat on her back, eyes closed. Every so often, Sunday watched her, fascinated by the thin trail of smoke from her cigarette, which was curling up into the cloudless blue sky to form strange animal-shaped patterns. And all around, people were strolling about in their Sunday best, mums and dads with babies in prams, young men arm in arm with their girlfriends, small children on scooters and tricycles, and elderly couples watching it all from the comfort of a park bench, reliving their lives all over again. Finsbury Park had never looked more radiant. It was a beautiful day. A perfect day for everyone – especially a child. Sunday was seven years old. And yet – something was not quite right. There was no sound. Sunday couldn't hear the ducks and seagulls fighting over her scraps of bread. She couldn't hear the other children laughing and yelling as they played hide and seek with each other around the boat house. And she couldn't hear what her mum was singing to herself, even though she knew it must be one of her favourite hymns. But there was something more. The surface of the lake – it looked different. No longer the blue reflection of the sky above, but a dark grey, and then black. And then a face. The face of a man – a young man, staring at her from beneath the surface. Gradually, it was rising up out of the water. It was horrifying. It was unreal. It was – Ernie Mancroft. Sunday screamed out as loud as she could. But no sound. She couldn't hear her own scream. No sound! Ernie was laughing at her. And again – she screamed!

Sunday's eyes sprang open with a terrified start. The first thing she saw was a window. It was dark outside, but rain was streaming down the glass panes. She tried to move. But her body was aching all over and burning-hot. She was lying in bed, but not her own bed, and she was soaked in perspiration.

It was several minutes before any logical thoughts formed in her mind. Yes, she was Sunday Collins all right. But she wasn't seven years old. She was seventeen, a young woman, a beautiful young woman, with all her life ahead of her. But who *were* these people peering down at her, dabbing the sweat from her forehead, smiling sweetly, sympathetically. Why couldn't she hear what they were saying to her? A nurse. A man in a white jacket. A doctor? Hospital? This was a hospital? And then she remembered. Slowly she remembered. The Bagwash. The sound of the flying bomb. The explosion. The screams. The silence.

'You're all right, Sunday. Everything's going to be all right.'

Sunday had no idea what the doctor – if that's what he was – was saying.

'You've had a terrible experience, Sunday,' said the nurse, who was holding Sunday's left hand, and stroking it tenderly. 'We're going to get you fit and strong.' She turned briefly to look up at the man in the white jacket. 'Isn't that right, Doctor?'

Despite the feeling of numbness throughout her body and limbs, Sunday was getting irritated that she couldn't hear one single word they were saying. 'What did you say?' she said, but she couldn't hear her own voice either. 'Why d'you have to whisper?'

The doctor and nurse exchanged an odd look.

Only then did Sunday realise that her head and ears were swathed in bandages.

'Just try to lie still, Sunday.'

The man in the white jacket was using his lips in an exaggerated way to try to form the words.

'You've got a lot of cuts and bruises, Sunday,' he continued, using his own hands to illustrate what he meant. 'And a nasty bang on the back of your head. A few days' rest and you'll be fine.'

As the nurse spoke, Sunday was very aware that she was using her tongue and teeth to spell out the words. And her lips were making the most extraordinary contortions. 'It's amazing how you survived at all, Sunday,' she said, a broad sympathetic smile on her saintly face. 'If it hadn't been for that boyfriend of yours—' She sighed deeply. 'It's too awful to think what might have happened.'

It was a good thing Sunday was unable to read the words being formed by the nurse's lips.

At that moment, Sunday's attention turned to the ward she had been taken to. Her eyes were still not focusing accurately, but through the cloud she could just see the rest of the patients in their beds, some of them with legs or arms suspended on pulleys, others heavily bandaged, and several of them with drip-feeds and oxygen masks. She was clearly in a casualty ward, although she was still too disoriented to know which hospital the ward was in. Distressingly, one or two beds were completely curtained off, and only then did memories of those last few terrible moments at the Bagwash start flooding through her brain: the droning sounds throbbing in the sky above, the silence, the rush of air, and the astonishing sensation of being caught in the middle of a gigantic explosion, followed by a complete blackout. From that moment on, however, she couldn't remember a thing. Oh, if only Pearl were there to tell her.

At that moment, Sunday felt someone kissing her gently on the cheek. Although it was painful to turn her head, her spirits rose when she saw who was stooped over her. 'Mum,' she said, tearfully, without being able to hear the sound of her own voice.

'Oh Sunday.' Madge was gently stroking her daughter's hand as she spoke. 'My dear, dear baby. Our Lord has answered my prayers.'

Sunday had no idea what her mum was saying. All she knew was that tears were running down the poor woman's cheeks.

'We'll have you home in no time,' said Madge, holding Sunday's hand with both her own, and finding it very difficult to be brave. And her face crumpled up in tears as her tongue and lips tried to form the words, 'I love you so much, Sunday.'

Her mum's odd behaviour was beginning to unnerve Sunday. 'I can't hear what you're saying,' she said, not realising that her own voice was raised. 'Why can't I hear you?'

Madge swung a quick glance to the doctor, hoping for some kind of help. But the doctor, aware that Sunday was watching everyone's reactions, was careful not to indicate anything by his expression. However, the look in his eyes warned Madge to be cautious.

'Where's Pearl?' Sunday asked, suddenly. 'I want to see Pearl.'

Madge bit her lip anxiously, and squeezed her daughter's hand tightly.

Sunday was panicking. Her whole body felt as though it was burning up. 'What's going on!' She had no idea she was shouting out loud. 'Why can't I hear you?' She was breathing faster and faster. 'I want to see Pearl!'

Sunday's shouts caused everyone in the ward to swing an anxious glance towards her bed. Madge leaned over, and tried to soothe her by gently stroking her face with her fingers.

And then Sunday felt pain, a searing pain which engulfed her entire body from head to toe. Inside her head, she could feel a thumping sensation as though someone was pounding her with a sledgehammer. But most of all, it was the sudden feeling of intense pressure deep inside her ears that really scared her; it felt like someone's fingers were pushing hard into them, tearing through her temple and almost touching her eyes. The only release she had was to scream out in pain at the top of her voice.

Her panic was so great, she hardly felt the needle that was being pushed into her arm.

It was several days before Sunday had regained enough strength to be transferred to the Ear, Nose, and Throat Ward which was in a separate wing of the Royal Northern Hospital. Once the bandages around her head had been removed, she was immediately subjected to a series of exhausting tests which would determine the extent of the injuries to her ears. For Sunday it was a painstaking, depressing experience, for since that first moment of regaining her faculties, she had had to come to terms with the agonising reality that she was unable to hear anything more than low, distant humming sounds. The flying bomb explosion had not only perforated her eardrums, but had also caused serious infections to both her middle and inner ears. And despite a specialist's assurances that there might be the possibility of an operation to partially restore the hearing in one ear, Sunday was shrewd enough to know that the prospect was bleak. And if that wasn't bad enough, she was getting more and more concerned that no one could tell her anything about what had happened to Pearl. It was finally left to Madge to break the news. Pearl was dead – killed in the flying bomb explosion together with five other 'Baggies'. Ma Briggs was amongst the dead.

Sunday was devastated. Pearl was her friend, her very best friend. They were like sisters, always laughing and joking together, always standing up for each other whenever Ma Briggs tried to throw her weight around. For at least a day after she was told, Sunday had refused to believe what had happened. Not to Pearl. Not to *her* friend. It had to be a mistake, it just had to be. OK, so Pearl was chubby. But she was strong. She was really strong. If she'd been buried under that wreckage, she'd never have just given up – and died. As she lay in bed, her pillow soaked with tears, all Sunday could do was to keep repeating Pearl's name to herself over and over again. 'Pearl. Pearl. Pearl. Pearl. Don't do this to me, Pearl. Don't leave me. Don't *ever* leave me.'

* * *

The trauma of coping with Pearl's death, together with the prospect of being deaf for the rest of her life, was too much for Sunday. Even though she was full of drugs to combat the pain in her head and ears, her mind was in turmoil, and, despite the strenuous efforts of her doctors and nurses, she refused to cooperate in trying to learn even the most basic ways to communicate, such as reading and writing messages on a note-pad at the side of her bed. She spent most of the time sitting in a chair in the day room at the end of the ward, with a fixed stare at all the activity around her – movement, doctors and nurses talking to their patients, a WVS helper serving tea from a trolley, exchanging a comforting word with a seriously ill air-raid victim, patients sitting up in bed listening through earphones to the Home Service on the wireless. Nothing different about any of it, except that she couldn't *hear* the voices, couldn't *hear* the laughter, couldn't even *hear* the shuffling of feet on the bare lino floor of the ward. She was living in an alien world, a world that was stark and unreal, like the nightmares she was now having every night. She wanted no part of it. She wanted things to be like they used to be, when she and Pearl went dancing up the Athenaeum every Saturday night. She wanted to wake up from this nightmare!

Sadly, Madge Collins was no help at all to her daughter. Despite the endless flying bomb raids that were now taking place every day of the week, she never missed a visit. But after sitting with Sunday for just a few minutes, and making unsuccessful attempts to communicate with her, the poor woman's eyes would well up with tears, which meant that she had to spend the rest of the hour holding Sunday's hand and saying prayers to herself. After a time, Sunday began to dread her mum's visits. Not because she didn't want to see her, but because she only made things worse. Some of the neighbours from 'the Buildings' also came to see her, but they weren't much help either, for they always used the visiting hour as an excuse to have a good old chinwag about the war, and to slag off Churchill and Roosevelt for giving Hitler the chance to use his flying bombs on poor old 'Olloway. Doll Mooney didn't improve matters either and had to be restrained by the Ward Sister, because she was convinced that the only way to communicate with Sunday was to shout at her. Nonetheless, Doll meant well, for she bought Sunday a lovely sixpenn'th of white daisies from the florists' shop in Caledonian Road, and also a tasteful 'Get Well' card from herself, Joe, and the kids.

Sunday's spirits were temporarily raised, however, when one

evening she received a visit from Bess Butler. Madge had only just left the ward when she arrived, and as Bess knew only too well that Sunday's mum had never approved of her, she made quite sure there was no chance of them coming face to face.

Sunday's expression lit up when she saw Bess approaching her. The older woman looked dressed to kill, for she was already made-up for her night's 'work' outside the US Servicemen's Club in the 'Dilly'. ''Ow d'yer like me new pong?' she asked Sunday, after kissing her on the cheek, and practically gassing the poor girl with the overpowering smell of perfume.

Sunday shrugged her shoulders and smiled weakly. Although she had guessed what Bess was saying, she hadn't watched her friend's lips moving.

'It's called "Moon Over Miami",' she said, her scarlet lips working hard to form the words. ''Ad ter work 'ard fer that, I can tell yer,' she said. 'Well let's face it, we 'ave ter look after our GI boys, don't we?'

Although Bess chuckled at her own joke, Sunday could only smile. It was a tired, strained smile, and it worried Bess.

'Yer've 'ad a rough time, Sun,' Bess said, sitting on the edge of Sunday's bed facing her young mate, who was propped up in a chair. 'It's about time we brought some colour back inter them cheeks, gel.' As she spoke, she gently pinched Sunday's cheeks, and gave her one of her great big comforting smiles. But in her stomach, she felt desperately concerned for the girl. 'Yer don't know what the bleedin' 'ell I'm goin' on about, do yer, mate?'

Sunday looked puzzled.

Bess leaned across, and took hold of one of her hands. 'Watch me, Sun,' she said. And as she spoke, she used a finger from her other hand to point at her lips.

Sunday understood. She lowered her eyes and focused on Bess's lips.

'Everything's – going – to be – all right,' said Bess, trying as hard as she could to signal the words. 'Can yer – understand me?'

Sunday looked absolutely blank.

Bess took hold of both of Sunday's hands. 'Watch, Sun,' she said, making intense eye contact. 'Just watch me – *please*.'

Sunday was doing her best to concentrate.

Before continuing, Bess used the tip of her tongue to touch her thick red lipstick. 'I said – it's going to be – all right. Yor'll get fru this – I promise yer will.'

Sunday screwed up her face in anguish. Unable to follow what

Bess was saying, she pulled her hands away, and buried her face in them.

'Sun!'

Bess waited a moment. Then she reached into her handbag, and brought out her small bottle of 'Moon Over Miami'. She unscrewed the top, took hold of one of Sunday's hands, poured some of the perfume on to the back, and gently smoothed it in.

Sunday slowly looked up at Bess. There was a suggestion of tears in the middle-aged woman's eyes. Bess gave Sunday a saucy wink, and raised the girl's hand up to her nose.

Sunday immediately smelt the strong aroma of the perfume on the back of her hand. Gradually, her face broke into a radiant smile. Then she looked up at Bess. 'It's – lovely.'

Bess bit her lip again. The bottom row of her teeth was now smeared with lipstick. Overcome with emotion, she broke into a broad grin, threw her arms around the girl and hugged her. Although Sunday's voice sounded odd and strained, at least she was making the effort to speak.

At the end of the third week, Sunday left hospital. As she stepped out with her mum into the warm July sunshine, the world around her seemed to be a totally different place. It was a silent world, where she could see everything but not hear it. All the familiar sounds must have been there – the electric hum of the trolleybuses, people's shoes hurrying along the pavements, a horse's hooves clip-clopping ahead of the groceries delivery van, motor-car horns, an ambulance with bell ringing as it left the hospital on another emergency call. But most of all – people. People just talking to each other as they passed by. Sounds that had been such an everyday part of Sunday's life. Sounds that she had taken for granted; they were always there all right, but they had never seemed important before. Not until now. And even though she could feel a cool breeze blowing through her hair, she couldn't hear it. It wasn't the same any more. Not until she could hear again. And she *was* determined to hear all those things again. After all, the specialist had conveyed to her that an operation might possibly restore the hearing in one of her ears. As far as Sunday was concerned, there was no such thing as 'possible'. She *would* hear again. There was no doubt in her mind about that.

Under normal circumstances, it was less than ten minutes' walk back to 'the Buildings', but to Sunday it seemed like hours. She felt totally disoriented, as though she found it difficult to keep her balance. The doctors had warned Madge that until Sunday had got used to walking without being able to hear, she might feel a little giddy, so for the entire walk back home, she linked arms with the girl and kept a firm grip on her.

They had hardly reached the Nag's Head when Sunday became aware that people everywhere were looking upwards, scanning the sky in every direction. She felt herself tense. Had the air-raid siren sounded? How would she know – how would she *ever* know that she should take cover? She had thought about it all the time she had been lying in her hospital bed. The memory of what had happened to her at the Bagwash on that ill-fated morning nearly a month before had heightened her awareness of the fact that flying bombs were now plunging down on to London practically every day of the week. Her nervousness had turned to sheer terror, for she realised that from now on, she would have to rely on other people to warn her of the approaching danger.

'Come on gels! Get yerselves under cover!'

Sunday could see that the special constable was talking to them, but as his face was turned away from her she couldn't read his lips.

'Over here, Sunday!'

Again, Sunday didn't hear what her mum said to her, but she felt her arm pull her into the doorway of a shoe shop.

'Down, Sunday! Get down, dear!'

Madge pulled Sunday down into a crouching position, and they both shielded their heads with the small suitcase of clothes Sunday had brought with her from the hospital.

As they crouched there, Sunday could see everyone else scattering for any cover they could find. It was a bizarre, unreal sight. But it was enough to send a chill through Sunday's entire body.

Within a few minutes, her attention was drawn to a young boy sheltering with his older brother in the next doorway. He was shouting excitedly, and pointing up at the sky. Soon, other people were doing the same, whilst others crouched for cover, and, for all the good it would do, shielded their heads with their hands.

And then Sunday saw it. The long black shape with its burning, murderous flame billowing out behind, approaching high above Holloway Road from the direction of Highbury Corner. She had never seen a flying bomb in daylight before, and somehow it looked even more menacing than at night, with its sinister shape and clipped wings. Once again she felt herself tense. She could see, but not hear. And yet, that droning, throbbing sound of its engine was tearing into her mind. How soon would it be before those few moments of dreaded silence heralded the inevitable explosion?

She did not have to wait too long. The 'doodlebug', as Londoners had now nicknamed the flying bomb, rapidly disappeared over the rooftops of Seven Sisters Road, and within seconds Sunday felt the ground vibrate beneath her.

Aunt Louie was very unpredictable. Although Madge knew what an emotional person she was, Louie had always been careful to conceal her true feelings. But on the day Louie heard about the explosion at Briggs Bagwash, she was quite inconsolable. For two days and nights she practically lived in her bedroom, spending most of the time sobbing her heart out and trying to study form in the *Sporting Times*. Charitable as she was, Madge secretly put her sister's grief down to guilt. During all the years when Sunday was growing up, Louie had never said one kind or encouraging thing to her, which clearly turned the child against her at an early age. But, even though she had never attempted to visit Sunday in hospital, she had made up her mind that as soon as her young niece came home, she was going to make amends.

'Hallo, Auntie,' bellowed Sunday, in her strange new way of speaking.

Louie turned one cheek towards Sunday, and allowed her niece to kiss it. 'You're feeling better then, are you?'

'Oh, I'm much better, thanks.' Ever since Bess had helped her to start reading people's lips, Sunday had made rapid progress. 'Once I've had the operation I'll be as good as new.'

'Then there's no need for you to shout like that, is there?'

Madge swung a glare at her sister. 'Louie!'

'Don't be silly!' snapped Louie. 'She's got to learn to speak properly. It's no good shouting.'

Despite understanding precisely what Aunt Louie had said, Sunday did not take offence. 'I'm sorry, Aunt,' she said, lowering her voice. 'You see, I can't really hear myself. You'll have to tell me when I'm shouting.'

Sunday's reasonableness irritated Louie. She grunted and sat down at the parlour table.

'I'm going to make us a nice cup of tea,' Madge said, quickly. It was always her way of changing the conversation. Then, making quite sure Sunday could read her lips, she added proudly, 'I've made you a bread pudding. Jack Popwell got me some dried fruit on the black market.'

Sunday's face lit up as her mum disappeared into the kitchen.

'She's going round the bend, you know.'

As Sunday wasn't facing her aunt as she spoke, she hadn't heard what she had said.

Louie waited for Sunday to sit down opposite her at the table before speaking again. 'Did you hear what I said?' Now she was the one who was raising her voice. 'I said, I think your mother's going round the bend.'

Sunday looked puzzled.

'You don't know the half of what's been going on around here.'

'What d'you mean, Auntie?'

'Her gentleman friend, that's what I mean!' She took out her tin of tobacco and started to roll a cigarette. 'He's been coming round here. She thinks I don't know. But I *do*.'

Although Sunday couldn't understand every single word her aunt was saying, she did just manage to make out the words, *gentleman friend*. 'D'you mean Mr Billings?' she asked.

'I've no idea what his name is,' replied Louie sourly. 'All I know is that every time I go to the pictures on a Wednesday afternoon, she's had him round here. You can always tell when a man's been inside the place. You can smell 'em.'

Before she arrived home, Sunday had also had good intentions about being nicer to her Aunt Louie. But she really didn't like the way that this woman was talking about her mum. 'Honestly, Auntie,' she said, trying to make sure that the level of her voice was not raised too much, 'I don't think it's any of our business who mum sees – do you?'

Louie stopped licking the gummed edge of her cigarette paper for a moment, and leaning across the table, replied, 'I don't care *who* she sees,' she snapped. 'It's what they get up to that worries me.'

For a brief moment, Sunday said nothing. Then suddenly, she roared with laughter. The sound she was making was very odd, and not a bit like the way she used to laugh before her loss of hearing. But she found it hilarious that her aunt was suggesting that Madge was having some kind of passionate affair with someone from the Salvation Army. And the more she thought about it, the more absurd it seemed.

'Oh you can laugh,' growled Louie indignantly, making quite sure Sunday could read her lips. 'But just wait 'til he asks her to marry him. Then you'll laugh on the other side of your face!'

To Sunday's astonishment, her aunt got up from the table, turned, and stormed off in a huff to her bedroom.

Despite all Aunt Louie's good intentions, nothing had changed.

# Chapter 7

Ernie Mancroft looked at himself in the broken piece of mirror that was propped up on a ledge above the stone sink in the scullery. He liked what he saw, good strong features, a pug nose, and piercing dark eyes that almost perfectly matched his hair and pencil-thin moustache. The cut above his left eye was still a bit raw, and as he dabbed it with one of his fingers he still marvelled at the way he had managed to survive the blast from that 'doodlebug' explosion down the Bagwash. But then Ernie was one of life's survivors. When he was only six years old he was beaten up by some of the kids down his street, but when he got home his old man had warned him that if he ever allowed such a thing to happen again, he'd kick him out of the house. Ernie never did allow it to happen again. Since his mum had died of consumption when he was a small kid, Ernie was brought up by his punch-happy old man and his four elder brothers, and it was they who had taught him how to use his fists. In fact, he became a 'bruiser' in every sense of the word, always trying to prove himself by bashing up anyone who dared to cross his path, who ever dared to come between him and his girl. And Sunday *was* his girl. That's why he'd shielded her from the falling debris with his own body. That's why he'd saved her life.

Now once he'd togged himself up in a white shirt and tie and the only suit he'd ever possessed, he left the filth and grime of his old man's house in 'The Bunk' up Campbell Road, and strutted briskly along Tollington Road.

On his way to 'the Buildings', Ernie Mancroft reckoned that it was about time Sunday Collins knew that she owed him one.

During the few days since she left hospital, Sunday had made very little effort to adjust to her new silent world. She spent most of her time sitting at the window of her tiny bedroom, staring down into the backyard below, watching the neighbours entering or leaving their flats, kids laughing and chasing each other and kicking their football against a back wall. And as she watched, in her mind she tried to *hear* the sounds that were being made, and what those sounds used to be like before her eardrums had been blown in by the flying bomb explosion. It was extraordinary how lonely she felt, even when people were trying to communicate with her.

Her worst problem was not being able to hear the air-raid siren, so Madge had to make arrangements that whenever she and Aunt Louie were out at the same time, either Jack Popwell or Doll Mooney would let themselves in with their spare keys, and take Sunday off to the downstairs shelter. Sunday absolutely hated having to rely on other people to protect her, and several times she refused to leave the flat despite the danger. And although she was gradually getting to grips with lip-reading, the effort of doing that thoroughly depressed her. Worst of all, of course, was the fact that she was unable to listen to the wireless. Her mind was endlessly tuning in to all her favourite programmes, especially those featuring music by the big bands. Every so often her foot would tap out a rhythm, and for a few exhilarating moments she could imagine that she was gliding around the dance floor back at the dear old Athenaeum. The summer was passing by, but the hot sun outside was wasted on her. The only thing that could sustain her now was the hope that once she'd had her operation, her hearing would at least be partially restored.

'You've got a visitor.'

Although Sunday couldn't hear Louie talking to her, she could feel the tips of her aunt's bony fingers tapping on her shoulders from behind.

'A visitor.'

This time, Sunday was able to read Louie's lips. And her heart sank. She hated people calling on her, with that sickly look on their faces which always meant that they felt sorry for her. 'Who is it?' she asked.

Louie, now getting used to the laboured sound Sunday was making as she spoke, shrugged her shoulders, and left the bedroom.

Sunday left the window, and slowly made her way to the parlour.

'Wotcha, Sun. Good ter see yer, mate.'

Sunday froze as Ernie Mancroft beamed across at her. Her first instinct was to turn around, go back into her bedroom and lock the door. But she stood her ground. 'What are you doing here?' she asked nervously.

For a brief moment, Ernie was taken aback by her distorted speech. Then he relaxed, and took a confident step towards her.

'I've missed yer, Sun,' he said, his face breaking into a fixed grin. 'I couldn't come and see yer in 'ospital. Didn't feel too good after that bang. You know 'ow it is.'

'If you speak too fast, she won't understand you,' scowled Louie, moving off towards her own bedroom door. 'She can only read your lips.' She opened the bedroom door, and turned. 'So it's no good if she can't see your face.' With that, she disappeared into her room and closed the door behind her.

Left alone with Ernie, Sunday felt a moment of panic.

Obeying Louie's instructions, he stood directly in Sunday's eyeline, and moved his lips slowly as he spoke. 'I'm sorry fer wot's 'appened to yer, Sun.' He rubbed his chin with his hand, as if feeling the stubble. 'Yer've 'ad a rough time.'

As Ernie took another step towards her, Sunday moved out of his path and made her way towards the kitchen door. When she got there, she turned and looked back at him. 'You shouldn't have come here,' she said, her voice sounding as though she was swallowing her words. 'You had no right.'

Ernie's face hardened. 'In case yer 'adn't noticed, I saved yer life.'

Sunday briefly turned her head on one side, something she had taken to doing when she couldn't quite lip-read every word that was being said.

Ernie moved back slowly towards her, but stopped at the parlour table. 'Your mate, Pearl,' he said, leaning both hands on the back of a hardback chair. 'She got killed.'

As Pearl's name formed on Ernie's lips, Sunday closed her eyes in anguish. When she opened them again, Ernie was still staring at her.

'She weren't the only one eiver,' continued Ernie, who seemed quite unperturbed that his remark had upset Sunday. 'A coupla your mates went up the chimney too. An' wot about the old gel, eh? Old Briggs? Took a packet all right! They din't dig 'er out 'til late at night.'

Sunday could only just follow what Ernie was saying because he was gabbling again, so she pushed the kitchen door open with her back.

'It coulda bin you, yer know, Sun. Yer know that, don't yer?' Ernie seemed to think that by raising his voice, Sunday could hear him. 'If it 'adn't bin fer me, you'd be lyin' six foot under.'

Sunday glared back at him. Even though she couldn't follow all he was saying, his hostile facial expressions were telling her all she needed to know. 'Why me?' she asked timidly.

Ernie stared at her. 'Why you?' he replied. Then he walked around the table and slowly approached her. 'Why you?' he asked again, making quite sure she could clearly see his lips moving. 'Because I love yer, Sun. I've always loved yer. Ever since the first day I set eyes on yer.' He paused a moment, and from a few yards' distance, stared directly into her eyes. 'D'yer understand wot I'm sayin'?'

To ensure a quick getaway, Sunday had her back pinned against the open kitchen door.

'Why can't yer love me too, Sun?' he asked, almost like a child. 'If my old man, if my bruvvers 'eard me talkin' ter yer like this now, they'd smash me face in. But they don't know. They don't know that I've never felt like this about anyone – but you.'

Sunday was concentrating really hard to try to understand what he was saying. And, as on previous occasions when she was with him, her nervousness was tinged with a certain perverse attraction for his brutishness.

'I saved yer life, Sun – because I don't want yer ter die. I want yer ter live. I want yer ter live, and learn not ter turn away from me every time yer set eyes on me.'

Although Sunday tensed as Ernie moved another step closer to her, something inside prevented her from retreating into the kitchen.

Now within an arm's reach of her, Ernie was extra-careful to ensure that she could read his lips. 'It makes no difference ter me, Sun. It makes no difference that yer can't 'ear wot I'm sayin'. I'll take care of yer, Sun. I promise I'll always take care of yer.'

'Go away, Ernie.'

Sunday's sudden response was harsh, and it clearly struck home deeply, for Sunday noticed he had clenched his fists at his side.

'You owe me one, Sun,' he growled. 'You're never goin' ter get away from me – never!'

Sunday was scared. She had seen that cold look in Ernie's eyes before. And when he made a quick start towards her, she immediately backed out of sight into the kitchen, and slammed the door straight into his face.

Ernie made no attempt to follow her. For a moment, he just stood right where Sunday had left him. Then, his knuckles white with tension, he thumped both his clenched fists just once on the door, turned, and left the flat.

* * *

The hospital waiting-room at the Ear, Nose and Throat Clinic was a dreary place. Grubby white walls that hadn't seen a paint-brush for years, hard wooden benches, a pervading smell of ether and iodine, and coloured posters that were pinned to a large notice-board which gave details of evacuation procedures in the event of an air-raid.

Sunday still had another ten minutes to wait before her appointment with Mr Callow, the ear specialist, so she and Madge passed the time sizing up all the other patients, wondering who they were, where they came from, and what was wrong with them. Madge was particularly interested in the small children who were having a wonderful time playing tag with each other, quite oblivious to the cotton wool swabs stuffed in their ears or up their nostrils. Madge smiled a lot at them, especially at one little girl in a wheelchair who had a heavily bruised eye, together with ear swabs, stitches all along the bridge of her nose, and one arm and one leg both encased in plaster. The current 'doodlebug' campaign was clearly taking its toll. Rather pointedly, however, Sunday carefully avoided casting her gaze towards a family of deaf and dumb people, who were using sign language to communicate with each other.

A few minutes later, Sunday found herself in the consultant's room, being examined by the redoubtable Mr Callow, who despite a heavy frame, bushy eyebrows, metal-rimmed spectacles, and a starched collar that was cutting into his neck, touched her ears with the sensitivity of an artist.

'Excellent,' he finally proclaimed. 'No more discharge.' Madge beamed, and communicated the good news to Sunday.

Mr Callow returned to his seat by a small table, and started to write endless notes. But it was his face that Sunday was interested in; she was watching for any possible expression that would give her a clue to the news she was really waiting for.

'And so, young lady.' The bushy eyebrows flicked up, and the eyes beneath them stared directly at Sunday's face. 'Now we have to plan for the future.'

Sunday was so tense, she couldn't make out his words. But when she swung around to her mum for explanation, Mr Callow took hold of her hands, which immediately brought her gaze back to him.

'From now on,' he said gently, and using his tongue and lips slowly and with precision, 'you start all over again.' Before continuing, he paused and waited for her reaction. 'Do you understand what I'm saying, Sunday?'

'When will I hear again?'

Even though he was used to these tragic moments, Mr Callow found it difficult to keep looking into Sunday's eyes. All he could do was to shake his head slowly.

Sunday panicked, and immediately pulled her hands out of his. 'Operation!' she demanded.

Mr Callow again shook his head.

'You promised!' Sunday's whole body was tensing.

Madge quickly rose from her seat, put her arms around Sunday's shoulders, and hugged her.

'Watch me, Sunday. Watch me carefully.' There was now a stern look on Mr Callow's face. Using his fingers to illustrate what he was saying, he continued. 'The explosion has severely damaged what we call the *labyrinth*, the inner part of your ear. There is no operation available that would repair that damage, no operation that would restore your ability to hear.' He leaned as close to Sunday as she would allow. 'Do you understand what I am saying, Sunday?' he asked, slowly and very deliberately. 'Do – you – understand?'

Sunday's eyes were suddenly watery, a sign of her intense fear.

Mr Callow looked past her, first to Madge, and then to someone who was sitting in the corner behind her. 'Mrs Davies,' he said.

The woman he was addressing rose quietly from her seat, came across to Sunday and crouched in front of her. 'Hallo, Sunday,' she said with a smile. 'My name is Jennifer. We're going to be working together.' As she spoke, her hands were very animated. 'I'm going to show you how to listen with your eyes, with your hands, and with your fingers.'

Madge hugged Sunday tighter.

The woman, still crouched in front of Sunday, looked up directly into the girl's eyes. 'It's going to be like learning to walk all over again.

Watched carefully by both Mr Callow and Madge, the woman gently took hold of the girl's hands. But Sunday, almost mesmerised as she struggled to read the woman's lips, shrank back into her chair.

Jennifer Davies then made the mistake of turning to address her next remark to Madge. 'Don't worry,' she said, with a well-meaning smile. 'In a few years' time she'll have forgotten all about what it was like to listen with her ears.'

The words were hardly out on the woman's lips, when, quite unexpectedly, Sunday pulled her hands away and sprang up from the chair. 'Operation!' she spluttered, in deep distress, addressing her remark directly to Mr Callow. 'You promised me! Operation!'

By the time the consultant had come back to her, Sunday had broken away from her mum and made a wild dash for the door.

'Sunday!' called Madge, rushing out of the room to chase after her daughter. 'Come back, child! Come back!'

But it was too late. Within seconds Sunday had disappeared from the clinic, and dashed straight out into the August sunshine.

Sunday had no idea in which direction she was running. All she knew was that she was winding her way in and out of the afternoon shoppers, knocking into them in her rush to get away from everything that was connected with clinics and hospitals, and people who lied to her and didn't keep their promises. As she ran, life all around her seemed to blur. She knew that cars and lorries and buses and trams were streaming past her on the road alongside, but how could they be real when she couldn't even hear them? So many images were flashing through her mind: cold, metal instruments being poked into her ears, hypodermic needles being shoved into her arms, tablets resting on her tongue before starting the long voyage down into the depths of her stomach, X-rays, and tests, tests, and more tests. And Mr Callow scribbling down notes, horrible endless notes that would tell how Sunday Collins would never hear again.

''Allo, Sun.'

Sunday stopped running. Someone was standing right in front of her. Until her vision had cleared, all she could see was a blurred outline.

'You all right, mate?' It was Jack Popwell from 'the Buildings'.

Sunday, fighting for breath, didn't answer. For a brief moment she just stood there, gradually bringing him into focus.

''Ow d'yer get on down the 'ospital then?' he asked.

But before there was any chance of a response, Sunday had dashed off again.

Jack watched her go. It had scared the life out of him to see the state she was in, with her face drained of all blood, her hair all over the place, and sweat streaming through her clean white blouse. 'Sun!' he called, knowing only too well that there was no way the poor girl could hear him.

Sunday hurried on her way, refusing to look back over her shoulder. And as she passed the Savoy Cinema, her mind was flooded with happier days when, only a year before, she had queued up with the crowds to watch *Gone with the Wind*.

By the time she was passing under the railway bridge which

crossed Holloway Road opposite the Tube Station, she was completely out of breath.

The first thing she noticed was the smell of urine coming from the men's lavatories beneath the bridge, so she held her nose and hurried on. On the other side of the bridge, she decided to cross over the main road, and without a moment's thought just dashed across, not looking to see if the road was clear. There was an immediate cacophony of motor-car horns, and an angry bus-driver shouting out, 'Yer silly cow!' from his cabin window. Even if Sunday could have heard him, it would have made no difference, for at that moment, all she could see was the other side of the road.

Without considering what she was doing, Sunday rushed straight into the dingy interior of Holloway Road Tube Station. She had always hated the place, with its grubby, stifling atmosphere and depressing brown wall tiles, and as she had always tended to suffer from claustrophobia she kept well away from the antiquated lift, ignored buying a ticket at the tiny booking office, and made her way straight to the spiral staircase.

When she was a child, Sunday loved to count out loud to her mum every step of this staircase from top to bottom, and as she did so she could hear the sound her feet were making on the heavy wrought iron, which echoed down into the very depths of the station. Now she could hear nothing, and she felt as though she was descending towards the gates of Hell. With each step she took, the steep staircase seemed as though it was trying to swallow her up and drag her down. And once again there was the smell of urine, the usual leftover from some drunk's night out at the boozer. The journey down seemed to take forever, and Sunday was feeling giddy, her ears were throbbing, and because she was having difficulty in keeping her balance she had to hold on tightly to the long, cold, curving metal rail.

When Sunday finally reached the bottom of the staircase, the lift doors were just opening to deposit the few passengers who had left at the same time as herself. None of them even noticed her, for their main preoccupation was to get to the train that was due any moment. She was now streaming with sweat, and after her ordeal on the spiral staircase, her legs felt as though they couldn't carry her any further. But gradually she made her way towards the platforms, oblivious to the vast array of posters along the curved walls. By the time she reached the first platform, the rush of air from an approaching train was already pounding against her body.

Although there were very few people along the platform, there was already that odd feeling of panic and anticipation which prompted everyone to take up their rightful ground at the very edge of the platform. Sunday was no exception. But, although no one had even registered her existence, her feet were much closer to the painted white line of the platform edge than theirs. In fact, her toes were suspended over the railtrack itself.

The train was now only seconds away, and all the passengers had to brace themselves against the strong rush of air that was roaring through the darkened tunnel ahead of that train.

As Sunday waited, her eyes became transfixed on the track beneath her, and in particular on the deadly live rail which had powered the London Underground tube-trains for so many years. Gradually, the lethal rail became blurred, and in its place she could see a succession of images: Pearl's chubby cheeks, with those sparkling emerald eyes staring up at her; kids in the backyard of 'the Buildings', kicking their football against the wall; the flame burning at the rear of the flying bomb as it chugged menacingly over Finsbury Park at night; and the kind, familiar faces of her mum, Bess Butler, Jack Popwell, the Mooneys, and poor Harry Smike – all stretching out their hands as if trying to help her. But it was only their faces she could see. She couldn't hear what they were trying to tell her, what they were begging her not to do.

As the headlights of the approaching train started to snake along the tunnel walls, Sunday's feet began to move further across the painted white line along the edge of the platform. For those few reckless moments, it was only that stark narrow line that held her between life and death.

Sunday was now crazed with desperation. One more image joined the others. It was Mr Callow, the ear specialist, slowly shaking his head. Sunday couldn't bear it. Her own head started to do the same, shaking violently back and forth. There was only one thing to do, only one way to end the nightmare. As the images started to fall away into a large black pit, her body slumped forward.

With a mighty roar and a powerful gush of stale air, the tube-train suddenly burst out of the tunnel and raced along the track.

On the platform, a woman screamed out loud.

Sunday heard nothing. All she felt was a strong pair of arms around her waist, and the next moment she was stretched out on the cold stone floor.

The train screeched to a halt along the platform.

'Come on little lady!' gasped the posh voice of a middle-aged man who was pinning Sunday down on the platform floor. 'It's not worth it!'

Within seconds, a crowd had gathered around Sunday, including both the train-driver and guard. Although Sunday couldn't hear one word of the rumpus she had caused, she knew only too well what everyone must have been saying.

Quite suddenly, she started to sob. She couldn't hear any of it, of course, but her stomach was lurching up and down in distress, and soon tears were streaming down her cheeks. She hadn't cried since she had heard about Pearl. She hated crying. She had always hated crying. But at this precise moment, it was the only thing her body knew what to do.

An elderly Cockney lady, still wearing her working apron and grimy flat cap, knelt beside Sunday and tried to comfort her by cradling the young girl's head in her lap. 'It's all right, darlin',' she said soothingly. 'It's all right.'

Sunday's eyes slowly opened. Towering all above her were faces, anxious, blood-drained faces, caring, concerned, perplexed. But as she lay there, flat on her back on the cold stone platform floor, her eyes gradually focused on something spread out on the curved platform wall behind them. It was a large coloured poster showing a farmer talking to a young girl who was wearing a green sweater and fawn-coloured breeches. Her hands were holding on to the bridle of a horse.

'*We could do with thousands more like you*,' the farmer was saying. '*JOIN THE WOMEN'S LAND ARMY*.'

# Chapter 8

At the start of winter, the wide, open fields of North Essex were bare and wet with thick, muddy clay. After a prolonged early drought, the summer of 1944 had been difficult for the local farmers, with hay and stover crops well below normal, a shortage of agricultural labour to lift the potatoes, and a great deal of the new season's wheat still not planted. October had brought quite a lot of rain, which had left many gardens and allotments soggy and tough to dig, and now the early November mists were clinging to the horizon, defying the sun to break their hold on the bleak rural landscape. Before she left 'the Buildings', Sunday had been told that the Essex countryside was very flat, but as she peered out through the charabanc window she could see quite a few gentle, undulating hills, many of them dotted with trees that had now shed their dead leaves.

It hadn't been an easy decision for her to leave home. But even though everyone thought the idea of a deaf girl taking a job in the Women's Land Army was crazy, Sunday knew it was at least an opportunity to learn how to survive on her own terms in her new silent world. The greatest obstacle, of course, had been her mum. Ever since Sunday was a baby, Madge had never parted with her, and the idea of her own daughter living in a billet with a whole lot of other girls horrified her. But Sunday was determined to have her own way. During the early part of October she had had her eighteenth birthday, and this had given her a new sense of purpose and independence. To her surprise, Mr Callow, her ear specialist, and Jennifer Davies, her therapist, had both supported her idea, but only on condition that she make a concerted effort to perfect her lip-reading technique and to start learning basic sign language. The greatest support, however, had come from Bess Butler, who was shrewd enough to know that if Sunday was going to come to terms with the trauma of going deaf, she had to get away from the pressures of an over-protective home life. But as Sunday rested her head back on the seat, and stared out aimlessly through the misted-up charabanc window at the passing grey countryside, in her mind's eye she could still see the tiny forlorn figure of her poor old mum, standing on that friendless platform back at Liverpool Street Station, with red, tear-stained eyes, waving to her, bewildered, lost, and wondering whether she would ever see her child again.

'This is your stop, young lady.'

Sunday's attention was miles away, and she hadn't even noticed that the village bus had drawn to a halt outside a country pub called the Waggon and Horses.

'Cloy's Farm is up that way,' said the elderly country man sitting next to her. As soon as Sunday had got on the bus outside Braintree Station, the old boy had realised that the girl was deaf, so, being a little hard of hearing himself, he had made quite sure she could see his lips as he spoke. 'About 'alf a mile up the road,' he said, standing up to let her pass. 'Five or ten minutes' walk at the most,' he added with a rascally smile, raising his checked flat cap.

By the time Sunday had got off the bus, the driver had already retrieved her suitcase from the baggage hold and left it for her on the pavement. As soon as she had picked it up, the bus was on its way, and quickly disappeared with a grunt and a rattle off the main road, narrowly missing what seemed to be a huge old oak tree.

It took only a few minutes for Sunday to realise that the length of a road in the country was clearly quite different to that of Holloway or Seven Sisters Road, for after walking uphill with her suitcase for over ten minutes, there was no sign of the Cloy's Farm Hostel she was expected at.

'Oh no, dear,' said the first passer-by she came across, who was walking her bicycle down the hill in the opposite direction. 'Cloy's is Ridgewell. This is Yeldham, Great Yeldham.'

As the ruddy-faced woman was not looking straight at her, Sunday could only guess that she was miles from the place she was looking for. From the way the woman was wrapped up in a heavy winter coat and headscarf, it was quite apparent that the locals knew how to protect themselves against the biting cold of the countryside far better than Sunday herself.

Continuing in the direction the woman had pointed, Sunday slowly made her way up the hill towards the village of Ridgewell. The only signs of life she saw on the way were an old man with a small boy, both struggling up the hill on rusty-framed bicycles, a pre-war Morris Minor belching out thick black exhaust fumes, and a US Army truck racing down the hill in the opposite direction.

After half an hour, Sunday began to regret what she had let herself in for. As it was, it had taken all her energy to persuade the recruiting officers at the Women's Land Army Committee back at Islington Town Hall to let her take up a job on a farm. The idea of a young deaf girl working on or near dangerous farm machinery concerned them enough to delay their decision for several weeks. But, mindful that farm labour was in desperately short supply, and after a strong letter of support from the Ear, Nose, and Throat therapists at the Royal Northern Hospital, the Committee had decided to give Sunday the chance of a three-month probationary period at a WLA Farm Hostel, where she would work alongside one or two other disabled girls of her own age.

After walking a short distance further, Sunday found herself at the top of the hill. From there she could see for miles, for it was now early afternoon, and the mist was slowly releasing its grip on the horizon. Out of breath, she put her suitcase down on to the grass verge beside the roadside path, and sat on it. Her ears were numb from the cold, so she cupped her hands together, blew warm breath into them, then covered them over her ears. And as she sat there, she felt as though she was in another world. No cars, trams, or trolleybuses, no crowds of people out shopping with their kids, and no terraced houses and towering blocks of flats for as far as the eye could see. And no flying bombs, nor murderous V-2 rockets which the Germans were now targeting on London each day, bringing death and destruction without a moment's warning. Yes, out here in Essex it was another world, a place where there was only peace of mind. And for the first time in her life, she felt close to all the things her mum believed in – fields and hedgerows and trees and grass and birds – all the things that were such an essential part of life.

But after sitting there for a moment or so, she had a premonition. It was as though something was creeping up on her from behind, trying to touch her. As she slowly turned to look over her shoulder, a giant shadow quite suddenly engulfed her, and when she stood up in panic, the glistening silver shape of a huge warplane tore across the sky just above the trees. By the time she had thrown herself to the ground, the great monster, with wheels already down, had disappeared behind a group of thatched cottages and appeared to land in the field beyond.

For several moments she lay stretched out on her stomach on the cold path, shielding the back of her head and ears with her hands. She was shivering with fear, partly because her premonition had come true, and also because she hadn't been able to hear the roar of the plane's giant engines.

The next thing she felt was a pair of hands trying to lift her up from the path. As she turned to look, she found that she was being helped by a girl of about her own age, who was wearing the belted overall coat of the Women's Land Army.

'Are you all right, girl?'

Although Sunday was staring directly at the Land Army girl, she was too unnerved to be able to read her lips, and couldn't know that the accent was Welsh. All she could do was shake her head.

'No need to be scared, you know,' said the girl in uniform. 'It was only a Yank. One of ours, believe it or not.'

Sunday, nonplussed, again shook her head. But this time she grunted a few unintelligible words. 'Terrible. Shouldn't . . . shouldn't . . .'

The girl in uniform understood immediately. 'You've got to be Sunday,' she said. Then, positioning herself so that Sunday could read her lips, she repeated, 'Sunday. You're Sunday Collins, aren't you, girl?' Then, giving her a huge smile which revealed two rows of dazzling white teeth, she added, 'We've been waitin' for you.'

A few minutes later, Sunday found herself sharing a horse-drawn cart with the Welsh girl and a loadful of muddy potatoes.

'The name's Jinx,' said the girl. 'Jinx Hughes.' She had to turn from holding the horse's reins to face Sunday every time she wanted to talk to her. 'It was me old man's fault, see. All 'cos he reckoned me mam had put a curse on him for not 'avin' a rugby-playin' son!'

When Sunday saw the girl roaring with laughter, she immediately felt at ease. 'I like the name,' she said. 'It's different.'

Jinx didn't answer, because the horse who was pulling them started to slow down. 'Come on, 'Oratio!' she yelled, impatiently. 'We 'aven't got all day!' Then she turned to Sunday. 'Got a will of 'is own, this one.'

This time it was Sunday who laughed.

It was something she hadn't done for quite a long time.

Cloy's Farm was set in the middle of flat, arable land that had been ploughed and tilled for over three hundred years. The farmhouse itself was quite large and built around a cobbled yard, which contained stables for three working horses. The few cows still remaining on the farm were kept in their own shed, as were other livestock such as pigs and hens. Apart from the Land Girls, who were billeted in a converted barn well away from the main house, there were no agricultural labourers working the land there any more, for all of them had long ago decided to forego their right to exemption from military service. Their reason for doing so was perfectly clear to anyone who knew the farmer who ran the place, Arnold Cloy.

'A real mean old sod!'

Jinx was never known to mince her words, and as she watched Sunday unpacking her suitcase in the Land Girls' billet, she certainly wasn't doing so.

'D'you know, when we first moved in 'ere, those beams up there were riddled with woodworm, and the place was full of mildew from top to bottom. An' if they 'adn't come down from Lond'n and made 'im put in some windows, we'd 'ave been livin' in a bleedin' cellar!' Sunday had been too busy hanging her clothes in a narrow bedside locker to pick up everything Jinx had been telling her. But as she looked around at the bleak interior of the thatched seventeenth-century barn, she had a rough idea of what she was going on about.

'I tell you, girl,' Jinx continued, arms crossed as if in a perpetual rage, 'the reason this place is so cold is because the old sod won't let us light up the paraffin stove 'til we get back from the fields. An' durin' the winter months, 'e keeps the electric turned off 'til four in the afternoon. Sometimes longer. An' as for the bog – ha! A bucket in a freezin'-cold shed out back! If 'Eadquarters knew 'alf what 'e gets up to, they'd cut off 'is goolies an' feed 'em to the pigs!'

Jinx suddenly noticed the anxious look on Sunday's face. So she went and stood in front of her. 'Take no notice of me, girl,' she said reassuringly. ''Round 'ere they all call me the old moaner. Complain about everythin' I do. But if you don't, you don't get nothin' in this world. In't that right?'

Sunday nodded, and smiled. As she watched Jinx's lips moving, she tried to imagine what the voice sounded like, and if it matched her tall, lanky figure, pointed nose, bony face, and slightly slanted eyes.

'Even so,' said Jinx, adjusting the turban around her short, bobbed brown hair. 'Don't ever be tempted to rub the old sod up the wrong way. Unfortunately, 'e's the one in charge 'round 'ere. 'E's the one we 'ave to answer to.'

Again Sunday nodded that she understood, then looked around the room at the other beds. 'How many are we?' she asked.

Jinx only just heard what she was saying, for Sunday had been told so many times how loud she was speaking that she had now lowered her voice more than was necessary.

'Six includin' you,' replied Jinx. 'We're all very different, but we get on ever so well together.' She moved to the bed next to Sunday. 'This is me here. An' on the other side of you is Ruthie. Comes from a posh place she does – somewhere down south. She's an epileptic, but you'd never know. 'Asn't 'ad an attack for more than six months.' She moved on to the beds opposite. 'An' this is Sue,' she said, stopping at the first bed. 'She's from just outside Birmingham. Bit of a snoot, but means well.'

Sunday strolled across to the next bed Jinx was approaching, where she picked up a small teddy bear which had been propped up on the pillow. She looked up at Jinx for an explanation.

'Ah yes,' said Jinx, with a bit of a smirk. 'That's Algie. Belongs to our Sheil. It's her baby really. Poor girl, she's a bit round the bend. But we can cope.' She took Algie from Sunday, and replaced him on the pillow. 'Lost all her family in the Blitz. Round your way somewhere. Well – Lond'n anyway.'

The two girls moved on to the third bed. But Sunday's expression changed immediately when she noticed a chart showing a two-handed alphabet on the wall behind.

'Now this is someone you'll do well with,' proclaimed Jinx, proudly, standing beside the chart, and talking directly at Sunday. 'Bit of a mascot is our Maureen. Deaf an' dumb all her life. Takes it all in her stride though.' And leaning forward to Sunday, she added with a beaming smile, 'She'll teach you all you want to know about usin' sign language.'

Sunday immediately felt herself shrivel up inside. She smiled weakly, and moved away from Maureen's bed.

'Oh – and by the way,' said Jinx, following Sunday and then stepping round in front of her. 'I'm from Swansea – capital of the whole bloody world!'

Sunday laughed with her. But her mind was really still on that wall chart.

Although it was not yet four o'clock in the afternoon when Sunday was called across to the house to meet Farmer Cloy, it was rapidly getting dark. The sun, which had struggled all day to break through the damp November mist, had finally given up the struggle by deserting the landscape with a watery golden glow, and now a light coming from the window of the farmer's office on one end of the house was beginning to cast huge shadows across the stable-yard.

Sunday was met in the back porch by young Ronnie Cloy, the farmer's fourteen-year-old son, who had just returned from school in nearby Sible Hedingham. Sunday thought he was quite small for his age, but she liked the way he smiled at her, and kept crinkling up his nose as he talked. And to her surprise, he did talk well, because, unlike so many people who tried too hard, he moved his lips in a perfectly natural way that was so much easier to read.

'D'you like butterflies?' Ronnie asked, almost the moment he set eyes on her.

'Yes,' replied Sunday, taken aback. 'They're beautiful.'

Ronnie's face lit up. 'If you like, I'll show you my collection. I've got ten different species all under glass.'

That wasn't quite what Sunday had been expecting. She hated the idea of anything being captured and killed and put on display. Since losing her hearing, she had felt very much as though the same kind of thing had happened to her. However, she was grateful that the boy had wanted to share something with her that he prized so much. 'I'm a bit worn-out tonight,' she replied in her low voice. 'Some other time perhaps?'

Ronnie didn't take offence. In fact, he didn't take offence to anyone except his own father, who had only ever looked upon his son as an intense irritation.

'Is it true what they say about you?' he asked, with innocent curiosity. 'Can't you hear anything at all?'

Sunday wanted to answer that she wasn't entirely deaf, that at times she could hear just a little. But it simply wasn't true, and she knew it, although she was determined, whatever she told others, never to admit it to herself. 'It's true,' she replied, nodding her head.

'No need to worry,' said the boy brightly. 'You can count on me. If you want, I'll show you round Ridgewell. I know a pond where there are loads of newts.' To Sunday's surprise, he offered her his hand to shake. 'Friends?'

Sunday was taken aback by this sudden act of kindness from someone she had only just met. 'Friends,' she returned, shaking the boy's hand.

'Ronnie!'

Sunday had no idea Farmer Cloy was standing in the doorway of his office behind her, until Ronnie's expression changed abruptly. 'See you later,' he said to Sunday, soundlessly moving his lips.

As he rushed off, Sunday turned around to see a massively built man beckoning to her. 'In here, please,' he said curtly. But as he was standing with his back to the light, Sunday couldn't see what he was saying. But she guessed, and moved into the office.

The first thing she noticed was how warm it was. There was no doubt that the log fire burning in the grate had been warming the room all day.

The huge man moved behind his desk and sat down, before beckoning Sunday to do the same on a chair placed in front of it.

'I want you to understand, young lady,' he began, 'that whilst you are on my land, you are my direct responsibility. Do you understand?'

Sunday didn't understand, only because she couldn't read the man's lips, which seemed far too slight for his bloated face. 'I'm sorry,' she replied. 'Would you mind repeating that again, please?'

Cloy looked irritated. He picked up a pen, scribbled something on a scrap of paper, then showed it to her.

Sunday looked at the message which read, *Do you understand what I am saying?*

Sunday smiled back at him courteously, and answered, 'If you speak slowly.'

Cloy tried again. 'You are here to work, and to work hard. This country needs all the food we farmers can produce. Without us there is no bread, no vegetables, no milk, no meat. The Women's Land Army have provided me with you girls so that my levels of food production are fully maintained.'

Whilst he was making his speech, Sunday's eyes kept flicking up to look at the small but prominent veins on his ruddy cheeks. There was no doubt in her mind that Cloy liked his drink, for she had seen plenty of boozers with a complexion just like that back in The Eaglet pub in Seven Sisters Road.

'I want you to remember that whilst you are resident on *my* land, you are on probation.' Cloy was now exaggerating his style of speech even more than when he started. 'During this time,' he continued, 'I expect not only a full day's work for a full day's pay, but the highest levels of behaviour.'

Sunday understood what he was saying all right. A full day's work for a full day's pay meant to her ninepence an hour, rising to a shilling when she reached nineteen. Slave labour in the name of maintaining food production, or rather *his* own standard of living.

Cloy put his hands on the desk, and leaned across at her. 'Now I fully accept that you face particular difficulties with regard to – your disability. In which case I expect you to treat that disability with respect, and not involve me in unnecessary concern for your safety. Do you understand what I am saying?'

Sunday nodded. 'Yes, Mr Cloy.'

'Good. That's all I have to say. Do you have any questions?'

Sunday looked down at her lap for a moment, then almost instantly looked up again. 'Yes,' she said, her voice barely audible. 'What sort of work will I be doing?'

Cloy sat back in his chair, and crossed his arms. 'You'll be on milk call, tomorrow at five.'

Sunday's eyes widened. 'Five? You mean five o'clock – in the morning?'

Cloy was getting irritated. 'That's what you're here for, young lady. We have to earn our living in the country.'

With that, he got up from his seat, went across to the fireplace and warmed his rump in front of it. It was his way of saying that Sunday's first interview with him was now over.

For a brief moment Sunday sat where she was without moving. She watched Cloy as he collected a pipe from the mantelpiece behind him that was crowded with framed family portraits and snapshots. Only then in those few split seconds did she take in the cosy lifestyle this man had sustained for himself, with a fire in the grate, a half-eaten bar of American candy on his desk, and several bottles of liquor on a shelf above the wireless in the corner.

Finally, she got up and made her way to the door. But she turned briefly to look back at her new employer, who, from what she'd just seen, might well make Ma Briggs back at the Bagwash seem like a saint. 'Thank you,' she said.

That was all she said before leaving the room. She didn't wait for a reply.

Even in the unlikely event that there might have been one.

By the time Sunday got back to the barn, it was already pitch-dark outside. But to her relief Jinx had lit the paraffin stove and the sharp cold she felt inside the place earlier was gradually capitulating to the cosy glow coming from the burning flame of the saturated wick. And as it was now after four o'clock, the electricity had been turned on, and two solitary low-watt light bulbs in faded yellow shades were dangling from each end of the beamed ceiling.

Jinx immediately introduced Sunday to the other girls, who had just returned from lifting potatoes out in the fields. Although she had been dreading this moment all the time she was on the bus, it turned out better than she expected. In fact, despite being dead on their feet, all the girls made Sunday feel welcome, with the exception of Sue from Brum, who was too tired to talk to anyone, let alone make the effort to communicate with a deaf girl.

Apart from Jinx, the girl Sunday took to most was the epileptic, Ruthie. Jinx had talked of her being a bit on the posh side, so as soon as Ruthie launched into conversation, Sunday imagined that she spoke with a plum in her mouth. She was not to know, of course, that it was quite the reverse, for although Ruthie came from a 'good family' down south, ever since she left school a few years earlier, she had worked hard for a living as a sales assistant in a shoe shop.

'You chose a good night to arrive,' called Ruthie, who was a few years older than the other girls, with a full flock of naturally curly brown hair, which just touched the shoulders of her sturdy, well-proportioned figure. Then she disappeared into the kitchen to start her stint as the evening's cook. 'Roast pork and crackling!'

'What did she say?' asked Sunday, who certainly couldn't read lips on the far side of the room.

'It's her turn to cook,' explained Jinx. 'We take it in turns. Roast pork and crackling tonight.'

Sunday was flabbergasted. 'Roast pork!' she spluttered incredulously. 'I haven't had that since last Christmas. Where d'you get the coupons?'

There were a few sniggers around the room before Jinx explained again. 'You're on a farm now, girl. We may be livin' in absolute 'ell, but at least we eat well!' And to prove it, she cut herself a thick slice of bread, and started to toast it on a fork over the paraffin stove.

During the course of the evening, Sunday gradually got to know all the girls. Without any inhibitions, they told her about their lives back home, their boyfriends, their wartime experiences, and what they wanted to do when, as Jinx put it, they'd finished digging up bloody potatoes for 'old fart-features'. With the place consumed by the succulent smell of pork roasting in the open kitchen range, everyone seemed to be telling Sunday the story of their life. But despite the hard work and bleak living conditions, none of them seemed to be particularly homesick. Sheil seemed the only really complicated one of the group, for she spent most of the evening combing the threadbare fur on Algie, and talking to it as though it were her child.

The meal itself was a dream come true for Sunday, for not only had Ruthie cooked the best roast pork and potatoes she had ever tasted, but Sue had made apple sauce from cornflour and saccharin tablets, with apples nicked only two weeks before from Cloy's own orchard.

There was, however, one tense moment which very nearly ruined the warmth of the evening. It came soon after the meal was over, and Sheil was making everyone the last cup of tea of the day. The problem was caused, unwittingly, by Maureen, the deaf and dumb girl, who Sunday thought was the most attractive girl of the bunch, with her soft, light brown hair combed seductively behind her ears, and wearing only a slight suggestion of make-up. All through the meal Maureen had watched and admired every move that Sunday had made, so much so that she was impatient to communicate with her. Eventually, her moment came. Putting her hand on Sunday's arm, she started to point first to her own mouth, and then Sunday's. Then she used both her hands to convey some kind of a message.

Sunday's expression changed immediately.

'Mo's askin' you somethin', girl,' said Jinx, who turned back to try to work out what Maureen was trying to communicate. 'Oh – that's right, Mo,' she said triumphantly. ''Ave a go, girl.'

'What does she want?' Sunday asked brusquely.

Ruthie turned to face Sunday. 'She wants to know if you can read sign language.'

'No!' Sunday's snapped reply took the girls by surprise.

Maureen looked puzzled, and turned to Ruthie for an explanation. Ruthie looked embarrassed, and by shaking her head towards Maureen indicated Sunday's reply.

Maureen, looking most surprised, came back immediately. 'Why not?' she asked, using her hands in coordination with her lips to get across her question.

Ruthie turned back to Sunday to relay Maureen's message.

But Sunday had understood only too well, and dismissed Maureen's question with an angry wave of the hand. 'It's *my* business!' she snapped, her voice raised again for the first time in several weeks. 'Tell her I don't need to learn sign language. Tell her I'm not deaf – not for ever. One day I'm going to hear again. All the doctors told me so. Go on, tell her!'

There was a tense silence around the table. The moment was only broken by Maureen, who smiled and gently put her hand on Sunday's arm. She wasn't hurt. She wasn't hurt at all, because she understood. More than anyone else in the room, she understood.

Luckily, the incident passed quickly and by the time the girls turned in for the night, Jinx had gone through her entire repertoire of dirty jokes, which caused uproar and gales of laughter right round the ancient beams in the high ceiling.

At nine o'clock on the dot, Farmer Cloy turned off the electricity, and apart from the light from a torch which Sue always used to read a magazine before turning in, the place was plunged into darkness.

For the first hour or so, Sunday didn't sleep too well. Her bed was as uncomfortable as hell, and the solitary pillow felt like concrete. So she just lay there, wondering why she'd come to such a place, and what her mum and Aunt Louie were doing now back home in 'the Buildings'. If she wasn't exactly homesick, she was certainly bewildered. Bewildered to be sharing her bedroom with five other girls, with no privacy, and no sense of belonging to anyone. But as her eyelids gradually began to feel dry and heavy, her mind started to race. She thought of everything that had happened to her that day, about the massive silver plane swooping down low across the hedgerows just above her head, about Jinx and the girls, about Ronnie Cloy and his butterflies. For a moment or so she also remembered the flying bomb, and Pearl, and Ma Briggs. She could see them – and hear them. But as her eyelids flickered just one more time, those images soon disappeared.

By the time she fell into a deep sleep, she remembered nothing. Absolutely nothing.

# *Chapter 9*

During November, the Allied invasion of France was gaining momentum. Despite heavy opposition, there were advances on all fronts, and speculation was growing that by the New Year a heavy battle would be taking place well inside Germany itself. Unfortunately, however, the Allied success had not yet stemmed the daily onslaught on London by Hitler's latest secret weapon, the V-2 rocket, and Prime Minister Churchill's statement to Parliament that 'the casualties and damage had so far not been heavy', was far from the truth. Islington had been one of the first of the London boroughs to be hit, when a rocket came down on a residential back street causing devastation and the loss of many innocent lives. After the D-Day landings in Normandy back in June, the initial euphoria that the war was almost over had vanished. Even in 'the Buildings' the mood of fear and depression had returned, and like all the rest of their neighbours, Madge Collins and her sister Louie never knew from one day to the next whether they would survive an explosion caused by one of the giant rockets crashing down on them from the sky.

In North Essex, too, the skies were constantly streaked with the trails of rocket vapour. Ever since September, there had been rumours of V-2s dropping on Chelmsford and Clacton, of others that had exploded in midair or in the sea off the Essex coast, and many more tearing their way across the skies to wreak even more havoc on London.

By the end of her first week at Cloy's Farm, Sunday had seen very little of the lethal rockets that were passing over the stubble fields each day. Because she had received no formal training for her duties from the War Agricultural Committee, she had to learn the hard way. That meant getting up at four every morning, waiting until the cold bathroom was free, swallowing a quick cup of tea and a slice of bread and marge, and rushing out to the cowsheds where Farmer Cloy's wife, Angela, was waiting to show her the rituals of milking. To her surprise, Sunday took an immediate liking to

Angela Cloy, who not only had a beautiful outdoor complexion, but who seemed to work just as hard as the rest of the girls. Once the milking was done, Sunday then helped out in the grain sheds, before going on to join her Land Army pals who were still lifting potatoes from the heavy clay, a tedious and freezing-cold job that had been badly delayed by the shortage of farm labour.

Although she adapted to the hard working conditions much quicker than she had imagined, the one great obstacle she found difficult to overcome was the sight of dozens of American bomber planes taking off night and day from the runways of the US Air Force Base at Ridgewell. The base was within easy sight of the farm, and hardly a day went by without a crippled plane swerving low over the field in which she was working. Sometimes the huge plane was flying in on one engine, other times it had lost either one or both the wheels from its undercarriage, which usually resulted in an emergency landing, sometimes with fatal casualties amongst the crew. There were also times when dozens of planes took off, one after another, with hardly a moment's interval between them. Every time Sunday watched the huge birdlike machines rise up gracefully into the air, she felt a strange feeling in her stomach, not only because she couldn't hear the roar of their powerful engines, but because the whole spectacle brought back so vividly her memories of the Blitz at home in 'the Buildings', and that one deadly flying bomb that had changed her life so dramatically.

But during these first few weeks, Sunday's life was changing in more ways than one. Most important of all was that she was allowing herself to be drawn out of the shell she had been hiding in ever since she had lost her hearing. At last she was beginning to mix with people who were totally different from herself, people who came from a different way of life to her own.

Two weeks after she arrived, Sunday finally agreed to go down and have a drink with her Land Army pals at the local pub, the King's Head. It wasn't a very big pub, and as it was a Saturday evening the place was jammed to suffocation point with locals and American servicemen from the Ridgewell USAF Airbase. Since going deaf, Sunday had acquired an acute sense of smell, and as soon as she entered the pub the pungent smoke from the mixture of British and American fags nearly choked her.

'That's the trouble with this place,' called Jinx, making quite sure she could be heard as she pushed a way through the already well-oiled crowd of khaki uniforms and flat Essex caps. 'Bloody Yanks think they own it!'

Sunday didn't even know she was saying anything, for she and the other girls were too busy trying to follow on behind.

'Mind you,' contined Jinx, turning briefly to look at Sunday as they reached the counter, 'I never object to a nice bit of lease an' lend from time to time. Especially the lease. I mean, we've got to keep up Anglo-American friendship, 'aven't we!' She didn't wait for a reaction before bursting into one of her loud, raucous laughs.

Amidst all the crush, Sunday couldn't fail to notice that some of the young servicemen and their local girlfriends were bopping around in time to the old upright pub piano, which was being pulverised by a young GI who was attempting to get as much boogie rhythm out of it as he possibly could. For a moment or so, Sunday just stood quite motionless, trying hard to imagine what the music sounded like, whilst casting her mind back to Tommy Dorsey and Glenn Miller and all those bands that used to be such a part of her life.

Whilst Jinx was ordering the drinks, Maureen, the deaf and dumb girl, studied the forlorn expression on Sunday's face. So she twisted herself round to look straight at her, and moved her tongue and lips slowly and clearly to say, 'You look wonderful, Sunday. I love the way you've done your hair.'

Sunday looked embarrassed, and subconsciously raised a hand to smooth her strawberry-blonde hair which she had tied with a ribbon behind her head. It hadn't really occurred to her to imagine why she had decided to take so much trouble with her appearance.

Maureen spoke again. But as it came so naturally to her, this time she used both her hands to express what she was saying, as well as her tongue and lips. 'The boys from the base can't keep their eyes off you.'

The moment Sunday saw Maureen's hands fluttering in front of her, she felt ill at ease. Instead of being flattered by Maureen's remark, she shrugged her shoulders indifferently. But she knew only too well that as soon as she had entered the pub, quite a few heads had turned towards her, and even now a group of young airmen were eyeing her up from the other side of the bar.

'Two shandies!' called Jinx, turning from the counter with two glasses. 'A port for you, Sue. An' a delicious G and T for Mama Jinx!'

Ruthie took the two glasses of shandy from Jinx, and gave one of them to Sunday. Then Sue took her small glass of port.

Sunday sniffed the small amount of alcohol in her lemonade.

Then she sipped it and discovered that it wasn't nearly as horrible as she had been expecting.

'Doesn't Sheil like coming to the pub?' she asked, quite innocently.

'Hardly ever,' replied Ruthie, who, at thirty-one, was the oldest amongst the Cloy's Farm girls. 'She's a funny kid. Spends most of her spare time listening to classical music on the wireless, or drawing pictures on old bits of paper.'

Sunday was curious. Watching Ruthie's lips carefully for a reply, she asked, 'She draws pictures?'

'Does she!' snorted Sue, in her rich Brum accent. 'Everywhere you look you find something she's been scrawling on. Newspapers, magazines, cigarette packets – even on the kitchen wall.' As she sipped her port, she patted the mass of thick dark hair that was packed tightly beneath a fashionable thick black hairnet. 'She's a pain in the neck, that one,' she said haughtily, her heavily made-up eyes constantly scanning the bar to see if any of the young airmen had noticed her. 'It's time she grew up.'

Sunday didn't catch every word Sue had said because she spoke too fast. But she did get the feeling that she was being a bit unkind about someone who had to cope with life so soon after losing her family in the Blitz.

'Mama baby!'

Sunday had no idea what the pug-nosed airman had said to Jinx as he pushed his way through the customers and threw his arms around her.

Jinx allowed him to give her a full, tight kiss on the lips, before snapping, 'Where've you been, you bloody tike! You were supposed to 'ave been 'ere 'alf an hour ago!'

'Listen, honey. If you want us guys to win this war for you, you've got to give us time to drop a few Christmas presents for Adolf.'

'*You* win the war for *us* – ha!' Jinx's voice could be heard all around the bar. 'Bloody Yanks! If it wasn't for us diggin' in our 'eels, you'd 'ave 'ad the jackboots marchin' down bloody Times Square long ago!'

Sunday caught the gist of the exchange, and laughed along with the others around her.

'Anyway, stop boastin',' sniffed Jinx, 'and say 'allo to my friend.' Turning to face Sunday, she said, 'Sunday, this is Erin. 'E calls 'imself my boyfriend, God 'elp me!'

Sunday laughed, and shook hands with the pug-nosed American.

'Bombardier Erin Wendell at your service,' he said, bowing

low, and removing the remains of a cigar stub from his mouth. 'Heard all about you, Sunday,' he said. 'You're not a bit like Jinx here described you. You're much more of a chick. Lemme get you a drink.'

Jinx slapped him one on the top of his head. 'She's already got one!'

Even though Sunday was concentrating hard on Erin's lips, she found it hard going trying to read them. But he had a good face, a humorous one which reminded her a bit of Edward G. Robinson in a gangster film she'd once seen. Which meant, of course, that he wasn't as young as Jinx! Sunday even detected a slight paunch beneath his short leather combat jacket.

'Anyway,' continued Erin, still looking Sunday over, 'anytime you get too much flak from Mama baby here, you just—'

To Sunday's surprise, the Bombardier's lips suddenly stopped moving, and his expression changed.

'Excuse me, miss. Can I buy you a drink?'

Sunday had no idea that someone was talking to her, for her back was turned towards the young airman. But she was able to read what the Bombardier's lips were now saying.

'The lady already has a drink, buster. Get lost.'

Sunday turned with a start. Standing behind her was a young American airman in uniform. He was black.

Sunday was at first taken aback. Apart from the pictures, it was the first black man she had ever seen. Once the fact had registered, she smiled. 'I'm sorry,' she said, not realising that her voice was raised. 'Did you say something?'

The young airman had a stern, defiant look on his face. 'I asked if I could buy you a drink?'

The Bombardier took a step forward, but was quickly restrained by Jinx. A sudden silence descended on the bar, as several groups of American servicemen turned to witness the exchange.

Sunday was puzzled and bewildered by the tension she could feel, especially from the Bombardier, who was sharing a look of mutual hate with the young black airman. Even Jinx was shaking her head at her, and she couldn't understand why.

'"Doodlebug!"'

Sunday didn't hear the landlord calling from behind the counter, but it certainly broke the tension, for everyone suddenly made a wild dash for the door. Everyone that is, except Sunday herself, the Bombardier, and the young black airman, who stood right where they were, just staring at each other.

Before she knew what was happening, however, Sunday was led out of the bar by Ruthie and Sue, whilst Jinx had practically to force the Bombardier to go with her.

Outside the pub, the customers were looking up into the dark night sky, where the familiar droning sound of the 'doodlebug' flying bomb was echoing across the quiet unlit countryside.

Sunday couldn't hear the deadly sound that she knew only too well, and she was hesitant about glancing up at the burning tail of the machine, with its fiery glow that was now reflected in the anxious eyes of all who were watching and waiting to see where it would fall. After all, it was not the first time Sunday Collins had ever seen a flying bomb.

It was, however, the first time that she had seen a black man.

Digging turned out to be Sunday's least favourite type of work. For a start, Cloy's Farm was a holding of eighty acres of land, and as Arnold Cloy himself was an independent farmer, the place possessed very few agricultural machines that would take the pain out of the many essential back-breaking jobs. And now that the winter frosts had set in, the clay soil was particularly hard to break down. However, Ronnie Cloy had confided to Sunday that some Italian soldiers from a nearby prisoner-of-war camp would soon be coming to the farm to help out on the land, so there was hope that the digging was only temporary.

'I'm sorry about what happened at the pub last night, girl.' Jinx was hoeing alongside Sunday, and had to tap her on the arm whenever she wanted to talk to her. 'The Blacks usually keep themselves to themselves. Erin says that bloke's an engineer or somethin', doesn't even come from the base. Anyway, it's best not to get involved in all that.'

The incident had been on Sunday's mind all night, and she was still bewildered by what had gone on between Erin and the young black airman. So she stopped digging for a moment and asked, 'What d'you mean?'

'Like I say – that Blackie.'

'What about him?'

Jinx didn't know why she felt awkward, but she did. 'The Blacks and the Whites don't get on. That's why they keep them apart – in different camps.

Sunday was shocked. 'Different camps?' she said, totally horrified. 'How can they do such a thing? I thought *all* the GIs over here were supposed to be American.'

Jinx didn't quite know how to answer that one. But she tried. 'Apparently it's the same over there, Whites and Blacks at each other's throats all the time. Chalk and cheese.'

'It's all racial discrimination,' said Sue, taking off her gloves for a moment to rub some warmth into her hands. 'You'd never catch that sort of thing happening over here.'

'Don't you believe it,' called Ruthie, over her shoulder. She was just ahead of the others, and having a hard time breaking down a huge lump of rock-like clay. 'My father used to work out in the West Indies. He said the English always considered the Blacks inferior.'

'Well they are, aren't they?' asked Jinx. 'I mean, what I heard was that their minds can't move faster than a bloody snail.'

'That's not fair, poor buggers,' said Sheil, chiming in whilst sipping a cup of hot tea from a vacuum flask.

'Don't be such a hypocrite,' said Sue, putting on her gloves again. 'They're different to White people, everyone knows that.'

Sunday, who had been trying to follow what was being said, felt uneasy and slightly disgusted. 'That man last night. *He* wasn't different – well, not really. He was nice. He only wanted to buy me a drink.'

'Yes, and all the rest, girl!' griped Jinx. 'You'd soon find out 'ow nice 'e is if 'e got you round the back of the pub on your own on a dark night!'

With the exception of Sunday, all the girls roared with laughter. Even Maureen joined in with a huge beam on her face, despite the fact that she hadn't taken in a word of what anyone was talking about.

Sunday had a sinking feeling inside. She found it difficult to understand why everyone was being so unfair about the black man, who seemed to be no more troublesome than half the blokes she used to knock around with back home in Holloway Road. In fact, she'd trade Ernie Mancroft in for him any day of the week.

A few minutes later, Jinx, Ruthie, Maureen, and Sue made their way back to the barn for lunch, leaving Sunday and Sheil to follow on in their own time. Before they put down their shovels, the two girls watched the rapid progress of a V-2 rocket as it streaked across the gaps in the dismal grey sky, leaving in its wake a long thin trail of exhaust. Neither girl said anything. But they were both thinking a great deal. Thinking about the rocket's final destination, and how many more people's lives it would destroy.

After a moment or so, Sunday was the first to speak. 'What will you do after the war, Sheil?'

Sheil hesitated a moment, then turned to look at her. 'I can't fink that far ahead,' she said. 'I can only fink of today.'

'Don't you want to get married?'

Sheil grunted wryly. 'I'm not the marryin' type.'

'Why not?'

Sheil looked away briefly, then turned back again. 'Because the only man I ever loved was me bruvver.'

Sunday was more curious than shocked.

'We used ter sleep in the same bed tergevver,' she said, looking straight into Sunday's eyes without any trace of anxiety or guilt. 'We din't do nuffin' though – if yer know wot I mean. We just cuddled up tergevver, that's all. 'E was a year younger than me. Got killed wiv me mum and dad in the bomb.' She turned her eyes away to stare aimlessly across the horizon. ''E was a lovely feller. I miss 'im like 'ell.'

Sunday knew exactly what Sheil felt. She didn't know how or why, only that she felt an affinity with this strange little creature, with her mousy hair that was short and uncared for, tiny breasts that were barely noticeable beneath her chunky knitted sweater, and wellington boots that were one size too big for her. There was something about Sheil that reminded Sunday of Pearl, about the close bond of friendship that had always existed between the two 'Baggies'. Was it the grief she still felt, the loneliness, the despair of not having Pearl around any more to confide in? As she and Sheil stood together and felt the frosty air biting into their flushed cheeks, a large flock of green-and-white-coloured birds swooped down low and skimmed the field just ahead of them, finally coming to rest on a mutually agreed site where they immediately began the arduous task of beaking the muddy soil. Sunday couldn't hear the strange little call they were all making, and had no idea what they were actually searching for. But, like herself and Sheil, she knew it had to be for something.

On Saturday, Sunday had the afternoon off, so she decided to stroll down to the village shop and buy herself a new tablet of soap. Since she had arrived at the farm, she had got to know the shopkeeper, Ken Johnston, quite well. He was a lovely, rotund man, who seemed to have a perpetual smile on his face every time Sunday saw him. The only problem was that he had a moustache, and for one reason or another, Sunday found that difficult when trying to read his lips.

Therefore, whenever Sunday came in to buy something, he usually had a few scraps of paper ready so that he could write down anything that she couldn't understand. Sunday was always amazed whenever Ken failed to ask for her ration book, especially for soap, which had often been in short supply back in London during the war. But then, she soon got used to seeing more things available in Ken's shop than she ever saw back home. In the countryside, people ate well.

'So, 'ow d'you reckon you'll make out with the *Ities*?' asked Ken, ringing up the penny bar of soap on his till.

Sunday looked puzzled. What the hell did he mean?

As usual, Ken obliged, and scribbled down, *Italians. POWs*. Then he looked her straight in the face, and said, 'I 'eard they're bringin' some of 'em over to your place on Tuesday.'

Sunday gradually understood, and nodded her head. 'Good,' she answered. 'We could do with some help.'

'Lazy lot though, them dagos. Got to keep an eye on 'em – if you know what I mean.'

Sunday did know what he meant, and because Ken was a bit of an 'old woman', it brought a smile to her face. 'We'll keep an eye on them all right, Mr Johnston,' she replied. 'No need to worry about that.'

Ken smiled back, delighted that he had mastered the art of communication without resorting to too much scribbling.

Sunday picked up her soap, slipped it into the pocket of her warm uniform topcoat, and turned to leave.

''Ang on a moment, Sunday,' he called softly. Taking something out from beneath his counter, he came round and discreetly popped it into one of Sunday's coat pockets. It was a one-ounce bar of plain chocolate. 'Mum's the word, eh, dear?' He took a quick glance out through his shop window to make sure that he wasn't under surveillance by M.I.5, then quickly returned behind the counter.

'Thank you very much, Mr Johnston,' said Sunday, who was really very touched by his gesture. 'It's very good of you.'

As soon as Sunday got outside the shop, it started to rain. Luckily, she had her umbrella with her, and as she rarely seemed to go anywhere these days without wellington boots, she wasn't too worried about getting wet.

It was almost twenty minutes' walk back to the farm, so she decided to take the short cut along a small back road that bordered the airbase. For Sunday, walking in the rain had now become a whole new experience. No longer could she hear the raindrops pelting down on to her umbrella, like the time when she went to listen to her mum playing in the band at the Salvation Army meeting. Even if there was thunder rumbling across the entire sky, she wouldn't hear it. There was no longer any threat, no longer any menace. The momentary feeling of despair suddenly turned to anger, and in a fit of bitterness and rage she took down her umbrella, turned her eyes up towards the sky, and walked along with the rain pelting down on to her face.

Whilst she was hurrying along the narrow muddy path, the rain was driving down so hard that she could hardly see where she was going. Soon, a stream of water came rushing down the path against her wellington boots, and she had a struggle to keep her balance on the slippery mud. A thin veil of rain mist gradually covered the bare trees, and after a moment or so she couldn't even see any of the USAF planes in front of their hangars in the distance. With her headscarf now saturated, she put up her umbrella again. But as she did so, she was unable to hear the rapid approach of a motor vehicle just turning round the bend on the path ahead of her.

There was a sudden screech of brakes, followed by the angry wail of a motor horn.

Sunday looked up, and just managed to dodge out of the way as the US Air Force jeep skidded in the mud alongside her.

'You stupid broad!'

The young airman who leapt out of the jeep looked as though he was going to hit Sunday. But his outburst was caused more by anxiety than anger.

'Don't you ever look where you're goin'? You could've been killed stone-dead!'

With both of them now soaked to the skin, Sunday just stared at the airman with total uninterest.

'Well, don't just stand there, for Chrissake! Say somethin'!'

Sunday had no idea what he was ranting on about. All she could see was a face distorted in anger. So she decided it was safer to ignore him, and continue on her way.

The young airman watched her go in sheer disbelief. There he was, practically up to his knees in mud, rain soaking his cap and uniform, and she just walked on as though she had nothing to do with the whole darned thing.

'Goddamn Limey!' he yelled. Then he got back into his jeep, slammed the door, and started to move off. Unfortunately, however, the wheels were now stuck in the mud.

By this time, Sunday was well on her way back to the farm. She didn't even bother to look over her shoulder at the hotheaded airman who had nearly knocked her down.

'Stupid Yanks!' she said to herself. 'Think they own the country!'

# *Chapter 10*

24 November 1944

Dear Sunday, You may or may not be interested to know that your poor mum has been injured by a V-2 rocket that fell on a pub up near Hackney.

Aunt Louie's scribbled note shocked Sunday. For the past week or so, she had suspected that something was wrong, for, since she left home her mum had written to her twice a week, but during the last week she had heard nothing. So, once she had got Jinx to clear compassionate leave with Farmer Cloy, she was back on the village bus to Braintree, and then the train to Liverpool Street.

During the journey, Sunday imagined all the worst possible things that might have happened to her mum. Every day the newspapers were full of reports about V-2s dropping on all parts of London, and despite the insistence that casualties were light, she knew only too well what it was like to be buried alive in falling debris from one of those devastating explosions.

Doll Mooney was the first person Sunday saw as she entered the backyard of 'the Buildings'. And, as usual, Doll was full of high drama and pessimism. 'I don't know 'ow we survive, 'onest I don't,' she said, trying to keep an eye on her two eldest kids who were making snowballs from the first light fall of the winter. 'I tell yer, Sun, I'm sick of it. One minute they tell us the war's practically over, and then all of a sudden these bleedin' rocket things start it all over again.' Then she wiped her running nose with one finger, and asked gloomily, 'Did yer 'ear about the one that came down on Smiffield Market? Loads er people copped it, poor devils. Terrible!'

Luckily, Sunday hadn't taken in half of what she had been saying, for most of the time Doll had forgotten to let Sunday lip-read.

A few minutes later, Sunday had climbed the stone steps, and was letting herself into the flat with her own key. What she found inside was hardly what she had been expecting.

'Sunday! Oh . . . oh . . . Sunday!'

Madge was out of her chair at the tea table in a flash, and throwing her arms around Sunday in a warm, tight embrace. 'Oh, my dear, dear little girl!' she whimpered, over and over again, her voice cracking with emotion. 'I've missed you so much. Let me look at you.'

She stood back to look at Sunday, her eyes streaked with tears. 'I've been so worried about you. They said on the wireless it's the coldest winter in fifty years. Is your bed warm? Have you been wearing enough clothes?'

'I'm all right, Mum,' said Sunday, embarrassed by the fuss, and surprised to find the old lady looking so well, with only a few signs of cuts and bruises. Once again, Aunt Louie had exaggerated. But the moment Sunday had entered the parlour, her attention had been drawn to the elderly man who had got up from his seat at the tea table.

'Oh – I'm sorry, dear,' said Madge, only just realising that she hadn't introduced her visitor. 'This is a very good friend of mine – Mr Billings.' She turned to the grey-haired man still standing by the table, and held out her hand towards him. 'Stan,' she said rather shyly. 'This is my daughter, Sunday.'

Mr Billings came across, and shook hands with Sunday. 'Lovely ter meet yer, young lady,' he said, making quite sure Sunday could see his tongue and lips moving. 'Yer mum's told me so much about yer.'

Sunday tried hard to smile, but she found it difficult. All she could bring herself to say was, 'Hallo.'

'Why didn't you let me know you were coming home, dear?' asked Madge uneasily. 'I'd have got things ready.'

Sunday felt odd, a mixture of hurt and resentment. 'Aunt Louie wrote that you'd been injured in a rocket explosion up at Hackney.'

Madge sighed. 'Oh dear. Auntie shouldn't have done that. We were having a Bible meeting in the local Army Hall. But it was several streets away. I just got a little shook up, that's all.'

'Actually, yer mum was very brave,' interrupted Mr Billings. 'All the windows blew in. She was blown off her feet, poor thing.'

'Don't be silly, Stan,' said Madge. 'I was perfectly all right.'

For some reason or other, Sunday felt all twisted up inside. It was partly because she felt excluded from something, as though her mum had been carrying on with this man behind her back, just like Aunt Louie had told her. It was also because she had never met him before, and certainly couldn't remember ever having seen him up at the Salvation Army Hall in Highbury.

'Anyway, let's all have a nice cup of tea,' said Madge, before making her way back to the table to collect the teapot. 'I'll go and put the kettle on.'

'Don't bother about me, Madge. I'll be on me way,' said Mr Billings, picking up his trilby hat from the sofa. 'You two've got a lot ter talk about.'

Madge looked disappointed. 'Oh, are you sure, Stan?' she asked, as she went across to him.

For a brief moment, Sunday felt guilty. After all, the man had done nothing wrong. He had every right to like her mum, even fancy her if he wanted. In fact, Sunday found Mr Billings quite a likeable old chap. He had a kind, cheery face, and the most beautiful head of white hair she had ever seen on a man of his age.

'I 'ope I see yer again, young lady,' said Mr Billings, once more shaking hands with Sunday. 'You're like yer mum all right – oh yes, no doubt about that. Strong as an ox too, I bet – especially after all you've been through. Gord bless yer, Sunday.'

After Sunday had shaken hands with him, she was surprised to see him lean across and peck her mum on the cheek. Again, she felt a twinge of resentment.

'God bless you, Stan,' said Madge, opening the front door for him. After he had left, she called down the stairs, 'See you soon.'

Before her mum had returned from the outside landing, Sunday picked up her small holdall, and went into her own bedroom. It was an odd feeling for her to be back home again. Nothing had changed. Her room was exactly the same as the day she had gone away, including a magazine she had left open at the side of her bed, and a packet of hairpins she had left behind on the pillow. It was as if she had died, and Madge had just wanted to leave everything intact. And that was how Sunday felt at this precise moment, as though she was coming back from the dead. The flat seemed to feel even smaller than she remembered it, with that overpowering smell of carbolic everywhere, and the three mantles of the gas fire in the fireplace with their flickering blue flames. Sitting on the edge of her bed and looking around, she couldn't believe that she had slept in this same place all her life. Although she had only been away from home for a matter of weeks, living in the countryside had spoilt her. There she could breathe and move around as free as the wind itself.

She turned with a start as she felt her mum's hand on her shoulder.

'Oh, Sunday,' said Madge, 'I can't tell you how wonderful it is to have you home again. I knew it was wrong for you to leave like that. I knew you only did it to run away from all the suffering you've had to endure.'

Still perched on the edge of the bed, Sunday looked straight up into Madge's eyes. 'I've not come home for good, Mum,' she said, articulating her words slowly and with precision. 'I'm only staying a day or so.'

Madge's face crumpled up.

Sunday got up from the bed, and faced her. 'You've got to understand something, Mum,' she said. 'I'm not the same person you used to know, the same person I used to be before – before what happened to me.'

She went to the window and looked out. In the backyard of 'the Buildings' below, she could just make out the tiny figure of Mr Billings slowly making his way out towards the Holloway Road gate. From this height, he seemed such a vulnerable old thing.

'I need to do things,' she continued. 'I need to work things out in my own way – even if I make mistakes. I don't want to be deaf for the rest of my life, Mum. I want to be able to hear the sounds of life again – all kinds of life. Dogs barking, people talking, rain pelting down on my umbrella, traffic in the road, birds on the trees, Doll Mooney yelling at her kids. I want to listen to *I.T.M.A.* on the wireless, and the bands and the singing. I won't ever believe that I'll never hear again. It's not as though I was born this way. I know what it's like to hear all those things, and I want them back. Why me, Mum? It's not fair. It's just not fair.'

Madge could feel her heart breaking. But just as she was about to move towards Sunday and throw her arms around her, Sunday suddenly swung around to look directly into her eyes.

'Mum,' she said tensely. 'Why didn't you tell me about Stan Billings?'

Madge was taken aback.

'You've been seeing him for a long time, yet you've never really talked about him to me. Why not?'

'He's only a friend, Sunday.'

'A boyfriend?'

Madge was now embarrassed. 'Stan is nearly seventy-four, Sunday,' she spluttered. 'I'm seventy-two.'

'Age has got nothing to do with it!' Sunday's voice was now

raised. 'If you're having an affair, I have the right to know about it!'

'Sunday!' Madge was horrified. 'How can you say such a thing – to your own mother!' She turned and walked back into the parlour.

Sunday followed her. 'Are you going to marry him?' she called. 'Tell me, Mum. I want to know.'

Madge stopped by the table, and leaned on it to keep her balance. Then turning to look back at Sunday, she said, 'Stan and I are friends, Sunday. Just friends. We meet at Bible readings on Tuesday evenings, and he comes here for tea on Wednesday afternoons.'

Sunday was about to interrupt, but Madge raised her hand to stop her.

'You're young, Sunday,' said Madge, establishing eye contact with her daughter. 'Despite the terrible thing that's happened to you, you're young. You still have your life ahead of you, and it can be a good one if only you'll give yourself the chance.' She sat down at the table. It was clearly difficult for her to talk, but she knew she had no alternative. 'Stan's my companion. I haven't had anyone like him to talk to since your dad died.'

'You have Aunt Louie.'

Madge shook her head. 'I love your auntie, but it's not the same. Stan's different. He's strong. He gives me confidence. And he makes me laugh.' Her face broke into the faintest smile. 'It's been a long time since I laughed, Sunday.'

There was a moment's silence between them, which was only broken by the ticking of a small alarm clock on the mantelpiece. During that silence, Sunday was suddenly consumed with guilt. For the first time in her life she was jealous of her mother. She didn't know how or why, only that the blood was rushing through her veins and sending totally illogical thoughts to her brain.

'Just tell me something, Mum,' said Sunday, her voice barely audible. 'Do you love Stan Billings?'

Madge restored eye contact with Sunday again. 'If it's love for two old people to enjoy being in each other's company, then yes, I love Stan. And he loves me.'

Sunday hesitated a moment. Then, quite impetuously, she rushed across to her mum, threw her arms around her, leaned down, and kissed her on the top of her head.

In Madge's bedroom, her sister Louie had her ear pinned against the door.

She had clearly heard more than she had bargained for.

* * *

Overnight there had been almost an inch of snowfall. But by mid-morning a weak sun had succeeded in breaking through the heavy grey cloud, and soon turned the snow to a dirty black slush. People shuffled along the Holloway Road, doing their best to keep their balance on the slippery pavements, and there were very few cars or trucks around to brave the perilous road conditions.

Sunday, who was now used to getting up at the crack of dawn, was out of the flat early, so that by the time she reached the pile of snow-covered debris that was once Briggs Bagwash, it was still hard and crunchy underfoot. This was the first time she had been back to the place since she and Ernie Mancroft had been pulled out of the wreckage, and as she looked at the scene now before her, she felt cold and numb. It was impossible for her to imagine in which part of this wide, open space on Holloway Road she had once worked, scrubbing at one of the three huge washing tubs, or pushing wet clothes through the mangle. A few months before, this place and all her 'Baggie' mates she had worked with, had been such an important part of her life. Now all that was left were memories – memories of steam rising up from the washing tubs; of Ma Briggs with hands on hips and fag dangling from her lips, watching over her 'Baggies' with eyes of steel; of the 'Baggies' themselves, slaving away in the heat of the day, scrubbing, mangling, laughing and giggling with each other about their boyfriends, and telling coarse jokes that would have raised eyebrows even amongst the most broadminded of male customers at the local boozer. But most of all, she could see Pearl. Her own, dear, precious Pearl, with those large emerald eyes glistening through the steam, and a chubby smile that was unequalled anywhere. It was unbearable. Sunday could see them all so vividly, as though nothing had changed. Except that it *had* changed, for she would never see any of them again.

After a moment, she carefully climbed up on to the first pile of debris she came to. Just behind her, huge thick icicles had claimed their place, hanging stoically like giant teeth from the window ledge of what was once a high inside wall. In the hope of finding some small remnant from her past, she stooped down and used her hand to clear away an obstinate layer of snow. But there was nothing, just a heap of frozen earth, bits of parched wall laths, chunks of timber and stone, and fragments of bright red chimney pots. It was a depressing sight, and if it hadn't been for the intense cold, she would have burst into tears right there and then. But just as she was about to turn away, her hand touched something that felt vaguely familiar. The top edge of it was still buried quite deep below the surface, so Sunday had to persevere. Eventually, however, her fingers frozen to the bone, she managed to recover the object. It was a scrubbing brush.

'Wouldn't 'ang 'round 'ere if I was you, mate.'

Sunday didn't hear the voice talking to her, for it was coming from behind. But the moment she felt a hand on her shoulder, she turned around.

'The coppers say the 'ole place could cave in any minute.'

Standing behind her was a snotty-nosed kid no more than eight or nine years old. With him was another boy a bit younger. They were each holding an aluminium pail containing ack-ack shrapnel.

'Me and my bruvver used ter come up 'ere all the time,' sniffed the first boy, wiping his runny nose on his sleeve. 'Dug up all sorts er fings we could sell.'

'We found a gold bracelet just over there,' said the younger boy, pointing to a further heap of debris. 'Mum made us give it in ter the coppers.'

'We don't come no more, do we?' asked the older boy, as he turned to his brother. 'It's too dangerous.'

The younger boy nodded in agreement. Then he turned to Sunday. 'A "doodlebug" come down 'ere, yer know,' he said dramatically. 'A load er gels got killed.'

The two boys turned and disappeared as silently as they had arrived.

Some time later that morning, Sunday went up to the Highgate Cemetery, and found her way to Pearl's grave. When she got there, a small family group were putting some chrysanthemums into a glass vase, so she kept out of sight until they had gone.

The huge chunks of earth were still in the process of settling, which meant that there was not yet any headstone. Sunday had to shield her eyes with one hand, for she was dazzled by the sun now reflected on the carpet of snow covering all the surrounding graves.

When she reached the foot of Pearl's mound of earth, she stood in contemplation for a moment or so. It was a strange experience not to be able to hear the sound of distant traffic rolling down Archway Road, or the seagulls that paid frequent visits from the Leg of Mutton Pond up at Hampstead. But at least, in her mind, she could still hear Pearl's tiny voice that night, outside the pub after going to see *Henry Hall's Guest Night*: 'You're the best friend a gel could ever 'ave, Sun. An' that's the 'onest troof.'

Sunday closed her eyes for a moment, and just stood there in the biting cold, ears covered by her headscarf, and her face exposed to the bright winter sun. When she opened her eyes again, the first thing she saw was the small glass vase containing the bunch of different coloured chrysanthemums, which was wedged into the hard earth to form a bright contrast with the stark white snow. She didn't know whether to cry, or to say something to Pearl. But it didn't make sense. Nothing made any sense. Pearl had gone and she would never come back.

She crouched down at the side of the grave, and with both hands started to scrape away a small hole in the middle of the earth. When she was satisfied that it was the right depth, she put her hand into her coat pocket, and took out the scrubbing brush which she had retrieved from the debris of Briggs Bagwash.

Without ceremony, Sunday placed the brush into the hole she had just dug, covered it up, and quietly went home.

Alf Butler dozed in his favourite armchair by the fire, his legs tucked up in a blanket which his wife, Bess, had covered over him just before Sunday arrived. All his life, Alf had been a frail sort of man, full of ailments from lumbago and rheumatism, to the flu and cataract problems. But just a year before, his health suddenly deteriorated when he collapsed with a stroke. This meant that he had had to give up his job as a door attendant at the Savoy Cinema across the road, which had deeply distressed him. But in the sixteen years that he had been married to Bess, he had been a good husband, despite the fact that he was over twenty years older than her. Now in his early sixties, he had resigned himself to a sedentary life, pottering around the flat doing odd jobs, and reluctantly leaving Bess to be the breadwinner. How she really earned her living, however, was quite another matter, for, as all her neighbours in 'the Buildings' knew, it had always been far removed from the hotel receptionist job she told Alf she went to most nights of the week.

''E's 'ad a slight stroke,' Bess mouthed.

She wanted to avoid waking Alf, so it was useful only having to move her tongue and lips to talk to Sunday.

'Gone numb down one side of 'is face. Luckily, it 'asn't really affected 'im anywhere else. Poor old boy.' She kissed him gently on the forehead. 'Always in the wars.'

She nodded to Sunday, who followed her into the kitchen.

''E ought ter be in a nursin' 'ome or somefin',' Bess said, as she quietly closed the door behind Sunday. 'But I fink it'd kill 'im off in a coupla weeks. 'E relies on me, Sun – that's the sad part. Sits at that window night an' day, waitin' for me ter come 'ome.' She moved to the kitchen table, pulled back a chair for Sunday to sit down on, then sat down opposite her. 'Mind you, I rely on 'im too, yer know. Oh yes. 'E's a stupid ole sod, but I'm a lucky woman to 'ave a man to love me like 'e does.'

Sunday crossed her arms and leaned them on the table. 'Do you love him too, Bess?' she asked.

Bess took out her packet of fags and lighter from her dress pocket and put them on the table in front of her. 'I don't know what love means any more,' she said. 'Every night of the week some Yankee boy or uvver tells me 'e loves me. Until 'e finishes wiv me after an 'our or so.' She flicked open the fag packet. 'It's not like that wiv Alf though. I love *'im* in quite a different way.'

She took a fag out of the packet, and then pushed it across to her friend. Sunday shook her head, and passed it back again.

Bess was surprised. 'Wot? Given it up already?'

Sunday shrugged her shoulders. She had only started to smoke in the first place because all the other 'Baggies' seemed to do it, and because it seemed glamorous and sexy to be seen by a feller with a fag drooping out of sticky red lips, just like a film star. But ever since she lost her hearing, smoking just didn't matter to her any more.

Bess lit herself a fag, and for the next half-hour or so, she sat there listening to how Sunday had been coping with her new life in the country. Bess hung on every word Sunday said, for before the girl had joined up in the Women's Land Army, she had made no secret of the fact that, in her opinion, getting away from the stifling atmosphere of living with two elderly women was Sunday's only hope of survival.

Sunday loved her little chats with Bess. For some reason, she felt totally at ease with this larger-than-life character who didn't care a damn what anyone thought of her. Most odd, however, was the fact that the two of them spoke about sex quite openly. Bess told Sunday everything about her exploits with her GI customers in the West End, and in turn Sunday confided in her about all her most intimate physical problems. In that sense, despite her free and easy ways, Bess was more of a mum than Sunday's own mum, for Madge had always shied away from discussing any 'worldly' matters with her daughter. However, Bess suddenly mentioned one particular matter that caught Sunday completely off guard.

'So tell me about this Ernie Mancroft.'

Sunday was startled. 'What about him?'

'Who is 'e?'

Sunday moved about restlessly on her chair. 'He used to work at the Bagwash. He and I – we were dug out together.'

''Ad a bit of a ding-dong, 'ave yer?'

For the first time ever, Sunday took umbrage at one of Bess's remarks. 'No, Bess! Don't say things like that. You make it sound like we're friends. Don't ever say that again. I hate Ernie Mancroft.'

Bess looked both surprised and curious. But she had retained a lungful of smoke for longer than she had anticipated, and it made her cough. 'Don't foller yer, Sun. It don't make sense.'

'What do you mean?'

Bess got up from the table, stubbed her fag out in the sink, and threw the stub into the waste bin below. Then she returned to the table, but remained standing. 'From what I 'ear, 'e's been 'anging round your place quite a lot since yer left. Yer Aunt Louie's been seein' quite a bit of 'im. Accordin' to 'er, this bloke says you an' 'im – are a couple.'

Sunday's lips went dry.

'As far as I can make out, Louie gave 'im yer address in the country.' She pulled another fag out of the packet and placed it between her lips. But she didn't light up. 'Sounds ter me like 'e's got the 'ots for yer, mate, 'cos 'e's coming out to Essex to look yer up.'

All the colour drained from Sunday's face.

# Chapter 11

The journey back to Ridgewell took Sunday twice as long as when she had originally set out. There had been such heavy falls of snow that not only was the train from London running late, but the poor old driver of the village bus had to get out several times to clear the road with a shovel. But for Sunday, it was a magical sight. This was the first time she had ever seen the countryside completely covered in snow, and in some places, where the wind had blown drifts against the bordering hedgerows, the entire landscape looked just like one massive white blanket.

As there was currently a great shortage of both salt and grit, the roads in and around the farm had been cleared by GIs from the base, who had used their own powerful tractors to keep their road transport vehicles on the move. Later, Sunday learnt that they had also been a great help to the surrounding villages by delivering essential food supplies such as bread, milk, and fresh meat.

Like every other farm in the district, Cloy's was also under several inches of snow, and when Sunday finally reached the barn on foot she found Jinx and the other girls feverishly digging themselves out.

'When the war's over, I can always get a job as a navvy!' yelled Jinx when she saw Sunday approaching. Then, with a nod towards the farmhouse, she added, 'At least I'd get more than in this crummy dump!'

Sunday laughed with the other girls, even though she didn't take in exactly what Jinx was saying. A few minutes later, she had changed into her wellington boots, and was outside joining in. To her it was a novelty scraping snow away to clear a path. Living all her life in 'the Buildings', it was something she had never been called on to do. Although she couldn't hear the banter and laughter going on between the girls, she thoroughly enjoyed the exhilarating feeling of release that was so lacking during her short, inhibiting trip home.

That evening, Sunday had her first taste of rabbit and vegetable pie. She wasn't exactly mad on it, but at least it was a hot and warming dish after her long journey from London in the cold. What she hadn't liked, however, was to watch Jinx preparing the poor creature for the pot, for she had to skin and gut it, and then remove its head. Although, like Sunday, Jinx was a town girl, she had soon got used to country ways, especially as rabbit was readily available food. This one had only been shot by Farmer Cloy that very morning. 'Rather 'im than me!' laughed Jinx, as she popped the rabbit's head and entrails into a waste bin.

During the few weeks since Sunday had been working at the farm, she had got to like and trust Jinx. In Sunday's mind, there was something about the Welsh girl that appealed to her, whether it was her spirit of total independence, or her firmly held idea that life was for living. Whatever it was, more than once she had wished she could be like her. But the more she got to know Jinx, the more she realised that there was, like with most people, another side to her. Her outward face was obvious: big, brash, a laugh a minute, but as tough as old nails. This part of her nature was a throwback to her childhood, learning to fend for herself in the slums and poverty of the Swansea dockyards. Inside, however, it was quite a different story. Contrary to popular belief, Jinx did care what people thought of her, and most of all, she could never cope with the idea of being rejected. Therefore, it came as no surprise to Sunday when, after she and the girls had polished off the last of the rabbit pie, Jinx told them all that she had an important announcement to make.

'You're all goin' to be aunties!' she proclaimed proudly, making quite sure that she was turned towards Sunday and Maureen so that they could both read her lips.

Jinx's smile became fixed when she suddenly realised that her news had been greeted by the girls with shocked silence.

'Well, don't all rush to congratulate me!' she quipped.

Sunday was the first to get up from the table, and go to her. 'It's wonderful, Jinx,' she said, kissing her tenderly on the cheek. 'How far gone are you?'

'About a month. I've known for a couple of days.'

'But you're not even married.' This piercing remark came inevitably from Sue.

'What difference does that make, boyo?' snapped Jinx, trying to make light of it all. 'I'll find someone eventually.'

'You mean – you don't know who the father is?' asked Ruthie, more out of concern than shock.

Jinx let rip with one of her chesty laughs. 'Don't be daft, Ruthie!' she roared. 'Of course I know. I been walkin' out with 'im for the last year, 'aven't I?'

'So it *is* him,' sniffed Sue haughtily. 'That bombardier.'

'Don't you talk about my Erin like that, Sue Partin'ton! 'E's a lovely darlin', an' I won't 'ave a word said against 'im.'

The news was too much for Sheil to take in, so she quietly got up from the table and went across to join Algie on her bed.

'What does Erin say about it?' asked Sunday.

''Aven't told 'im,' she replied quite casually. ''E's got enough on 'is mind, poor sod. I don't want to lumber him with a kid when 'e's out on dangerous missions all the time.'

Ruthie was now very concerned. 'Jinx,' she said, leaning across the table to her. 'You *must* tell Erin. After all, he's responsible. It's his child as much as yours.'

'What do Yanks care about kids?' added Sue, sarcastically. 'All they care about is a quick night's bash, and home again where nobody can find them.'

'Come off it, Sue,' said Jinx wickedly. 'Given 'alf a chance, you wouldn't mind a quick night's bash with any of 'em yerself!'

Everyone laughed except Sue, who sat back in her chair and decided not to contribute anything more to the discussion.

Jinx got up from the table, and started to collect the dirty supper plates. 'Anyway, it makes no difference,' she said. 'As soon as I get the chance, I'm goin' to get rid of it.'

Ruthie clasped her hand to her mouth in horror.

Sunday immediately picked up Ruthie's shocked reaction. 'What did you say?' she asked Jinx. But when Jinx didn't reply, she turned back to Ruthie and asked her, 'What did she say?'

'She's going to get rid of it.'

Now Sunday was shocked. She had heard of this sort of thing happening all the time to girls back home, but she was distressed by the thought that Jinx was going to do the same thing.

Ruthie got up from the table and started to help Sunday and Maureen to clear it. She couldn't believe how calmly Jinx was handling such a crisis. 'Are you doing this – because of what your family back home might say?'

'Not at all!' insisted Jinx. 'Me mam an' dad couldn't care less what I get up to. Especially me mam. We're very broadminded down in Wales, y'know.' Without another word, she picked up her pile of supper plates, and swiftly disappeared off into the kitchen.

Sunday watched her go, then exchanged an anxious glance with Ruthie.

During the night, Sunday was woken by someone gently shaking her shoulder. It was pitch-dark in the barn, so she had to reach for her torch on her bedside cabinet. When she turned it on, Maureen's face was staring down at her in the beam. She was clearly very disturbed, for she was using her lips and hands in an attempt to get Sunday out of bed.

'What is it?' whispered Sunday, knowing only too well that in the dark, Maureen was unable to lip-read.

When she reluctantly got up, her feet were freezing-cold as they touched the bare floorboards. But Maureen had grabbed hold of her hand, and practically dragged her across to the next bed, which was where Jinx slept, but was now deserted.

'Where is she?' asked Sunday, pointing the torch at her own face so that Maureen could read what she was saying. Then she immediately turned the beam back on to Maureen, who was shrugging her shoulders.

Hoping that there was some logical explanation, Sunday quickly slid into her bedside slippers, and, taking care not to wake any of the other girls, went out to look for Jinx, first in the kitchen, then the bathroom, and finally the outside lavatory. There was no sign of Jinx anywhere.

Sunday was now just as anxious as Maureen, so she got dressed quickly, putting on her green uniform pullover and beige breeches, a heavy woollen scarf tied over her head, and her WLA duffle coat. Try as she may, she couldn't do all this without waking the others, so after she had told them what was going on, she took her torch and went outside to search for Jinx.

The weather was atrocious, and the path that the girls had only cleared during the early afternoon, was already covered in another layer of thick, wet snow. Sunday didn't know in which direction to go, so she used the beam from her torch to pick out everything from the farmhouse to the outside buildings. She wanted to call out, but even if she were able to hear a reply, it would be too risky, for if she woke Farmer Cloy all hell would be let loose.

To make matters worse, a blustering wind was twisting around her entire body as she made a supreme effort to keep on the move, and snowflakes were fluttering straight into her torch beam, to end up covering her face, headscarf and coat. She felt as though she was trudging across the North Pole.

After checking the various outbuildings which flanked the farmhouse stable-yard, Sunday eventually found herself inside the cowshed. An all-night oil lamp was hanging from one of the overhead beams, and the light was casting huge eerie shadows across the sleeping cattle who were all huddled together trying to keep warm. Sunday was a little nervous being in the shed on her own in the middle of the night, and after her torch beam had moved from one direction to another, she almost gave up hope of finding Jinx before morning. But just as she was about to make her way out into the blizzard again, she saw a girl's figure huddled up in the corner on a pile of hay.

'Jinx!'

Jinx raised her head, and squinted into the torch beam.

Sunday rushed across and squatted down in front of her. Only then did she realise that the girl had no topcoat on, and was shivering with the intense cold. 'What is it, Jinx?' she asked. 'What are you doing out here?'

Jinx slowly lifted her head. Her eyes looked red and sore from crying. 'I don't want to get rid of it, Sunday,' she said. And as she spoke, her face crumpled up in anguish. 'I don't want to get rid of my baby.'

'Oh, Jinx!' Sunday pulled her into her arms and hugged her. 'Of course you don't have to, if you don't want.' Then she faced her again. 'We'll sort this out for you, Jinx,' she assured her. 'We'll all help you to find a way out of this.'

Jinx shook her head. 'You don't understand,' she said, rubbing her eyes with the back of her hand. 'When me mam and dad find out, they're goin' to kill me. 'Specially me mam. She's a regular at Chapel. She'll never forgive me for humiliatin' her.' She shook her head again. 'They'll never let me 'ave the kid, Sunday – not in a million years.'

Sunday was astonished to think that Jinx was talking like this. It was such a different side to her character, the complete opposite to the rumbustious, outgoing girl she had taken her for. 'Listen to me, Jinx,' she said, clasping her by the shoulders and staring straight into her eyes. 'It's not your people back home you should be thinking about – it's you. You're the one that has to cope with all this, you're the one that has to make the decisions – not them. And if you want to keep the kid, then you must keep it.'

''Ow can I, girl?' asked Jinx, cupping her cheeks in her hands. ''Ow can I bring up a kid on my own? Where would I go? What would I do for money? I'd be an unmarried mother, an outcast in everyone's eyes.'

Sunday could see that Jinx was shivering from top to bottom

with the cold, so she took off her own duffle coat, and draped it around her shoulders. 'You must tell Erin – as soon as possible,' she said.

'I can't,' replied Jinx, shaking her head. 'What we did was my idea. I 'ave no right to put the blame on 'im.'

Sunday took Jinx's hands into her own and tried to rub some warmth back into them. 'It's got nothing to do with blame, Jinx. He has a right to know.'

Jinx lowered her head, and pulled the duffle coat snugly around her neck.

Sunday put her hand under Jinx's chin, raised it, and again looked straight into her eyes. 'Look,' she said. 'If it'll help, I'll be with you when you tell him. Nobody needs to know about this – not yet – not even your mam and dad.' She moved closer. 'We can keep it a secret, between you, me, and the girls. OK?'

Jinx smiled weakly, and nodded.

Sunday smiled back. But as she did so, a voice boomed out from the open barn door.

'What the hell's going on in here!'

It was Farmer Cloy.

A few days later, the thaw set in, and although the roads were once again more passable, the heavy slush made both driving and walking hazardous adventures.

In May 1943, after the RAF had handed over their airbase at Ridgewell to the 381st Bomb Group of the Eighth US Air Force, some of the local villagers got together and set up a Forces' Canteen for the visiting servicemen on the upper floor of an old Victorian redbrick Congregational chapel, which sat snugly in the middle of its own crumbling graveyard on Ridgewell's Chapel Green. The GIs found it a quaint place to get a cup of tea and a home-made rock cake, and they were grateful that the 'Limeys' were prepared to show them such warm hospitality and friendship, which they fully reciprocated.

Not long after Farmer Cloy had blasted Jinx and Sunday for disturbing his cows in their shed in the middle of the night, the two girls trudged their way in the slush to the chapel canteen, where Jinx had arranged to meet up with Erin. To their surprise, the Bombardier was already there, comparing notes with his pals about the coffee, which was made with a very bitter chicory and coffee essence. The air-crew guys let forth a stream of wolf whistles and catcalls when Erin broke away from them and walked straight over to greet his 'Brit' girlfriend with a hug and a long, firm kiss right on the lips.

'Hey, Sunday!' gasped Erin when he came up for breath. 'Got someone right here who's waitin' ter meet you.' He turned around and called back to his group. 'Gary! Get yer butt over here, man!'

Sunday hadn't realised that Erin had been addressing her, so that when he beckoned to one of his group to join them, she looked a bit confused.

'Sunday,' he said, at last remembering to face her. 'I'd like to have you meet my best buddy, Gary Mitchell. Gary, say hi ter Sunday.'

The young American serviceman in front of her held out his hand. 'Hi, Sunday,' he said with a warm smile, and speaking straight at her as though already briefed to do so. 'Good ter know you.'

Although Sunday shook hands, also with a smile, she was a bit reticent about doing so. He was a good-looking fair-haired feller all right, in his Air Force-issue fur collar flying jacket, scarf, crush hat, and fawn-coloured trousers. But the last time they had met, when he nearly knocked her down in the pouring rain, he had a very different look on his face.

'I guess I owe you an apology,' he said, 'for what happened outside the base the other day.'

Sunday shrugged her shoulders, trying to make light of it.

'I had no idea about – well. If I'd known about your—' With one finger he pointed first to one of his own ears, and then the other. For a moment he felt awkward, then trying hard to think what to say next, he launched into a fluent sign language with both hands.

Sunday's smile faded quickly. She turned immediately to Jinx and Erin to look for some kind of explanation, but they had already left the canteen, and she could see them just disappearing down the stairs making for the chapel door. When she turned back to look at the young airman again, his hands had stopped moving.

'I'm sorry,' he said, speaking directly at her again. 'I thought you could read this stuff.'

Sunday shook her head brusquely.

The airman looked a touch embarrassed. 'Oh well. No harm in trying.' Not sure of his next move, he scratched the overnight stubble on his chin. 'How about a cup of coffee – whoops, sorry – tea!'

Sunday relaxed a little, chuckled and nodded. She could see the airman looked relieved as he went across to the counter, exchanged a few quick words with his buddies, and ordered a cup of tea from a smiling village lady at the tea urn. After a moment, he returned with two cups, one for himself and one for Sunday.

'I have a hunch coffee doesn't go down too big in this country,' said the airman. He took a sip of his bitter-tasting coffee, and pulled a face. 'No wonder you only drink tea!'

This made Sunday laugh, which in turn helped to break the ice.

To calls of 'See you, Gary!' and 'Take it easy, guys!' the other airmen left the chapel. Now alone, Sunday and Gary wandered closer to the paraffin stove, which seemed to be the only source of heating in the whole building.

'Do you come from California?' asked Sunday, her louder-than-average voice echoing around the hollow interior of the old church.

The young airman spluttered over his coffee, and shook his head. 'Not with this white-sheet complexion,' he joked.

'I thought most Americans came from California,' she said, only half meaning it. 'At least, most of them at the pictures do.'

The young airman chuckled again. 'Yeah – well, don't believe everything you see in the movies.'

For a moment they sipped from their cups in silence. But the young airman frequently took sly admiring glances at Sunday over the top of his cup. 'You'll have ter forgive this,' he said, drawing her attention to the stubble on his chin. 'I haven't had a chance to shave since I got back. Active duty last night. Only got back an hour or so ago.' He wasn't quite sure if she knew what the hell he was talking about, so he tried to elaborate. 'I'm a tail-gunner. B17s. You know what a B17 is?'

Sunday looked blank.

'Flying Fortress. They're really big guys.'

Sunday kind of understood, or at least pretended to.

'Erin told me about the tough time you've been having,' he continued, now gaining more confidence. 'I mean, about the flying bomb and all that.'

Sunday lowered her eyes, and sipped her tea.

The young airman touched her arm with his hand, which prompted her to look up again. 'War can be hell at times,' he said, talking directly at her again. 'I guess the only thing we can be grateful for is we're still alive.'

Sunday smiled, and half nodded in agreement. Then, for another moment or so, the two of them sipped from their cups in silence.

On the other side of the room, the tea lady was in animated gossip with some of her village friends, whilst washing up cups and saucers in a bowl of hot water. Despite its vast size, the chapel was quite a dark place, and the only real light available was coming from a solitary electric light bulb dangling from the high beamed ceiling.

Sunday was taking in the rather plain and simple surroundings of the old chapel, when the young airman eventually spoke to her again. 'You're probably wondering where I learned how to use sign language?'

Sunday felt herself tense again, but she smiled blandly.

'My mother was deaf,' he said. 'From the day she was born. Never heard a damn thing all her life.'

Sunday tried to disguise her interest.

'When I was born, the doctors thought there was a chance I'd be exactly the same. But it didn't happen. Nor to my kid sister. Just Ma. Poor old Ma.' He sipped the dregs from his cup of coffee, and put the cup down on to a chair. 'Still, she led a full and active life. Never heard anything, so she didn't know anything any different. Better that way, I guess. What you've never had, you don't miss. But, at least we were able to talk to each other – in a manner of speaking, that is. Thanks to these, of course.' He held up his hands in front of her. 'Ma gave me my first alphabet sign lesson when I was just six years old. I learnt the British two-handed SL as well as the American. Came as easy as using my own voice.'

Sunday felt uneasy. Still sipping her tea, she started to stroll around the room, which had once been the chapel gallery. The young airman strolled with her.

For a few moments, they stood together in quiet contemplation, staring up aimlessly at the church eaves. Both of them clearly had a great deal on their mind. Sunday was thinking about Jinx, who at this very moment would be breaking her crucial news to Erin, and at the same time she was also feeling an odd sense of affinity with the young airman standing next to her. It was the same for Sergeant Gary Mitchell. There was no doubt that he was drawn to this girl, this strange and distant creature. For some inexplicable reason, he had known it the moment she walked into the chapel, as though he had known her all his life.

The few moments' silence came to an end when the young airman quietly turned to Sunday, and, facing her, said, 'I'd like to see you again, Sunday.'

Sunday looked into his eyes. They were soft and undemanding.

'If you want, I could help you. Like I told you, I know the British two-handed system as well as the one we use back home.'

Sunday looked puzzled.

'You're holding back, Sunday. There's a whole world out there. You have to be part of it.' He took hold of both her hands, and, despite the fact that the village ladies were still gossiping non-stop, his voice echoed gently in the hollow atmosphere. 'Let me teach you,' he said. Then, raising his hands in front of her, he whispered, 'Let me teach you how to speak – with these.'

Sunday looked at him as though he was mad, and stepped back from him as though he was a threat to her.

'I am not going to be deaf for the rest of my life,' she said, her voice now raised so much that it spiralled up to the chapel roof. 'They said I'd never hear again,' she bellowed. 'But it's not true! It's not true!'

With that, she put her cup down on to a chair, turned and rushed off down the stairs. Reluctantly, the young airman let her go. His inclination was to follow her, but his common sense warned him otherwise.

Sunday hurriedly left the chapel and disappeared on to the green outside.

The village ladies stopped talking abruptly and watched with absolute fascination at what they were sure must have been a lovers' tiff.

When Sunday got back to the farm, a message was waiting for her to go and see Cloy. After the incident in the cowshed a few days before, she feared the worst, but whatever happened, she was determined that she was not going to let Jinx down. However, as she entered Farmer Cloy's office, it was apparent that the interview was nothing to do with the cowshed incident, for there was also someone else in the room waiting to talk with her.

'Miss Collins,' said Farmer Cloy rather formally. 'I believe you've already met this lady, Mrs Jackson, from Divisional Headquarters WLA. She's come up from London to have a few words with you. Please sit down.'

As she sat in the usual chair on the other side of Cloy's desk Sunday's heart sank. The woman in the uniform of an official of the Women's Land Army was one of the board who had interviewed her when she applied to do the job of working on the land.

The woman brought up a hard chair, and placed it directly beside Sunday, so that the girl could see her as she talked. 'Sunday,' she said, lips moving laboriously slowly, 'our information is that you have not responded to any of the requests made by Colchester Hospital for a therapy training appointment. Is that correct?'

Sunday sighed and nodded.

'Why is that? Can you tell me?'

Sunday paused before answering. 'I can understand without having to learn sign language. It's not necessary.'

The woman official stiffened visibly and leaned closer towards Sunday. 'Please watch me, Sunday,' she said precisely. 'And watch me clearly. When the WLA gave you the opportunity to take up work on the land, it was on the strict understanding that you avail yourself of therapy which is essential to your communication progress. You were sent to this farm because Mr Cloy here wants to do his best to help those with disability problems. There are two other girls working with you who are cooperating, and you must do the same. Do you understand what I am saying?'

Sunday nodded reluctantly. But she was curious. She already knew about Maureen, the mute girl, but who was the other 'disabled' girl who was taking therapy?

'Let me ask you one thing, Sunday,' the woman continued. 'Why are you so hostile to the idea of learning further communication skills? Can't you understand that it is for your own protection?'

'It would be a waste of time,' insisted Sunday. 'I'm not completely deaf.'

The woman was taken aback by Sunday's remark, and exchanged a puzzled look with Cloy. 'What do you mean?' she asked. 'Are you telling me that you have – partial hearing?'

Sunday took a deep breath and replied, 'Yes.'

The woman exchanged another look with Cloy. 'Sunday,' she said, trying to appear as understanding as possible. 'Sunday, I have spoken to Mr Callow, your specialist, several times, and he has assured me that there is absolutely no possibility at all that your hearing will be restored. You should know that you are now registered as a disabled, deaf person.'

'No!' snapped Sunday, suddenly rising from her chair. 'I'm not deaf! I won't be deaf! I'm going to hear again! I won't be dictated to! I won't!'

The woman official felt distressed. She stood up and, taking hold of Sunday's hands, said, 'This is difficult for you, Sunday, but if you are going to put your life together again, you must face up to the truth.'

Sunday tried to pull her hands away, but the woman held them tight.

'Remember this, Sunday,' she said, facing her directly. 'We gave you three months' probation here, three months to find your way back into the community. Now it's up to you whether you carry on working with the WLA. If you don't, then we shall have to say that this experiment has failed. It's up to you, Sunday. It's up to you.'

# *Chapter 12*

Early in December, there were ceremonies and parades throughout Essex to mark the stand-down of local Home Guard units. But despite the fact that many of the stringent wartime restrictions were gradually being lifted, the war itself was far from over, for flying bombs and V-2 rockets were still causing persistent havoc in East Anglia and London. Also, the skies above Ridgewell and all the surrounding villages were constantly filled by armadas of American Flying Fortress bomber planes, heading out towards the Continent on dangerous missions to obliterate the enemy's V-1 and V-2 launch pads in Holland, and to back up the Allied invasion which had now crossed the River Rhine in the very heart of Germany itself.

It was still very cold, and the snow around Cloy's Farm was now frozen hard. But for several days there had been no more heavy snowfalls, which gave Sunday and the other girls the chance to get on with their farm duties, consisting mainly of looking after the livestock. Many a time, however, Sunday and Maureen found themselves being rugby-tackled to the floor as the other girls heard the drone of a stray flying bomb suddenly cut out, and end up with a loud explosion in some distant field. It was lucky that Sunday could never hear the frequent barrage of ack-ack guns from the base that were always targeting the 'doodlebugs' or V-2 rockets as they passed overhead at regular intervals day and night. But there were many times when she lay awake at night, watching the endless flashes of gunfire as they filtered through the blackout curtains and lit up the barn.

However, these days Sunday had more on her mind than flying bombs and rockets. The best news was that as soon as Jinx had told her GI Bombardier about the baby she was expecting, he had asked her to marry him. And furthermore, he wanted to do it as soon as possible, before Christmas. Jinx, who had gone through so much anguish and torment about what she had done, was overjoyed by the responsible way in which Erin had taken the news, and especially the exhilaration he had shown at the prospect of being a father.

And Sunday's estimation of the Bombardier immediately soared, for until that moment she had thought of Erin as nothing more than a gangster from the wrong side of Jersey City.

Sunday's own problem was now her main cause of concern. The visit from the WLA official, which had thrown her into such a panic, meant that unless she made an effort to improve her communicating skills, her days at Cloy's Farm were numbered. And yet, the moment she agreed that she had any future need to learn about sign language and everything else about living as a deaf person, it meant that she had accepted that she was going to remain deaf for the rest of her life, and that was something she had vowed never to do. However, as each day passed, the reality of her situation was becoming only too clear. The truth was that she had not heard even the faintest sound since before the explosion at Briggs Bagwash, and despite her initial determination to hear, she now had very little confidence of ever doing so again. So why was she holding back from improving her quality of life? Was it fear of doing something so alien to her? Was it the feeling that she was having to step back in time by going back to school to learn something? Or, more likely, was it just stubborn pride? Whatever it was, Sunday knew that if she wanted to grasp this opportunity of learning how to stand on her own two feet without her mum and Aunt Louie watching her every move, she had to think rationally. But *how*?

On these Saturday winter afternoons, Sunday had taken up young Ronnie Cloy's invitation to let him show her around the place. She found him great company, for he seemed to have such a love for everything he did that, even though half the time she couldn't catch everything the boy was saying, he somehow always managed to communicate such enthusiasm for wanting to share with her everything he knew.

'I once saw the Home Guard take this German pilot prisoner. Actually there was two of them, but the other one got killed when his parachute didn't open and he crashed down through the roof of the old Dairy near Clare.'

Ronnie was in a sprightly mood. For the past hour or so, he and Sunday had been on a trek through the woods around the village, and he was greatly enjoying his role as a country guide. At times, Sunday found it hard going, for the snow had turned to ice, and they spent a lot of the time trying to avoid falling over.

'We've had a lot of bombs 'round here, you know.' Only occasionally did Ronnie forget to look directly at Sunday as he talked to her. ''Specially when the war started. They had a big one over near Meadows Farm, and quite a lot at Halstead. We had a flying bomb at Hedingham,' he said, as they climbed a snow-covered stile, and then added ghoulishly, 'and a rocket that killed loads over Chelmsford.'

Sunday forgave him for the way he related the morbid details of local air-raids. She knew only too well that all boys his age had a morbid fascination with war, even that snotty-nosed lot back at 'the Buildings'. To them, death and destruction was all part of one big adventure. Nonetheless, it did cross her mind to wonder how he would cope if he were to live much closer to the daily human tragedies of war, in a town or city, like London.

They trudged across a wide stretch of field, their feet leaving deep imprints, and crunching in the snow as they went. When they reached the edge of some thick woods, Ronnie came to a halt and paused for a moment. Turning round to gaze out at the snow-covered landscape behind them, he said, 'This is my favourite view. I always come here when I want to get away from Dad.'

The sun was just managing to squeeze out from behind the clouds, and quite suddenly the whole scene before them was transformed into a dazzling glare.

Sunday relished the moment of warmth on her face, which prompted her to pull down the hood of her duffle coat. 'Don't you like your dad?' she asked Ronnie.

The boy swung a look at her. 'Are you joking!' he spluttered, his face crumpled up in disdain. 'He thinks I'm a cissy. But I'm not!'

'Why does he think that?' asked Sunday, curious.

''Cos I don't like living on the farm,' he answered. Then he took out a packet of chewing-gum, and offered her one. 'Gum?'

Sunday looked surprised. She hadn't seen chewing-gum for a long time. So she took one.

'We get lots of it from the Yanks,' he said, his mouth already moving rapidly as he softened the gum with his teeth. 'They give us a lot of things – sweets and stuff. My dad's always on the fiddle. Gets petrol off the ration, and all sorts of buckshee things.'

Sunday had guessed as much the moment she saw that half-finished bar of American candy on Cloy's desk. 'Why don't you like living on the farm, Ronnie?' she asked, her voice even more difficult to understand as she chewed the gum.

'I don't like seeing things killed,' he said, before stooping down to roll himself a snowball. Then looking up, he added, 'Pigs and chickens. I give them names. They're like pets to me. Then *he* sends them all off to be slaughtered.' He stood up and threw his snowball as far as he could. 'D'you know what he did once?' he said, turning back to Sunday again. 'He brought a chicken out into the yard, and told me to watch. Then he cut off the poor thing's head right in front of me. I couldn't bear it. He knew I couldn't. That's why he did it. I ran away.'

Sunday felt a wave of maternal fondness for the boy.

'D'you know why I come here?' Ronnie asked.

Sunday shook her head.

'See that house over there?' he asked, stretching out his hand and pointing with one finger across the field. 'That red house – just to the left of that big tree that's bending over to one side.'

Sunday nodded. She could see the house he was indicating on the far side of the field in the distance, distinctively red-coloured, the only one set in the middle of a row of white distempered cottages with thatched roofs.

'I used to come here with my dog, Rupert. He was a golden Labrador. We used to have a smashing time. While I spent the time looking at the house and wondering why it was the only one painted red, Rupert used to sniff around for rabbits. I like that house. I like it 'cos it's different.' Ronnie sighed. It was the only time he revealed his true feelings. 'Dad made me get rid of Rupert. He said he didn't want him chasing the pheasants. Dad doesn't like things that move. He just has to shoot them. By the way,' he asked, 'are you a Cockney?'

Sunday was taken aback by the boy's sudden change of mood. 'In a way – yes,' she replied, a little flustered. 'But I wasn't born close enough to the sound of Bow Bells.'

'I knew some Cockneys once,' said Ronnie, stamping the heel of his wellington boot on the hard crust of the frozen snow. 'There was this man, used to live over Toppesfield way. Came from this place called Walthamstow, or somewhere like that. 'Course, they weren't real Cockneys, but they liked to think they were 'cos he used to have a pub, spoke all sort of funny-like.'

The boy's observation amused Sunday.

Ronnie responded to Sunday's smile with a smile of his own. 'I like you, Sunday,' he said without any awkwardness. 'Will you be my friend?'

This remark confirmed to Sunday what she had begun already to know. In his own adolescent way, the boy was attracted to her.

'We *are* friends, Ronnie,' she replied, holding out her hand to shake his.

Ronnie beamed brightly as he shook hands eagerly with her.

Suddenly, however, there was an explosion in the distance, which caused the ground to shake, and snow to come cascading down from the branches of the leafless trees. In one swift movement, Ronnie seized hold of Sunday, dragged her to the ground, and shielded her with the upper part of his own body.

As soon as the ground and snowfall had settled, Ronnie helped Sunday to sit up.

'Sorry about that, Sunday,' he said, worried about how she would react. 'In the distance, over there. Can you see?'

Sunday looked to where the boy was pointing, and in the distance she could see a tall funnel of smoke rising up from the snow-covered landscape.

Ronnie tried to explain exactly what had happened. But rather than use words, this time he illustrated that the explosion had been caused by a 'doodlebug' or a V-2 rocket. This hc did by using both his hands to show a vivid imitation of the clipped wings and burning tailplane flame of the 'doodlebug', and then went on to do the same with an animated illustration of a V-2 rocket.

Sunday, her face and duffle coat covered with snow, watched the boy with intense fascination. Suddenly, in a reaction that bewildered Ronnie, she grabbed hold of both his hands, stared hard at them for a moment, and held on to them.

Ronnie thought his new friend had gone mad.

For Sunday, however, it was a moment of enlightenment.

Soon after Sunday arrived back at the barn, Ruthie suddenly collapsed to the floor, suffering from an epileptic fit. Sunday's first response was fear, for she had never seen such a thing before. But as only Maureen and Sheil were present at the time, she had to think quickly what to do.

'Sheil!' she called. 'Give me a hand – quick!'

Sheil, who until this moment had been curled up on her bed drawing her umpteenth sketch of Algie, shook her head and retreated towards the kitchen door.

'Get back here, Sheil!' yelled Sunday angrily, whilst kneeling down beside Ruthie to try to calm her.

But Sheil ignored Sunday's pleas for help, and rushed out.

Sunday then turned to Maureen, who was by this time also kneeling on the floor at Ruthie's side. 'Maureen,' she said, using her hands to show that Ruthie needed a pillow.

In what to her was a perfectly natural response, Maureen used sign language back at Sunday to show that she understood, then rushed across to Ruthie's bed, brought back a pillow, and whilst Sunday gently raised Ruthie's head, Maureen placed the pillow beneath it.

'It's all right, Ruthie,' said Sunday several times. 'Just try to lie still, and we'll get some help.'

All this time, Ruthie, unaware of what was happening, lay twitching and jerking on the floor. Soon after Sunday arrived at the farm, Jinx had briefed her that should she ever have to deal with this kind of situation with Ruthie, then the first thing she should do would be to force something between Ruthie's teeth to prevent her from biting her own tongue. But, quite instinctively, Sunday thought this a risky thing to do, and decided to just keep Ruthie as calm as possible.

Whilst this was going on, little Maureen tried to soothe Ruthie by placing one of her cool hands on Ruthie's forehead. This greatly impressed Sunday, who, without fully realising what she herself was doing, spoke not only with words to convey what she wanted to say to Maureen, but also her hands, which she used as a rough and simple attempt at sign language. 'I think she's going to be all right now,' was what Sunday seemed to be saying.

Maureen's face beamed when she recognised the effort Sunday was making to communicate with her. So she nodded eagerly and accompanied her reply with sign language that indicated that she understood perfectly what Sunday was saying to her.

By this time, Ruthie had calmed down completely and was fast asleep.

A few days later Gary Mitchell called on Sunday at the farm, and asked her out to have a meal with him. After the way she had treated him when they last met, Sunday felt a little guilty. But Gary was very persuasive, and early that evening he took her to the British Restaurant in the nearby town of Halstead. It was quite an austere establishment, but as the country was still in the grip of food rationing, there was very little choice. When they got there they found the lower floor dining-room crowded with young evacuees from London, who were encouraged to use it as a common feeding place by the local District Council. However, once Sunday and Gary had climbed the stairs to the second floor, there was a table available by the window overlooking Trinity Street below. The three-course meal they collected from the counter consisted of soup, roast beef, Yorkshire pudding and veg, and baked milk macaroni and jam, which cost Gary the princely sum of two shillings and threepence.

Once he had handed over a half-crown to the ebullient elderly lady cashier, he collected his threepence change, and followed Sunday back to their table.

'I'm sorry for the way I behaved at the canteen the other day,' said Sunday, before she had even started on her tomato soup. Although she had already apologised once to Gary, the guilt was still preying on her mind. 'I'm amazed you should ever want to see me again.'

'Just try and stop me,' replied Gary.

For a brief moment, their eyes met. Sunday noticed his for the first time. They were pale blue, and his eyelashes were just as fair as his short wavy hair.

The meal wasn't exactly what the Sergeant had in mind for his first date with Sunday, but at least it gave him a chance to take a few admiring glances at her, and to get to know her better than the last time thcy had met.

'You haven't told me yet where you come from,' said Sunday, struggling to cope with her tiny ration of tough roast beef.

'Ah!' replied Gary. 'Good point.' He put down his fork, and leaned back in his chair. 'Ever heard of Montana?' he asked.

Sunday shook her head.

Gary then leaned forward and rearranged the table so that he could illustrate with his own style of map. 'U.S. of A,' he said, making an outline on the tablecloth with one of the prongs of his fork. 'Idaho State on – this side,' he said, placing his knife on the outline. 'North and South Dakota – on that side.' He did the same with his fork. 'And right here in the middle,' he plonked down his glass tumbler, 'Whitefish, Montana.'

'Whitefish!' exclaimed Sunday incredulously. 'What's that!'

Gary stiffened. 'A little respect for my home town, if you please, ma'am!' His strict reprimand was soon accompanied by a broad grin. 'We may not have the Crown Jewels and Yorkshire pudding, but we have mountains – beautiful, snow-capped mountains. And not too far away we have our "Big Muddy" – the good old Missouri river.'

Sunday thought for a moment, then asked, naïvely, 'Is it anything like the River Thames?'

Gary, shaking his head, was amused. 'No, ma'am. Our river is big, wide, and deep. When I was a kid, my dad used to take me fishing there.'

'Is that where you caught your whitefish?'

Gary went along with Sunday's teasing. 'White, blue, yellow, brown. You name it, I caught it.'

They both laughed, and whilst they carried on eating, Gary told Sunday everything about his life back home in Montana, about his father, who worked as a track-layer on the Great North-Western Railroad, about his kid sister, Jane, who was so bright at college that she was clearly heading for a career in Law, and about his mother, who took part in nearly every social activity in the town that you could think of, despite the fact that she had been deaf since birth. Sunday read Gary's lips with rapt attention. Everything he was telling her was totally alien to anything she had ever experienced in her own life, and he made it all sound so much more appealing than life in 'the Buildings'. She also told him about herself, about her mum and the Salvation Army, and Aunt Louie, and Pearl, and her time at Briggs Bagwash. Most of all she told him how she had always missed not having a father, someone who could have helped her to balance out her life between a well-meaning mum and a domineering aunt.

When they had both finished their meal, Gary offered Sunday a cigarette. Her first reaction was to shake her head. But quite suddenly, she had second thoughts and took one. As they were lighting up, two of the evacuee kids from the downstairs dining-room came chasing each other up the stairs, and when they saw Gary, they immediately shouted out to him, 'Got any gum, chum!' The cashier lady was furious, and chased them down the stairs again. 'Sorry about that, sir,' she called to her GI customer. 'Those Cockney kids are such cheeky little . . . !'

Gary laughed. He wasn't at all offended. 'Is that true?' he asked, turning to talk directly to Sunday again. 'Are you Cockneys all as cheeky as that?'

Sunday looked puzzled. The first cigarette she had smoked since before the explosion tasted awful, so she quickly stubbed it out in the ash-tray. 'What makes you think I'm a Cockney?' she replied.

'You come from Lond'n, don't you?'

'You don't have to be a Cockney to come from London.'

Gary pulled on his cigarette, held the smoke in his lungs for a moment, then exhaled what was left, making quite sure he didn't let it drift into Sunday's face. 'Can I ask you a question?' he said, staring straight at her with a look of genuine care. 'Why do you shout when you talk?'

Sunday was at first taken aback by his question. But she quickly answered it. 'Do I?' she said.

Gary nodded. 'Yuh. It's not easy, I know, but there *are* other ways of making conversation with people.'

To his surprise, Sunday answered, 'Then why not tell me about them?'

Gary's face changed immediately. For a split second he stared right at her. 'The last time I offered—'

'The last time you offered,' interrupted Sunday, 'I should have accepted.'

Again, Gary just stared in silence at her. Then he broke into a warm smile, and after resting his cigarette on the edge of the ash-tray, he held up both hands in front of her, as though he was a magician who was about to show her a trick.

'*A*,' he said, at the same time touching the thumb of one of his hands with the forefinger of his other hand.

Sunday pulled down a small handkerchief from the sleeve of her pullover, and wiped her hands on it. Then she held up both her hands, and did exactly thc same as Gary was showing her.

'This is called the two-handed alphabet,' he said. 'Just watch and copy everything I do.'

And for the next half an hour or so, Sunday did exactly that. At the start, it was an exhausting process, for her eyes were fixed on his eyes, his lips, and his hands. Time and time again both her hands formed a close union with each other, as she twisted them into strange shapes to make a different letter of the alphabet. As she did so, Gary's lips would curl into, 'That's it, Sunday! That's it!' and just occasionally, 'No, Sunday. Bend that finger more – no, *more*.'

After a while, the lady cashier started to turn off lights around the dining-room. 'Sorry, dears,' she said. 'It's 'alf past eight. We're just about ter lock up.'

The young couple were so engrossed in their sign-language lesson, it hadn't occurred to them that, apart from themselves, the dining-room was now deserted.

A few minutes later, Sunday and Gary were strolling down Trinity Street. Even though it was still only mid-evening, there weren't many people around, for there was a hard frost and it was biting-cold. Unlike some parts of the county, where there was now a relaxation of the blackout, the streets of Halstead were still plunged into winter darkness, and the only light they saw came from a chink in the foyer curtain at the Savoy Theatre. But as they made their way up the High Street hill, a bright icy moon floated in and out of the heavy night clouds, and sent a dazzling shaft of light all along the rows of ancient beamed houses and shops.

At the top of the hill, they had to wait quite a while for the bus that would take them back to Ridgewell, and even when it arrived, they had an uncomfortable journey ahead of them, for there was no interior lighting or heating.

Apart from the driver, there were only three other people on the bus, a farm labourer who had spent the last couple of hours with his mates in the Royal Oak pub at the corner of Pickering Street, and two women who had been visiting a seriously ill relative in Halstead Hospital just round the corner in Hedingham Road. Gary and Sunday found their way to the back seat, and snuggled up together to keep warm. As the bus chugged along the lonely country roads, the young couple made no communication with each other. But there was plenty going through their minds, for the evening had made an impact on them both, for quite different reasons. Although Sunday couldn't see Gary's face in the dark, she could feel the gentle beating of his heart as she rested her head against his shoulder. There was something about this man that was quite unexpected. He wasn't at all like any of his 'buddies' back at the base, or at least, not like the ones she had met so far. In many ways he was quite shy, and when two girls back in the restaurant had smiled at him, he quickly turned away in embarrassment.

Gary was thinking an awful lot about Sunday too. He liked her independence, the way she refused to take anything at face value. But he was also attracted to the sheer vulnerability of the girl, the way she kept trying to conceal her true feelings. In the dark country fields and woods that were flitting past outside the bus window, every so often strange dark shapes were suddenly illuminated, caught in the act by the glaring white moon, which revealed just how ordinary and natural they really were. For Gary, however, the ice-cold atmosphere inside the bus didn't even exist, nor the endless chatter of the two female passengers sitting in the front seat. No. All that mattered to him was the warmth of the body at his side, and the breath that was escaping through those lips and drifting up towards his face. If he had had the nerve, he would have kissed those lips right there and then.

After they had got off the bus at Ridgewell Village Green, Gary decided to walk Sunday back home to the farm. They took the long way, past the base perimeter, where in the distance they could see the giant B17 Flying Fortresses already lining up on the runway for the night's bombing. Although Gary had pointedly not discussed any of the missions he was regularly involved in, Jinx had often told her of the great dangers all the air-crews faced each day and night, some of them never to return.

When they finally reached the barn, Sunday took out her torch and directed the beam on to her own face. 'It's been a lovely evening, Gary,' she said. 'Thanks a lot.'

Gary took hold of her hand, and directed the torch beam on to his own face. 'We've got a lot of work to do, Sunday,' he said, squinting in the torchlight. Then, holding out his hands in front of the bright beam, he used his fingers to form a word that he had earlier taught Sunday to recognise: 'persevere'.

Sunday acknowledged the young airman's challenge.

But to her, the word meant a great deal more.

# *Chapter 13*

With Christmas now only a week or so away, Sunday began to think a lot about home. In her mind's eye she could see all the flats in 'the Buildings' with their Christmas trees, home-made paper chains, and cotton wool stuck around the inside of every window pane, and the smell of her mum's mouthwatering mince pies cooking in the oven. Christmas in 'thc Buildings' was always special, because everyone talked together and went into each other's place to have a Christmas Eve drink and a singsong. Yes, whatever 'the Buildings' was like at any other time of the year, Christmas was special all right. The only trouble was, this year people were just as nervous and ill at ease as they were during the darkest moments of the great 1940 Blitz. V-1s and V-2s were still coming over in their droves, and from one day to the next no one ever knew whether one of the murderous things had their name on it. Only a few weeks before, Sunday had heard about the V-2 rocket which had come down on a terrace of houses near the Archway, and despite the fact that the Allies were getting closer to the flying-bomb and rocket launch pads in France and Holland, the deadly machines still kept coming. More than ever before, Sunday feared for her mum's safety.

The war also continued in North Essex, where the wide, open skies were constantly being savaged by 'doodlebugs' and V-2 rockets. Rumours in Ridgewell and the surrounding villages told of V-2s exploding on farmland and residential property right across the district, and one evening whilst they were passing through nearby Sible Hedingham, Sunday and Jinx narrowly missed a flying bomb, which came down close to the centre of the village, causing severe damage to the local school, the Gas Office, and several houses and shops. And as each day and night passed, stories of courage and tragedy filtered out from the US Airbase, where severe losses amongst air-crew on combat duty over enemy territory, and accidents on take-off and landing, were becoming only too frequent.

But even in the midst of all this anguish, there were lighter moments, and good things to look forward to. For a start, despite opposition from his commanding officer, Bombardier Erin Louis Wendell was reluctantly given permission to marry his Welsh girlfriend, Jinx Daphne Lloyd, who was now twenty-one and who luckily didn't have to ask *anyone's* permission. The ceremony took place on the penultimate Saturday before Christmas, and just prior to the Base Mission Dance, and as Erin was Jewish and Jinx a non-practising Welsh Chapel, for obvious reasons the service had to be a low-key inter-denominational ceremony, conducted by the Air Force Chaplain on the base itself. To her surprise, Sunday was asked to be maid of honour, but she only accepted when she was assured that she wouldn't have to say anything. Gary was Erin's best man, and the chapel was full of his Air Force 'buddies' and even a couple of the WAAC admin girls. Apart from her Land Girl mates from the farm, on Jinx's side there was only her dad up from Wales and her elder brother, Eddie, who was in the Navy and came down on a few days' compassionate leave from Scotland. As expected, the one person missing from the proceedings was Jinx's 'mam', who had been so disgusted with the news of her daughter's pregnancy that she wanted no part of what she considered to be Jinx's mad rush to the altar.

The ceremony itself was short and to the point, and Erin positively glowed with pride as he kissed his bride, who in his words looked 'a knockout' in a pink, knee-length wedding dress, which had been loaned from the base in a generous American gesture of Christmas goodwill to any brides who were serving in the women's forces, Civil Defence, or Women's Land Army. When the ceremony was over, everyone made their way back to the Sergeants' Mess, where a slap-up meal was provided, with a fair amount of bottled ale which had been smuggled in from a local off-licence. As best man, Gary made a very moving speech about how 'Limeys' and 'Yanks' were made for each other, how Erin was a 'lucky sonoverbitch', and, turning to Sunday to illustrate what he was saying in sign language, he expressed the hope that when the war was over, everyone would find what they were looking for in their life. Jinx cried all the way through the speech. In fact, she had not stopped crying since the start of the wedding service, which meant that every so often she had to keep rushing off to the girls' room to fix her make-up. And when it was all over, everyone had a wow of a time swapping stories about their own lives back home, from Selly Oak to Kansas City, Swansea to Jersey City, and from Bagshot, Surrey, to Pea Green, Iowa! The celebrations ended with a British knees-up which somehow perfectly matched a selection of bawdy American baseball songs.

In the evening, however, Sunday had to face up to her hardest challenge of the day. The Mission Dance.

Her first sight of the inside of the giant hangar sent a shiver through Sunday's entire body. Laid out before her were probably two or three hundred GIs dancing with girls who had been trucked in from local villages all over the district. On one side of the stage was a huge Christmas tree glistening with coloured lights, seasonal decorations hanging from the walls, and vast nets suspended from the ceiling, all bulging with hundreds of coloured balloons. And even though she couldn't hear anything that was going on, over the tops of the dancers she could just see the Air Force Dance Band beneath a banner reading, 'MERRY CHRISTMAS'. Sunday was transfixed by thc sccnc and found herself holding back by the door through which she had just entered.

'A few months ago we had Bing Crosby giving a show in here,' said Gary, proudly surveying the packed dance floor. 'Over four thousand guys, and babes from just about everywhere.'

'Isn't it fantastic, girl!' yelled an excited Jinx over the sound of music booming out from the hangar tannoy system. She was quite a sight herself, for her lipstick was smeared all over her chin from the number of times she'd been kissed by her new husband. 'Fancy 'avin' Bing Crosby right 'ere in Ridgewell!'

'Huh! That's nothin'!' added Erin. 'We've had loadsa movie stars round here. Edward G. Robinson, Vivien Leigh, Clark Gable, James Stewart . . .'

'James Stewart!' squealed Jinx. 'You saw *the* James Stewart!'

'Sure I saw him!' bragged Erin, chewing on the butt of a half-finished cigar. 'I rubbed shoulders with the guy, fer Chrissake!'

Jinx gasped and turned to face Sunday directly. 'Did you 'ear that, Sunday?' she spluttered breathlessly. 'James Stewart right 'ere where we're standin' now! I can't believe it!'

'I'm sorry, Jinx,' Sunday replied, looking nervous and agitated. 'I – I've got to go. I – I . . .' She was already backing to the door. 'I'll see you . . . see you later. I – I don't feel too well.' To everyone's surprise, she pushed her way out through the crowd, who were still swarming in through the main entrance door.

Jinx was upset and bewildered. 'Gary?' she asked anxiously.

Gary was already on his way back to the door. 'Don't worry,' he called. 'Leave it to me.'

Sunday rushed out of the hangar, and hurriedly made her way

across the apron area where a clutch of giant B17 Flying Fortress bombers were being loaded with high-explosive bombs all ready for the night's mission over enemy territory. There was quiet but concentrated activity everywhere, with bomb trolleys being wheeled towards the various undercarriages of the huge bomber planes, fuel trucks filling the wing and reserve tanks, and ground engineers checking out every part of the planes with various members of the air-crews who were about to embark on yet another night's dangerous combat duties.

'Restricted area, miss!'

Sunday didn't hear the armed white-helmeted military policeman calling to her, so she just continued winding her way in and out of the apron activity.

Receiving no response, the MP caught up with her and grabbed hold of her arm. 'You're out of bounds, miss!' he said, firmly this time. Then pointing her in a return direction, added, 'The party's back there – in the hangar.'

Because of the sparse lighting on the apron, Sunday couldn't read what he was saying. So, as she was agitated, she tried to struggle with him. 'Let me go!' was all she could say.

'It's OK, Mike,' called Gary, as he approached. 'The lady can't hear you. I'll take over.'

The MP looked a little concerned, but when he recognised Gary, he released his hold on Sunday's arm, and left her to him.

'Sunday!' Gary said firmly, knowing only too well that where they were standing in the half-light, she couldn't see what he was saying. So he took hold of her around the waist, and quickly led her towards a position directly beneath the nose of one of the B17s which was lit up by a mobile maintenance lamp.

The first thing he did was to stand directly in front of her, and hold up the finger of his right hand in a vertical position, which he accompanied by saying, 'Bad, Sunday! What the hell's got into you?'

Although she could understand what he was saying, Sunday tried to pull away.

'Don't fool around with me, Sunday!' snapped Gary, holding on to her. Then he let her go and stood facing her. He knew there was no way she was going to understand his hectic sign-writing, but he still used it to accompany what he was saying. 'Why d'you do that?' he snapped, slamming the fingers of one hand against either the fingers or palm of his other hand. 'Why d'you run out on Jinx like that?'

'I can't do it!' Sunday pleaded, her face racked with anguish. 'I can't go into that place and see it all, see what they're doing . . . seeing without hearing, without being able to do something I've loved all my life! Why can't you understand? Why can't *anyone* understand?'

If Sunday expected a sympathetic response from Gary, she didn't get it. 'Tough shit!' he said, pummelling his fingers against each other. 'Is that all you can think of? *You*? Just *you*?'

Although Sunday had now spent several sessions learning the basic structure of sign language, she clearly had a long way to go before she got to grips with it. But, as her eyes flicked back and forth from Gary's lips to his hands, she knew what he was saying to her.

'For Chrissake, Sunday – this is your best friend's wedding day. It's *her* day, not yours! OK! So dancing means a big deal to you, so it tears you apart because you can't hear the music any more. But that doesn't mean you have to spoil other people's pleasure, it doesn't mean that you have to just – cut off!'

'I'm not cutting off!' yelled Sunday. And as the sound of her distorted voice rose up from the apron, one of the four great engines of a nearby B17 was beginning to chug into life. 'Don't you understand, Gary,' she continued, 'I'm scared. I'm scared to go into that – that place, and see people doing all the things that I should be doing, all the things that I *want* to be doing. Why *me*, Gary! Why does it all have to be taken away from me?'

One by one, the engines of the B17 were now starting up. But as it was Gary's lips and hands that Sunday was concentrating on, he didn't have to raise his voice to cap the overpowering noise.

'Let me tell you something, Sunday,' he said, his fingers moving much more calmly than before. 'I'm scared too. And d'you know what of?' He pointed one finger to the B17 they were standing beneath. 'Of this,' he said, letting her read his lips. 'All of it.' He turned slowly, and with Sunday watching him, he took in all the warlike preparations going on around them. 'I'm scared,' he continued, looking back at her again, 'because every time I go up in one of these things, I'm convinced I'll never come back.'

Gary paused, allowing Sunday time to consider what he'd said. 'Come back with me, Sunday,' he said, hands flicking back and forth in the light from the apron lamp. 'Come back to the hangar.'

Sunday, her face twisted in anguish, slowly shook her head.

'If you don't stop thinking of yourself, Sunday, there's no future for you. You've got to stop thinking of the past. It just doesn't exist any more. Tomorrow starts right now.'

Whilst they were standing there, one of the B17s started to taxi off along the runway. As the giant heavy bomber plane turned, the backdraught from its four engines caught up with Sunday and Gary, and they had to hold on to each other and bend their bodies against the rush of air to keep their balance.

One by one the Flying Fortresses taxied along the hard concrete runway, and gradually their speed increased, and the eerie dark shapes took off into the dark night sky, like huge eagles off to hunt their unsuspecting prey.

When Sunday and Gary got back to the hangar, the lights were turned low, and a spotlight was picking out a huge crystal ball suspended from a steel girder in the centre of the ceiling, sending a torrent of tiny dazzling lights across the dance floor.

Although she couldn't hear the music, Sunday knew at once that the dance was a waltz, for the vast crowd of dancers were clutched to each other and moved their feet and bodies in perfect unison to the one, two, three tempo. As the tiny lights from the crystal ball flicked across her face, she couldn't help feeling a sense of deep yearning inside, a yearning for all those happy Saturday evenings at the Athenaeum back home in Islington, a yearning for the times when she gave her body freely to the sway of her favourite music.

In the middle of the swarm of dancers, Sunday was just able to pick out Jinx, who seemed to be transported to another planet as she hugged her Bombardier around the neck, eyes closed in ecstasy, and her feet shuffling around the heavy concrete floor. Amongst the dancers, Sunday also caught a glimpse of her other pals from the farm, all enjoying an evening they would never forget. Not far away, Ruthie was enjoying a chat with a bright-eyed young airman she was dancing with, and who looked at least half her age. And even Sheil had managed to take the floor with a rather large master sergeant, who insisted on dancing with an unlit cigar in his mouth. Sue, however, was the exception. She had found herself the perfect partner, a full-blooded Air Force colonel, and she spent most of the time looking all around her to make quite sure that everyone was aware of the fact.

Sunday closed her eyes and hardly moved a muscle. All she wanted to do was to try to *hear* the sound of the music in her own mind, to see every instrument that was bringing it all to life. When she opened her eyes again, however, she was startled to see

Gary standing right in front of her, facing her, his hand outstretched towards her.

She knew what he was suggesting and immediately panicked. Shaking her head firmly, she started to back away. But Gary quickly grabbed hold of her hand, gave her a gentle, reassuring smile, and calmly led her on to the dance floor.

Her entire body shivering with fear and apprehension, Sunday reluctantly took up her dance position with Gary. Her brain was rejecting this. If she couldn't hear the music, how would she be able to move her feet without the rhythm and tempo? But as soon as Gary started them off by moving the first step forward, she responded immediately by simultaneously moving her own foot backwards. Their two bodies were soon clasped tightly together, and as Sunday began to feel the rhythm surging through Gary's body, her feet instantly responded to the tempo of the slow, shuffling waltz. Gradually, Sunday felt the life seeping back into her. It was as though nothing had changed, as though everything that had happened to her over the past few months had been nothing more than a horrific nightmare. This is where she belonged, right here on the dance floor, and if she couldn't actually hear the sounds that were bringing her feet to life again, she could certainly *feel* them.

On the other side of the dance floor, Jinx and Erin watched Sunday dancing cheek to cheek with Gary. Erin liked what he saw; a deaf girl dancing with a pretty regular guy was, in his book, a great end to his wedding day. And as for Jinx – well, from the way she was watching Sunday with her young air-crew sergeant, swirling around quite naturally amongst the vast throng of dancers, it looked certain that she would soon be off yet again to the girls' room to check her make-up.

In the run-up to Christmas, the Ridgwell Airbase was still suffering heavy casualties amongst its air-crews, many of whom had not returned from hazardous combat missions over enemy territory. At Cloy's Farm, Sunday and the girls were often in despair as they watched battle-scarred B17s crash on take-off, and early every morning their eyes scanned the sky, as they anxiously awaited the return of the previous night's mission. There were several occasions when they watched in horror as one of the giant airplanes limped back over the rooftops of the surrounding villages, sometimes with part of a wing or tailplane missing, sometimes chugging in desperately on one remaining engine only to end up as a blazing inferno in a frosty field at the end of the runway. Every take-off and landing Sunday watched distressed her. Since coming to Ridgewell, she had lived amongst these almost childlike young men, and found it unbearable to accept the inevitable fact that so many of them would never return to their families and homes.

However, despite the anxieties, these last two weeks before Christmas had been some of the happiest Sunday had ever known. Getting to know Gary was beginning to change her whole attitude towards life, for not only was he helping her to develop a whole new style of communication, but he was also giving her back her confidence, her will to live. Yet, most important of all was the fact that she was falling in love with him, even if she didn't realise it.

A few days before Christmas, Sunday and her pals from the farm were asked to help out at a Christmas children's party to be held at the base. Despite the fact that this was the season when the girls' farm duties were somewhat fewer than throughout the rest of the year, as it was during official working hours, Farmer Cloy was none too pleased to give the girls the time off. However, as he had no wish to fall out with his contacts at the base who were keeping him supplied with a regular flow of luxury goods that he would never have been able to get on his family's ration cards, he reluctantly decided to give the girls permission to have a few hours away from the farm.

The Christmas party started with Santa Claus stepping out of a B17 Flying Fortress, which had landed on the runway to be greeted by over four hundred children from all parts of the district and neighbouring counties. This was followed by a slap-up tea party in the base canteen where Sunday and her pals joined officers and other ranks to serve the kids with Spam sandwiches, cookies, candy bars, ice-cream, and gallons of a funny drink they had never heard of before called Coca Cola. And when they had filled themselves up so much that they could hardly move, they all settled down to the entertainment which included games of musical chairs and hide-and-seek, followed by a mass singsong, with Jinx doing her best to sing louder than all the kids put together. Then, led by servicemen and women of every rank, all the excited youngsters formed a line and jigged around the canteen doing the hokey cokey. Jinx and Erin quickly joined them, and Gary found a place in the line for him and Sunday. When that was all finally over, it was time for the highlight of the afternoon – the distribution of Christmas presents by Santa Claus.

'This is where I need your help,' Gary said, suddenly grabbing hold of Sunday's hand and dragging her up to the front of the surging mass of young party-goers. On the way, he also collected Sunday's pal, Maureen.

Santa Claus was already on the small, makeshift stage, and when he was quite sure that everyone was quiet enough to hear him, he yelled out, 'Hi, kids!'

With Sunday and Maureen standing either side of him, Gary simultaneously conveyed Santa's words by launching into brisk, animated sign language. It was directed straight towards a small group of bright-eyed deaf and dumb kids, who were all huddled together to the left of the stage.

A great roar came back from the kids, 'Hi, Santa!' For Sunday, however, the most overwhelming response came from the small group immediately in front of her, all of whom had replied in sign language.

Santa, in reality a tail-gunner with thc 381st Bomb Group, looked duly pleased. So before getting to the important part of the proceedings, he asked, 'Have you all been good boys an' girls this year?'

Another great roar echoed around the canteen, accompanied by a frenzied activity of hands from the deaf and dumb group. 'Yes!'

Spurred on by his success, Santa bellowed out one last question, 'An' do you believe in Santa Claus?'

The final response nearly raised the canteen roof, 'YES . . . !'

With that great roar, coupled with the flutter of small hands from the special front-row group, Santa was convinced that it was now time to open up his many sacks of Christmas presents.

For the next hour or so, Sunday helped Gary and Maureen to hand around dozens of small packages containing candy, Hershey chocolate bars, chewing-gum, all kinds of toys including model USAF jeeps and trucks, and dolls, and compact puzzle games, and so many things that these wartime kids had had to do without for so long. Sunday was totally immersed in the excited, happy atmosphere as she handed out presents and received eager thanks by mouth and hands from the sea of young faces, some of whom were orphans from the London Blitz. Nearby, a group of young blind kids were receiving similar treatment, and they laughed excitedly as several of the GIs placed Santa's gifts in their hands. For Sunday, it was an astonishing, wonderful occasion. During those past few hours she had learnt so much, as she watched Maureen conversing in frantic sign language with her own group of kids, and Gary doing likewise, using his lips and hands to tease and joke with them, pulling funny faces, turning their paper hats back to front, and making them all feel very special. Before the party came to an end, Santa Claus led all the kids in a singsong of Christmas carols, and as a finale, the place echoed to the sound of 'Jingle Bells'.

It was already dark when the young party-goers, clutching their presents from Santa Claus and a whole array of coloured balloons, finally swarmed out of the canteen and filed excitedly back on to the USAF buses that were to take them back home to their various towns and villages. Sunday and Gary stood with Jinx and Erin as they and all the young servicemen and women waved the kids off.

'You know somethin',' said Jinx, as she wandered off with Erin. 'This one afternoon's been worth not 'avin an 'oneymoon.'

'Speak fer yerself!' answered Erin, as he put his arm around Jinx's waist, and leaned forward to bite and kiss her neck.

A few minutes later, Sunday and Gary strolled off together. It was already turning out to be a typical winter's evening, with a freezing fog swirling across the runways, and parked vehicles looking as though they were entombed in a thin web of frost. As they walked, the dimmed headlights of an Air Force jeep passed close by, casting strange patterns and shadows on to the stifling grey wall of fog that had engulfed them.

When Gary entered the Sergeants' Mess with Sunday, there was hardly anyone there, just two men playing cards at a corner table, and another man fast asleep with his half-finished cigarette still burning in an ash-tray. Not surprising, for with the aerodrome now fog-bound, the night's missions were cancelled, leaving air-crews the chance to get some well-deserved shut-eye. Strictly speaking, Gary wasn't allowed to bring visitors into the Mess, especially a female guest, but as there was little chance that anyone was going to complain on a night like that, he threw caution to the wind and found them a table by a shuttered window.

Gary took off his peaked cap and placed it on to the empty seat beside him. Then, for a brief moment or so, the two of them just sat and looked at each other. Both were now aware of a strong feeling between them, a warmth that was difficult to define. But what they did know was that during the times that they were apart, they thought a great deal about each other.

Gary made the first move. He held up his hands, and started to animate the sign-language alphabet.

Sunday shook her head. 'No lessons tonight, please, Gary,' she said. 'I'm too tired.'

Gary understood, and smiled. Nevertheless, he still continued to use sign language as he talked to her. 'I was wondering,' he asked tentatively, 'whether you'd like to come over here on Christmas Eve. They're showing a Bing Crosby movie. Have you seen *Holiday Inn*?'

Sunday shrugged her shoulders, and looked a little pensive. 'I haven't been to the pictures since – before . . .'

The moment she hesitated, Gary continued. 'Then now's the time.'

'What's the point, Gary? I mean, if I can't hear it, I won't know what's going on.'

'You'll know *everything* that's going on – believe me.'

Sunday shook her head. 'I'd like to, but I have to go home for Christmas. Just a few days. My mum – well, it wouldn't be the same for her without me.'

Gary leaned forward and covered her hands with his own. 'That's different,' he said. 'But I'm warning you, next Christmas – you're mine.'

They turned with a start as the sleeping sergeant suddenly began to snore loudly. Both laughed.

'What makes you think you'll still be here next Christmas?' Sunday asked, facing Gary again. 'The war's nearly over.'

Gary grinned at her. 'Whether the war's over or not, nothin's goin' to keep me away from you, Sunday – nothin'.'

Sunday wanted to say something, but she didn't know what. For the first time in her life, she was completely at a loss for words.

Gary leaned across the table. 'I want to tell you something, Sunday,' he said, looking straight into her eyes. 'I've known girls in my time. But none of them has been like you.'

Sunday felt embarrassed, so all she could do was laugh. 'Oh yes?' she quipped. 'How many times have I heard that at the pictures!' The moment she said it, however, she wished she hadn't.

For a moment Gary looked hurt, and averted his eyes. But he quickly recovered, looked straight at her again, and squeezed her hands which were still resting on the table. 'When I was a kid,' he continued, 'I used to know this girl. Her name was Margie. She was a friend of my sister, came from a well-stocked family who had a farm just outside town where I lived. Margie and I were in love with each other. She was six years old, I was seven.' He leaned back in his chair, took out a cigarette, and lit it. 'Margie and I used to go toad huntin' together – well, not exactly huntin', more like observin' 'em.' He drew on his cigarette and inhaled deeply. 'Anyhow, we used to find most of these toads down by the old pond on the edge of McCauley's land. Not many people went there because it was pretty deep and muddy, and in the fall the place was infested with 'squiters – mosquitoes.' For a moment or so, he had lost eye contact with Sunday, and was staring down quite aimlessly at the ash-tray. 'One day after Sunday mornin' church service, we was down this pond, and Margie fell in. I panicked, tried to get her out, but her hand was too full of mud, and she just – fell away straight under. There was nothin' I could do.' Quite impulsively, he stubbed out his just-lit cigarette in the ash-tray. 'It wasn't fair, it just wasn't fair.' He looked up at Sunday, and talked directly at her again. 'You see, Sunday,' he said, 'I trusted Margie. She trusted me. We shared all our secrets together, and never let on to no one.' He paused a moment, then took a deep breath. 'Right from that time, I vowed I'd never trust anyone else. Margie'd meant too much to me, and look what happened. An' I never have let myself trust anyone else. Not 'til now.' He took hold of both her hands, and held them. 'Don't ask me why, Sunday, because I don't know.' He kissed her hands gently.

Sunday watched him closely, and as he sat upright in his seat again, she then took his hands and kissed them. Then both of them broke into a broad smile.

'Oh, by the way,' Gary said suddenly. 'I almost forgot.' He stretched into his topcoat pocket and took out a small packet. It was wrapped in Christmas paper. 'Since I won't be seeing you at Christmas, this is for you.'

Sunday took the packet and looked at it. 'What is it?' she asked.

'I'm an old-fashioned boy, Sunday,' he quipped. 'Open it on Christmas morning and find out!'

Early on the morning of Christmas Eve, Sunday was on stable duties with Jinx, Ruthie, and Sue. It was her last job before the Christmas holiday, for she was catching the afternoon train back to London.

'You know what?' called Jinx, who was cleaning out one of the horse stalls. 'I've heard that in Lond'n, some people 'ave been eatin' these things.'

'Don't, Jinx,' said Ruthie, who was helping her. 'That's a terribly sick thing to say. Horses are such beautiful creatures.'

'I know they are,' Jinx called. 'No offence meant,' she said, talking straight into the horse's ear. Then after picking up some soiled straw and putting it into a sack, she added, 'But I wonder 'ow they cook 'em? Roast or boil?'

Ruthie shivered. 'Jinx – please!'

'It's true,' called a voice from the stable door. 'They do cook horses. Not young ones though. Only the old'uns that cost too much to keep.' It was young Ronnie Cloy.

Sunday waved her sponge as she caught a glimpse of him from between the legs of the horse which she was rubbing down.

'Hallo, Sunday,' Ronnie said, crouching down to talk to her. 'I've come to ask if you want to come to Clare with me. Not 'til you've finished, of course. I'm going over on my bike to see the Christmas Bazaar at the pub there. You can borrow my mum's bike. She won't know 'cos she hardly ever uses it.'

'I'm sorry, Ronnie,' replied Sunday. 'But I'm going back home on the afternoon train.'

Ronnie's face crumpled. 'Home?' he said. 'You mean – London?'

Sunday nodded. 'Just a few days. Back after Christmas.'

Ronnie seemed deep in thought for a moment, then said something quite extraordinary. 'Is that Yank going with you?'

Sunday looked at him in astonishment, and even the other girls stopped what they were doing.

'What do you mean, Ronnie?' she asked.

'That Yankee bloke you've been knockin' around with. Is *he* going to London with you?'

Sunday stood up and came around from behind the horse to face him. 'No, Ronnie. I'm going home on my own. To see my mum.'

Ronnie shrugged his shoulders. The boy was clearly irritated. 'They're not worth it, you know. All these Yanks are the same. They all go after the girls and give them babies.'

'Oi!' yelled Jinx, over the top of the stall she was working in. 'You're not old enough to talk about things like that, young man!'

'It's true,' snapped Ronnie defiantly. 'I know girls in the village who've been to bed with Yanks, and they've all ended up in the family way.'

Jinx was outraged, and exchanged a shocked look with Ruthie.

'That's not a nice thing to say,' said Sunday. 'The Americans are very good to us. They're here to protect us.'

'Is that what your Yankee boyfriend's doing?' he snapped sarcastically. 'Is *he* protecting *you*?'

'Ronnie!' called Ruthie. 'Stop that!'

'Well, it's true,' yelled Ronnie, who was clearly upset. 'If she thinks a Yank's going to look after her and take her back to America and give her a good time, she doesn't know what she's letting herself in for.' Then turning to face Sunday directly again, he said, 'I thought you were supposed to be *my* friend? I thought you were different to all the rest of them. But you're not.' Then, close to tears, he yelled, 'You're just a bloody Yankee's girl!'

With that, he rushed out of the stable, leaving the door open behind him. Sunday and the other girls watched him go, all absolutely astonished and bewildered.

Sunday was too upset to say anything, so she turned back to carry on rubbing down the horse she was grooming. Inside, she felt a deep sense of sadness, of guilt, of not understanding the boy's feelings for her. But Ronnie was wrong. Whatever he thought about Yanks, he had no right to talk about Gary like that. Gary was special, he was different. He had made her feel like someone he could trust, and she would never betray that trust. Not as long as she loved him. And she *did* love him.

Her quiet moment of thought was suddenly interrupted by someone's hand touching her on the shoulder. She swung around with a start.

'Erin,' she said with surprise.

Jinx's bombardier husband was standing there. But the expression on his face was unlike anything she had seen before. It was grave and drawn.

'Erin?' Jinx came across to meet him. 'What's wrong?' she asked, immediately concerned.

But Erin was still looking straight at Sunday.

'Erin?' Sunday asked. 'Tell me?'

'I'm sorry, Sunday,' he replied, his lips almost too dry to move.

The moment he spoke, Sunday knew what he had come to tell her.

# Chapter 14

It was still dark when Sunday's eyes sprang open. She imagined it was about four o'clock in the morning, for that was the time of her daily alarm call back at Cloy's Farm. But when she switched on the small bedside lamp, her clock was showing that she had overslept, for it was already six forty-five and she could see the first chink of morning light filtering through the side of her blackout curtains. On the previous afternoon, when she arrived back home at 'the Buildings', all she had wanted to do was to go straight to bed and shut herself away. But her mum had been so excited to see her again that, after a Christmas Eve meal of boiled scrag-end of mutton and mashed potatoes, they and Aunt Louie had sat up talking until nearly eleven o'clock at night. However, despite the lateness of the hour, Sunday had slept very little. The news that Gary had been listed Missing in Action in a night raid over Berlin had absolutely devastated her. Although she had known him for just a few weeks, he had been the first man that had ever really meant something to her. As she lay awake for hours on end, tossing and turning restlessly in her bed, she found it hard to believe that her short young life could be so full of ups and downs. If what Erin had warned her was true, if the Air Force jargon really meant that Gary had been killed, then not only had she lost someone she had come to love and trust, but she had also been deprived of the one chance to restore her own self-respect.

A few minutes later, she got out of bed, put on her old towelling dressing-gown, and went into the parlour. Her mum was clearly already up, because the curtains had been drawn back, but as it was a fairly grey morning outside, the early-morning light was quite dim. But, unlike getting out of bed at this hour back at the barn, the place was warm and cosy, for the gas fire had been lit and was throwing out a welcoming glow around the room. As usual, there was the small Christmas tree on a table at the side of the sofa, decorated with tinsel, cotton wool, and home-made paper chains, and the mantelpiece was proudly displaying a selection of Christmas cards.

Despite all this, however, Sunday found it hard to believe that this was Christmas Day. Every year at this time she had always got up to the sound of church bells ringing out on the wireless, followed by carols and the regular Christmas morning programme, *Postman's Knock*. Then it was time for scrambled (powdered) eggs and skinny bits of streaky bacon for breakfast with her mum and Aunt Louie, and a trip up to the Salvation Army Hall for the Christmas morning service. But this year it was different. This year she could hear none of the wondrous sounds of Christmas that she had been brought up to love and cherish – the kids in the next door flat, yelling with delight as they woke up at the crack of dawn and excitedly searched the Christmas stockings filled for them by Santa Claus; and the parties and knees-ups in every flat throughout 'the Buildings'. This year, and every year from now on, her Christmas Day would be reduced to silence, pictures with no sound.

Whilst she was warming her hands in front of the fire, she suddenly felt her mum's arms hugging her from behind. She turned around to face her.

'Merry Christmas, my dearest Sunday,' said Madge, whose expression revealed elation and sadness.

'Merry Christmas, Mum,' replied Sunday, hugging her back.

Madge sat down in her favourite armchair by the fireplace. 'Sit with me for a moment, dear,' she said. 'There's something I want to tell you.'

Sunday knelt down on the rug in front of her.

'I want to tell you about Mr Billings,' she said, exaggerating her lip movements. 'You remember Mr Billings, don't you?'

Sunday nodded. She had a hunch she knew what was coming.

'He's asked me to marry him.'

Sunday's hunch was right, and she sank back on to her heels.

'I told him I couldn't,' Madge continued.

Sunday looked surprised.

'Not because I don't want to, but because I think it wouldn't be right for either of us.' She turned to stare into the glow of the gas fire, and the blue flame was reflected in her eyes. 'You see, I want us to be friends, just like we've been all the time. If we got married, it would be different. We'd have – obligations to each other, vows. I don't want to go through that at my time of life.'

Sunday found it hard going trying to read her mum's lips, for the old lady had got out of practice, and just occasionally turned away from her.

'But we both want to go on being friends. And if anything should happen to me, he's promised to keep an eye on you.'

Sunday was taken aback. 'What d'you mean – if anything should happen to you?'

'Nothing, dear,' Madge replied quickly. 'But nobody lives for ever, do they? After all, I'm not as young as I used to be.' She looked down at Sunday, smiled and stroked her hair affectionately. 'You know, I've always regretted that you were too young to get to know your dad before he died. You'd have got on so well together. He could have helped you so much. Especially now. Children need a dad as well as a mum. When you have problems, being part of a family always helps.'

Sunday lowered her eyes.

Madge put her hand under Sunday's chin, gently raised it, and looked directly at her. 'This boy you told me about last night,' she said suddenly. 'He sounded quite special to you?'

Madge's unexpected question caught Sunday off guard. So she lowered her eyes, and hesitated before answering. 'Yes,' she said, raising her eyes again. 'Very special.'

'Then you mustn't let him down,' said Madge. 'If somebody has meant that much to you, then you must never forget to ask yourself why. In my case, it's always been our Lord God. I know you think I'm a silly old fool, just tramping around the streets in my Salvation Army uniform, trying to bring His word to all those drunks in the pub on Saturday nights. But I could never have done it unless I was sure it was the right thing to do. I could never have done it without asking myself questions, lots of questions. I used to ask myself why I loved your dad so much. It was because he respected me for what I am. It was because he never tried to hold me back from doing all the things I knew I had to do.' She leaned forward, and cupped Sunday's cheeks between her hands. 'What you've had to go through hasn't been fair, Sunday. But to be given the chance to love someone, even for five minutes, is a great gift. Love is strength. Will you try to remember that?'

Sunday nodded.

A little later, Sunday, her mum, and Aunt Louie all sat down to breakfast together. There was Madge's customary pre-meal prayers, of course, which always irritated Aunt Louie. But soon after breakfast was finished, Jack Popwell arrived with his traditional bottle of sherry, which was the only thing that ever brought a smile to Aunt Louie's face. However, the latest gossip Jack brought with him was hardly welcome news for a Christmas morning.

'Joe Mooney's 'avin' a ding-dong wiv some bus-conductress from Stepney,' he announced, as though he had scored a coup. 'Wait till Doll catches up with him. She'll do 'er nut!'

'You mean, she knows about it?' asked Louie imperiously.

'Well, she don't know fer definite,' replied Jack. 'But from what *I* 'eard, she's got a good idea.'

'But didn't you say, Mum,' asked Sunday, 'Doll's expecting another baby?'

Madge didn't answer. There were some things she just didn't want to know about, and this was one of them.

'They're supposed ter be good Catholics,' Jack continued, milking the drama for all it was worth. 'Wot is it this time? Baby number five? Or is it six?'

'Disgusting!' snorted Aunt Louie.

'Wait till the Pope 'ears about this one!' quipped Jack, roaring with laughter at his own joke.

'Oh Jack,' was Madge's only comment. 'I wish you hadn't brought such sad news on Christmas morning.' With that, she collected the three breakfast plates, and disappeared into the kitchen.

As she watched her go, Sunday noticed for the first time that her mum was limping badly. It worried her, for although Madge had suffered from phlebitis for some years, it had never affected her movements as much as this.

'It's what I've always said,' said Louie cryptically. 'Never trust a man. He'll stab you in the back as good as look at you.'

Jack looked quite put out. 'Come off it, Miss Clipstone,' he sniffed. 'We ain't all the same, yer know. Anyway, it's probably just a flash in the pan. Doll and Joe ain't stupid. It'll all come out in the wash.'

Louie lit one of her rolled cigarettes, sending a cloud of bitter-smelling smoke across the breakfast table. 'If I had a husband who went sleeping around with whores, he'd be out of my front door quicker than he came in.'

Jack came back at her in a flash. 'Yeah, well there ain't much chance of that, is there, Miss Clipstone?' he snorted indignantly. 'I mean yer don't 'ave no 'usband.' Then added pointedly, 'Nor ever likely to.'

Before she went off to her Christmas morning service, Madge handed out a few presents from around the Christmas tree. Jack was delighted to be given a shaving brush from Madge and a safety razor from Louie. Sunday bought her mum a new pair of carpet-slippers, which she had managed to buy without coupons from a shoe shop back in Halstead, and for her Aunt Louie, an ounce of her favourite tobacco for rolled cigarettes. To her surprise, Aunt Louie gave her a pair of warm gloves, which she had actually bought with her own ration book in Woolworth's. Madge had bought two presents for Sunday. One was a beautiful leather purse from Jones Brothers' Department Store just across the road. But the second present was more unusual, for it was a photograph of Sunday's adopted father, mounted in an ornate brass frame which Madge had bought for a shilling at the Salvation Army Christmas Jumble Sale. Sunday spent several moments looking at the snapshot portrait of the man who had died so many years before. It was a strangely youthful-looking face, and after what her mum had told her about him, he was clearly a good and decent man. And yet, there was something that worried her about the photo.

It made her want to ask questions about her real father.

Holloway Road on a Christmas morning was pretty much like it was on most other days. Not so many people around perhaps, but, despite the endless bomb-blasts during the 1940 Blitz, and now the V-1 and V-2 campaigns, everything looked exactly the same as always. As she made her way to the Salvation Army Hall up at Highbury, there was a moment when Sunday couldn't help wondering what this great inner London road to the north looked like during the days when Queen Elizabeth I stayed in the Nag's Head Inn and hunted deer in The Hollow Way. Sunday tried to picture what must have once been green fields bordered by dense woods, and the Virgin Queen galloping on horseback through this rural idyll on the outskirts of her capital city. For a brief moment, a smile came to Sunday's face as she pondered on what the old Queen would have thought of 'The Hollow Way' Road of today, with its myriad shops, tall terraced houses, council estates, cinemas, pubs, and a railway bridge that spanned one of the busiest parts of the road outside the Tube Station. And as she strolled along the ice-cold pavements, acutely aware of the seductive smells of Christmas dinners roasting in ovens, her mind contrasted the colourful well-trodden streets of her own part of London with the wide, open spaces of agricultural Essex, and the people who toiled on the land there. And then she thought of Jinx and Erin, and the girls with whom she was sharing a new and different life. But most of all she thought about Gary, and what he had meant to her, and why fate had continued to treat her so unfairly.

When she reached the Regent Cinema, it saddened her to see how squalid the outside of the place had become. She remembered the times when she was taken to the Saturday morning kids' film shows there, the serial Westerns and thrilling adventure epics. And in her mind's eye she could still see the narrow auditorium, and the steep rake of the rows of seats that swept down towards the stage, so that anyone sitting anywhere near the front had to crane their necks to look up at the screen. Sunday still cherished memories of those wonderful, glorious times at this now painfully neglected old picture house, and the days when she could hear as well as see.

Next door to the cinema, she stopped briefly to look at a poster outside the Northern Polytechnic, which announced an impending production by the Amateur Operatic Group of *The Mikado*. But just as she was about to move on, she found herself facing an all-too-familiar figure.

'Merry Chris'mas, Sun!'

It was a shock for her to see Ernie Mancroft again.

'It's good ter see yer again, Sun,' he said. As usual, he was without a topcoat, though, despite his strong physique, he had to blow into his cupped hands to warm them up. 'Yer aunt told me yer was comin' 'ome for the 'olidays. She said yer was bound to go up to the 'All for yer mum's Chris'mas service.' For a moment, he just carried on looking at her, hoping for a reply. 'Come on, Sun. This is Chris'mas. Ain't yer got nuffin' ter say ter me?'

Sunday shook her head. 'Ernie, we've got nothing to say to each other,' she replied. Subconsciously, her gloved hands were moving about wildly in a simple attempt to illustrate what she was saying. 'I'm grateful for what you did, but that's all in the past now. You've got your life to live, and I've got mine.' Sunday hated having to talk this way, especially on Christmas Day, but if she was going to prevent Ernie pestering her for the rest of her life, she just had to say it.

Ernie smiled. 'I've bin called up,' he said, adjusting the white scarf around his neck. 'Goin' off first fing in the New Year.'

'Good luck to you, Ernie.' Sunday made a move to walk on.

'I wanna see yer again, Sun,' he said, blocking her path.

'I don't want to see *you*, Ernie,' Sunday replied firmly. 'Why can't you understand that? Why can't you understand that you and me have nothing in common – absolutely nothing?'

Ernie's smile disappeared. He looked crushed. 'I've never loved anyone before, Sun,' he said, with almost a look of pleading in his eyes. 'Everyone deserves ter be loved, one way or anuvver.'

As they stood there, a cheerful family of two adults and three children hurried by, all clutching wrapped-up presents, and all clearly on their way to a relation for Christmas dinner. 'Merry Christmas!' yelled the smallest of the children, a greeting that was immediately taken up by the rest of the family.

Sunday smiled weakly, but as she hadn't heard them, she didn't answer.

'Look, Sun,' Ernie continued, ignoring the family as they made their way past them. 'This war's cut up a lot er good people – 'specially you, I know that. But we all 'ave ter 'ave somefin' ter cling on to. Know wot I mean?'

Sunday tried to move on again, but this time Ernie gently held her back by taking hold of her arm.

'D'yer remember that first time, Sun?' said Ernie, talking directly at her, determined to make sure she was taking in what he had to say. 'That first time we met – down the Bagwash? Yer give me the eye – remember?'

Sunday stared in disbelief at him. 'Ernie, what are you talking about?'

'You an' Pearl was out the backyard tergevver, 'avin a good ole chinwag about Muvver Briggs. I came fru wiv a big bundle of washin', an' as I passed, I give you the eye, an' you turned 'round an' smiled at me.' He was staring hard into her eyes, desperate for some kind of recognition. 'Yer do remember – don't yer?'

Sunday's body tensed. Suddenly it all came back to her. Yes, of course she remembered. But she had dismissed it from her mind long ago. Inside, she was tearing herself apart for being so stupid. Why, why, why had she been so stupid? Why had she let herself lead Ernie on like that?

'Ernie, please listen to me,' she said. 'I was wrong to do that. I was wrong to let you think that – whatever you thought I meant. You've got to understand something,' she continued, not realising that as she spoke her voice was raised again. 'You talk about what the war's done to people. Well, you're right. It *has* cut them up. But in my case, it's also taught me a lesson. It's taught me to grow up. If I looked at you in the way you say, then I was being dishonest. The person who did that to you, Ernie, doesn't exist any more. Please understand that, Ernie. Please try to forgive me.'

Once again, she tried to move away. But this time, Ernie dug his fingers into her arm, and held it in a steel-like grip.

'Just who d'yer fink you are anyway?' he growled, reverting to the type of mood Sunday was more accustomed to. 'Miss High-and-Bleedin'-Mighty, Miss Cut-Above-Everybody-Else-in-the-'Ole-Wide-World! Not good enuff fer the likes of you – is that it?'

'No, Ernie!' protested Sunday, trying to pull away. 'That's not what I'm saying . . . !'

'Lemme tell yer somefin', Miss Sunday bloody Collins. I got me pride – see! I got the right ter be loved just the same as anyone else. Now yer may not fink yer love me, but I know different. I need yer, Sun,' he said, pulling her close and exchanging a pulverising contact with her eyes. 'An' *you* need *me*.' He released his grip on her and stood back. 'Don't ever ferget that, Sun. 'Cos wherever yer are, I'll find yer. Whatever yer do, I'll be there.' He made a move to go, but suddenly stopped and turned back briefly to look at her. 'Yer shouldn't muck around with people's feelin's, Sun. It's dangerous.'

Sunday watched him stride off down the street. However, he had only gone a few yards when he stopped again and turned. 'Oh, an' by the way – Merry Chris'mas!'

With his hands in his trousers pockets, Ernie Mancroft hurried off, and within a few moments he had disappeared out of sight, turning off down Hornsey Road.

Sunday watched Ernie go. This time, she wasn't angry, just sad. But most of all – she felt guilty.

By the time Sunday had reached the Salvation Army Hall, the Christmas morning service had already begun. So she found a seat at the back of the Hall and tried to make herself as inconspicuous as she possibly could.

The Hall itself was beautifully decorated, with lovely coloured paintings of the Nativity done by children from the Sunday school, and home-made paper chains draped across the stage and all around the walls. As ever, the huge Christmas tree was most impressive, and was lit by the same lights that had been used since Sunday was a little girl. Soon after she entered, everyone stood up to sing a Christmas carol, but as she couldn't hear the words, she had no idea which carol it was. But she soon found the order of service sheet, and it took her very little time to feel the mood and tempo of 'Hark the Herald Angels Sing'. It was an odd experience for her, for practically every Christmas morning of her young life she had come to this Hall and joined in the hearty festive singing with all her Salvation Army aunts and uncles. Now, like so many other things, she could only hear the music and words of the carols in her own memories.

On stage, the band was clearly at full throttle, and it was easy for Sunday to pick out her mum, whose cheeks were puffed out at the mouthpiece of her euphonium. Sunday always got a lot of fun out of watching Captain Drew conducting the band as though it was some vast symphony orchestra, and now that she was unable to hear anything, it had given her a greater awareness of certain things that she had taken for granted all her life. The energy that the singing had radiated throughout the Hall was somehow a potent force, a force of inspiration. Salvationists loved music, they loved to sing and play their instruments, and most of all they rejoiced in sharing it with each other. Sunday's own mum had been a perfect example of what true dedication was all about. Madge had devoted years of her spare time in the service of poor people, of people who had lost their way in life and had nowhere to go, and the only reward she had ever received for her unselfish contribution had been to bring up Sunday as her own daughter. As she stood there, watching all those Christmas worshippers sway to and fro to the carol music, Sunday thought about her mum. In fact, she thought about her now more than ever before.

When the carol came to an end and everyone sat down, Sunday was able to catch a fleeting glimpse from behind of a white-haired man who was seated just a couple of rows in front of her. It was her mum's 'gentleman friend', Mr Billings. And a couple of rows in front of him was Jack Popwell from 'the Buildings'. Seeing so many familiar faces all around her gave her a feeling that she was spending Christmas with a far bigger family than she had ever been used to. In some ways, it helped to erase some of the guilt she felt about the turbulent meeting she'd just had with Ernie Mancroft. Colonel Faraday then stood up to give the Christmas Day address. As he was so far away and she was unable to read his lips, Sunday couldn't understand what he was saying. So it gave her a chance to come together with her own thoughts. Seated next to her were an elderly couple who absolutely fascinated Sunday because they were holding hands all the way through the service. But then, she thought, why shouldn't elderly people hold hands if they want to? Surely there should be no age limit between two people who love each other?

For the next few minutes, the Hall remained quite motionless, listening in rapt attention to the homespun message from the portly, ruddy-faced Salvation Army Colonel. Most years, this was always the part of the service when Sunday spent much of the time scanning the Hall for something – *anything* – that would take her mind off all the boring words that always seemed to be bouncing off the high ceiling. But not today. Today was quite different. At this precise moment, Sunday seemed to be assessing her own life, and what the future would hold for her once this seemingly endless war was behind her. She closed her eyes. The first and only image she saw – was Gary. He was sitting opposite her at that table in the Sergeants' Mess, his short, wavy blond hair catching the glow from an electric light bulb dangling from the ceiling above them. And she could see that smile – that devastating, mischievous smile, caressing and comforting her, and bringing a warm flush to her pallid cheeks. '*I want to tell you something, Sunday.*' Gary's words suddenly entered her head, and whirled around in a soft but distant echo. '*I've known girls in my time. But none of them has been like you.*' Sunday, her eyes closed tightly, leaned forward in her chair, head bowed low. In her mind, she was reading those lips, watching those hands make words that she wanted desperately to understand. '*. . . I'm warning you, next Christmas – you're mine.*' Gary's words were haunting her. She tried so hard to imagine what his voice would have sounded like. Would his accent have been soft and gentle, or clear and sharp? If only she could have heard it with her own ears, just once. If only. It was also hard to believe that Gary was not right there beside her now, willing her to stop feeling sorry for herself and urging her to get on with her life. But it was even harder for her to believe that she would never see that face again, nor read the lips and hands that would remain a burning image within her for the rest of her life. As she sat there, hunched up in her seat, she felt her stomach start to shake. Everything inside her was telling her to cry, to release all the frustration and sense of loss that she was unable to cope with. But the tears just wouldn't come. Like all the emotions she had been born with, tears were elusive. '*Oh, by the way. I almost forgot.*' Once again, Gary's voice soared through her troubled brain. '*Since I won't be seeing you again before Christmas, this is for you.*'

The moment she heard those words, Sunday's hand dug deep into the pocket of her duffle coat. Slowly, she brought out the small packet that Gary had given her and asked her not to open until Christmas morning.

Opening her eyes, she looked down at the present, and after holding it tightly in her hand for a moment, opened it. Inside she found a jewellery box containing a gold locket surrounded by mother-of-pearl and set on a fine gold chain. In the centre of the locket was a tiny snapshot photograph of Gary in cap and uniform. He was smiling. It was a typical mischievous Gary smile.

Sunday placed the small locket in her palm, and after studying it closely for a moment, she closed her hand tightly around it.

At long last the tears came. And it helped.

# Chapter 15

So far, it had been a lousy Christmas for Doll Mooney. For a start, the week before she had trudged the streets of Holloway to find a turkey, but because there weren't many of them around this year, she had to make do with a chicken that looked as though it had died of old age. Then on Christmas Eve, the kids had kept her awake half the night waiting for Father Christmas to come down the blocked-up chimney with their presents. And if that wasn't bad enough, just as she was getting to sleep, her husband Joe, who had come home blind-drunk from the Nag's Head, tried to have sex with her. Already two months gone with her fifth, she soon put a stop to that! Luckily, however, Joe always managed to sober up fairly quickly after a night out, and at the crack of dawn Doll was relieved when he went off to an early-morning Mass at the Roman Catholic Church in Upper Holloway. Anyway, once the old-age pensioner bird had been devoured by an army of hungry mouths, Joe was off again. Doll knew where he was going, but pretended she didn't. So once he'd gone, she sent the kids off to play with their pathetic wartime toys in their own bedroom, got rid of her own mum and dad for an afternoon nap in her and Joe's bedroom, and then settled down herself to a cup of tea and a piece of Woolworth's Christmas cake with Sunday, who had just popped in for a quick visit.

''E's got this woman up at Stepney,' Doll gabbled, as she smoked a Gold Flake fag, sipped some tea, and ate a piece of fruit cake all at the same time. 'Conductress on the buses, can you believe! I mean, yer'd fink 'e could do better than that. Someone wiv more class at least!' She roared with laughter at her own joke, then flicked her fag ash into her saucer which was balanced precariously on the arm of the sofa where she was sprawled out.

Sunday was amazed how calmly Doll had reacted to Joe's unfaithfulness. 'When did you find out about all this, Doll?' she asked.

'Oh, right back last summer I knew 'e was 'avin' a bit on the side.

In fact, 'e's always 'avin' a bit on the side – lots er bits. That's the trouble wiv Joe – sex-mad!'

'But don't you mind?'

'Wot's the point?' Doll replied, unwittingly dropping a few currants on the floor as she munched her piece of cake. 'Joe's always 'ad an eye fer a bit of crumpet – even when I first met 'im. Men are like that. Always got an itch in their trousers.'

Sunday found it a bit difficult to follow Doll, because as she spoke she had a habit of turning away. 'But if he's unfaithful,' she asked, 'why don't you just kick him out?'

'Don't be silly, Sun,' Doll spluttered, her mouth full of cake. 'Why would I do that when I love 'im?'

Sunday was bewildered. Most people in 'the Buildings' had always known what an odd couple the Mooneys were, but how could Doll humiliate herself by holding on to this man?

'I look at it this way,' Doll continued, putting her feet down on the floor and sitting up straight on the sofa. 'Joe's been a good farver to 'is kids, never lets 'em want – nor me neiver, come ter that. But if yer try ter tie 'im down, yer've lost 'im. An' the trouble is, I don't want ter lose 'im.'

As Sunday watched Doll pulling on her fag and again flicking the ash into her saucer, it suddenly occurred to her what an attractive woman Doll must have been in her younger days. But after four kids and another one on the way, she had let herself go, for these days she hardly even bothered to put a comb through her straight shoulder-length brown hair; her whole appearance suggested neglect and a lack of interest in how she looked.

'But surely you can't keep going on having kids, knowing Joe's out with other women all the time?' asked Sunday.

'Oh, don't you worry, Sun,' replied Doll instantly. 'This is the last – make no bones about that! I told 'im last night, from now on 'e's got ter tie a bleedin' knot in it!'

They both laughed, but as they did so, there was the sound of a rumpus coming from the kids' bedroom.

Doll leapt up from the sofa, rushed across to the bedroom door, and called, 'You lot wake up yer nan and grandad, and I'll separate all of yer from yer bleedin' breff!'

Although Sunday couldn't read exactly what Doll was saying, she had a pretty good idea, and it made her laugh.

'I'll tell yer somefin', Sun,' Doll said when she returned. 'This war does funny fings ter people. I mean, a few munffs ago we fawt it was all over. An' then these bleedin' planes wiv their arses on fire come along. Then the rockets. An' suddenly, we're all back ter square one. I tell yer, I've not seen people so fed up – not since the Blitz.' She sat down on the sofa again, and curled her legs up beneath her. 'Yer know, it's not bin easy fer my Joe.'

Sunday put down her cup and saucer on a small table beside the armchair she was sitting in. 'What d'you mean?'

'Bein' Irish an' all that. Sometimes 'e feels like a square peg in a round 'ole. 'Specially durin' wartime. If 'e 'adn't bin a Caffolic, I fink 'e'd 'ave gone off 'is chump. Some people in the Buildin's don't go a bunch on the Paddys. They reckon they should've bin interned for the duration of the war, like the Jerrys and the Dagos.'

Sunday knew exactly what Doll meant. When the war broke out, it was common knowledge in 'the Buildings' that certain residents resented the presence of some Irish people who lived in the district, suspecting them of having sympathy with the Nazis. It was because of this prejudice that the likes of Joe were often treated with suspicion, and never allowed to work near 'sensitive' wartime establishments.

'Anyway, Joe knows I'll never desert 'im,' Doll continued, lighting up another fag. 'As long as he goes on lovin' me, 'e can 'ave as many flings wiv 'is women as 'e wants.' She pulled deeply on her fag, held the smoke briefly in her lungs, then exhaled very, very slowly.

'But if the time comes when *I* stop lovin' *'im*,' said Doll, 'it'll be a very different matter.'

On Boxing Day there was a brief fall of sleet. It didn't last long, and the moment the sun popped out from behind grey clouds, there was a quick thaw, and the roads and pavements glistened with a slippery, wet surface.

After a midday meal, Aunt Louie went off to play cards at a Ladies' Bridge afternoon at a house up in Liverpool Road. So Sunday agreed to go with her mum to Archway Central Hall, where the Salvation Army were giving a tea party for people who had been bombed out of their homes, and also for the usual sad crowd of down-and-outs. Madge and Sunday were collected by Mr Billings, who took them in his old Morris Minor car, but it was a tight squeeze in the back seat because Sunday had to share it with one of her Salvation Army 'aunties', who had to bring along two aluminium teapots and a bucket full of party balloons, paper hats, and song-sheets. On the way up Holloway Road, Sunday took a wistful look out at the poor old Gaumont Cinema, once the pride and joy of the entire neighbourhood, but now reduced to an empty shell thanks to the 'doodlebug' which had landed on its roof during the previous August.

The party itself turned out to be far less solemn than Sunday had expected, for most of the people there were determined to have a good time. She even joined in the knees-up with a group of elderly people who had been bombed out of their homes by a V-2 rocket which had fallen on nearby Grovedale Road. The fact that she couldn't hear the piano playing made very little difference, for all she had to do was copy what everyone else was doing. But, as much as she entered into the spirit of things, it was no patch on the good time she'd had on Boxing Day afternoon the previous year, when she and Pearl had paid ninepence each up in the 'gods' at the Finsbury Park Empire, where, alongside a theatre full of kids and their families, they hissed the villains and cheered the heroes in the annual Christmas panto, *Babes in the Wood.*

To Sunday's surprise, one of the elderly guests at the party turned out to be Pearl's grandmother. The old lady was a real character, a widow for over twenty years who had lived for the best part of her married life in a terraced house in Grovedale Road.

'Pearl thought the world of you,' said the old lady, who soon discovered the secret of speaking close and directly at Sunday, whilst clinging on to the girl's arm. 'She told me so just a couple er nights before she got killed down the Bagwash.'

'I thought the world of her too,' replied Sunday. 'I miss her so much.'

The old lady smiled at her. Despite her age, she had young eyes, and in many ways they reminded Sunday of Pearl herself. 'I want ter tell yer somefin', dear,' she said. 'Can yer keep a little secret?'

Sunday nodded and allowed the old lady to pull her closer so that she could smell the pickled onion she had just been eating with her cheese sandwich.

'The night she come ter see me, she told me she was gettin' engaged. Not official like, she was too young fer that. But she said she was in love wiv this boy, and that 'e'd asked 'er ter marry 'im. D'yer know the boy I mean? 'Is name was Lennie Jackson.'

Sunday felt her stomach turn over. Of course she knew Lennie Jackson, and she suddenly felt consumed with guilt that she had ever wanted Lennie for herself.

'Yes,' she said, smiling weakly. 'I used to know him.'

'She never told her mum, yer see,' said the old lady, trying to straighten her party hat which was already torn halfway through. 'That's the trouble wiv that daughter of mine. Too busy finkin' of 'er own problems ter worry about 'er own kiff and kin. My dear lil' Pearl.' The old lady's eyes were misting up, and she had to dab them with her handkerchief. 'I was the only one she could talk to, the only one she could confide in.' She looked straight at Sunday again. ''Cept you, of course, Sunday. In 'er eyes, you was always special. Like 'er own sister.'

The old lady took hold of Sunday's hands, and squeezed them in a firm grip. Then Sunday threw her arms around her, and they hugged each other.

Behind them, Madge and her Salvation Army friends were leading the party-goers in a spirited rendering of 'Nearer My God To Thee!'

But as for Sunday, still hugging the old lady, she felt closer to Pearl than she had done since they had last met.

Soon after Sunday had returned home to the flat, her mum and Aunt Louie had a blazing row. This was a new experience for Sunday, for she could never remember a time when her mum had even dared to answer her domineering elder sister back. The trouble started when Madge decided to bring Mr Billings back for a cup of tea and a Spam and pickle sandwich. Louie, in a sour mood after losing two shillings and threepence at her ladies' card-playing afternoon, bitterly resented what she saw as an intrusion into the family's privacy on a Boxing Day evening. However, Madge was having none of it, and temporarily putting to one side her Salvationist ideals about love and compassion, told Louie that if she, Madge, wanted to have a visitor in her own home, she certainly wouldn't ask her sister first. Poor Mr Billings was most embarrassed by the whole incident, and offered to leave, but Madge practically ordered him to take no notice of 'the slight misunderstanding' between herself and her sister, and to stay right where he was. Although Sunday couldn't take in everything that was going on, she thoroughly enjoyed the tough battle of wills between the two women. In fact, it cheered up her Boxing Day no end!

Early that evening, Sunday was able to slip away from home so that she could call on her old friend, Bess Butler. But when she eventually arrived at the corner flat on the third floor of 'the Buildings', it was Bess's husband, Alf, who peered around the front door.

'Come in!' Alf said, his face brightening up the moment he recognised Sunday on the doorstep.

As soon as she entered the flat, Sunday smelt greens boiling in the kitchen. It was a pungent smell, sour and overpowering.

'My Bessie got me a nice pig's trotter up the Cally Market on Christmas Eve. Got a lot er meat on it. Not bad for a tanner, eh? I'm goin' ter 'ave it wiv boiled potatoes an' some nice spring greens.'

Sunday always found Alf such an affable old boy. In all the years she had known him, she had never heard him complain or criticise anyone. The only problem was, he had not really mastered the way of talking directly at her, and spent a lot of the time correcting himself with, 'Oh, sorry, Sun. What I was sayin' was . . .' and then having to repeat everything he said.

''Fraid she's gone off ter work,' he said, disappointed that Sunday didn't have the time to share the pig's trotter with him. 'Dunno wot I'd do wivout that gel,' he added, adjusting the jet-black toupee that had never really fitted him. 'Werks every night of the week, summer an' winter, never any time off ter relax.' For a moment he looked downcast, and shaking his head, said, 'She shouldn't 'ave ter do it, yer know. She shouldn't 'ave ter spend 'er life supportin' a useless old fart like me.'

Sunday felt deeply for him. She knew only too well how inferior Alf had always felt because he was so much older than Bess. 'You mustn't talk like that, Alf,' she said, trying to reassure him. 'Bess wouldn't do it if she didn't love you.'

Alf, trying not to be upset, took a deep breath. 'Trouble is, my Bessie's got an 'eart of gold. Night work at an 'otel ain't easy werk, y'know – oh no. But she don't care 'ow 'ard it is, as long as the money keeps comin' in.'

Sunday lowered her eyes. She prayed Alf Butler would never know the truth about where that money really came from.

There was something unreal about Piccadilly Circus on Boxing Day evening. It was like a Jack-in-the-box that was straining to be let loose before its time. Lying at the heart of London's West End, 'the Dilly' was clearly impatient to have its highly dazzling neon lights restored after such a long blackout, and although there had recently been some easing of restrictions, until there was no longer any danger of further enemy air-raids, a return to its full glory had to be delayed.

Sunday hadn't been 'up West' for over a year, when she and Pearl had queued for nearly an hour outside the tiny Ritz Cinema in

Leicester Square to see *Gone with the Wind*, which seemed to have been running at the same place all through the war. As she made her way up the steps from Piccadilly Circus Tube Station, there were hordes of people around, either queuing up for the evening film performance in front of the exotic façade of the London Pavilion, or just strolling along Coventry Street heading off in the direction of Lyons Corner House and all the cinemas in Leicester Square, and the posh West End theatres in and around Charing Cross Road. Winding her way in and out of the crowds, Sunday was practically engulfed by men in uniforms from Allied and Commonwealth countries, and as she brushed shoulder to shoulder with GIs who were kitted out in their superior-styled khaki uniforms and peaked caps, she thought of Gary, and the sinking feeling inside her stomach reminded her that she would never see him again.

By the time she reached the corner of Shaftesbury Avenue and Piccadilly Circus, Sunday was already keeping her eyes open for Bess Butler, for this was Rainbow Corner, the club for American servicemen, once the site of one of London's most famous restaurants, Del Monico's. As she expected, there were young girls and women of all ages hanging around the place, most of them on the make for a good dinner and a one-night stand. Earlier in the day, when she had made up her mind that the one person she was desperate to see was Bess, it depressed her to think of what she might find. She also knew that she was taking a chance by calling on Bess at such a time, for although Bess had often confided in Sunday about how she was earning her money, it was quite a different thing for her to make an appearance during her older friend's 'work hours'.

It was nearly nine o'clock when she passed the Rialto Cinema and the bombed-out entrance of what was once the fashionable Café de Paris. The winter cold was biting deep again, so she pulled the hood of her duffle coat over her head and pushed her hands deep into her pockets. In her search for Bess, she peered into every shop doorway, every back alley, and at the face of every woman who passed by. Realising that she herself was being paced by two servicemen from New Zealand, she took a sharp turn into Windmill Street, and after crossing over Shaftesbury Avenue, found herself in the seediest part of Soho.

Outside the Windmill Theatre, a long queue of servicemen had formed on the pavement, waiting to see the latest girlie revue. Sunday hurried past as quickly as possible. Not far away she approached a pub, which was jammed to suffocation, with a crowd of GIs overflowing on to the pavement outside. Watching them from a vantage position on the opposite side of the road were two white-helmeted US military policemen, so although Sunday couldn't hear what the men outside the pub were saying, she was grateful that they were somewhat subdued. At that moment, she caught her first glimpse of Bess, who was with two or three other women, laughing and drinking with the GIs in the middle of the crowd. For several minutes, Sunday tried to catch Bess's eye, but every time she did so, some of the GIs did their best to get her to join them.

'Sunday!'

Bess finally noticed her, left the crowd, and hugged her.

'Oh God, Sun!' she said with incredulity. 'I can't believe it! I just can't believe it! What yer doin' 'ere, mate?'

When Sunday looked at her old friend, she was shocked to see how gaunt she had become. And despite the bitterly cold breeze, Bess was wearing only a flimsy above-the-knee party dress, with her hair piled on top of her head, and thick sticky make-up plastered all over her face.

'I'm sorry, Bess,' Sunday said. 'I'm going back to the country the day after tomorrow. I just had to see you.'

Bess hugged her again. 'I'll just get my coat,' she said, not forgetting to speak directly at Sunday. 'Let's get away from this lot.'

It was fairly deserted along the Victoria Embankment down by the River Thames. The only people around were the 'regulars', the tramps who slept out rough in all weathers. Although it wasn't even ten o'clock, most of them had already taken up residence on any spare bench that was still unoccupied, and the rest of them stretched out either on the open pavement, or beneath the railway bridge at Charing Cross. Sometimes there was a fight amongst them, usually when a kind passer-by had offered one of them a penny for a cup of tea or the remains of a half-eaten sandwich. Others, who occasionally roamed the streets at night, had often been victims of the air-raids, dying on the pavement where they lay, buried beneath the debris of a bombed building.

'I love walkin' down 'ere,' said Bess, 'especially at night. It's always so – cut off from everythin'. No hassle, no bobbies ter move yer on. I love the peace.' She turned to Sunday, who was warming her hands on the mug of tea Bess had just bought her at the all-night refreshment stall. 'Actually, I've scored down 'ere a coupla times. I even 'ad this official. Come from the LCC over there at County 'All. Randy old sod 'e was. Still, 'e paid well.'

Sunday was just able to make out what Bess was saying, for they were standing directly beneath a rather dim lamplight on an open parapet overlooking the river. Just being in Bess's company again cheered Sunday up no end, for she was the one person to whom she could pour her heart out. And that is exactly what she did, recounting everything that had happened to her since she arrived out at Ridgewell, and how wonderful it was that, after meeting Gary, her life had taken on such a new meaning, only for her to be devastated again by his being lost in action.

'Yer know somefin', Sun,' Bess said, after peering down into the fast-flowing river beneath them. 'All me life I've tried ter keep on the move – just like that river down there. Stand still an' I'm finished.'

A small group of customers were now crowded around the refreshment stall behind them, including two Black GIs.

'It 'as ter be the same wiv you, Sun,' Bess continued, balancing her mug on the parapet wall whilst she searched around in her coat pocket for her fags. 'Yer can't keep still, mate. Yer can't just go under 'cos somefin's changed. 'Specially someone your age.' She took out her fags and offered one to Sunday.

Sunday shook her head and sipped her tea.

Bess lit a fag, then retrieved her mug of tea, the rim of which was heavily smeared with lipstick. 'I look at it this way. We all 'ave ter make somefin' of ourselves even if fings don't go the way we want 'em to. Take me fer instance. When Alf 'ad ter give up 'is job 'cos of 'is stroke, I couldn't just sit down an' say, "Ooh, 'ow terrible. That means we're goin' ter starve."' She shook her head, pulled deeply on her fag, and released a funnel of smoke which curled up into the dark night sky. 'Fact is, Sun, I just 'ad ter get up an' do somefin', din't I? That's 'ow I got on the game.'

'But surely you could have done something else?' asked Sunday. 'Isn't it too big a price to pay – what you're doing?'

'I needed money, Sun – lots of it. When the 'ospital told me Alf 'ad only got a year ter live, I decided there an' then that 'e'd 'ave the best bloody year of 'is life.'

Sunday lowered her mug. She was stunned. 'Alf? Going to die?'

'It's over a year since they told me. 'E's already livin' on borrowed time.'

Bess was aware that one of the two Black GIs was eyeing her

over the sausage roll he was eating. Without making it too obvious, she responded with a grin.

'I know yer may fink I'm bonkers doin' all this for an old geezer nearly twenty years older than me. But the fact is, Alf loves me. An' I love 'im. When 'e took me on all those years ago, I was nuffin' – absolutely nuffin'.' Before she continued, Bess lowered her eyes and stared aimlessly into her mug. 'Yer see, I've made a lot er mistakes in my life, Sun, stupid mistakes.' Then her eyes flicked up pointedly to look directly into Sunday's eyes. 'I couldn't've got through it all wivout Alf – oh no. That stupid old sod! 'E give me everythin'.'

Although Sunday was not quite sure what Bess was trying to say to her, she felt a strange closeness to this warm-hearted woman.

'I suppose wot I'm tryin' ter tell yer, Sun, is that when somebody yer love ain't around no more, it don't mean yer 'ave ter stop lovin' 'em.' She took one last pull on her fag, then flicked it into the river. Then she put her mug down on the parapet wall, and turned back to Sunday again. 'You're 'avin' a rough time, mate, don't fink I don't know it.' Her eyes were glistening in the cold. 'But yer've got a good 'ead on yer body. Just always remember that yer 'ave ter do wot yer 'eart tells yer ter do. An' never ever look back over yer shoulder.'

Sunday and her old friend turned to look down into the river. With elbows leaning on the parapet wall, they could just pick out the strange patterns the lamplight was creating on the fast-flowing tidal water beneath them. On the south bank side, a coal barge was chugging its way upriver, and just before it reached Westminster Bridge, it sounded its warning horn.

A few minutes later, Bess bundled Sunday off into a taxi, and paid the driver three shillings to take her back to 'the Buildings'. Once the taxi had disappeared off in the direction of Blackfriars Bridge and Ludgate Circus, Bess returned to the refreshment stall to share a fag with the two Black GIs.

It was the start of yet another hard night's work.

# Chapter 16

When Sunday got back to Cloy's Farm, one of the first things she did was to register for speech and sign language therapy at the Colchester General Hospital. This involved attending evening sessions twice a week at a clinic in Halstead, and together with other patients, she started to build on what she had already been taught by Gary. It was a slow, laborious task, for the therapist in charge of the sessions did not have the real flair needed to bring the complications of two-handed sign language to life.

Meanwhile, during the Christmas holidays, Jinx and Erin had managed to take a belated weekend honeymoon to Clacton-on-Sea, and, with the exception of Sheil, the other girls had spent the time at home with their respective families. When everyone got back to the barn they had quite a shock, for Sheil had decorated the place with all the sketches and coloured drawings she had been working on. The sketches were absolutely beautiful, and ranged from portraits of the girls themselves to winter landscapes and cows grazing in the meadow. It had taken Sunday a long time to forgive Sheil's behaviour on the evening when Ruthie had suffered an epileptic fit. At the time, she had no idea that Sheil had been undergoing psychiatric treatment for the trauma she had gone through during the London Blitz, and that on three separate occasions she had tried to kill herself. Since then, Sunday had felt tremendous sympathy and compassion for Sheil, and recognised that she was using her sketches and drawings to release all the complicated tensions that were pent up inside her. In fact, Sunday was fighting the same kind of battles within herself, for it had now emerged that Gary's B17 had been shot down, with little chance that any of the crew had survived.

The first few days of the New Year soon turned into a nightmare. During the Christmas period there had been little or no activity from V-1s or V-2s, but quite suddenly all that changed, and the skies above East Anglia were again streaked with the trailing flames of these final attempts by the *Luftwaffe* to turn the tide of the war.

And as if that were not bad enough, it started to snow again, and within just a few hours, drifts had reached almost a foot deep, cutting off roads and villages within a wide radius, and causing extensive power cuts throughout the region. Ridgewell Airbase was one of the first casualties, with all planes grounded and a lengthy cessation of combat raids on enemy-occupied territory.

Heavy manual help was now desperately required to clear the deep snowdrifts from the roads leading to and from the airbase. And at Cloy's Farm, the girls had a real struggle to retrieve cows and sheep that were stranded in the fields. This problem was eventually solved when a group of Italian prisoners of war were sent over from the Golden Meadow Camp in Halstead. Although some of them were resistant to helping out in any way, most of the men, aware that their country was now being occupied by the Allies, were only too willing to do what they could.

Sunday got her first glimpse of the POWs in their distinctive green battledress uniforms and topcoats when she and Jinx were desperately trying to shovel a path through the snow to rescue a small flock of sheep who had taken refuge in the woods beyond Cloy's now bare sugar beet field. In the far distance, the POWs looked like a pack of green insects cutting their way in a single line across the densely covered meadow, where a herd of cows were huddled together in a panic trying to keep warm. Behind them followed a snowplough from the aerodrome, operated by a couple of GI maintenance men who had been loaned by their commanding officer to help out in the emergency.

'Bloody lazy lot, those dagos!' gasped Jinx, as she struggled to free one of the sheep, and herd it and the rest of the flock back towards the farm. 'That's why they've lost the war. Too much like hard work for them, fightin' our boys!'

Sunday didn't really catch what Jinx was saying, but she guessed that, as usual, she was complaining about something.

Nearby, the cows who had just been rescued from oblivion were making a hell of a row, protesting strongly at the Italian POWs who had finally succeeded in herding them along the path they had cleared for them. But once the poor, terrified creatures were safely back in the farmyard area again, one of the Italians returned to help Sunday and Jinx with the sheep.

'You leave to me, lady,' said the young POW, whose sharp Latin features were only just visible behind a green woollen balaclava.

As Sunday was busy struggling to contain a terrified sheep, she hadn't seen what the man was saying to her.

The POW looked puzzled, and tried again. 'Lady?' he asked. 'You need help?'

'She can't 'ear yer!' snapped Jinx tartly, at the same time pointing to her own ears.

The young Italian still looked puzzled.

'She can't 'ear yer!' she yelled. 'Can't yer understand, boyo? My friend is deaf!'

The POW finally understood, but looked shocked. 'Oh,' he said dolefully, as Sunday looked over her shoulder at him. 'I sorry.'

Now it was Sunday's turn to look puzzled.

Without saying anything more, the young Italian grabbed hold of the sheep that was bucking up and down in Sunday's arms, and pushed it off with his foot towards the path that the plough had now forged in the snow. Once the panicking creature had escaped, the rest of the small flock followed.

'Thanks,' Sunday said to the Italian.

'Lady.'

The young Italian half bowed to her. He wanted to stay and speak with her, but one look from Jinx persuaded him otherwise. So he turned, and walked back towards his comrades, who were now rejoining their British Army supervisor.

Sunday watched him go. There was something about him that fascinated her.

Jinx thought otherwise. 'Bloody dago!' she sneered. 'That's wot 'appens when you eat too much spaghetti!'

It was almost a week before Ridgewell Airbase became operational again. Once the runways were cleared of snow for take-off, it was only a matter of waiting for the freezing fog to disperse before orders were received to recommence bombing raids over Germany. And when that order finally came, the heavy winter skies were immediately jammed with wave after wave of B17 Flying Fortresses from the 381st Bomb Group. As Sunday watched the great silver birds heading off towards the East Anglian coastline, she thought of Gary, and of all those air-crews who risked their lives day after day, night after night, many of whom would never return.

Despite the constant Allied onslaught by land, sea, and air, North Essex still faced danger from enemy attacks by V-1 and V-2 rockets. This meant that everyone in the region, including the people of Ridgewell, had to remain on a full state of alert, and after the lull in enemy aerial attacks over the Christmas and New Year period, the reality that the war was not yet over was brought home only too well. It happened early one morning, when Sunday was alone in the chicken huts, cleaning out the runs after the annual slaughter of birds for the Christmas ovens. Unbeknown to her, a sudden barrage of anti-aircraft guns from the aerodrome was blasting the sky with shells and tracer bullets, attempting to bring down a stream of V-1 'doodlebugs' that had infiltrated the coastal defences, and were now making their way through to the London area.

'Sunday!'

Sunday only turned to see that it was young Ronnie Cloy who had entered the hut, because there was a sudden rush of cold air coming through the door behind her.

'You've got to take cover, Sunday!' he spluttered urgently. 'They're shootin' down "doodlebugs" – a whole lot of them!' His hands and arms were waving about wildly. 'We've got to get down the shelter!'

Sunday was flummoxed. The last person she expected to see at this hour was Ronnie, for it was the first time he had spoken to her since his jealous outburst on Christmas Eve. Panicking, she quickly followed him out of the hut.

Outside, it was still dark, but as clear as a bell. Up above, the sky was streaked with vapour trails and puffs of small artificial clouds from ack-ack fire, and jagged pieces of shrapnel were plopping down into the snow all around the farmyard.

Ronnie had grabbed hold of Sunday's hand, and was dragging her as fast as he could towards the air-raid shelter beneath ground at the rear of the girls' billet. 'Quick as you can!' he yelled, trying to make sure that Sunday could read what he was saying. 'This stuff's white-hot . . . !'

He had hardly spoken when he and Sunday were virtually blown off their feet by a massive explosion in the nearby potato field. In the towering wall of snow that cascaded across the farmland towards them, windows all around the farm were shattered, tiles and thatch ripped off the roofs, and farmyard machinery toppled over like pieces of cardboard.

When the cascade of snow had finally settled, Sunday and Ronnie found themselves sprawled out face down on the ground, covered by an inch or so of snow and ice.

Ronnie was the first to recover. 'Sunday!' he yelled, pulling her up from the snow. 'Sunday, are you all right?'

Sunday was shaking from both the sheer terror of the incident and also the severe cold. 'W–what happened?' she asked, clearing the snow from her face and hands.

'I think they shot it down,' replied Ronnie, helping Sunday to her feet. 'In Father's potato field at the back.'

Almost as he spoke, there was the sound of people shouting from the air-raid shelter, and from the farmhouse. And at the same time, fire engine bells were clanging excitedly as they came racing out from the aerodrome making straight towards the farm.

'Sunday!'

Jinx was yelling out at the top of her voice. Behind her came the other girls, who were all emerging in a panic from the air-raid shelter.

'Sunday! Are you all right? Are you hurt, girl? Are you?'

Sunday, still trying to recover from her ordeal, nodded her head. 'I'm all right,' she said, trying to allay everyone's fears.

Behind them, there was pandemonium in the stables, the sheep- and cowsheds, and amongst the few remaining pigs and geese who had survived the Christmas slaughter.

Meanwhile, Maureen was doing her best to draw everyone's attention to the front of the farmhouse, where a fire had broken out on the roof.

'Fire!' yelled Ruthie, who was already rushing back to the barn to collect one of the stirrup pumps.

Within moments, the whole area was frantic with activity, as people rushed back and forth trying to work out what needed to be done. Although bewildered and disoriented, Sunday refused Jinx's offer to lead her back inside the barn. 'I'm all right,' she insisted, immediately looking around to see what she could do to help.

'Over here!'

Everyone turned their attention towards the rear door of the farmhouse, where Arnold Cloy's wife, Angela, had appeared and was shouting out almost hysterically.

'Help me!' she yelled again. 'Arnold's been hurt!'

Ronnie Cloy immediately sprinted off towards the house. Whilst he was doing so, two fire engines from the aerodrome came speeding down the main farmhouse approach, emergency lights flashing, warning bells buzzing.

Sunday had no idea what was going on when she saw everyone rushing towards the house. So she just stood where she was, clutching her ears with both hands and closing her eyes, and telling herself inside that it was happening all over again. She felt as though she was going out of her mind as she clenched her fists and shook them angrily up at the sky. 'When is it going to end!' Her strange new voice boomed out loud above the chaotic sounds all around her. 'For God's sake tell me – *when*!'

High above her, white vapour from a V-2 rocket streaked across the entire expanse of the gradually lightening sky.

The Parish Church of St Laurence in Ridgewell was so crowded that some people had to stand at the back. Every pew had been taken by local villagers and men and women of the United States 381st Bomb Group from Ridgewell Airbase, all of them there to pay tribute to civilians and air-crews who had given their lives in what had now become known as 'the endless war'. Sunday and her Land Girl friends were there too, sitting in a neat row halfway back just behind Farmer Cloy's wife, Angela, whose husband was recovering in hospital from injuries incurred during the 'doodlebug' explosion in the field at the back of the farmhouse. Young Ronnie Cloy was sitting alongside his mother, and Sunday was aware of how ill at ease they both were in each other's company, for at no time did they communicate or even exchange a glance.

Although Sunday couldn't hear anything of the service taking place, her eyes constantly scanned the grey stone walls of the old church, which set off so dramatically the sea of khaki uniforms and the two huge Union Jack and Stars and Stripes flags which were draped across each other above the altar. It was a poignant occasion, and Sunday's thoughts were miles away, drifting back to those few brief weeks of happiness she had spent with Gary. It was the same for Jinx, who was very emotional and tense, as she tried to picture in her mind where Erin might be at that very moment, bottled up inside his giant B17 aircraft on yet another hazardous daylight bombing raid over enemy territory. And Sunday even felt sympathy for Angela Cloy who had suffered such anguish in the aftermath of the 'doodlebug' explosion, which had caused considerable damage to the farmhouse roof.

When Sunday first read the order of service card, she knew only too well that, although she wouldn't be able to hear the service, the last part was going to be the most harrowing. This would involve a schoolgirl reading out the names of local villagers missing or killed in action, and a young GI doing the same for his own fellow air-crews from the base. When it came to the readings, some people wept unashamedly, including Jinx, who had to be comforted by Sunday.

When the service was over, the girls from the farm piled into the back of a US Army truck, which was giving them a lift. But Sunday told Jinx that she wanted a few moments to herself, and would walk back in her own time.

The church emptied very quickly, and soon there was a procession of jeeps and trucks heading back towards the aerodrome. For a short while after, a few villagers walked around the graves in the churchyard, stopping briefly to clear the snow from the headstones of their relatives, and spending a short time there in silent contemplation. Sunday waited for them all to go, but just when she thought that the place was deserted, young Ronnie Cloy appeared from inside the church porch.

'Hallo, Sunday,' he said awkwardly, his hands buried deep inside his raincoat pocket.

'Hallo, Ronnie,' she answered, aware that the boy looked uneasy. 'Where's your mum?'

'Gone home,' Ronnie replied. 'I told her I was going down to the pond.' He moved a few steps closer to her, so that she could read his lips. 'When it gets iced over, I make a hole – to let the fish breathe.'

Sunday didn't quite know what he meant, but she smiled and nodded as though she did.

'Did you like the service?' he asked.

Sunday lowered her eyes. 'It was very sad.'

'Too sad. People always cry when they're sad. I don't see the point.'

Sunday thought that was a curious thing for him to say. But then it occurred to her that she had rarely ever seen Ronnie himself cry.

For a moment, Ronnie stared at his feet. Then he looked up again. 'I'm sorry, Sunday,' he said, even more awkwardly, 'for the way I talked to you – on Christmas Eve. I didn't mean to, honest I didn't. It was just the way I was feeling that day.' He lowered his eyes guiltily. 'I shouldn't have talked to you like that.'

Whilst they were standing there, two robin redbreasts swooped in and out of the church porch just behind them, jostling each other for territory and ending up on the headstone of a neglected grave close by.

'Sometimes,' said Sunday, 'we all say things we don't mean. But by the time we say them, it's too late.'

'Is it *too* late, Sunday,' the boy said, a pained expression on his face. 'Does it mean we're not friends any more?'

Sunday smiled and held out her hand for him to shake.

Ronnie took hold of her hand and shook it vigorously.

Behind them, the two robins, with puffed-up bodies to keep out the cold, were preening themselves in competition on the ridge of snow along the top of the headstone. Sunday and Ronnie moved off together, and wandered slowly through the churchyard.

'How's your dad getting on?' Sunday asked. 'Is he still in pain?'

'He's all right,' replied the boy, casually. 'Mum said he'll be in hospital for at least three or four weeks.'

'Have you been to see him?'

Whilst they strolled, Ronnie turned to look at her. 'Why should I?' he asked.

Sunday was shocked. 'Ronnie! He's your dad.'

'I know he is,' replied the boy, digging his hands deeper into his raincoat pocket. 'But I still couldn't care less.'

Sunday came to a halt, and stared at the boy. 'You mustn't say things like that, Ronnie,' she said. 'Your dad was very nearly killed the other day.'

'I wouldn't've cared if he was.'

Ronnie's calm but piercing reply shook Sunday to the core. 'How can you say such a thing?' she asked.

'Look, Sunday. What's the use of lying? I've told you before, my dad doesn't care about me, and I don't care about him. In fact, I hate him. I hate everything about him. So why should I lie?'

Behind them, the vicar was just leaving the church, and when he caught sight of Sunday and Ronnie, he waved at them. Sunday and Ronnie waved back, and watched the black-and-white clerical robes he was wearing flutter off along the snow-cleared path towards his vicarage.

'Shall I tell you something, Sunday?' the boy said suddenly. 'One of these days, I'm going to get away from him, away from my father, away from home.'

'Don't be so daft, Ronnie,' said Sunday, firmly, but clearly anxious.

'It's true, I tell you. As soon as it gets warm again, I'm going to go to London. I won't have much money, so I'll probably have to hitch a ride somehow.'

As Sunday looked into the boy's soulful eyes, she felt deeply sad and sorry for him. Ronnie was such a strange, lonesome kind of boy. Never had she seen him knocking around with kids his own age, doing all the things that he should be doing, such as kicking a football around with his mates or something, just like she'd seen the boys do back home in 'the Buildings'.

'Will you help me, Sunday?'

Sunday flinched. 'What d'you mean?' she asked.

'Will you help me get away from the farm? Oh, I don't mean give me money, but – well, tell me how to do it, where to go, that sort of thing.'

Sunday began to feel panic. How *could* she help Ronnie to do such a thing? She wasn't old enough to advise, she wasn't grown-up enough herself to show this boy the way out of his own childhood. 'You can't do it, Ronnie,' she said, quite calmly. 'If you go to London, what will you do? Where will you go? Without money, or people to go to, you could end up sleeping out rough on the pavements or something.'

'I'd sooner do that than go on living under the same roof as my father. I'd sooner be dead than let him go on resenting me for the rest of my life.'

Reacting to the casual determination in the boy's face, Sunday felt quite numb. 'Your mum, Ronnie,' she asked softly. 'What about your mum? Can't you talk to her?'

Ronnie's lips curled up in a wry grin. 'She's not much better than him,' he said. 'You should hear them sometimes. At night I listen to them from upstairs in my room. Always drunk on black-market booze, always fighting like cat and dog. Then they talk about me. And they laugh. I hate it most when they laugh about me. They make me feel dirty. But I'm not. They're the ones who are dirty – not me.' He suddenly realised that he was upsetting Sunday, so his face quickly brightened up as he asked, 'Will you come and see the pheasants with me some time?'

Once again, Sunday was taken aback by Ronnie's ability to change the mood so quickly. 'Pheasants?' she asked. 'Where?'

'In the woods, on the other side of the 'drome. There are hundreds there. They hide from the farmers' guns. Mind you, they shot a lot of them just before Christmas, so there might not be so many now. But I like to see them. I like to let them know that not everyone wants to kill them. Will you come with me some time, Sunday? Will you?'

Sunday found herself nodding.

'Aw – thanks, Sunday! Thanks! Maybe next Saturday?' he asked eagerly. 'Is Saturday afternoon OK for you?'

Again Sunday nodded.

Before she could say another word, Ronnie was rushing off out of the churchyard. But he suddenly stopped, turned, then came back to her. 'By the way, Sunday,' he said, returning to a brief expression of guilt. 'I'm sorry about – about that bloke. You know, that friend of yours – the Yank? I didn't mean what I said about him – honest I didn't.'

With that, he was gone.

As Sunday stood for a moment, watching young Ronnie stride off through the churchyard, the first signs of a freezing fog began to drift across the village green on the other side of the road. It was an eerie feeling to be left alone in such a place, with an icy blanket gradually wrapping itself around the thatched roofs and smoking chimney pots. But at least Sunday could still make out the USAF jeeps and trucks parked outside the King's Head pub just down the road, which made her feel far less isolated knowing that her friends from the farm were having a lunchtime drink there.

The churchyard itself was now blending in with the stark grey fog, and the scattering of white headstones were protruding out of the ground like hands and arms reaching up for life. But the churchyard had its own special atmosphere to offer, and Sunday felt nothing but peace and confidence there. She started to move amongst the stones, but many of them were so old that the inscriptions were too difficult to read. It was now getting colder than ever, and she had to pull up the hood of her duffle coat to protect her ears from the frost.

Realising that the weather was now closing in on her, Sunday paused for only enough time to savour that special link which always exists between the living and the dead. Although she could hear no sound, in her mind she could hear all those voices that had always meant so much to her. And not only human voices, but cats and dogs and birds, and band music, and just about every sound of everyday life in her entire experience. Strangely enough, she felt no sadness, only joy. A smile even came to her face, and she found herself looking around as though all those voices from her past were lining up to encourage her. But then, something inside told her to stand still without moving.

The freezing fog was gradually engulfing the entire churchyard, and slight flurries of snow began to drift down on to the hood of Sunday's duffle coat.

At that precise moment, she felt the urge to turn around. Before her was now a blanket of sinister grey fog which threatened to swallow her up and cast her off into the wilderness. But then, she saw a figure emerging from the mist. At first it was nothing more than a distant shadow, closing in on her, as if in slow motion in a cinema picture. She became mesmerised by the image, all the time agonising whether she should back away and escape while she still had time. But as the figure drew closer, blood surged through her entire body, and she felt like shouting out as loud as she knew how. The figure was now no longer walking, but rushing straight at her. At that moment, Sunday realised that she knew that walk, she knew it better than any other in the whole wide world. Unaware of what she was doing, she found herself rushing forward, arms outstretched in greeting. A moment or so later she had been lifted off her feet, and was being whirled around in the miserably grey ice-cold fog. When her feet finally touched the ground again, two bodies were clasped against each other, and Sunday could feel the warmth of a man's lips pressed firmly against her own. She couldn't hear what was being said to her, and the visibility was too poor to enable her to read those lips. But she knew what was being said. Yes, in some extraordinary moment of intuition, she just knew.

'Oh God, Sunday! I'll never leave you again. Never!'

The arms, the lips, the voice, the warmth. They all belonged to Sergeant Gary Mitchell.

# *Chapter 17*

Sunday had always wanted to go to Thorpe Bay. She had no idea why the place appealed to her, except that she had once read about the beaches there in an old *Picture Post* magazine. It was an odd ambition, she knew that. After all, most girls of her age yearned to go either to the East-ender's favourite day-trip paradise at Southend, or to the swankier Essex resorts of Leigh or Westcliff-on-Sea. Perhaps it had something to do with the sound of the name – *Thorpe Bay*. It sounded so exotic, like Hawaii or Scarborough, although Sunday hadn't the faintest idea where either of those two resorts were. No, Thorpe Bay was at the top of her dream list, and it was ironic that it took a young American airman to make that dream come true.

In reality, exotic Thorpe Bay turned out to be quite ordinary – delightful and charming, but ordinary. Situated right on the tip of the Thames Estuary, it was flanked on one side by the hectic amusement arcades of Southend, and on the other side by Shoeburyness, which was mainly a restricted area as there was a top-secret army camp there. Since the beginning of the war, there hadn't really been many holiday visitors, and even though a lot of the barbed wire had now been removed from the beaches, a cold, frosty weekend along the seafront in the middle of January was not to everyone's taste.

'It's hard to believe there's a different country on the other side of that sea,' said Sunday, her face tinged with a bright rosy glow from the biting-cold breeze that was curling across the bay to create a shimmer of small white patches of foam on the surface of the water.

'Not just one country, Sunday,' replied Gary, his arm tucked firmly around her shoulders to keep her warm. 'Just a few miles from where we're standing, there's a whole continent, with all kinds of people with different ideas, and different ways of life. When this hell of a war's over they're going to have to learn how to live together, without tearing each other to pieces.'

As if to emphasise Gary's point, high above the sea wall from where they were staring out to sea, the clear blue sky was streaked with several white vapour trails, all heading over the Essex coastline towards their final destination in London. And behind them, the pounding of anti-aircraft guns was shaking the foundations of the old seafront houses and small hotels, as the Army did their best to bring down the seemingly endless stream of V-1 'doodlebugs' and V-2 rockets before they could reach any populated areas.

Even after Gary had finished speaking, Sunday continued to stare up at his face. She loved to watch his lips moving. Not only were they easy to read, but they were so firm and sensuous. As she leaned her head on his shoulder, her arm around his waist, she gazed out to sea, telling herself over and over again how lucky she was to know that he was alive and holding her in his arms at that very moment. The story of Gary's survival had sent a chill down her spine as he told her how his plane had been shot down over enemy-occupied territory, and how, despite the fact that the entire crew had managed to bale out, he had been the only one to find his way back to the Allied lines in Belgium.

'Do you really have to fly again?'

Gary paused a moment before answering Sunday's question. When he finally did speak, he pulled her gently round to face him. 'Look, honey,' he said, talking with lips and sign language, 'I've got two weeks' furlough. Let's make the most of it, huh?'

Sunday's eyes were anxiously taking in every part of Gary's face. 'But how can they send you back when—'

Gary stopped her saying anything more until he had made her take off her gloves, so that she could use her hands for sign language.

Sunday's hands struggled to continue what she wanted to say. 'But how can they send you back? You were very nearly killed.'

'I have to go back, Sunday. That's what I'm here for. It's my duty.'

Sunday knew she was breaking her promise to him not to be anxious. But she couldn't help herself. 'You've done your duty, Gary,' she said, trying desperately to find the right fingers for the letters and words he had been teaching her. 'It's other people's turn now.'

This irritated Gary. With a scolding expression, and after wagging a finger at her, he answered, 'It's up to all of us to end this war, Sunday. And that includes me.'

For a brief moment Sunday looked hurt. So she turned to gaze out towards the sea again. In the distance, a flock of seagulls was swooping down into shallow water just off the beach. She couldn't hear the screeching and squealing sounds the gulls were making, but she guessed that a shoal of fish had strayed into their view.

Gary, concerned that he had upset Sunday, turned her round to face him again. 'You know what,' he said, a warm smile on his face. 'One of these days I'm going to take you across to the other side of that water. Have you ever been there?'

Sunday smiled, and shook her head. 'My Aunt Louie went there once. Before the war. She said they eat snails and frogs' legs.'

This made both of them laugh.

'I prefer fish and chips,' said Sunday, impressing Gary with the accuracy of her sign language.

'I prefer you,' replied Gary. He pulled her to him, and kissed her full on the lips.

A special constable nearly fell off his bike as he passed them by. 'Bloody Yanks,' he said to himself. 'Overpaid, oversexed, and over here!'

Mrs Baggley bought her house on the seafront long before the war. In those days Thorpe Bay was very popular with holiday-makers, and there was hardly a day during the summer months when every room in her Hotel de la Mer wasn't taken. Since the war started, however, it had been a different story, for, with the constant threat of enemy invasion, most seaside resorts had been more or less declared restricted areas. But she did get the occasional guests, usually soldiers and their girlfriends down for a dirty weekend. However, Gary was the first American visitor she'd had, and when he had checked in earlier in the day with his 'companion', she had gone to the most enormous trouble to assure him that he had booked into a 'truly international establishment'.

'I'm sorry you can only stay for the weekend,' said Mrs Baggley, as she poured tea for her only two guests in her downstairs parlour. 'Thorpe Bay has such a lot to offer the holidaymaker. In my humble opinion, our beaches are some of the finest in the whole of East Anglia. And you can get a really wonderful suntan.'

Gary exchanged a look with Sunday, but resisted taking a glance out through the window, where it was now snowing quite heavily.

'And we've had our share of Jerry's bombs, yer know.' The hospitable hostess was determined to get as much out of her tea party as she possibly could. 'Oh yes. It was terrible during the early part of the war, planes going over day and night. My dear hubby nearly copped it when a parachute bomb come down on a pub just along the road. Blew him right off his feet into my neighbour's vegetable garden.'

Gary enjoyed talking to Sunday in sign language in front of Mrs Baggley, mainly because the old lady was so fascinated to watch him doing it. 'Mrs Baggley says Thorpe Bay was bombed at the beginning of the war.'

Sunday nodded her head, indicating that she understood.

'Oh yes indeed!' Mrs Baggley was determined to make a meal out of her wartime experiences. 'We've had everything here – including these terrible "doodlebug" things, and now the V-2s.' She leaned across to Sunday, to make sure she could read her lips. 'And have you heard about the butterflies?'

Sunday looked puzzled, and shook her head.

'Don't tell me you haven't heard about the butterfly bombs? These terrible things 'Itler's dropping to kill poor little kids?'

Sunday swung a questioning glance at Gary.

'They're a small explosive device, usually dropped in rural areas. They're really booby-traps, designed to kill civilians, especially kids.'

Sunday was horrified. 'But that's wicked!' she said.

'Oh yes, dear,' said Mrs Baggley, patting her head of tightly permed ginger curls. 'It's wicked all right. If anyone ever tries to tell me that it's wicked to bomb Germans in their own homes, I always remind them that it wasn't us who started this war, thank you very much. And when you think of what they do to us! Those poor people in Halstead today.'

Sunday swung a startled look at Gary.

'Pardon me, Mrs Baggley,' said Gary. 'Did you say – Halstead?'

'Yes, dear,' she replied. 'My hubby's a special constable down the Police Station. They heard there's a V-2 come down there. Sounds like it's done a lot of damage.'

She suddenly realised that her two guests were looking shocked and anxious.

'I'm sorry, my dears,' she said. 'I hope it's not anywhere near where *you* come from.'

Although the King's Head pub at Ridgewell was ten miles or so away from Halstead, most of the people drinking in there had heard the explosion from the V-2 that had dropped there earlier in the day. In fact, the blast had been so powerful that some of the old timber-framed cottages had shuddered, as if in an earthquake. Despite the fact that V-1s and V-2s were still crossing the east coast every day and night of the week, the suddenness of the powerful Halstead bomb had shocked everyone.

'Somebody's got to stop those bastards!' snapped Jinx, who was playing darts with Erin and some of the other crewmen from the base. 'I thought this bloody war was supposed to be over. And yet Jerry keeps sendin' those things over from France without anyone doin' anythin' about it!'

'They ain't comin' from France,' sniffed Erin, a smoking cigar butt protruding from his lips as he aimed his dart at a double eleven. 'They're hidden in underground bunkers on the Dutch coast.'

'I don't care where they are,' Jinx grumbled, as she watched Erin remove his unsuccessful darts from the board. 'Somebody's got to find them and get rid of them!'

'Fer Chrissake, Jinx!' growled Erin. 'What the hell d'yer think we're tryin' ter do day after day, night after night?'

'That's right, Jinx,' said one of Erin's buddies, who was lining up his own darts for a double six and a two. 'It's like lookin' for a needle in a haystack. But we'll find those goddamn rocket sites – sooner or later.'

'I'm sorry boys,' said Jinx, guiltily. 'It's all right for me to go on while you lot go out there and risk your lives. But finding those things later is going to be too late if they go on much longer like this. That rocket in Halstead was a real killer.'

''Scuse me, mate. Could I 'ave a quick word wiv yer?'

The young British soldier who had made his way across the bar to talk to Jinx waited until after she had thrown her third dart.

''Allo, darlin'!' said Jinx, with a huge smile. She had already noticed the young conscript in rough British Army serge as soon as he had entered the bar. The place was usually so full of GIs from the base that it made a change to see a local on the scene, especially a good-looking local like this!

'What can we do for yer, Tommy?' asked Erin, sourly.

The 'Tommy' smiled and, without turning to look at Erin, continued to direct his questions to Jinx. 'I was told yer work up at Cloy's Farm?' he said in a distinctive London accent. 'I was wonderin' whevver yer could give me some 'elp – ter find a friend of mine.'

'*I* could be a friend, darlin',' quipped Jinx, mischievously, unable to take her eyes off the boy's newly grown Clark Gable 'tache. 'Where yer from?'

Erin glared at her, but only jokily. He had come to know only too well how his new wife liked to tease him.

'Shoeburyness,' replied the soldier-boy. 'The barracks on the uvver side of Soufend.'

'I know where Shoeburyness Barracks are, kiddo,' interrupted Erin. 'What's the fascination with Ridgewell?'

Again the boy soldier answered to Jinx, without turning to look at Erin. 'Like I said. I'm lookin' fer this friend of mine – a very old friend. She's in the Women's Land Army. Gel named Collins? Know 'er by any chance?'

'Sunday?' gasped Jinx. 'D'you mean *our* Sunday? Sunday Collins?'

'Yeh, that's 'er. Sunday Collins.'

'Good 'eavens, boyo! 'Course I know Sunday. My best friend. Maid of honour at my weddin'! Erin!' she said, all excited. 'Get this boy a drink!'

Erin was relieved when the boy shook his head and said, 'No, fanks. I've got one waitin' for me at the counter.'

The boy's intervention had clearly brought the game of darts to a halt. Even so, a small group of Erin's buddies were gathered around, curious to see a 'Limey Tommy' in what they had considered to be their own out-of-camp pub.

'So 'ow d'you know our Sunday?' asked Jinx, desperate to know more about this boy, whose strong muscular build, dark cropped hair, and devastating smile were driving her mad. 'You come from those "Buildin's" she lives in? Up London?'

'Somefin' like that,' was all the boy would tell her. 'Where is she now?' he asked. 'Know where I can get 'old of 'er?'

'You're out of luck, boyo,' replied Jinx. 'At this precise moment, she's otherwise engaged!'

This comment brought hoots of dirty laughter from Erin and his buddies, which somehow spread to the rest of the customers in the bar. The rowdiness immediately prompted one of the locals to start playing the pub's piano, and in no time at all, everyone started singing 'Bless 'Em All'.

The boy soldier was not amused, and continued to stare at Jinx with a fixed look of suppressed anger.

'Take no notice of this lot,' said Jinx, knowing only too well how the Yanks always tended to take the piss out of anyone who wasn't one of their own. Then leaning closer, so that he could hear above the singing, she said, 'Sunday's gone away for the weekend. Won't be back 'til tomorrow night.'

'Fanks a lot,' replied the boy soldier. 'When yer see 'er, could yer tell 'er I've bin lookin' for 'er.'

'My goodness!' purred Jinx, who was beginning to irritate Erin by pretending that she fancied this guy. 'Sounds like you're a really *good* friend of our Sun,' she quipped, nudging him in the ribs with her elbow.

'Oh yeah, we're good friends all right,' replied the boy, coolly. 'As a matter of fact, me an' Sun are goin' ter get married.'

The shilling that Gary had put into the gas fire meter was lasting longer than he and Sunday had thought, for their sparse bedroom in the Hotel de la Mer was far more snug and warm than they had dared to expect when they first arrived. For Sunday, this had been one of the happiest days she had had for such a long time. She had even enjoyed the journey down from Ridgewell, during which she and Gary had had to change trains twice and wait endlessly in the freezing cold on bleak railway station platforms for their connections. But the best part had been taking a taxi from Southend along the seafront, and feeling the excitement swell up inside her stomach as the broken-down old banger gradually made its way towards the holiday resort of her dreams – glamorous, exotic Thorpe Bay. And if Mrs Baggley's evening meal of boiled chicken, boiled potatoes, boiled carrots, and boiled greens hadn't been exactly the dream menu of all time, well even that went down a treat on a frozen winter's night.

But the best part of the dream was just lying there in Gary's arms, and feeling the warmth of his body against her own. The huge double bed with its rock-hard mattress may not have been the most comfortable in the world, but at least it was warm, with their feet sharing the heat from a hot-water bottle, and a thick eiderdown to cover their naked bodies right up to their shoulders. Making love with Gary was not like anything Sunday had experienced before, mainly because it really was love, and not just sex. Before they even started to do anything, Gary had gently caressed her body, planting his kisses on her mouth, her ears, her breasts, and her stomach. And she did likewise to him, exploring as much of his flesh as she dared, moving her lips sensuously over the stubble on his face and chin. And when he finally lowered himself on to her, she gave herself to him willingly, utterly convinced that this man really loved her, and that she loved him more than any other person in her entire life.

After it was over, they lay back together in each other's arms for what seemed like hours. The room was not entirely in darkness, for they were bathed in a bright white glow from a wintry moon, which was bursting through the windows and transforming night into day. Sunday hoped that these precious few moments would never end. Unfortunately, however, it was not to be.

'Sunday.' Without warning, Gary suddenly sat up in bed and looked down at her. 'I have to tell you something.'

Sunday was unable to read what he was saying, because his face was turned away from the direct moonlight. Realising this, Gary turned on the small bedside lamp.

'There's something I want you to know,' he said, pulling himself up into a position where Sunday could watch his lips.

Even though the combination of electric and natural light was dazzling her eyes, Sunday could see the anguished expression on Gary's face.

'I once killed someone,' he said, staring straight into her eyes. 'It was a long time ago.'

A cold chill shot up and down Sunday's spine. Slowly, she pulled herself up. 'What d'you mean?' she asked.

For a brief moment, Gary carried on staring at her, finding it almost impossible to say what he knew he would some time have to say to her. Clearly agonising, he pulled back the sheets, and got out of bed.

Sunday watched him in bewilderment as he retrieved his uniform trousers from a hardbacked chair, and started to put them on. All the joy she had succumbed to over the past few hours started to evaporate as she saw his naked buttocks gradually disappear into the well-tailored army-issue trousers.

Gary searched around for a cigarette. He found one, lit it, then went to the fireplace to crouch in front of the antiquated gasfire. Sunday waited a moment, then got out of bed, put on her old towelling dressing-gown, and kneeled in front of him.

Gary inhaled as much smoke as his lungs could cope with, and exhaled the residue. When he looked up again, he was face to face with Sunday, so he rested his cigarette in a small glass ash-tray in the hearth. 'When I was sixteen,' he said, his hands suddenly bursting into life with sign language, 'I used to have a motor-cycle. My dad bought it for me. It was his way of helping me grow up like a *real* guy.' He picked up his cigarette again, pulled on it, and blew out a funnel of smoke away from Sunday's face. 'I didn't really want the bike. I just didn't feel right on it. But Dad wanted me to have it. It was his way of tryin' to stop me foolin' around with poetry.'

Sunday was puzzled. She had been trying hard to follow the signs

Gary was making, but frequently returned her attention to reading his lips. 'Poetry?' she asked.

'I like to read it,' he said. 'An' I like to write it. Pretty dumb for one of Uncle Sam's Army Air Corps, huh?'

Sunday didn't really understand what he meant, so all she could do was to shrug her shoulders.

Gary exercised his fingers before explaining. 'In my dad's eyes, poetry doesn't add up to being a guy in a guy's world. And Dad should know,' he added bitterly. 'He's been pretty much of a roughneck all his life.'

He picked up his cigarette from the ash-tray, and pulled on it. 'Anyway,' he said, stubbing it out unfinished. 'I got to usin' the goddamn thing more an' more, because that's what my old man wanted me to do. Until one evening, I had one hell of a bust-up with him, and the only way I could get the steam out of me was to go out on *his* bike, and tear the guts out of it. Trouble was, it was raining hard, and the roads were full of grease and mud and hell knows what else. So when I turned this sharp bend, just past Mr Peterson's service garage, a truck came out of nowhere, headlights blazing straight into my eyes. All I remember is that I swerved, and my hands just kind of – left the bike handles.' For a moment, his hands stopped moving, and his eyes were too distraught to meet Sunday's. But he continued as suddenly as he had stopped. 'There was this kid,' he said. 'A girl. Not more than ten or eleven years old . . .'

Sunday grabbed hold of his hands, and stopped them from talking. She knew the rest and didn't want to know any more.

The light from the gas fire was flickering now, and when Sunday looked down to see how low the flames were on the mantles, it was obvious that the shilling's worth of gas was at last running out. So she reached for the tap at the side of the fireplace and turned it off.

Whilst she was doing this, Gary got up from the floor and strolled across to the window. Sunday joined him, put her arm around his waist, and leaned her head against him.

As they stood there, they were flooded with ice-cold moonlight, which turned them into two ghostly, statuesque figures. 'Tell me about the poems you write,' said Sunday, as they looked out on to the bay, with the sea bathed in light but calm and still as a pond, no gales, not even a breeze.

Gary paused before answering. Then he turned and looked at her. 'I killed someone, Sunday. A kid who hadn't even begun her life.'

'It was an accident,' Sunday replied, looking directly into his eyes. 'You must have killed an awful lot of people in this war. You and every soldier, or sailor, or airman. Some things are meant to happen.'

Gary suddenly pulled away and turned to face her. 'It's not like that, Sunday,' he said tensely. 'That's why I had to tell you. If I'm asking you to love me, you had to know.'

'Well now I do know,' replied Sunday, trying to reassure him. 'Gary, we all have things that we have to live with. But you can't go on blaming yourself for the rest of your life.'

'That kid!' Gary snapped, grabbing hold of Sunday's hands and holding them in a vice-like grip. 'She was from the local Deaf School. Don't you understand? She was like my own mother. She was like you. And *I* killed her!'

Sunday suddenly felt like she looked, a stone-cold statue bathed in dazzling white moonlight.

Outside, the bright flame of a V-2 rocket headed towards the bay from the open sea, and darted high across the black sky, only just missing the galaxies of tiny twinkling stars that did their best to impede its journey.

Not many people saw it, nor wanted to. But they knew it was there.

# *Chapter 18*

Ernie Mancroft's visit to the King's Head at Ridgewell caused quite a stir amongst Sunday's pals at Cloy's Farm, and by the time she had got back from her weekend with Gary, the place was buzzing with rumours. Sunday was horrified to hear that Ernie had called on her, and absolutely furious to be told by Jinx that he had presented himself as her future husband. But the person she blamed most of all was her Aunt Louie, who had stirred up all the trouble in the first place by giving Sunday's address to Ernie.

'Forget all about 'im, girl,' was Jinx's advice, as Sunday washed out her smalls in the bathroom sink. 'If 'e comes back—'

'Not *if*, Jinx,' interrupted Sunday. '*When*. You don't know Ernie. He's persistent.'

'Stop worryin' yerself, girl!' insisted Jinx. 'If 'e turns up again, we'll just tell 'im to bugger off back where 'e comes from.'

Sunday shook her head. 'There are things you don't know about him, Jinx.'

Jinx let out a dirty laugh. 'I know that if it weren't for Erin, I'd be shackin' up with that lovely bit of arse quicker than I could get me drawers down!'

For once, Sunday couldn't share Jinx's sense of humour. 'He's not like that, Jinx,' she said, turning from the sink to stare directly at her. 'Ernie's got a thing about me. He's always been so – possessive. There was a time once when he nearly killed someone I was going out with. I tell you, he scares me, he really does. I've often thought that he could kill me too.'

Sunday's concern persuaded Jinx to take things more seriously. 'Look, girl,' she said, putting her arm around Sunday's shoulder, 'if anyone ever tried to harm you, we've got enough fellers 'round 'ere to deal with 'im.'

Again Sunday shook her head. 'Ernie's made of iron, Jinx. Back home he was always getting involved in brawls with people, then beating them up till they had to go to hospital.'

'But, honey,' replied Jinx, picking up on some of Erin's slang, 'he won't stand a chance against that lot at the base. They'll make mincemeat out of him!'

Sunday was still shaking her head. She was unconvinced. 'Let me tell you something, Sun,' said Jinx, caringly. 'No 'arm can ever come to you as long as you've got someone to love you. An' you've got Gary now.'

Sunday thought about this for a moment, and about what Gary had told her in the bedroom at the Hotel de la Mer the previous evening. Yes. Until that moment she had been absolutely sure that Gary did love her. But now she questioned *why* he loved her. Was it for herself, or was it guilt for having killed someone who was handicapped, just like herself?

''E'll look after you, girl,' Jinx said reassuringly. 'Gary Mitchell is one hell of a nice bloke. Mark my words – 'e won't let you down.'

Sunday did her best to feel reassured. But it wasn't going to be easy. Especially when Gary heard about Ernie Mancroft.

Towards the end of January, the blizzards which had ravaged East Anglia for so much of the winter gradually began to ease off. There was still plenty of snow, in some places drifts up to four feet deep. In Ridgewell, the villagers were getting tired of having to dig themselves out every morning, and at the Base snowploughs were in constant use on the runways. Sunday also began to worry more and more about her mum, for in her letters Madge had talked about the endless gas and electricity cuts caused by the bad weather, and how difficult it had been for everyone in 'the Buildings' to keep warm. But the thing that was worrying Sunday most of all, however, was knowing only too well how her mum would be sacrificing her own personal comforts in favour of her sister, Louie. In fact, even when she had been home during the Christmas break, Sunday had noticed how her aunt had ignored the Government's appeals to use as little bathwater as possible, and continued to have her regular evening bath filled to the brim with piping-hot water.

These were difficult times for Sunday. Since the start of the New Year, so much seemed to have happened to her. What with Gary's return from the dead, that revealing weekend away with him at Thorpe Bay, and the worrying thought that Ernie Mancroft was determined not to leave her alone, her mind was in turmoil. Sooner or later, Gary's buddies were bound to tell him about Ernie's appearance at the pub in Ridgewell, and his assertion that he and Sunday were going to get married. How was she going to be able to explain Ernie's actions to Gary? Would he ever believe her? And what about Gary himself? Could she really trust *him*? Or was he merely trying to use her to ease his own feelings of guilt? What would happen if he were to ask her to marry him? Would she really want to go all the way to America and start a new life amongst the type of people she had only ever seen at the pictures? Surely it just wouldn't make sense, it wouldn't be natural. And if Gary wasn't the person she thought he was, what would happen if he left her alone in a strange country, with no way of getting back home?

And what of Ernie? How would she ever be able to break free of him? What if he should turn up again and turn nasty on her? What could she say or do that would rid her of him for ever? Then she thought about going home after the war. How would she be able to settle down to life again in 'the Buildings', with her well-meaning mum and Aunt Louie? How would she be able to cope with the prospect of being deaf for the rest of her life? As she tossed and turned in her bed, unaware that Jinx was snoring loudly in the bed next to her, she suddenly yearned for someone she could confide in, a dad she could really call her own, not an adopted one, not just a face in a snapshot photo. And then she got to thinking about what her real dad would have been like, what he would have told her to do when she had such painful problems. And her real mum? Who *was* that strange creature who had turned her back on such a tiny baby? Who *was* this woman? What did she look like? So many questions. Why? Why? Why?

As the long nights gradually began to get shorter, there were signs that the number of 'doodlebugs' and V-2s passing over from the coast were becoming fewer. During March, however, a handful of German bomber planes broke through the coastal defences and started to attack local airfields, including the Ridgewell Airbase. There were also warnings from the Civil Defence that small decoy bombs had been dropped in the area, and that local people should exercise the utmost caution if they came across such lethal weapons.

During February and the early part of March, Sunday saw very little of Gary, for after his two-week furlough, he had very quickly been returned to his unit for active combat duties. However, whenever they did meet, Sunday spent a lot of the time trying to get to grips with her sign-language therapy. Gary turned out to be a determined teacher, and there were times when he became really angry with her increasing lack of concentration. This was never more apparent than on one occasion in the Forces' Canteen in the Congregational chapel, when, in front of Jinx, Erin, and the girls from Cloy's Farm, Sunday was displaying tantrums, protesting over and over again that she was sick to death of trying to learn sign language, and that it meant absolutely nothing to her.

'Concentrate, Sunday!' Gary scowled, taking hold of both her hands and slamming the palms together. 'Think with your hands, for Chrissake!'

'I don't want to think with my hands,' she snapped back. 'I want to hear with my ears!'

'You're stupid!' yelled Gary, straight at her. 'I always took you for a bright young dame,' he said, his own hands working frenetically to illustrate what he was saying. 'But you're nothin' of the sort. You're just plain stupid!'

'If I'm so stupid,' Sunday yelled back, 'then why the hell d'you bother with me!'

'Because I happen to love you, you stupid broad!'

'I can't learn sign language!' insisted Sunday. 'It's just not in me!'

'Don't be so silly, girl!' interrupted Jinx. 'You've got a far better 'ead on you than all us lot put together.'

'Mind your own business, Jinx!'

Jinx was a bit taken aback by Sunday's temper. 'Well, pardon me for breathin'!' she said.

'Look here, you dumb blonde!' growled Gary, grabbing hold of Sunday's wrist. 'D'you want to go around for the rest of your life living in a dark, silent world?'

'I *am* living in a dark, silent world,' blasted Sunday, whose own distorted voice was far louder than anyone else's in the place. 'I'm the one who's got to live with it, not you.'

'Sunday, you don't have to live with it, believe me,' Gary replied, trying to be more conciliatory. 'Why can't you realise how important it is for you to communicate in a language that people like yourself can understand?'

'I *can* communicate!' insisted Sunday. 'In my own way!'

'No, Sunday,' Gary replied firmly, staring directly into her eyes. 'Your way is not the right way.'

Sunday tried to pull away from him, but he held on to her.

'Look guys,' said Erin, chewing hard on the remains of a cigar butt. 'Don't you think we could call a truce or somethin'?'

'Keep out of this Erin!' snapped Gary.

Erin hunched his shoulders in guilt. Now it was his turn to be snubbed.

Sunday tried to struggle with Gary, but he suddenly grabbed hold of her arm, dragged her to the stairs, and led her outside the chapel.

Jinx, Erin, and all the servicemen in the canteen watched them go in utter bewilderment.

'Isn't love won'erful?' said Jinx, with a sigh.

There was plenty of snow around on the Chapel Green outside, for despite a slow thaw, it was still cold enough to turn the surface of what snow remained into a hard, crunchy crust.

'What's got into you, Sunday?' asked Gary, as he brought them both to a halt on the path between the chapel and two small white-plastered cottages. 'Why won't you make the effort?'

Sunday tried to turn her back, but he walked around to make her look at him.

'Sunday?' he asked tenderly.

Sunday slowly raised her eyes to look at him. 'I don't have the strength,' she replied more calmly.

'You don't need strength to communicate,' he said, once again talking with both mouth and hands. 'You need faith.'

Sunday lowered her eyes again, but Gary put his hand under her chin, and slowly raised it so that she couldn't avoid looking straight into his eyes.

'You've learnt the signs,' said Gary, articulating carefully with his lips and hands. 'Now be excited by them. Make them come to life as though they're the most natural thing in the world. Use your eyes to see how beautiful these signs are – yes, and to *hear* them too. In my country, we can bring them to life with just one hand. OK, so over here it's different. But whether you use one hand or two, at least you're *talking*!' To emphasise this, he held up both his hands, the palms facing towards her. 'And believe me, Sunday – we *can* make our hands talk!' he said. 'All we need to do is to use our own thoughts, our own imagination.'

Sunday suddenly tried to pull away from him again.

'For Chrissake, Sunday!' he snapped, struggling with her. 'What the hell d'you want to do with your life?'

Sunday immediately glared into his eyes. 'Why are you doing this for me, Gary?' she asked intensely. 'Is it because of what you told me? Is it because of what you did to that child?'

Gary was stunned by her response. He stared at her in disbelief for a moment, then stood back and asked, 'Is that what you think, Sunday? Is that what you really think?'

Sunday felt the blood drain from her body. What had she

done? What had she said? 'I – don't know what to think,' she replied.

Gary turned and started to walk off.

This time, it was Sunday who went after him. 'How am I expected to know?' she called. 'After what you told me, I didn't know what to think. I knew there was a reason. There had to be a reason.'

Gary suddenly came to a halt, and swung round on her. 'You stupid broad!' he yelled. 'Don't you understand that when two people love each other, they have no right to keep secrets! I told you because I love you!' In the cottages on the side of the path, curtains were discreetly drawn apart as faces peered out to watch the lovers' tiff.

Gary, his brown leather shoes now covered in snow, strode off.

Sunday had a brief moment of panic, so she let him go. What did he mean about 'no right to keep secrets'? Was he trying to tell her something? Was it something to do with what his buddies had told him about Ernie Mancroft's bragging in the pub at Ridgewell? If so, why hadn't Gary come out with it? Why hadn't he given her the chance to deny Ernie's wicked lies? 'Gary!' she yelled, rushing after him and bringing him to a halt. Then standing right in front of him, she slowly raised her hands, and with great care and precision started to spell out some letters in sign language. 'For–give me,' she said, with hands and lips. 'I love you, Gary.'

They stared in silence at each other, until finally breaking into broad smiles. Then, quite impulsively, they threw themselves into each other's arms, and hugged and kissed. Her head pressed firmly into Gary's shoulder, Sunday breathed a sigh of relief, and she suddenly felt confident enough to tell him about Ernie Mancroft. But before she had a chance to do so, they were interrupted by a round of applause from Jinx, Erin, and all the GI canteen customers who had gathered around the chapel gate.

And once again, Ernie Mancroft's name wasn't mentioned.

A few days later, Sunday received an intriguing letter from her old mate, Bess Butler. It was a strange thing for Bess to do, for she had left school when she was fifteen years old and had hardly ever written a letter in her life.

number 7

deer sun

thawt I woold rite you a letter to find out how you are geting on. I miss you a lot becos theres nobody else I can have such a good chinwag with like you.

saw your mum and your aunt louie the other day. funny pair they are, never even pass the time of day with me but who cares I dont. trouble is thow your mum dont look too well these days shes ever so tired lookin. I woold be too if I lived with that old cow of a sisster of hers.

anyway sun the reel reezon I am ritin this to you is to tell you somethin that I have done that you shoold know about. as you know Ive made quite a bit of cash out of my 'work' and as alf gets all he needs Im keepin some of it safe for you in a puddin basin in my kitchen cubbord. alf nos where it is so all you have to do is to ask him for it. its only fiftey quid but it mite come in handy sum time. mind you by the time you collect it there mite be some more becos bisness is very good these days.

pleez dont be ofended sun. I want you to have this cash becos you are a good mate to me and Ive never dun anythin for you so let me do it. you meen a lot to me sun more than youll ever no.

got to go now becos its time for my evenin shift! alf sends love as I do now and awlways.

keep your warm drawers on mate.

luv from bess. xxx

Sunday read Bess's letter several times before putting it in the same drawer in her bedside cabinet as the framed snapshot of her adopted dad. She loved the letter because she could almost hear Bess talking as she wrote it. But she had very quickly made up her mind not to take her old friend's hard-earned fifty quid. Furthermore, as soon as she got back home, one of the first things she intended to do was to try to talk Bess into giving up her secret way of life. Earning her living in such a way was not only dangerous, but also humiliating for a woman who was one of the most generous and warm-hearted people Sunday had ever known.

Young Ronnie Cloy was madly in love with Sunday. He didn't know it of course, but she did. The other girls at the farm knew it too, but they were quite amused by it, and put it all down to 'puppy love'. Despite that, Sunday respected the way the boy felt, for even though he was only fourteen, he had some feelings that were the same as anyone else who was several years older. There was also no doubt that she enjoyed going for walks with the boy, who knew every path, every pond, and every copse in the entire district. Her favourite walk was to the woods on the far side of the main road, where she and Ronnie would spy out on the great gathering of pheasants that were always breeding there. Sunday adored watching the beautiful creatures pecking around in the snow, the males with their colourful red faces, dark green heads, and long, pointed tails, and the brown-speckled bodies of the smaller female birds. She found it so difficult to understand why anyone should want to shoot them; they seemed to be such a natural part of the rural surroundings.

Young Ronnie himself was in a brighter mood these days, gratified that Sunday clearly enjoyed his company a great deal. She also told him a lot about London, especially about Holloway and 'the Buildings' where she came from. But even as she chatted to him about her life back there, she felt uneasy, for it was making the big city seem far too attractive to the boy. This became only too apparent one Saturday afternoon when they were quietly watching a family of hares who were just emerging from their shallow nests in the snow.

'When I go to London,' Ronnie said, 'I want to live near the zoo, so that every day I can go and see the animals.'

'I think you'd soon get fed up going *every* day,' replied Sunday, relying on Ronnie to help her keep her voice down.

'Oh no I wouldn't,' he said, his voice soft and low, but lips moving succinctly. 'I like animals better than people – *most* people that is, not all,' he added, looking pointedly at Sunday. 'The thing is, I get on well with animals. I'm not scared of them.'

'But they're scared of you,' replied Sunday, as she watched a hare with long ears and legs emerging from the family nest.

'Oh no they're not!' Ronnie was quite firm about that. 'Animals know about me. All of them 'round here know I wouldn't hurt them. See those hares over there?'

Sunday turned to look at them. 'Yes,' she replied.

'If I stood up and went over to them,' he said, once Sunday was reading his lips again, 'they wouldn't run away. Shall I show you?'

Sunday had no time to reply, for Ronnie was slowly raising himself up from the snow. Once he was standing, he looked out towards the hares, careful not to make any sudden movement. 'See?'

Sunday peered out cautiously between the snow-covered hedgerow. Once the huge hare had recovered from the initial surprise movement, Sunday was astonished to see the whole family resume their frolicking in the snow.

Ronnie looked down at Sunday. 'Animals are only scared of you if you're going to hurt them. They know I'd never do that.' He held out his hand for her. 'Come on,' he said quietly. 'We can go a bit closer. But don't make any sudden movement.'

Sunday took hold of his hand, and he helped her to her feet. Moving very slowly, they gradually picked their way in the snow towards the hare family.

'I reckon you're going to be a vet when you leave school,' whispered Sunday whilst they walked.

Ronnie shook his head. 'I'd be too upset,' he whispered. 'I wouldn't like to see injured animals being put down. People don't realise how many cats and dogs have been killed in the war. I once saw them pulling a dead spaniel out of a bombed house in Colchester.'

As Sunday and Ronnie drew closer and closer to the family of hares, none of them seemed to take any notice. Coming as she did from the crowded streets of London, Sunday knew very little about wildlife out in the countryside. But what she had read was that hares were supposed to be some of the most timid creatures alive. When she and Ronnie finally came to a halt, they could see the huge buck hare quite easily, sitting up on his long hind legs, nose sniffing, as if in some kind of greeting. For a moment, Sunday and Ronnie stood absolutely still, just watching the huge grey hare, and trying to wonder what he was thinking about them.

'He's beautiful,' said Sunday, doing her best to keep her voice low. 'Why is he so tame?'

Ronnie turned slowly to look at her. 'Because he knows you're with me. He knows you wouldn't hurt him.' He was now staring her straight in the face. 'You wouldn't – would you, Sunday?'

Sunday shook her head.

Ronnie smiled. 'Stay where you are,' he said. 'Don't move.'

He started forward slowly, very, very slowly towards the hare. Although Sunday couldn't hear the crunching of his feet in the hard, icy snow, she could see the heavy footprints he was making.

Ronnie eventually reached to within six or seven yards of the buck hare, who was still perched up on his hind legs, almost as though giving permission for the boy to approach. Very slowly,

Ronnie lowered himself on to his knees, and carefully stretched out his hand towards the furry creature.

At that moment, the sound of a rifle shot cracked through the air, and the huge buck hare was immediately cut down by the bullet, right in front of Ronnie.

'No . . . !' The boy screamed out in anguish, as the rest of the hare family went racing off in terror towards the nearby woods. 'No, no, no . . . !' Ronnie's voice was echoing out across the snow-covered field, as he turned back to see his father at the hedgerow behind, with rifle still poised after firing the deadly shot.

Although Sunday was unable to hear the shot, she was horrified to see what had happened.

Ronnie, in deep pain and anguish, rushed forward to pick up the poor dead creature, which now had blood gushing out from the bullet hole. But it was too late. 'He trusted me!' the boy yelled out hysterically, holding the hare's lifeless corpse high above his head. 'He trusted me – and you killed him!'

Farmer Cloy did not react at all to his son's turmoil. He merely turned away and made off in a different direction.

To Sunday's consternation, Ronnie then dashed off, across the field towards the woods, shouting frenetically as he went, 'He trusted me! He trusted me!'

'Ronnie . . . !' yelled Sunday, as she set off to follow the boy. 'Come back Ronnie!'

In the distance, the family of hares were scurrying off in all directions, desperate to find cover in the woods. Ronnie was doing his best to close in on them, but by the time he reached the woods, the hares had disappeared.

'Come back!' the boy called over and over again. His shrill, sobbing voice was echoing out across the snow-covered wheat fields. Then he also disappeared into the woods.

Sunday was still quite a distance from the woods when she saw a huge column of smoke and snow thrown up into the trees.

'Ronnie!' she screamed in horror, without even being able to hear the sound of her own voice.

Overhead, the explosion in the woods had caused a vast flock of pheasants to rise up steeply in alarm. They were a magnificent spectacle of red, green, and brown against the bright blue winter's sky.

# *Chapter 19*

Most of the villagers in Ridgewell considered it a tragic act of fate that young Ronnie Cloy should have been killed at a time when the war was at last drawing to an end. In a sense that was true, for the Allies had now crossed the River Rhine and the Russians were pushing their way to the outskirts of Berlin itself. Nonetheless, Sunday remained convinced that Ronnie's death was not accidental. To her mind, the boy had been murdered by his own father, whose bullet had not only killed a trusting buck hare, but had also sent his own son to his death. For Ronnie had known only too well of the danger in those woods, since the local Civil Defence had issued repeated warnings about small explosive devices which had been dropped by the *Luftwaffe* in the area.

Ronnie's funeral was a low-key affair held on a cold weekday afternoon in the village church in Ridgewell. Apart from Sunday, Jinx, and the girls from Cloy's Farm, there were several crewmen from the base amongst the congregation, including Gary and Erin. The chief mourners were Ronnie's family, who took up most of the front row amongst a scattering of other villagers. Throughout the entire service, Arnold Cloy never once looked at the small coffin that had been placed on a pedestal in front of the altar. His face, which was usually fat, blood-red, and heavily lined, was now grey and drawn. But his expression was, as always, dour and ungiving, which disguised his true feelings. The explosion in the woods had devastated him, and he had not slept a wink since it happened. However, it wasn't guilt he felt, just a sense of loss. But his real loss was not being able to say all the things he knew he should have said to the boy a long time ago. Sitting next to him was his wife, utterly distraught, and being comforted now by her own mother. As Sunday watched the Cloy family in their time of distress, she felt nothing but hate and despair.

Once the service was over, everyone gathered around Ronnie's grave in the churchyard outside. The vicar said a few prayers, and the mourners observed a few moments' silence. But as soon as that silence came to an end, Sunday astonished everyone by saying out loud, 'I'd like to say something.'

All eyes turned in shock as Sunday moved to the head of the grave. Then fixing her eyes down at Ronnie's small coffin, she began to use her voice and her hands to pay her own last tribute.

'Ronnie was my friend,' she said, her strained speaking voice echoing around the snow-capped graves. 'He was the best friend any person could ever have. Ronnie told me all about the countryside. He told me about birds, and rabbits, and frogs, and all kinds of things. If only he'd been given the chance, he could've been a friend to a lot of people.' As she continued to peer down into the grave, tears began to stream down her cheeks. 'I'll miss you, Ronnie,' she said, her voice cracking. 'Thanks for everything.'

Gary stepped forward, put his arms around her shoulders, and led her away.

Cloy and his family then turned, and after shaking hands with the vicar, started to leave. The other mourners slowly followed.

'May God forgive you,' Jinx said to Arnold Cloy, as he shuffled past her and Erin. 'No one else will.'

Later that day, Sunday asked Sheil if she would draw a picture for her. She said that what she wanted was a picture of one of her favourite views in the fields outside, a very special view that would help to remind her of her friendship with Ronnie.

During March, the first welcome signs of spring were everywhere. After the early crocuses had managed to push their way through the snow, frost, and ice, the familiar yellow daffodils took over, and as the sun grew a little stronger each day, they began to display themselves proudly in window pots and boxes around Ridgewell village, and in small clumps all along the perimeter fence of the base. Sunday loved the thought that the nights were drawing out again, for it meant that she and Gary would be able to stroll down to the King's Head together in daylight.

After Ronnie's funeral, Sunday, relieved that Arnold Cloy had not reacted to Jinx's bitter remark, saw very little of the farmer and his wife. Owing to the considerable repairs needed to the farmhouse due to the 'doodlebug' explosion, the couple had moved to a small bungalow on the far side of Cloy's land. This suited the WLA girls just fine, for it meant that the only time they saw Cloy was when he came along to assign them new jobs. The bulk of the building work on the house was carried out by a small local firm, who were helped by some of the Italian POWs under the supervision of an armed British soldier. Several times, Sunday exchanged a passing smile with the young POW who had once helped her to release sheep trapped in the snow, but they didn't speak again until one afternoon when Sunday was in the middle of feeding the pigs outside in the main farmyard.

'Lady?'

Sunday hadn't noticed the young Italian until he stood in front of her. 'Hallo,' she answered, with a smile.

'For you, please.' The POW held out something for her.

Sunday looked at the small bundle, which was wrapped up in a single sheet of newspaper. 'What is it?'

'For you, please. Gift.'

Sunday looked apprehensively at the bundle, and before taking it, she wiped her muddy hands on the dungarees she was wearing. Inside the bundle she found a cotton shoulder bag, complete with straps, made out of different pieces of coloured cloth. She looked up with a start. 'For me?' she asked.

The young Italian nodded his head. 'I make.'

'You – made this – for me?'

The young Italian nodded again. 'You like?'

Sunday was overwhelmed, and immediately hung the bag over her shoulder. Then she looked at him again. 'Why've you done this?' she asked.

The POW shrugged his shoulders, and shuffled shyly from one foot to the other. 'I like,' he said.

Sunday studied him for a moment. It was the first time she had seen his face properly, for the last time they had met it had been partly covered by a balaclava. But she liked his face, even though it wasn't particularly handsome. The best feature was his eyes, which were dark and smiling, and his worst was his nose, which was long and slightly hooked. She could just see that he had dark curly hair beneath his green POW cap, and his ears were slightly too protruding for his thin face.

'What's your name?' she asked.

The young Italian had difficulty understanding Sunday's drawled way of speaking. 'Please?'

'Your name? What's your name?'

'Oh – *si*! I am Mario. Mario Giuseppe Lambini.'

Sunday found it difficult to read the Italian's lips. But she got the Mario part of it. 'I'm pleased to meet you – Mario,' she said, offering him her hand. 'It's a beautiful present. Thank you.'

Mario first wiped his hand on his POW overcoat, then shook hands with her. 'Lady.'

Whilst they were standing there, some of the pigs Sunday had just fed were snorting through the gate of their pen.

'How long have you been in England?' Sunday asked.

Mario watched and listened very intently to what she was saying. 'Ah!' he said, relieved that he had understood. 'Almost one year.'

'One year?' replied Sunday. 'And soon you go home – yes?'

Mario pulled a face, and shrugged his shoulders.

'But you want to go home?'

'Maybe yes, maybe no.'

Sunday was puzzled by his reply.

'I love my family. I love Italia. Is wrong for my country to make war. But is wrong to make friends with Nazis.' He nodded up towards his fellow POWs working on the roof of the farmhouse. 'This is what Nazis do.'

Sunday looked up at the damaged house. 'Yes, I know,' she said pointedly. And as she did so, she realised what the young Italian was trying to say, for ever since she first arrived at the farm, she had heard stories of how Italian and German POWs in the area had been kept apart because of the deep animosity they felt for each other.

'Sometimes,' he continued despondently, 'I ask my friends from Italia for why we fight English people. People like you, you are our friends. You can laugh, you can talk, you can cry. But Nazi people . . .' He shook his head slowly. 'No,' he said, firmly. 'Nazis do terrible things, to you – and to me.' For a brief moment he lowered his head, before looking up at her again. 'You are angry for these terrible things?' he asked.

Sunday flicked her eyes before answering. 'Yes, Mario, I'm angry,' she replied. 'But the war's nearly over now. The likes of you and me have got to find a way of starting all over again. It won't do us any good to go on hating each other.'

At that moment, Mario noticed that he was being watched carefully from a distance by his British Army supervisor.

'Please, lady,' he said urgently. 'We talk again – yes?'

'If you want.'

'You have no sound,' said Mario, touching his own ears with both hands to explain what he was trying to say. 'But you *hear* so much.' Then he held out both his hands towards her. 'Lady – thank you.'

Sunday used both her hands to shake his. 'Goodbye, Mario.'

'*Addio*!'

With a broad smile on his face, the young Italian turned and hurried off.

It was only whilst he was making his way to join his friends working on the farmhouse building repairs, that Sunday noticed he was walking with quite a limp.

She was not to know that one of his feet had been amputated during a battle in the North African campaign, and had been replaced in a British Army Hospital by an artificial foot.

Although the war was clearly entering its final phase, the 381st Bomb Group at Ridgewell was kept as busy as ever, for the last remaining German military installations were being pounded night and day by B17 Flying Fortresses.

This was the time that Sunday feared most. Each morning was now getting lighter much earlier, and as she made her way across the yard with the other girls to milk the cows or feed the pigs, her eyes constantly scanned the weak grey sky in the hope that she might catch a passing glimpse of Gary's giant B17 that would just be touching down after yet another night's perilous mission. Her stomach churned at the thought of losing him at such a time, so close to the end of the war in Europe. Since meeting him, her whole life had changed. He had given her the will to live, the determination to face up to the hardship of being deaf. But Gary had his own fears too. Sunday was constantly aware that when they were together he only ever talked of the present, never the future. Over recent weeks, Gary's whole attitude to life had become fatalistic, and whenever he gave a parting kiss on the day before a mission, she always felt that he was saying goodbye for the last time. And each time that he returned, they seemed to grow closer and closer. Even though they had only managed to spend one night together, there was now never a time when she didn't think about their two bodies entwined, the touch of his lips against her own, and the warmth of his hands cupping her breasts.

Towards the end of the month, Erin reached the ripe old age of thirty-two, so he invited Jinx, Sunday, and the other girls from Cloy's Farm to his birthday party in the Mess Hall at the base. To say it turned out to be an unusual party would be an understatement, for the highlight of the evening was a musical entertainment provided by some of Erin's buddies. This included impersonations of the 'old groaner' Bing Crosby, who had himself given a concert at the base the previous summer, and a collection of some rowdy locker-room songs from the crew of *Jane Russell*, which was the nickname of

Erin's own B17 Flying Fortress. However, Jinx, Sunday, and the girls had quite a surprise in store when the main attraction appeared. This turned out to be Gary, dressed in top hat, white tie and tails, in the guise of Fred Astaire, introducing his 'sexy' dancing partner, Ginger Rogers, better known as Bombardier Erin Wendell. Needless to say, Jinx nearly had hysterics when she saw her husband step out wearing a ginger wig, high-heeled women's shoes, and a South American dancing outfit, and when Erin and Gary launched into a chaotic version of 'The Continentale', the laughter, jeers, whistles, and applause very nearly brought the roof down. Sunday thought it was the funniest thing she had ever seen, and her big regret was that she couldn't hear as well as see the whole bizarre performance.

Later in the evening, the tables were moved back, a gramophone set up, and everyone started to dance. Thanks to Gary, even Sunday felt confident enough to join in, but she gave up very quickly after Erin had swapped partners with Jinx and Gary, and, with a cigar butt in his lips and still wearing his Ginger Rogers outfit, he stomped around like an elephant with three feet. Under the circumstances, Sunday felt it better to sit that one out.

Although alcohol remained strictly off-limits on the base, some of Erin's buddies had sneaked in a few bottles of brown ale for the party, so when he and Sunday found a table at the back of the Hall, he made quite sure that they drank discreetly. What Sunday didn't know, however, was that Erin had a reason for getting her alone for a few minutes.

'Look, Sunday,' he said, looking pretty bizarre with his lips still plastered with lipstick from the Astaire-Rogers act. 'I know this is none of my business, but have you told Gary about this Limey creep who says he wants ter marry yer?'

Sunday struggled to read his lips. Then she shook her head slowly. 'Does he know?' she asked anxiously.

'Not yet, I don't think. But sooner or later, one of those guys is goin' ter let slip.' He drew closer, making sure that he couldn't be overheard. 'You'll have ter tell him, Sunday,' he said. 'It won't look good if yer keep it from him.'

Sunday nodded.

'This guy,' Erin continued, keeping his voice as low as possible. 'Did you know he's gone AWOL?'

Sunday shot him a startled, worried look. 'AWOL?' she asked. 'What's that?'

'He's vamoosed – you know, absent without leave. His name's come up on a Brit Army list of deserters. Apparently, he's been on a posting to some unit out in France somewhere. No idea what happened, but your guys are out gunning for him. When they catch up with him, it's a court martial – that's for goddamn sure!'

As they talked, Jinx, who was now almost five months gone, was launching into a hectic jitterbug dance with Gary and two of Erin's buddies.

Sunday, however, was looking concerned. 'He frightens me, Erin,' she said. 'Ernie's capable of killing a person. If he finds his way back here, I'm afraid what he might do.'

'If he's got any sense at all, Sun,' said Erin, 'he'll keep his butt away from here.'

Try as she may, Sunday was unable to feel reassured. She had prayed that after his appearance in the King's Head back in January, Ernie Mancroft would have forgotten all about her. But she knew she should never underestimate his determination to get what he wanted. And it was Sunday herself that he wanted, and nobody else.

'Look, Sun,' said Erin, leaning across the table to her. 'The guys 'round here are a pretty tough bunch. If that sonoverbitch tries to lay one finger on you, he'll regret the day he was born. But you've got ter tell Gary. For his sake, and for yours too.'

In the background, the dance had come to an end with a burst of rowdy, hooting sounds, jeers, and whistles.

'Ladies and gentlemen – if you'll pardon the expression!'

The place again erupted into jeers and whistles as two GIs helped Jinx to stand up on to one of the tables.

'Unaccustomed as I am to public speaking . . .'

More jeers and whistles as Gary went across to join Sunday and Erin at their table.

'As it so 'appens, I've got something I want to say to my 'usband – yes, and all his gang of thugs here tonight!'

Laughter and applause from everyone this time.

'I just want to tell you that I'm very proud to be a part of you,' Jinx said. 'Thank God this bloody war's nearly over, and it's thanks to all of you who've made it possible.' She looked around the sea of faces watching her, and for the first time in her life she felt herself becoming far more serious than she ever thought possible. 'Believe me, I know what you boys 'ave gone through since you come 'ere to Ridgewell two years ago. I also know what it's meant to all of you to lose your friends, your buddies, those wonderful people who've helped to keep us safe in our beds at night. All I can say from us girls, from us Limeys, is – thank you, fellers. When you get 'ome, your folks should be pretty proud of you. I know *I* am.' Then she turned to Erin. 'I know I'm proud of you – you ol' soak!'

This brought a storm of hoots and applause from Erin's buddies.

At the back of the Mess, Gary was busy using sign language for Sunday, to explain what Jinx had been saying.

'Hold it right there, Mrs Wendell!' called Erin, getting up from the table, and winding his way through the party-goers to join his wife. 'As it so happens,' he said, 'I have an important announcement to make.'

This brought a chorus of catcalls and whistles from his buddies.

From the inside of his uniform jacket, Erin took out a piece of official-looking paper, and held it high above his head. 'See this?' he called, looking first at the sea of faces watching him, and then up at Jinx. 'This is official confirmation that in two weeks from now, my wife, Mrs Erin Louis Wendell, will be sailing on the S.S. *Argentina*, bound for the good old U.S. of A.'

This prompted a huge roar of cheers, applause, and whistles from everyone.

Jinx, however, was so shocked, she nearly fell off the table she was still standing on. 'Erin!' she gasped. 'D'you mean it? D'you really mean it?'

Erin climbed up on to a chair at the side of her. 'Here,' he said, giving her the official military permit he was holding, 'take a look for yerself.'

'She's goin' home, folks!' he called to everyone present. 'To my home, my folks. An' lemme tell yer somethin', huh? When my kid's born, I want every one of you sonoverbitches to go out and toast him with a tank of Bud!'

'Him!' screeched Jinx, excitedly. 'Who said anything about *him*? If I 'ave anythin' to do with it, we're 'avin' a bloody girl!'

'Over my dead body!' growled Erin.

This brought the house down. But just then, one of Erin's buddies started to sing, 'Happy Birthday To You'. Soon, the whole Mess Hall was echoing to the rowdy sound of GIs bellowing out in a hell-raising chorus.

At the back of the Mess, Gary threw his arms around Sunday, and hugged her tight. Although it was a celebration that no one could fail to enjoy, at the back of her mind, Sunday still couldn't forget Ernie Mancroft.

Sunday woke up at about three o'clock in the morning. She wasn't sure of the exact time, because the wristwatch her mum had given her on her eighteenth birthday had stopped, so during the night she had to rely on her small alarm clock. But something woke her, although she wasn't quite sure what. It was pitch-dark, so she reached for her torch. After checking the time, she directed the beam around the other beds to make sure everyone was asleep. When she was satisfied that they were, she turned off the torch again, slipped out of bed, and put on her towelling robe and slippers.

She made her way first to the bathroom at the back of the sleeping quarters. Her torch beam scanned the old stone sinks, and the chipped enamel bath itself, where a large house spider had settled down for the night. Everything seemed to be in order, until she suddenly noticed that the outside door had been left slightly ajar. Before closing it, she peered outside. Her torch beam picked up nothing but the shadows of trees bending in a lively gale, which was making it seem far colder than it actually was. Nonetheless, she decided to explore just a little further, so pulling the towelling robe snugly around her neck, she stepped outside. The night clouds were racing across the sky, and every so often the moon managed to make a subliminal appearance, flooding the farmyard with light for no more than a second or so before hurrying back to safety again.

Sunday had no idea why she was being so brave. She had often seen girls doing this sort of thing in the pictures, putting themselves at risk as they roamed dangerous places in the middle of the night. But that was what she was doing right then, and like all those girls in the pictures, she was scared out of her life, scared because she could only experience all these strange, distorted images without sound. For her, the silence of the night was far more disturbing than the day. Why, oh why was she connecting this to Ernie Mancroft all the time? Yes, he was a brutal thug all right, but surely he wasn't the sort who would go around stalking girls just to frighten them? And in any case, what reason had he to frighten her? If he loved her as much as he was always saying, why should he want to harm her? However, no matter how hard she tried, she was unable to convince herself. She turned and hurried back inside the barn. Once she had closed the door, she paused for a moment, suddenly feeling quite stupid to have behaved more like a silly child than an eighteen-year-old.

When she got back to her bed, all the girls were still fast asleep, so she turned off the torch, removed her towelling robe and slippers, and quietly sneaked back under the covers. But as she laid her head back on to the pillow, and turned over to one side, she felt something cold against her cheek. She sat up with a start, reached for her torch, and switched it on.

The torch beam picked out what was lying on her pillow. It was a small snapshot of Ernie Mancroft.

A few days later, there was great excitement in the barn. Not only was Jinx regularly feeling her baby kicking around inside her stomach, but she had also received her tickets for the journey to New York, where Erin's entire family were planning to meet her at the dockside.

Ever since Erin's birthday party at the base, Sunday had talked a lot to Jinx about the new life in America that she was about to experience. Despite the caustic way her own mother had reacted to her wedding, Jinx's loyalties were divided. It seemed a crazy thought, but she still loved her mam and dad, and as the time grew closer for her to leave Blighty once and for all, she knew that, like all the other GI brides who were embarking on a strange new journey, she had misgivings.

'Of course, I'll come back from time to time,' said Jinx, as she showed Sunday the new maternity dress Erin had had sent over from the States. 'After all, whatever she says, my mam's goin' ter want ter see this.' She placed her hand on her stomach and gently rubbed it. 'Depends 'ow much money Erin's got in the kitty, I suppose.'

Sunday put her arms around Jinx and held her. 'Your mum'll have to get used to it,' said Sunday. 'The only things that are important in your life from now on are Erin and your baby.'

'You're right,' replied Jinx, looking up at Sunday. 'Stupid, in't it? But I really love Erin, ugly lookin' goat 'e is.' Even so, there was a touch of uncertainty on her face. 'You do like 'im too, don't you, Sun?'

'He's one of the nicest blokes I know,' replied Sunday. 'I can't believe there's another man in the whole wide world that you could trust more than Erin.' Sunday had good cause to believe what she had just said, for Erin had been the only person she had told about the snapshot of Ernie Mancroft she had found on her pillow.

'Thank God they've at last finished those bombing raids,' said Jinx. 'At least I won't 'ave to worry about him being missing or killed in action any more. Unless they send 'im out to bomb the Japs in the Far East or somethin'. That's all I need!'

That same afternoon, Jinx received a call from the CO's office at the base, asking her to come along to see him. Erin had already warned her to expect this interview, for it was normal procedure for all war brides to be given a friendly but formal lecture before entering the United States. Nonetheless, Jinx was very nervous about the interview, and had to be persuaded not to put on too much make-up to meet the CO, just in case he got the wrong impression about her!

'She's making a big mistake,' said Sue, once she was quite sure that Jinx had gone off to her interview. 'These things never work.'

'What d'you mean?' asked Sunday curiously.

'Well, for a start, he's Jewish.'

Sunday was taken aback. 'So what?' she said.

Sue was perched on the edge of her bed, using the mirror of her compact to powder her nose. 'Jinx was brought up Welsh Chapel. They'll never accept her in the Hebrew faith.'

'That's absolute rubbish!'

Everyone was astonished to hear Sheil contribute to the discussion. It was something she had never done before.

'It doesn't matter what faith you belong to,' said Sheil, making a rare excursion away from squatting on her bed. 'If you're a human being, you've got the right to love anyone you want.'

'Romance has got nothing to do with it, Sheil,' Sue said, in her usual condescending tone. 'It's all to do with what you've been brought up to believe in.'

'I was brought up to believe in God,' replied Sheil, calmly. 'But He let me down. Now I only believe in me.'

Sunday was impressed with Sheil for saying what she felt, even if she didn't agree.

Some time later, Sunday went off to see if she could help Ruthie to feed the chickens. But when she got to the chicken runs, Ruthie had already left, so she decided to take a stroll along the public footpath close to the woods where young Ronnie Cloy had often taken her to see the pheasants.

The weather had at last broken, and the sharp, cold spring air had given way to a mild spell that was inducing tufts of grass everywhere to green up in the gradually warming sun. She felt a twinge of excitement as she looked around at the bare branches of the trees, knowing that within the next few weeks they would be bursting into life again after their long winter sleep.

When she reached the woods, there seemed to be more pheasants than ever. But then, this was not the time of year to shoot them, despite the fact that once the new crop of wheat had been sown they would undoubtedly ignore the dumb scarecrows that were placed across the fields, and peck up as much seed as they could get their beaks into.

To her astonishment, Sunday noticed that someone was walking through the woods. It seemed an incredible thing for anyone to do, for even though the Civil Defence and USAF engineers had given the all-clear for explosive devices in the area, there was still an outside chance that one or two might remain.

She came to a halt for a moment, and after a while the figure emerged from the woods, and made straight towards her on the footpath. The encounter was making her quite nervous, until she suddenly identified the figure of Arnold Cloy. Unfortunately, there was no way she could avoid him, so she carried on walking in the direction she had started out. A moment or so later, Cloy brought her to a halt again, barring her way. She hadn't really seen him since Ronnie's funeral back in March, and thought he was looking much older and more frail. After keeping his eyes lowered to the ground for a brief moment, he raised them again and looked straight at her.

'You think you know, don't you?' he said, his voice strong and firm. 'You think I didn't love that boy?' He walked a few steps towards her, and stopped again. 'Well, you're wrong.'

With that, he brushed past, and headed off back towards his bungalow.

When she got back to the barn, Sunday was surprised to see a jeep waiting outside the front door. Recognising it as the one Gary had taken her out in once or twice, she started to run towards it.

Gary was just coming out of the front door when she arrived. She immediately wanted to throw her arms around him and hug him as tight as she could, but the look of anguish on his face told her not to.

'Jinx is inside,' he said gravely. 'She needs you, Sunday.'

Then he sighed. He was close to tears.

'Erin's been killed. A collision. Two B17s.' His voice was cracking with emotion. 'A goddamn bloody accident.'

# Chapter 20

The village railway station at Great Yeldham was bathed in warm spring sunshine. It seemed incongruous that the temperature for early April should already be hot enough for people to shed their jackets and pullovers, when just a few weeks before great clumps of ice-hard snow were still obstinately refusing to thaw.

As a small kid, Sunday had always loved railway stations. To her they had always seemed such vast, busy places, with people hurrying from one platform to another to catch their trains, and thick dark smoke billowing up from the funnels of dusty old engines as they puffed out of the station on the way to magical places, like Thorpe Bay. It was only when the war started that she'd realised that railway stations could be tragic places too, the places where families and lovers were parted, with the prospect of never seeing each other again. Although there was nothing vast about Great Yeldham, over the years this tiny village station had also had its share of grief and tears. Throughout the war the modest setting had played host to so many village women and their children who had gathered to wave farewell to their menfolk. Sunday felt a bit like that now as she waited with Jinx on the small sun-drenched platform.

'Funny, in't it?' said Jinx, her face pale and drawn as she gazed up the railway track for the first sign of her train. 'The day after termorrow, me an' Junior 'ere should've been on our way to fresh coffee and thick juicy steaks in the Brave New World. Now, it's back to tea an' oatcakes in good old Swansea.'

Sunday only caught part of what Jinx had said, but she knew how her mate was feeling. 'You know, Jinx,' she said. 'It won't be as bad as you think. I'm sure, after what's happened, your mum and dad will take good care of you and the baby.'

Jinx threw out a wry grunt. 'Oh, me mam'll do that all right. Now she knows there's no father around to compete with. I tell yer, me dad knew what he was doin' when 'e named me Jinx.'

Sunday put a comforting arm around Jinx's waist. She found it unbearable to recall everything Jinx had had to go through during the past week. The death of Erin had been such a cruel act of fate, to have been killed in a midair collision with another B17 after surviving nearly two years of hazardous bombing missions over enemy territory. Sunday knew that she would never forget those harrowing few moments when she stood beside Jinx and the men of the 381st Bomb Group, as they watched the giant Flying Fortress taking off from the runway at Ridgewell Airbase, carrying the bodies of Erin Wendell and his buddies back home to their last resting-places in America. No wonder Jinx never stopped stroking her stomach with such loving care. Her baby was all she had left now of a man with whom she had shared barely a year of her life.

‘’E was a good man, yer know, Sun,’ Jinx said, again feeling the tiny movement inside her stomach. ‘They all are, that bunch up the ’drome.’ And making quite sure that Sunday could read her lips, she added, ‘And that includes your bloke too.’

Sunday unconsciously bit her lip. As usual, Jinx had known exactly what was on Sunday’s mind.

‘Erin thought the world of ’im, yer know. ’E told me several times that if you two didn’t stick tergether, you’d be a couple of chumps.’ The strained smile she tried to offer looked odd without any of her usual smattering of make-up. ‘You won’t be a dumb idiot, will you, Sun?’

Sunday smiled weakly, and shook her head.

Although the sound of a train whistle was heard approaching from the distance, Jinx resisted the temptation to turn and look up the track. ‘In any case, I want you two to be Junior’s godparents!’

This brought a more relaxed smile from Sunday. ‘Then you’re still convinced it’s going to be a boy?’ she asked.

‘Don’t be so silly!’ Jinx replied. ‘If Erin says it’s goin’ ter be a boy, a boy it is!’

From the corner of her eye, Sunday caught sight of the train slowly chugging towards the end of the platform. It was the moment she had been dreading, and it prompted both girls to throw their arms around each other in a tight embrace.

‘I want to tell you something, Sunday Collins,’ Jinx said, pulling herself away just enough to be able to let Sunday read her lips. ‘I’ve only known you a few months, an’ yet I feel as though I’ve known you all my life. An’ that’s just what I want to do, girl. I want ter know you *all* my life. You’re the best I know. Please keep it that way, won’t you?’

Sunday was doing her best to stop the tears flowing down her cheeks.

Whilst they were standing there, thick black smoke from the engine momentarily engulfed them. When the train finally came to a halt, Sunday quickly opened the door of an empty compartment. Then, after helping Jinx to get her luggage on board, she slammed the door behind her.

Jinx immediately leaned out of the window, and stretched down to grasp hold of Sunday's hands. 'You better keep in touch, girl – or else.'

Sunday squeezed Jinx's hands. 'Just try to stop me,' she replied. There were only two other passengers boarding the train, but as the train guard at the end of the platform blew his whistle and raised his green flag, a young British sailor wearing tunic and bell-bottoms suddenly rushed along the platform. Jinx immediately took advantage of the boy's panic, and opened her compartment door for him.

'Thanks, mate!' said the sailor, as he leapt on board and took a seat by the window facing Jinx.

Jinx slammed the door behind him, and leaned out of the window again. 'Well now,' she said, with a touch of the old twinkle in her eye. 'Looks as though it's not goin' ter be such a borin' journey as I expected!'

Even though the train then started to move off, Sunday just had to laugh. It was the way she wanted to remember Jinx.

A few moments later, the train was easing out of the tiny station, winding its way through the friendly green landscape of the Colne Valley, and leaving behind a thin trail of dark black smoke which gradually rose up into the azure-blue sky.

Sunday watched the train chugging off for as long as she could, and she was still waving madly to Jinx as she caught her last sight of her. Then the engine picked up speed and headed out further and further into the valley. For a moment or so, Sunday just stood there, feeling very empty and lost. But then she started thinking about Jinx, sitting opposite that young Jack tar, all alone together in their compartment. And as she strolled off slowly along the platform, a comforting smile came to Sunday's face.

There was no doubt about it. Jinx Daphne Lloyd was going to be all right.

During the middle of April, East Anglia experienced a record heatwave. With RAF and USAF bombing raids on Germany now at an end, there was actually some spare time for the exhausted air-crews to enjoy the premature hot sunshine, and the main task was now to use the giant Flying Fortresses to bring home liberated Allied prisoners of war.

At Cloy's Farm, the girls were biding their time. With the end of the war expected within the following few weeks, all of them had decided to return to their homes. However, for their remaining workdays, they were given the arduous task of hoeing out the weeds in the freshly sown barley fields. Owing to the heatwave, the Essex clay was particularly rock-hard, and breaking it down whilst coping with temperatures in the 80s was tough going. There was also a great deal of anger amongst the girls, who had been told that on their release they would not be entitled to the same treatment as other conscripts, who could expect wartime gratuities, clothing and ration coupon allowances, and opportunities to take part in a free government training programme for other jobs.

Since the beginning of April, Gary had been relieved of any further operational flying duties, and this gave him and Sunday the chance to spend more time together than they had ever done before. With near-perfect weather and long hours of daylight, they used their time to cycle around some of the neighbouring villages, where time seemed to have stood still, and little churches that were tucked away behind ancient graveyards and whose bells were poised to ring out the end of a long and brutal war. Everywhere they passed, people were standing outside their cottages and houses, either taking in the hot evening air, or preparing their gardens for the oncoming season. In one small village called Stambourne, they stopped to talk to a middle-aged couple, known affectionately as Jessie and Ted, who even asked them in for a cup of tea and a piece of Jessie's home-made custard tart. It was at times like this that Sunday realised just how slow and different life in the countryside was from the congested streets of London.

However great her joy, Sunday knew only too well that these idyllic few weeks couldn't last for ever.

'They're sending us home, Sun – the whole 381. It's not for a couple of weeks yet, but I'm in the first group.'

Sunday had been expecting Gary's news ever since she was told about the death of President Roosevelt a few days earlier. Now that operational activities were winding down in Europe, it was apparently well known that the President's successor, Harry S. Truman, was keen to get his armed forces back home as quickly as possible. Sunday knew that it would only be a matter of time before Gary was amongst them. It was inevitable.

Until this moment, everything had been quite magical. They had taken almost half an hour to cycle up to Gosfield Lake, where they stretched out on the grass banks and watched the locals rowing and sailing their boats. The sun was so hot that, like most of the other people lapping up the heatwave there, Gary had immediately stripped off to the waist, and Sunday had removed her dress to sunbathe in her bathing costume. Gary had been dreading telling her his news, and he only did so when the two of them were idly cooling their feet in the cold water of the rather murky lake.

'I told them I wanted to stay behind,' he said, his arm around her shoulders, and making sure she could read his lips. 'They said it wasn't possible. The war's not over yet. I have to go back home first.' He sighed, then added sourly, 'I guess that's the way of good old Uncle Sam.'

Sunday reacted far better than she ever thought she would. 'There's not much we can do about it,' she said, trying to give him a reassuring smile. 'If you have to go, you have to go.'

Gary waited a moment, then removed his arm from around her shoulder. 'Then is that it?' he asked.

Over these past months, Sunday had got to know Gary well enough to realise that whenever he started to talk to her in sign language, there was something bothering him. 'What do you mean?' she asked anxiously.

'I'm asking if you care about my going home? I'm asking if you care that we could be apart for quite some time?'

Although Sunday was getting used to Gary's sudden mood changes, it still took her by surprise when his face tensed up, and his sign language was used with an aggressive slapping of fingers against his palms, or his fists were twisted on top of each other to show the white of his knuckles.

'Of course I care!' she said quickly, hurt that he should have even thought otherwise. Knowing that it would make him angry if she didn't make the effort to reply to him in sign language, she held her up her hands, and slowly replied, 'But what am I to think, Gary? It was bound to happen sooner or later.'

To her surprise, Gary suddenly took hold of both her hands, and held on to them. He had a stern expression on his face, and it worried her. 'Sunday,' he said, using only his lips to communicate with her. 'Why haven't you ever told me about this guy who's been tailin' you?'

Gary's question came like a bolt out of the blue, and Sunday felt herself tense. She knew only too well that she could have avoided this moment, but only now did she realise how stupid she had been. In those few seconds of panic she asked herself why she hadn't told him about Ernie Mancroft, and how he had pursued her obsessively even to the point of finding his way into the girls' billet in the middle of the night to leave a snapshot photo of himself. 'I'm sorry Gary,' was all she could say. 'I know I should have told you, but I just didn't want you to get involved.'

'Involved!' Gary pulled his feet out of the water and knelt beside her. 'Fer Chrissake, Sunday!' he snapped, again using aggressive sign language. 'A guy tells all my buddies you're goin' to marry him, and you tell me you don't want me to get involved! Have you any idea what a jerk you've made me look?'

'Gary, I'm sorry.'

'No, Sunday,' snapped Gary, his fingers slapping against the palms of his hands as he talked. 'I'm the one who's sorry. If somethin's been goin' on between you and this guy—'

'No, Gary!' insisted Sunday, grabbing hold of his hands. 'There's been nothing between me and Ernie Mancroft. Not now, not ever! I hate him. Can't you understand that? I hate the very sight of him!'

'Bullshit!'

'It's true, I tell you!' Sunday was now agonising, and didn't know how to convince Gary. 'Ernie came looking for me whilst you and me were down at Thorpe Bay.'

'Why?'

'Because he wants me. He's always wanted me – ever since we worked together in the Bagwash. I've tried to get rid of him. Time and time again I've told him to go away and leave me alone, but he just won't ever give up.'

'Tell me just one thing, Sunday,' said Gary, staring straight into her eyes. 'Did you ever give this guy any reason to believe that *you* wanted *him*?'

Sunday slowly shook her head. 'I've never given Ernie Mancroft anything but a passing smile.'

For a moment or so, Gary stared straight at her. Then he sat back on his heels, and tried to work things out in his mind. 'If what you're sayin' is true,' he said eventually, 'we have to do somethin' about it.'

Sunday shook her head. 'You'll never stop Ernie. He's dangerous, Gary. Believe me, he'd kill anyone who got in his way.' She also sat back on her heels. 'I'm very scared of him.'

The two of them were now facing each other.

Gary leaned across and took hold of her hands, held on to them, and looked directly at her. 'Watch what I'm sayin', Sun,' he said, talking gently with his lips only. 'As long as I'm around, you have no need to be scared of anyone, OK?'

Sunday nodded.

'Look,' he said. 'There are jerks like this all over the place. The world's full of 'em. But if we let 'em have their way, then they'll take over. The fact is, we're not goin' to let them take over.'

Sunday tried to speak, but he put his finger to her lips and stopped her.

'We can only do that, Sun, if we trust each other. But I have to know what's goin' on. Do you understand what I'm sayin'?'

Again Sunday nodded.

Gary drew closer, and with one finger cleared a few strands of her strawberry-blonde hair which had dropped across one of her eyes. 'You remember when I told you about what happened to me when I accidentally killed that kid back home?'

Sunday nodded.

'Well, that was a secret that I had no right to keep from you.' He looked deep into her eyes, and smiled reassuringly. 'You have to treat me the same way, Sun, because if we keep things from each other, there's no trust.' He moved even closer, held on to her hands, and talked calmly and firmly. 'Lemme tell you somethin',' he said. 'I hate the guy that's been doin' these things to you. But he won't win, because I won't let him. If he shows up again, I wanna know about it. Do we have a deal?'

Sunday smiled, and once again she nodded. Gary leaned forward and kissed her full on the lips.

The mother of the family nearby was shocked, and with both hands averted her kids' eyes from the disgraceful behaviour of the half-naked GI and his shameless English girlfriend.

'Kissing in public!' the local village woman said to herself. 'What *is* the world coming to!'

Mario Giuseppe Lambini much preferred the English summer to its winter. Not that it was officially summer just yet, for it was still only April and although the trees and hedgerows were gradually showing new buds, they remained obstinately stark and bare against the hazy spring sky. But Mario loved to feel the parched earth beneath his one good foot, and as he made his way along the narrow public footpath which ran by the edge of Cloy's newly ploughed wheatfield, it made him think of the dusty paths of the Tuscan countryside back home in his native Italy.

When he reached the door of the barn, he hesitated. He knew he was breaking the rules because Cloy had forbidden prisoners of war any direct access to farm buildings on his land without his permission. But, as this was Mario's last day in Ridgewell, he was willing to take the risk. He had no need to knock on the door, for Sunday, who was looking out of the window when he approached, came to the door immediately.

'Mario,' said Sunday. 'What are you doing here?'

'Lady,' he answered, with a broad smile which revealed a perfect set of solid white teeth. 'I come to say *addio*.'

Although she hardly knew the young Italian, Sunday felt a twinge of sadness. 'Oh,' she replied. 'I had no idea you were going so soon.' She came out of the barn, closing the door behind her. 'Does this mean you and your friends are going home?'

'Tomorrow,' replied Mario.

Sunday gave him a warm smile. 'I'm very happy for you, Mario.'

The young Italian smiled back shyly at her. During the few occasions the two had spoken together, Mario had told Sunday a lot about where he came from, and his yearning to see his wife and two young children again. Although she had always found it quite difficult to understand what he was saying, she could tell how much he had missed his homeland. In many ways, Sunday thought Mario should have been a writer or an artist, for when he talked, his hands were so full of expression as he described the red earth in the hills above the town where he was born, and the olive trees, and the small streams that dried up completely during the summer months. She also realised what it meant to him to lose his foot during a war in which he had never wanted to play a part. In that respect, both he and she shared the same anguish.

'Please, lady,' Mario said, as they moved out into the warm sunshine. 'Before I go, I ask you one question.' They came to a halt, but he continued to look directly at her. 'The first day – in the snow. With the cows, and the sheep. You speak with me. For why?'

Sunday looked puzzled. 'But – why shouldn't I speak with you? You were helping me with the sheep. All I said was *thanks*.'

Mario shook his head. 'No.' He pointed to his temple, and said,

'For me, you say much more. You say, everything is OK, Mario. You say, I have no hate.'

Sunday watched him intently. Whatever it was that this young Italian felt he had gained from the few words they had spoken together, the look of hope in his eyes couldn't fail to move her.

'*Addio*, lady,' he said, stretching out his hand for hers. Sunday offered it to him, and to her surprise, he took it with both his own hands and kissed it.

'I will not forget you – lady,' he said, letting go.

'Goodbye, Mario.'

The young Italian gave her one final look, turned, and slowly made his way back towards the footpath.

For a moment or so, Sunday watched him go. When he was finally out of sight, it suddenly occurred to her that she had never even told him her name.

The beach at Thorpe Bay was very different from the last time Sunday and Gary had been there. Although it wasn't quite as hot as during the recent heatwave, there was a warm, hazy sun, and now that the last curls of barbed wire had been removed, the sandy beach itself was overflowing with day-trippers.

This was the last weekend in April, and also the last couple of days that Sunday and Gary would spend together before his return to America on Monday morning.

At the Hotel de la Mer, Mrs Baggley was delighted to welcome the return booking of her American gentleman and his young lady. As she told her 'hubbie', if people are satisfied with nice clean board and lodgings, then they'll always come back. No doubt that was the reason why she felt perfectly justified in increasing her daily rates for B and B and evening meal by one and sixpence.

Despite the warm, muggy weather outside, Sunday and Gary spent most of Saturday afternoon in their room making love. For almost two hours they said hardly anything at all, and as they joined their bodies together as one, the joyous sounds of the beach drifted up to the open window of their first-floor room, and smothered them with happiness. When it was all over, they just lay there, resting on their sides towards each other, studying every single feature of their two faces – eyes, nose, lips, forehead, ears. They were two people in love, hopelessly, irretrievably in love, and for these few precious moments, there was no one else but them in the whole wide world. And yet, in the cold light of reality, Sunday knew only too well that this could be the last time she would ever see Gary, for once he had gone back home to America, it would be only too easy for him to forget. However, no matter what she thought in her heart of hearts, this particular moment belonged to her.

That evening, after one of Mrs Baggley's meals of toad-in-the-hole, mashed potatoes and red cabbage, Sunday and Gary made their way down to the beach. The day-trippers had long since gone, and all that remained now were one or two local residents walking their dogs, and a few elderly people taking in the warm evening air. Sunday and Gary strolled right round the complete curve of the bay, then ended up squatting on their heels at the rear of the beach with their backs to the promenade wall. It was an idyllic place to be at such an hour, for there was still plenty of daylight left as the hazy sun gradually turned into a huge ball of fire, and slowly dipped lower and lower into the sea. It was also an idyllic setting for the words Gary had been rehearsing all day.

'Sunday,' he said, sliding himself around on the sand to face her. 'What d'you say we get married?'

Sunday gasped and clutched a hand to her mouth.

Just in case she hadn't understood, he repeated what he had said in sign language.

'Well, what d'you say?' was his next question.

Too shocked for the moment, she just stared at him in disbelief. Then she used her hands to reply. First, the letter H, for which she tapped four fingers of her right hand against the palm of her left hand. For the letter O she used the forefinger of her right hand and tapped it against the index finger of her left hand. Finally, she entwined the fingers of both hands to show the letter W.

'*How*?' asked Gary, repeating the question with his own sign-talk. 'How d'you think! We find a preacher and get ourselves married.'

'What now? Before you go away?'

'Why not?'

Sunday found herself blushing. She had never considered acting so impulsively in her whole life. 'It's not possible,' she replied, with lips and hands. 'There's no time.'

'Are you telling me – you're not interested?'

Sunday shook her head. 'No. That's not what I'm telling you. But we can't, Gary. Not yet. I'm under-age, and, anyway, it wouldn't be fair.'

'Fair!' protested Gary. 'What the hell are you talking about?'

'It wouldn't be fair to you because when you get home, you might not get the chance to come back here again. And it's not fair to me because . . .' She hesitated. 'Because, after you've been home a while, you might want to change your mind.'

'Sunday,' he protested again, 'I love you.'

'I love you too, Gary. And I want to marry you,' she replied. 'But not until the war's over. Not until you come back.' Once she had finished sign-talking, she lowered her hands into her lap, and leaned her head back against the promenade wall.

Gary crawled back towards her side, and put his arm around her shoulders.

The sun dipped into the horizon, leaving the sea a burning, dark red. For a few moments, the two of them sat there, eyes closed, feeling the last warmth from the crimson sunset. Then Gary opened his eyes again, leaned across, and kissed Sunday full on the mouth.

'Have it your way, you obstinate young broad,' he said, once he came up for air. 'But I'll be back. With a ring, and a preacher, and a ticket on the *Queen Mary*. I promise you, Miss Limey Collins – I'll be back.' And with that, he bent down to kiss her once more.

'Wotcha, Sun!'

As Gary looked up with a start to find the silhouette of a young man standing between them and the rich-coloured sky, Sunday's eyes sprang open.

'Get 'round quite a bit, don't yer, mate,' the young man said coldly.

Sunday leapt to her feet immediately. 'What are you doing here, Ernie?' she snapped angrily. 'Just what the hell d'you think you're doing here!'

By this time, Gary had also raised himself up from the sand. 'Sunday?' he asked.

'Aren't yer goin' to introduce me to yer friend, Sun?' asked the young man, in a barbed voice.

'Ernie Mancroft, I presume?' asked Gary.

'I told you to keep away from me, Ernie,' shouted Sunday. 'I begged you! Why do you have to keep following me around everywhere? I don't want you! Can't you understand? I don't want you!'

Sunday's raised voice attracted the attention of an elderly couple, who were taking an evening stroll along the promenade just above them.

'Not very friendly, are yer, Sun?' said Ernie, who had clearly shed his army uniform, and was wearing an open shirt and old flannel trousers. 'It's no way ter treat the man you're goin' to marry.'

'Go away, Ernie! Leave me alone!'

'You heard what the lady said, feller,' warned Gary. 'Now why don't you call it a day, and get the hell out of here.'

'Ask 'er to show you the engagement ring I bought 'er,' said Ernie, quite calmly.

Sunday gasped, as Gary swung her a stunned look.

'Liar!' she yelled. Then she turned back to Gary. 'This is what he does all the time,' she spluttered. 'He tries to drive me mad by telling one lie after another about me!'

'*Did* he buy you a ring?' asked Gary, with uncertainty.

'Of course he didn't! He's made it up just to cause trouble between you and me!'

'Come on, Sun,' said Ernie, showing impatience. 'Stop all this shit, an' let's get out of 'ere!'

As he grabbed hold of her arm, Gary reached out and pulled Ernie's hand away.

This angered Ernie. 'Get your 'ands off me – Yank!' he snarled.

Gary stood his ground. 'Leave her alone, feller,' he said. 'Just beat it!'

'No, Gary!' yelled Sunday, trying to stand in between him and Ernie. 'Keep out of this – *please*!'

But it was too late. Ernie suddenly threw one hell of a punch at Gary, landing it full on his mouth. Gary was sent reeling back on to the sand.

The angry scene below proved too frightening for the elderly couple who were watching from the promenade wall, and they quickly rushed off.

Ernie grabbed hold of Sunday at the back of her neck, and started to frogmarch her along the beach.

'Leave me alone, Ernie!' shouted Sunday, who was doing her best to break loose from him.

By this time, Gary, with blood streaming from a gash in his lip, was pulling himself up from the sand. Wiping the blood away with the back of his hand, he then sprinted after Sunday, and, in true American-football style, threw himself straight at Ernie, bringing him to the ground.

Sunday's screams echoed out along the beach as the two men started to fight. Knowing the brutal strength Ernie had always used on anyone who had ever dared to challenge him, Sunday did her best to separate him from Gary. Despite her desperate calls for help, the two men flew at each other like bull-terriers.

This was a fight that was clearly going to be determined one way or another, and with Sunday looking on helplessly, the two men were soon slogging it out right down to the evening tide that was rolling in gently along the shoreline, two tiny figures silhouetted against the fading light of the horizon and the shimmering glow of a flaming-red sea. Every so often there were shouts of abuse from both of them, with first one of them flinching, and then another faltering. But what Sunday hadn't expected was that Gary, despite his lean physique, was landing one iron-hard blow after another on Ernie, who was constantly knocked off balance. After several minutes of this, Sunday thought that it was only a matter of time before both men killed each other. And as they fought, their feet were splashing around in the oncoming tide, sending up great sprays of crimson-coloured water which seemed to evaporate into the rapidly darkening sea.

Suddenly, however, the savage fight ended just as abruptly as it had begun. With one almighty right hook, Gary landed a decisive blow on Ernie's chin, which sent the boy with a great plop right into a gentle, rolling wave.

Sunday couldn't believe what she had been seeing, and the first thing she did was to rush down to Gary at the water's edge.

'Oh Gary!' she cried. 'I'm sorry. I'm so, so sorry!'

Gary, blood streaming from the cut in his lip, threw his arms around her and kissed her. Then, thoroughly bruised and exhausted, he waded into the water, grabbed hold of Ernie's hand, and dragged him back to the beach.

From the distance came the sound of police whistles.

# Chapter 21

On the day Gary flew back home to America, it was reported in the newspapers that Italy's power-crazed *Duce*, Benito Mussolini, had been captured by partisans, and executed. When she saw the headline in the *Daily Sketch*, Sunday immediately thought of the young Italian POW, Mario. She wondered if he had now arrived back home in his native Tuscany, and what he would find when he got there. She also wondered how his wife and young children would react to his disability, and whether they would have the strength to love and support him during the struggle he faced to rebuild his life.

Sunday had deliberately not gone to Ridgewell Airbase to see the departure of Gary's Air Force transport plane. Knowing that she might never see him again was pain enough, and to have to watch his plane disappear up into the huge white clouds was more than she could bear. That was why at ten o'clock in the morning, at the precise time that Gary's flight was due to take off, she made quite sure that she was doing work inside the chicken house where she was able to cut herself off from what was taking place on the runway less than a mile away.

Sunday had got to know quite a lot about Gary during their final weekend together at Thorpe Bay. Not only did she discover that, during his savage fight with Ernie on the beach, he possessed far more physical strength than she had imagined, but he also confessed to writing one short poem every day of his life, as a kind of diary. He even managed to capture a moment of that drama on the beach in a few lines which he had scribbled down on the back of an old envelope:

> Times past, times present, and times still to come,
> Love, fight, cry, we all are one.
> I knew the kid was wrong, but how could I be right
> To test my feelings' love in a senseless fight?
> Can love have an enemy that it is forced to bruise?
> I'll hold on to that love, a love I shall not lose.

However, when Sunday told Gary that she didn't really understand poetry because she had never read any, he answered by telling her that she should never close her mind to any experience, and that included learning to talk with sign language.

Knowing that Gary was no longer around was clearly going to leave a gap in Sunday's life that she would find hard to accept.

Sunday's decision to leave the Women's Land Army had been accepted by the authorities, mainly on the grounds of her disability, but also because she had been a volunteer and not a conscript. Even so, it wasn't easy for her to say goodbye to the girls at Cloy's Farm, for over the past six months they had become such a part of her life. In any case, she had come to hate goodbyes. Ever since she had been injured in the flying bomb explosion back at Briggs Bagwash, it had been nothing else. First it was Pearl, then young Ronnie Cloy, then Erin and Jinx, and now Gary. From beginning to end, the war had hurt deeply.

Sunday finally left Ridgewell after a tearful farewell with the other girls at Cloy's Farm. She was particularly sad to leave Maureen, the deaf and dumb girl whose sunny and cheerful nature had been such an inspiration, and the epileptic Ruthie, who often made her laugh by shaking her fist in anger at the sky every time she saw the vapour trail of a V-1 or V-2 rocket. But Sunday also knew that she was going to miss toffee-nosed Sue from Birmingham, with her disapproving ways and endless games of one-upmanship, and Sheil, strange disoriented Sheil, who showed every sign of remaining inside her shell for the rest of her life. Although all of them promised to meet up again one day, when Mr Barnes, the local taximan, arrived to collect Sunday and her baggage, the wrench she felt was unbearable, and she cried all the way to Great Yeldham. However, it wasn't until she was on the train to Liverpool Street, that she managed to pluck up enough courage to open Sheil's parting gift. It turned out to be what Sunday herself had asked for, a small, coloured crayon sketch.

It was of the red house across the fields, young Ronnie Cloy's favourite view.

'Have you heard about Hitler? Killed himself! In his bunker – in Berlin. Good riddance to bad rubbish say I!'

Aunt Louie was not renowned for her subtlety, but she was a great one for reading out newspaper headlines.

'Sounds like that Eva Braun woman was with him. The Russians say their flesh was all burnt-up.'

'Please, Louie!' gasped Madge, who found the description distasteful. 'I don't want to hear all that terrible talk when we're trying to have supper. Besides, Sunday's only just got home. We should be celebrating.'

'Well, I'm not celebrating 'til the war's over,' sniffed Louie, indignantly. 'Not 'til they've got the whole damn lot of them – Goering, Goebbels, Himmler!'

'It's all over bar the shouting,' said Madge, irritably, whilst trying to serve up mashed potatoes with the Spam fritters and dried peas. 'We've waited this long, we must just be patient.'

Sunday hadn't been watching either her mum's or her aunt's lips, so she had no idea what either had been saying. All she knew was that she found it deeply depressing to be home again. As much as she loved her home, the moment she walked through the front door and saw the warm afternoon sun creeping into the front parlour, she felt as though she was being shut away in a cell, and that her real 'home' was back there in the fields of Essex. On top of that, every time her Aunt Louie opened her mouth, it was like a red rag to a bull, and even her poor old mum's over-loving care was getting her down. All this and she had only been back at 'the Buildings' for less than two hours.

'It's good to have you home again, Sunday,' said Madge, once they had all settled down to the meal. 'I can't tell you how much we've missed you. Isn't that true, Louie?'

Louie pretended she hadn't heard, and started cutting up her Spam fritters.

'I've missed you too, Mum,' replied Sunday, who felt awful to know that she didn't mean it.

'We've been so proud of you, doing your bit for the war, despite everything you've been through. Anyway, I've cleaned out your room from top to bottom. You'll know the difference from having to sleep with a whole lot of other girls.'

Sunday smiled weakly and tried to swallow some mashed potato. If only her mum knew how she already yearned to be back at the barn, sharing her room with her friends.

'Not much to come back to, this place!' said Louie, with her mouth full of Spam fritter. 'Men sleeping with other people's wives all the time. It's disgusting!'

If she had been blessed with longer legs, Madge would have kicked her sister's foot under the table. 'Don't be so coarse, Louie,' she said. 'Doll and Joe must sort out their own problems. It's none of our business.'

'Joe Mooney's just like every other man,' snapped Louie. 'He's sex-mad, and has no right to treat his wife and kids like that. As far as I'm concerned, that *is* our business.'

This time, Sunday had managed to read her aunt's lips. 'Why do you hate men so much, Auntie?' she asked quite briskly.

Louie was caught off guard by her niece's sharp question. 'I don't know what you're talking about,' she said uncomfortably. 'I didn't say I hated men.'

'No, but that's what you meant,' Sunday quietly insisted. 'Some women behave badly too. I know I do sometimes.'

This remark prompted Madge to take a sly look at Sunday over the top of her thin-framed, oyster-shell spectacles.

'I wasn't talking about you.' And without turning to look at Madge, Louie added, 'I was talking about married people who have to go around with other married people.'

Madge ignored her sister's pointed remark.

'Even Jack Popwell's got himself a floosie.'

'Louie!' snapped Madge. 'That's a horrible thing to say. Ivy Westcliff is a nice, respectable woman. She's a widow and Jack's a widower. They're entitled to some companionship if they want it.'

'Yes,' snorted Louie, her back straightening as she ate. 'Provided that's *all* they want.'

For some reason, Aunt Louie's remark amused Sunday, who asked provocatively, 'Tell me, Auntie. D'you think it's wrong for people to sleep together before they get married?'

Louie straightened her back even more. 'I certainly do!'

'Oh, that's a shame,' Sunday replied mischievously. 'I've done it lots of times.'

Louie nearly choked on a forkful of peas, whilst Madge pretended that she hadn't heard anything.

Luckily, a difficult scene was avoided when a sparrow suddenly flew into the room through the wide-open window, and flapped all around the place in panic. This gave Madge a welcome opportunity to leap up from the table.

By this time, Louie, who was terrified of birds, was shielding her hair with both hands and screaming her head off. 'That's Jack Popwell!' she yelled hysterically. 'He's been feeding them out on his windowsill again!' She screamed out in panic as the poor, terrified little creature dive-bombed her across the table and shot right past her.

There was a huge grin on Sunday's face as she watched the drama, and when Madge finally persuaded the sparrow to escape out through the window again, she felt quite sad. In many ways, Sunday envied the small creature's successful dash for freedom.

The redbrick walls of 'the Buildings' were bathed in the magnificent dazzling light of morning sunshine, and as she made her way across the back yard, Sunday thought that the place had never looked better. She wasn't sure whether this had anything to do with the buzz of excitement about the imminent end of the war, or because the residents she saw standing around in their usual small groups were actually laughing and joking with one another. Whatever it was, however, the atmosphere had been completely transformed from the last time she was home.

Sunday had no idea what she was going to do with her life. It was one thing giving up her job in the Women's Land Army, but quite a different matter when it came to thinking about the future. On her first morning after returning home, her immediate inclination was to call on Bess, but aware that her old mate had only just got to bed after a night's 'work', she decided to take a stroll.

Holloway Road had suddenly come back to life. Ever since the threat of further V-bomb attacks had subsided, an air of confidence had returned and even though it was only a weekday, the shops were crowded with people, the windows had lost their protective sticky tape, and nobody was bothering to glance up anxiously at the sky.

Unfortunately, however, the happy mood amongst the shoppers was not matched by the window displays, for there were obvious signs of shortages everywhere. Sunday was convinced that some of the old-fashioned knee-length dresses in Jones Brothers' window had been there for months, and the so-called two-piece 'high fashion' women's suits in Selby's were so drab they could have been made for the inmates of Holloway Prison. And what about those prices! What a nerve! The brightest place was the good old 'threepenny and sixpenny' Woolworth's store, but even there Sunday found it pretty hard to find much for threepence or sixpence. But at the Nag's Head, she was thrilled to see a man selling ice-cream from his barrow again, and as the sun was beginning to hot up, she promptly bought herself a penny cornet.

When she stopped outside the poor old Gaumont Cinema, Sunday found the place in a pretty sorry state. Following the 'doodlebug' explosion there the previous year, every entrance and exit of the once beautiful tile-fronted building was now boarded up, and local thugs had desecrated the faded and torn film posters with a whole lot of stupid messages. Feeling despondent, she decided to make her way home. But, just as she was about to do so, in the distance she suddenly caught sight of Doll Mooney hurrying towards her from the Upper Holloway end of the road, bumping little Josie up and down in her pushchair on the way.

Doll didn't know whether to laugh or cry when she eventually reached Sunday, and threw her arms around her. 'Oh, Sun!' she spluttered, having forgotten that Sunday needed to read her lips to know what she was saying. 'It's wonderful ter see yer again, girl! I don't know why it is, but you've been on me mind now ever since yer joined up.' Finally, she remembered to face Sunday. ''Ow are yer, girl? 'Ome fer good now, I 'ope?'

Sunday smiled and nodded.

'Isn't it wonderful ter fink it's nearly all over? I can 'ardly believe it! They say Jerry might give in by the end of the week. Mind you, I'll believe that when I see it, but oh, Jesus, it'll be so good ter start gettin' our lives sorted out again.'

Sunday decided it wasn't worth saying anything, because Doll was chatting so fast she was hardly coming up for breath.

'Can't buy a flag, yer know. All gone! I walked all up Seven Sisters and Holloway Road yesterday, and I couldn't even buy a small Union Jack. All they 'ad left was a Chinese one or somefink. I ask yer, who wants ter put up a Chinese flag!'

'How's Joe, Doll?' Knowing how things were between Doll and her husband, Sunday hesitated about mentioning his name, but then thought it better to get it over and done with as soon as possible.

'No idea, love,' Doll replied, shoving little Josie's dummy back into the child's mouth. ''Aven't seen 'im since last Tuesday. Gone to his uvver bed in Stepney, I reckon.'

Sunday was amazed by Doll's indifference to her husband's infidelity.

'But, don't you miss him, Doll?' Sunday asked tentatively.

'Oh no, love,' Doll replied firmly. 'After all, what the eye don't see the 'eart don't miss. I've just taken Josie ter see 'er grandma, up Thorpedale Road. She says if Joe's old man was still alive, 'e'd bash the daylights out of 'im. But I told 'er there's no use worryin'. Joe'll be back when 'e's good and ready.'

Sunday shook her head. She was bewildered by Doll's attitude.

'It don't do no good,' said Doll, becoming more serious. 'This bleedin' war's turned a lot of people's 'eads. Joe's like a bleedin' sex machine. If I'd known what 'e was goin' ter be like when we got married, I might've fawt again. But then—' She sighed and tried to retie the ribbon holding her hair together on the top of her head. 'When yer fink of what might 'appen ter some people, like that poor woman in number seven—'

Sunday's eyes widened immediately. 'Number seven?' she asked anxiously.

'Yes. Mrs Butler,' replied Doll. 'Now I don't hold with – well, you know, the way she carries on an' all that. But I'd 'ate ter fink anyfin's 'appened to 'er.'

Sunday was going out of her mind. 'Doll!' she snapped. 'What are you talking about? What's happened to Bess Butler?'

'Din't yer mum tell yer? Everyone in "the Buildin's" is talkin' about it. Poor soul – she's gone missin'.'

Alf Butler showed Sunday into his parlour, which smelt of sweat, stale boiled cabbage, and fish. The flat was virtually in darkness, with the only light coming from a forty-watt bulb in the standard lamp at the side of the sofa.

'I 'aven't opened the windows or the curtains since I 'eard about Bess,' said the old boy, who clearly hadn't shaved for a couple of days either, and looked strained and distraught. ''Til I know she's safe, it's goin' ter stay like that.'

Sunday sat in a chair facing him. 'What's happened to her, Alf?'

'She just din't come 'ome one mornin'. I always know it's 'er when I 'ear the front door go, that's usually about seven. But when it got to after ten, I knew somefin' was up. Oh yes, I knew all right.'

'Did you – call the police?' Sunday asked tentatively.

Alf nodded. 'Some smartarsed bluebottle come round 'ere an' asked me a whole lot er questions. But I din't know what 'e was talkin' about 'alf the time. All I know is, two weeks ago last Tuesday, my gel went off ter work at her usual time, but she never come 'ome.'

Sunday bit her knuckle anxiously. Because of the dim light in the room, she was having great difficulty reading the old boy's lips. 'Did the police tell you what they're going to do about it?' she asked.

Alf shook his head. 'They're pursuin' their investigations,' he spluttered, making an attempt to adjust his ill-fitting false teeth. ''Til then, they're puttin' 'er on the Missin' Persons List.'

Sunday thought hard for a moment. What if the police started asking awkward questions? What if they should try to locate the hotel where Bess was supposed to have worked as a night receptionist? If Alf was told the truth about where the money had been coming from all this time, it would probably kill him.

'Now you listen to me, Alf,' she said, leaning closer so that he could see as well as hear her. 'You're not to worry, d'you hear? I'm sure there's a straightforward explanation for all this, and we'll find Bess – sooner or later, we *will* find her. OK?'

The old boy hesitated, then nodded.

'Now, how are you managing about food?' Sunday asked.

'The woman couple er doors down brought me in a kipper yesterday mornin'. It was good of 'er, seein' as 'ow sniffy they all are in this block. I ate a bit of it. But I don't eat a lot. No point. Not till Bess gets back.'

Sunday didn't see her mum until later that evening. It was soon after a Wednesday evening Salvation Army Band concert on Highbury Fields, which was well attended, for not only was the weather hot and muggy, but people had come along to treat it as a premature celebration for the end of the war.

The concert itself had been a roaring success, with crowds of onlookers joining in with the band and singers as they let rip with a selection of some of the most joyous hymns of praise. As usual, Sunday's mum was looking as pretty as a picture in her black and piped red uniform with matching bonnet and bows, although at times it was quite difficult to pick her out behind the rather large euphonium, which obviously required a great deal of puffing and blowing. Madge's friend, Mr Billings, wasn't far away either, for although he wasn't an official member of the 'Army', he was helping out by turning the sheet music for Captain Sarah Denning at the harmonium.

When the concert was over, everyone was invited to have a cup of tea at a stall which had been set up earlier in the evening by two of the 'Army' volunteers. Although there was a charge of a penny a cup, it was made quite clear that the proceeds were to go to the Salvation Army's fund for bombed-out war victims. However, Sunday didn't have to pay for her cup, for her mum had managed to sneak theirs out free of charge. The snag was that whilst they were drinking their tea, Sunday had to endure the ordeal of being smothered by well-meaning attention from several of her mum's 'Army' friends. Within a few minutes, the caring smiles and over-exaggerated lip-talk, which told her such things as she was 'a credit to Madge' and 'what a brave and courageous girl you are', drove Sunday mad. It was not that she did not admire these wonderful and unselfish people who had done so much to relieve the suffering of tragic war victims, but that by praising Sunday for the way in which she had coped with her disability, they were only making her feel different to everyone else, which is the last thing she wanted. So the moment they had finished their tea, she persuaded her mum to take a slow stroll with her across the Fields.

'Thank you for coming to the concert,' said Madge, making sure Sunday could see her lips moving whilst they were strolling. 'I know it embarrasses you when my friends say nice things about you, but I can't help feeling proud.'

'What are you proud *of*, Mum?' Sunday asked. 'I'm going to be deaf for the rest of my life.'

'I'm proud because you've learnt how to come to terms with it.'

'Stop it, Mum!' Sunday brought them to an abrupt halt. 'You should know that I haven't come to terms with anything. There's a battle going on inside me that keeps wanting to tear me apart.'

'Once the war's over—'

'It won't make any difference when the war's over, Mum,' Sunday insisted. 'I had nearly eighteen years of hearing the sounds of everyday life, eighteen years of answering people when I heard them talking to me, eighteen years of listening to music on the wireless, dogs barking downstairs in the backyard of "the Buildings", and people singing on the pictures. Have you any idea how I felt knowing everyone was singing their hearts out at your concert tonight, and *I* couldn't hear them? No, Mum. You don't give all that up without questioning whether life in the future is going to be worthwhile.'

They started to stroll again, and after a few minutes they came to the perimeter of the Fields facing Highbury Corner. From this position, Sunday had one of her favourite views, for this was where all the roads came together for traffic heading along Upper Street to the Angel, Islington, to Dalston, Hackney, and the City, and to Holloway, the Archway, and the Great North Road beyond.

'So where do you go from here?' asked Madge, more subdued now after all Sunday had confided to her.

'I don't know, Mum. I've got a lot of thinking to do.'

For a moment or so, they stood watching the evening traffic as it separated and made off in different directions. They looked out at the gap on the opposite side of the road which had once been the main post office, but was destroyed by a 'doodlebug', and the brewer's horse and cart which was just delivering a fresh supply of beer to the pub on the corner of Holloway Road and Upper Street. Best of all, were the street and shop lights, now back on for the first time since the start of the war. There seemed to be so much happening, that neither Sunday nor her mum said anything. But eventually, Madge knew that she just had to get something off her mind.

'Sunday,' she said reluctantly. 'Is it true what you said to Auntie and me last night? About – sleeping with someone?'

Sunday hesitated before replying. Then she said, 'You're the second person to ask me that question.'

'But is it true?'

Sunday was determined to evade her mum's enquiry. 'It's true that someone's asked me to marry him.'

Madge's tiny eyes widened behind her spectacles. 'Sunday! Is it the American boy you told me about when you were home at Christmas? The one who was missing in action?'

'Yes. But don't get too excited. He's gone back to America. I'll probably never see him again.'

'But you'd like to marry him.'

'Yes.'

'So you love him?'

Sunday sighed. 'Yes, I love him,' she said, wishing desperately that Gary was there right now to help her through this conversation.

'I'm so happy for you,' said Madge, taking Sunday's hand and clasping it tightly. 'But you should have told me. Sunday, why didn't you tell me?'

Sunday looked away for a moment. When she turned back again, her mum was still waiting for a reply. 'There are some things that I don't like to talk about,' she said. 'Just like you,' she added pointedly.

Madge was a bit taken aback by that remark. 'What do you mean?'

Sunday paused a moment. 'Mum,' she asked, 'why didn't you tell me that Bess Butler has gone missing?'

# Chapter 22

Winston Churchill delayed his announcement that the war in Europe was finally over until 3 p.m. on the afternoon of Tuesday, 8 May. By then, practically every windowsill in 'the Buildings' had a flag of some sort hanging from it, most of them the Union Jack of course, but also the flags of other Allied nations such as the USA, Russia, and France, and there was even a solitary Chinese flag hanging out from the top of Doll and Joe Mooney's kitchen window. There was red, white, and blue bunting everywhere, over every outside door, every gate, every tree, and right along the Holloway Road side of all the residential blocks. The end of more than five long tragic years of war had brought a surge of euphoria throughout the country, and everyone in 'the Buildings' intended to make the most of it.

During the morning, Sunday helped set up trestle-tables in the backyard, where a tea party for the kids was being held in the afternoon, and a knees-up for the adults in the evening. There was quite a lot of griping from some of the women residents, who were furious that the Government had not allowed any extra food rations for the celebrations, but luckily everyone chipped in with tins of Spam and pilchards for the sandwiches, and so many bowls of different-flavoured jelly that the kids could have floated in it – and some of them did! Earlier in the morning, during a heavy thunderstorm, Sunday had made a brief, emotional visit to the desolate bombsite of Briggs Bagwash. For a few minutes, she stood there alone in the pouring rain, with memories churning over inside, and raindrops pelting down on to her umbrella. Then she went on to Highgate Cemetery to place a small bunch of tulips and irises on Pearl's grave, where the earth had now settled, and a headstone fitted with Pearl's name engraved along with the words, 'A Loving Daughter'. Sadly, whilst she was arranging the flowers into an old jamjar, she had been unable to hear the sound of church bells which were ringing out in the distance across the rooftops of London for the first time since the start of the war. It seemed ironic that Sunday's tearful few minutes alone at her old mate's graveside should be in such marked contrast to the wild, abandoned joy that was now sweeping through all those who had survived one of the most fierce, ugly, and dangerous conflicts the world had ever known.

The evening VE Day party in the backyard of 'the Buildings' turned out to be the happiest and most carefree event the residents had ever seen. Once the tables had been cleared after the kids' tea party, the adults took over, out came the booze, and the knees-up began. Someone had provided an upright piano, and everyone sang their heads off. Sunday was amazed at the talent around, and she laughed herself silly as she watched the most unlikely residents teaming up to do everything from the old-fashioned waltz to 'Ballin' the Jack'. Doll Mooney was having the time of her life. Pissed as a newt and wearing a short party dress that was bursting at the seams, she hardly missed a single dance, leaving her husband Joe, back home from his sexual exploits in Stepney with the bus-conductress, to watch from the sidelines. However, the undoubted stars of the evening were Jack Popwell and his lady-friend, Ivy Westcliff, who showed professional expertise in their own interpretation of the tango. The only person who did not approve was Aunt Louie, who sat on a bench, smoking a cigar one of the men had given her, and chatting with two of her women friends from Swiss Cottage, all of whom were making wry comments about everything and everybody. Throughout the proceedings, there was an air of fervent patriotism, with frequent toasts to the King and Queen, to Princess Elizabeth and her sister Princess Margaret Rose, and most especially to the Prime Minister, '*Good ol' Winnie! Gord bless 'im!*' One teenager had even painted his own face in the colours of a Union Jack, and another had a huge VE printed on his forehead. Sunday loved it all, but by the time everyone had done their umpteenth 'Hokey Cokey' and 'Knees Up Mother Brown!', the strain of not being able to hear anything that was going on became too much for her, so she left.

In Holloway Road there were still puddles left over from the severe thunderstorm earlier in the day. But at least the storm had cleared the air, and as it was now almost midnight, Sunday found it quite pleasant to walk. There were plenty of revellers around, and it was clear that the street party celebrations would be going on all through the night. In many ways, it was like New Year's Eve, with groups of people wearing paper hats and blowing party favours, arms linked together as they sang and skipped deliriously up and down the pavement kerbs. All the fears and frustrations of more than five years of war were at last being released, and the streets of Holloway were bursting with exhilaration.

As she walked, however, Sunday couldn't help thinking about what life would be like after the 'night before'. At the outbreak of war she had been only twelve years old; as far as she was concerned, the trials and tribulations of adulthood meant nothing to her. Despite the Blitz and all the horrors of aerial bombardment, life in her early teens had been a great big adventure, it meant fun and dancing with her mates, and the traditional teenage contempt for anyone who told her what she should or shouldn't do. And in some ways, even the nights spent down in the public shelter at 'the Buildings' were exciting, because it gave her the chance to spend at least some time away from the claustrophobic atmosphere of her own tiny bedroom. But being grown-up was different. It meant taking things seriously and being responsible. And being deaf in a world full of sound was something even more alien.

On the pavement outside the Nag's Head pub, a crowd of customers in a boisterous mood were singing their heads off. Sunday was the only one who couldn't make out what the song was, but the streets around were echoing to the sound of 'There'll Always Be An England'. As she made her way down Seven Sisters Road, Sunday found it the same outside The Enkel pub and also further along, outside The Eaglet on the corner of Hornsey Road. Despite the lateness of the hour, there were crowds everywhere, and all the pavements were littered with coloured streamers and empty beer bottles. But it was such a joy to see the street gas lamps lighting up the shopfronts again.

Sunday decided to make her way back to 'the Buildings' via Hornsey Road. Although she couldn't hear any of the endless parties that were still going on in nearby Kinloch street, light was streaming out of open windows everywhere, as if in a final act of defiance to the long years of blackout.

When she had reached as far as Charlie Brend's sweet-shop, she stopped for a few moments to look at the darkened window with its huge V-sign picked out in white sticky tape. But as she did so, she suddenly realised that her own face was reflected there. Luckily, there was still a semblance of vanity left inside her, so she reached up with her hands to ruffle her shoulder-length strawberry-blonde hair. It was at that moment that she felt the real pangs of despair. Despair about her lack of direction, about not having Gary around to love and caress her, no Jinx or Pearl to confide in, and a home-life that was in danger of totally overwhelming her with cosiness. Unable to bear looking at her reflection any longer, she closed her eyes tight and thought of Gary, and of how he and his buddies would be celebrating the end of the war in Europe. Then she thought of Jinx and her forthcoming baby, and her mates at Cloy's Farm, and what they would all be getting up to on this one extraordinary night of their lives. Then she thought of her mum. And she tensed.

'Mrs Butler is nothing to do with us, Sunday.'

With her eyes still tightly closed, Sunday could vividly picture her mum's face, cold and taut, as she struggled to answer Sunday's awkward question.

'I don't know why she's gone missing. She led a very secret life. I'm not surprised this has happened.'

Sunday hated the way her mum was talking about Bess as though she was already dead. 'What *has* happened, Mum?' she had asked. 'What d'you know about it all?'

'I only know that God moves in mysterious ways, His wonders to perform.'

This had been the moment when, for the first time in her life, Sunday had seen her mum in a totally different light. She had always known how devoted to Salvation Army life her mum had been, but in these last months that devotion had become an obsession. '*God moves in mysterious ways*'? How could she say such a thing when by now Bess Butler could be lying in a back alley somewhere with her throat slit? Where was God's love now, where was His compassion?

'All we can do now for Mrs Butler is to pray, pray for her soul, pray for forgiveness. Most of all, we must pray for her husband, and give God's thanks for this poor man's tolerance.'

The image of Madge Collins's tight little lips forming a small circle as she spoke filled Sunday with despair and disbelief. The more she could see her, the more she wanted to know what was lurking behind the mask of the woman she had always known as her adopted mum.

Sunday's eyes suddenly sprang open, and she found herself staring straight at the reflection in Charlie Brend's shop window. But in her mind's eye, it wasn't the reflection of her own face that she could see.

It was of Bess Butler.

30 April

381 USAF
South Carolina
USA

My very own Sunday,

Oh Jesus, I can't tell you how much I've missed you! Ever since I got here, I've thought of nothing and no one but you.

Gary's first letter came like a bolt out of the blue, and it sent Sunday into raptures. She hadn't expected to hear from him ever again, and even to touch the very paper that he had written on made her feel as though she was being held in his arms.

The flight back was hell! Forty of us guys locked up in this broken-down transporter, and hardly enough chow to keep us going for more than ten minutes. I tell you, Sun, it made me wish I was back there eating with you at the good old British Restaurant in Halstead – yeah, *even* the British Restaurant!

Sunday read the letter over and over again. She loved it most of all because Gary wrote about everything he could think of, and that included a description of his new colonel, who, until recently, had been assigned to General MacArthur's command in South-east Asia. She was also especially interested to learn that Gary had been given forty-eight hours' furlough, which he used for a quick visit home to his folks back in Whitefish, Montana.

Told Ma all about you. *Everything* about you. She said you sounded pretty good. I said *pretty* good? Sunday is sensational! Anyway, both she and Pops are looking forward to meeting you, my sister Jane, too. Once we get the rest of this war over, I'll be back to kidnap you!

It was only when Gary mentioned 'the rest of this war', that she remembered that although it was all over in Europe, there were still the Japanese to contend with. For a moment or so, that brought a sinking feeling inside her stomach, for she hoped that, after all Gary had been through, the war for him would now be over. But by the time she had read eighteen pages of Gary's handwriting, she felt so cheered, it gave her the determination to think positively. And after she had kissed his scrawled signature on the last page, she was thrilled to see that there was still more to come.

PS Hope you're keeping up with the sign-talking. Don't let me down now!
PPS Some lines from Keats (he's a Brit, like you!) just so's you know that I'm mad about you!

> I cannot look on any budding flower,
> But my fond ear, in fancy at thy lips,
> And hearkening for a love-sound, doth devour
> Its sweet in the wrong sense:– Thou dost eclipse
> Every delight with sweet remembering,
> And grief unto my darling joys dost bring.

Don't forget me, Sun!

Sunday hadn't been to the Royal Northern Hospital since she was an outpatient at the Ear, Nose, and Throat Clinic. But her letter from Gary had spurred her into making an appointment with the Rehabilitation Officer, in the hope that she could receive some guidance about future career prospects. She knew it wasn't going to be an easy time to look for work, for now that the war in Europe was over, demobilisation was going to be a top priority for servicemen who were anxious to return to their old jobs. It was also not going to be easy to place someone who was so severely disabled.

Helen Gallop, the ENT Rehabilitation Officer, turned out not only to be very helpful, but she also had one or two friends who lived in 'the Buildings'.

'First of all,' she asked, using lips and hands, 'how've you been getting on with your sign language?'

Sunday demonstrated by answering with both lips and clear and precise signs, 'Difficult. But I'm doing my best.'

'Excellent! Splendid!' replied Helen. As the temperature was in the eighties outside, she had a small electric fan on the filing cabinet behind her, which helped her to cope with the perspiration on her forehead, which she wiped frequently with her handkerchief. 'You've obviously had a good teacher.'

Sunday had liked Helen on sight, because she was not much older than herself, and, unlike some people Sunday had come across, hadn't treated her like some kind of freak.

Helen took off her spectacles, and put them down on to the small desk in front of her. 'What sort of work would you like to do most of all, Sunday?' she asked.

Sunday shrugged her shoulders.

'No idea at all?' asked Helen.

Again, Sunday shrugged her shoulders. 'I had no idea that I was going to be deaf for the rest of my life.'

'What did you want to be – before what happened to you?'

'I wanted to teach dancing.'

Helen's face lit up into a bright smile. 'Really?' She got up and brought the electric fan across to her desk so that Sunday could feel its benefit too. 'What kind of dancing?'

'Anything. Dance-hall stuff, I suppose.'

'Marvellous!' Helen said. 'If that's what you want to do, you should do it.'

Sunday sat up straight in her chair. 'Pardon?' she asked, puzzled.

'There's no reason why you shouldn't teach dance if that's what you want to do.'

Sunday thought she hadn't understood properly, so, looking a bit taken aback, she asked, 'How?'

The office was small and airless, and Helen sipped from a glass of water before continuing. 'Do you like children?' she asked, with both lips and hands.

Sunday, puzzled, thought a moment. 'Yes,' she answered. 'Why?'

Helen perched on the edge of her desk. 'Teaching children can be quite rewarding. Especially children like yourself.'

Sunday was now even more puzzled. 'What do you mean?'

'Deaf children, Sunday. There's a school for deaf children in Drayton Park where you could be a great help.'

The word 'deaf' upset Sunday. 'But I'm no teacher,' she answered.

'You don't have to be. They're all quite young – mostly nursery age. All you have to do is to be with them, and be their friend.' Then she added pointedly, 'Teaching them how to dance would be a wonderful thing. It would be a way to show them that they're no different from anyone else.'

Sunday hesitated. It seemed such a crazy thing to ask her to do. And yet, wasn't that exactly what Gary had done for her back at the Base Christmas Dance? He gave her the confidence and determination to carry it through, and she did it.

'What d'you say?' asked Helen, eagerly awaiting Sunday's response. 'Think it's worth a try?'

Sunday hesitated briefly, then nodded her head.

Helen broke into a broad grin. 'Thank you,' she said, squeezing Sunday's shoulder. 'The pay's not much, I'm afraid, but at least you'll be doing something really worthwhile.' She got up from perching on the corner of her desk, and returned to her seat. 'Whatever happens, I promise you you'll not regret it.'

A few minutes later, Helen walked Sunday out towards the hospital reception. Before Sunday left, they stopped briefly.

'By the way,' said Helen, feeling confident enough to know that Sunday could understand her rather fast sign language. 'What's all this I hear about Ernie Mancroft?'

Sunday did a double-take. 'What d'you mean?' she asked rather tentatively.

'One of my friends in "the Buildings" told me about what happened down at Thorpe Bay. Is it true he was picked up by the Army, absent without leave?'

Sunday nodded warily.

'Then how come the court martial found him not guilty?'

Piccadilly Circus was looking very different from the last time Sunday had been there. Clearly VE Day had injected new life into the place, for people were milling about in the hot May sunshine, more cars and taxis were circling the boarded-up Eros site, and more neon signs such as GREYS TEA and GORDON'S GIN had joined the illustrious legends of BOVRIL and SCHWEPPES TONIC WATER.

When Sunday came up the steps of Piccadilly Circus Underground Station, the afternoon heat hit her like a steaming kettle, and she was glad that she had worn only a flimsy cotton dress instead of her well-worn lemon-coloured blouse and dark brown slacks. The pavements in Coventry Street were burning-hot, and she was not to know that behind her, in the Circus itself, some crank was trying to fry an egg on the steps below Eros.

Although it had been a couple of days since she'd had her interview with Helen Gallop, the news about Ernie Mancroft was still haunting her. How could he possibly have been let off by the Military Court who had tried him? Not only had he been AWOL, but he had stalked her right out to Ridgewell and Thorpe Bay, and also made an unprovoked attack on Gary. She was scared, really scared. If Ernie came looking for her again, he could be out to kill her.

But at this moment, her mind was on other things. Bess Butler was still missing, and something had to be done about it. That was why she had returned to the West End, to seek out some of Bess's old haunts, to try to find some clue. In Sunday's mind it just wasn't possible for someone like Bess to disappear without trace. Someone must have seen her somewhere, sometime, and if they were hiding her, there had to be a reason.

At Rainbow Corner, the usual groups of girls were hanging around the main entrance. Sunday thought some of them looked younger than ever, despite the fact that they had tried to disguise their age by plastering their faces with thick, greasy make-up. After a few minutes of sizing them up from a respectable distance, she decided whom she would approach first.

'Excuse me,' Sunday said, hoping that the young teenage girl with black hair piled on top of her head could understand her fractured speech. 'I'm looking for someone.'

'Aren't we all,' replied the girl, acidly, resentful that Sunday was trying to move in on her 'pitch'.

'You don't understand,' Sunday continued. 'I'm looking for my friend. She – works around here. Older than you.'

'Look, mate,' snapped the girl, pulling on a fag and leaving thick lipstick on it. 'If you're tryin' ter muscle in, I'll scratch yer bleedin' eyes out! Just bugger off!'

Sunday was not going to be intimidated. 'Her name's Bess. Bess Butler.'

The girl cringed visibly. 'Don't know 'er!'

'But she's often 'round here. Every night. Please, if you've seen her—'

'I said, I don't know 'er!'

Another girl, a redhead, joined them. She was older than the girl Sunday had approached, and with all the signs of quite a paunch, she had clearly had to squeeze into her above-the-knee, skin-tight dress. 'What's up, Jeannie?' she asked.

'Ask '*er*!' snapped the first girl, who hurriedly walked away.

Sunday spoke quickly. 'I'm trying to find my friend. She's gone missing, hasn't been seen for nearly three weeks. You must have seen her. *Somebody* must have seen her.'

'Wot's she like?' asked the redhead.

'Not very tall, dark curly hair, beautiful bluish-grey eyes.'

'Tits?'

Sunday was taken aback. 'Pardon?'

'What're 'er tits like!' the redhead snapped impatiently.

Sunday was embarrassed, but answered confidently, 'Very full. Please. Can you help me? I *must* find her.'

The redhead hesitated for a moment before answering. She spent a second or so sizing Sunday up. 'Tell me somefink,' she said. 'You deaf?'

Sunday stiffened, then nodded her head.

'I fawt so. Sorry about that, mate. Din mean no offence.'

'My friend's name is Bess Butler.'

As with the first girl, the redhead seemed to seize up.

'Why are you looking at me like that?' asked Sunday, fearing the worst. 'What's happened to her? Tell me!'

'I got nuffink ter tell yer, mate,' said the redhead, sympathetically. Then, after taking a cautious look over her shoulder, added, 'Sure, I know yer friend. But I ain't seen 'er around for a while.'

Sunday was about to ask more questions, but the redhead wouldn't let her.

'Take my tip, mate,' said the redhead, staring Sunday straight in the eye. 'A gel like you shouldn't be 'angin' 'round a place like this. It could be dangerous.'

'What's happened to her?' pleaded Sunday. 'Why won't you help me?'

'There ain't no 'elp for any of us, mate,' sighed the redhead. 'When we come out 'ere, we're on our own.' With that, she walked off.

For a few minutes, Sunday just stood there, surrounded by hordes of people swarming past her. She felt utter despair.

After searching the streets of Soho, Sunday decided to call it a day. It was obvious that the streetgirls were a close-knit community, and nothing in the world was going to persuade them to allow outsiders to penetrate their codes of silence. Feeling a desperate sense of frustration, she slowly made her way down Charing Cross Road past Leicester Square. Eventually, she reached Trafalgar Square, where people were feeding great flocks of greedy, fat pigeons with leftover scraps of bread, and as she headed off towards Whitehall, only once was she tempted to look up at the statue of Admiral Lord Nelson, standing proud and erect at the top of his Column, defying, as always, wind and rain, enemy bombs, VE Day and New Year's Eve celebrations, and, worst of all, hundreds of marauding pigeons.

At the Embankment, Sunday made straight for the refreshment wagon where only a few months before, she and Bess had sipped their tea whilst peering down at the fast-flowing waters of the River Thames. Apart from a couple of taxi-drivers, there were no customers at the wagon, so Sunday felt quite at ease as she approached the old bloke behind the counter.

'What can I do for yer, young miss?'

Sunday was only just tall enough to see over the top of the counter. 'I wonder if you can help me?' she asked. 'I'm looking for a friend of mine. A lady-friend.'

'Oh yes?' replied the old bloke, suspiciously.

Sunday was practically on tiptoe as she continued. 'I know it's been a long time, but a few months ago we came here and had a cup of tea together. She's older than me. Often comes here – she told me so.' She lowered her eyes when she added, 'Usually at night.'

The old bloke sized her up, then said, 'If it's that tart you're on about, I've already told the fuzz all I know.'

Sunday wanted to snap back at him, but she restrained herself. 'So – you haven't seen her in the last few weeks.'

'Who said I haven't?'

The old bloke's reply sent a rush of blood to Sunday's head. 'You mean – you *have* seen her?'

'Several times. The last time was just over a week ago, making 'er way over that bridge.'

Sunday swung around to look at Westminster Bridge, which was now bathed in early-afternoon sunshine. 'Are you sure?' she gasped excitedly. 'Are you absolutely sure?'

'Positive! Trouble is, by the time the fuzz got 'ere, she was gone.'

'Oh, thank you, thank you!' said Sunday, rushing off in the direction of the bridge.

The old bloke behind the counter watched her go and shook his head. 'These bloody gels. They'd sell themselves for a cup of char and a rock cake!'

The two taxi-drivers thought that was funny, and roared their heads off.

Once Sunday had turned the corner by the statue of Queen Boadicea, she was already on Westminster Bridge. When she was halfway across, she stopped and looked out downriver towards the Pool of London. Although it was still blistering-hot, there were signs that heavy thunderclouds were gathering, and that, hopefully, by that evening the air would feel a little more comfortable. In the distance she could see the dome of St Paul's Cathedral, nestling comfortably on top of Ludgate Hill, and her heart and mind went back to all those newspaper photographs of the Blitz, when St Paul's stood alone amidst the fire and smoke, a symbol of London's defiance. And further on, Tower Bridge, also a survivor of the war, despite everything that the *Luftwaffe* had tried to throw at it. She looked down into the water, and as she did so, she felt a surge of happiness sweep through her veins. Bess was alive! She was alive, and somebody had actually seen her. It was too good to be true. Whatever her mum said now would make no difference. God hadn't moved in 'mysterious ways' after all. Bess was alive! And as she stood on that bridge, with a pleasant, balmy breeze gently soothing her face, she felt like flinging her arms up into the air and shouting it out to the whole wide world: '*My mate Bess is alive!*'

Two days later, the police came to tell Alf Butler that they had reason to believe that the body of a woman they had just dragged out of the river was that of his wife, Bess.

She had been strangled.

# Chapter 23

The School for Deaf and Dumb Children in Drayton Park was set up in a semi-detached Edwardian house, just a stone's throw from the Arsenal Football Stadium. It was a fairly new enterprise, and operated mainly as a day centre for infants, of which there were no more than about two dozen regulars. As the Islington Borough Council were trying to cope with the huge bill for rebuilding in the aftermath of the war in Europe, the only funds that were available came from registered charities, such as the Royal School for Deaf and Dumb Children, and numerous private collections. The Principal was Mrs Eileen Roberts, who ran the place with her two assistants, Jacqui Marks and Pete Hawkins, all three of whom were deaf. Pete Hawkins was also mute.

When Sunday arrived for her first day at the school, she found it pretty hard going. It wasn't that she didn't like the people she was working with, but communicating with them meant that she had to use sign language more than she had ever done before, and as she had not been practising as much as Gary had asked her to, it was quite an ordeal. Unlike her colleagues, Sunday was not a trained teacher, so she took no real part in the children's education, and concentrated on their playtime activities.

For the first month, her task was to get to know the children. All of them were totally deaf, and half of them were also mute, but they played together as though there were no such things as the sounds of life. Sunday found the children irresistible, and as they gradually got to know her, they accepted her as one of their own. The hardest part of all was communication, and it took her a long time to learn their names. This she eventually achieved by following a technique suggested by Jacqui Marks, which was to identify each of the children as though they were a cat or a dog or some other animal, or a colour, or the sun or moon, or even an object such as a pencil or a storybook. But her greatest success occurred through a discovery which came to her quite by accident.

It happened one afternoon when she casually scratched her head whilst looking out of the window. When she turned back, she found all the kids scratching their heads, copying her. From that moment on, Sunday got them to copy practically every movement she made, from turning their heads side to side, clapping hands together, sitting down and getting up, and standing on their tiptoes. Even if she had been allowed to help teach them sign language, they were still a little too young to learn the hand alphabet. However, once or twice, she gave them an idea of what it was all about, when she got them to copy some of her hand-talk movements. The secret was imitation.

When it came to teaching them how to dance, it was obvious from the start that it was not going to be easy, and it took several weeks for the infants to understand what it was all about. The problem was that the kids who had been born deaf had no sense of rhythm, and it was difficult for them to imagine what rhythm actually was. Here Sunday enrolled the help of those kids who, like herself, had lost their hearing as a result of air-raid explosions. Beating time with her hands, she encouraged them all to partner one another, and they gradually swayed to and fro with the imaginary music, and copied Sunday as she danced with her partner, a small deaf and dumb boy named Joshua. Dancing then became a regular part of the kids' learning time, and when Sunday's Rehabilitation Officer, Helen Gallop, turned up to see how she was getting on, she was astonished to see a dancing session in progress, in which everyone was taking part, including the Principal and her two assistants.

By the middle of June, Sunday's work at the Deaf and Dumb School was already becoming a major part of her life. She was also making badly needed friends, for on several occasions she was asked out for the evening by either Helen Gallop or Jacqui Marks. Despite the new direction she was moving in, however, there were certain things that were still weighing her down.

After Bess Butler's death, Sunday was convinced that her world was about to fall apart. It was bad enough being told about the tragic circumstances of Bess's murder, '*raped and strangled by an unknown assailant, and dumped in the River Thames*', but it had been a fraught and heartbreaking experience to try to keep the real details of Bess's secret life from her husband, Alf. Luckily, the police had cooperated, and during their close questioning, had carefully avoided any mention of how and where Bess had made her money. '*Investigations are continuing*,' said the police, which meant that, like so many similar crimes committed during the war, there wasn't a hope in hell of convicting anyone for Bess's murder.

The cremation ceremony had been a particularly harrowing event, for only a handful of mourners had turned up, and none of them from 'the Buildings'. Sunday had felt the loss of Bess more than she had imagined she ever would. When she saw the coffin disappearing behind that unreal curtain, she somehow felt that a part of her own body was leaving her.

Sunday was also getting worried about Gary. Since he had arrived back in the States, she had received only a couple of letters from him. Every morning, she delayed leaving home until the postman had called, and when, by the middle of June, he had not written again, she gradually convinced herself that he was, after all, no different from all the other GIs who came to Britain, had a quick fling, and then disappeared without trace. But whatever happened, she promised herself that she would not pursue him, and that if he really loved her, he'd come back.

However, the postman did bring her one letter that managed to raise her spirits.

34 Ponreath Street — 16 June '45
Swansea

Dear Sun,

How are you, girl? I promised I'd write, so here I am.

Back home with Mam and Dad. Actually they've been pretty good to me – so far! The way me mam carries on, you'd think *she* was having the bloody baby. Still, if it keeps her happy, I don't mind. I've no doubt she'll do her best to play down the fact that Junior's dad was a Yank. Anyway, the little bugger's not due for another six weeks, so I'm going to lie in bed every day and have a good time for as long as I can. Isn't it wonderful not having to get up at crack of bloody dawn every morning!

Been thinkin' of you a lot just lately, you *and* Gary. When he gets back from the States, I hope he'll do the right thing and make an honest woman of you pronto. No point in hanging around this place, what with all this General Election rubbish and everything. When Junior's born, Erin's family want me to take him over there for a visit. The way I feel it would be more than just a visit! As a matter of fact, I wouldn't mind becoming a wealthy American widow. I rather fancy myself wearing silk Stars-and-Stripes knickers, what say you! Hey! Maybe we could both go on the same boat? Two GI brides together. What a hoot!

Got to fly now. Me dad's just got back home for supper. Everything stops for me dad!

Write soon. I'm dying to hear all your news.

Love – J and J (Jinx and Junior)

PS Have you heard from Gary lately? I hear they're sending some of the boys from 381 out to the Far East. Bloody Japs!

Jinx's letter cheered Sunday up no end, except the PS about sending out some of the boys from the former 381st Bomb Group at Ridgewell to join the Far East campaign. It was a reminder that the war with Japan was still going on, and that until that was over, Allied lives were in danger.

By the end of June, everyone was getting into a frenzy about the forthcoming General Election. Party political meetings were being held in Islington Town Hall, the Archway Hall, in Finsbury Park, Highbury Fields, Islington Green, and in just about every other public place where people were anxious to express an opinion. And everyone did seem to have an opinion, which is why Sunday was beginning to get fed up to the back teeth with having to watch the endless bickering between her mum, who had always voted Liberal, and Aunt Louie, a fervent and active Labour Party supporter. But for Sunday, the political divide between the two women had never been more embarrassing than during a heated discussion amongst some of the neighbours in the backyard of 'the Buildings'.

'If we throw Winnie out now,' warned Jack Popwell, sporting a huge blue rosette on the lapel of his summer jacket, 'it'll be the biggest act of betrayal this country has ever known.'

'Why!' growled Louie, who had just returned from shoving leaflets through people's letterboxes. 'Churchill's a warmonger. He knows nothing about the suffering amongst ordinary working-class people.'

'Come off it, Miss Clipstone!' retorted Doll Mooney, who had little Josie thrown across her shoulder trying to stop the child grizzling. 'Durin' the Blitz, Winnie was always the first to go 'round the East End comfortin' people who was bombed out.'

'I am not talking about the Blitz, Mrs Mooney,' replied Louie, rather condescendingly. 'I am referring to what this Prime Minister would do to help working-class people earn a decent living. For instance, what would he do about setting up a Public Health Service?'

'I think a Health Service is a very bad idea,' said Jack, rather dangerously. 'I mean, where's the money coming from?'

'From the rich, of course!' snapped Louie. 'God knows *they've* made enough money out of the war – one way or another!'

'Don't be silly now, Louie,' said Madge, embarrassed by her sister's simplistic opinions. 'I'm in favour of a Health Service too, but whoever the Government is, they won't find it easy to fund it.'

By now, people all over 'the Buildings' were hanging out of their windows listening to the rumpus going on down below. Everyone was moving their lips far too fast for Sunday, who found it almost impossible to understand what anyone was saying. But as she watched the heated exchanges, she couldn't bear the tense looks on people's faces, the way they screwed up their noses or glared at their opponent in rage or indignation. To her, it seemed incredible that just a few weeks ago these same people had been laughing and dancing with each other during the VE Day celebrations. What was it about politics that changed people from human beings into opinionated monsters? Sunday was glad that she was still too young to vote.

'Anyway,' said Doll, still trying to calm little Josie, 'they've been talkin' about an 'Ealth Service fer years. There's no way we're goin' ter get one.'

'Doll's right, ma!' called a man from the back of the group. 'The Tories are goin' ter sweep in next week. That's the last you'll 'ear about it.'

Louie swung round angrily on the man. 'Have you read this morning's *Daily Herald* by any chance?' she called.

'No, ma. I don't read the papers. It's bad fer me eyesight!'

'For your information,' growled Louie above the gales of laughter all around her, 'the *Daily Herald* is predicting a landslide for Labour. Mr Attlee will have a clear majority. *Then* you'll have a Public Health Service. Then people like my sister will be able to afford to have their phlebitis cured!'

This brought jeers from around the yard.

Madge was furious with her sister's remark, and without saying a word, she quickly left the group. Sunday watched her go, then followed her. Her Aunt Louie had brought her attention back to something that she had been noticing for some time. It was that her mum was now walking with a very definite limp.

After Madge and Sunday had disappeared into the block, Louie held the stage for as long as she could. To a hail of jeers, and sometimes applause, she took issue with everything that Jack Popwell, Doll Mooney, or anyone else challenged her with. But when she asked Joe Mooney for his opinion, the only support she got from him was, 'Sorry. I'm a Paddy. I'm not allowed opinions.'

Sunday had never seen her mum so angry. The moment Aunt Louie returned to the flat, Madge's lips practically spat out the words at her: 'You had no right to humiliate me like that! My ailments are to do with me and no one else! You have no right to tell everyone in these buildings that I'm suffering from phlebitis!'

'So what if I did?' Louie retorted. 'For weeks now you've been in pain, and that doctor's done nothing to help you.'

For once, Sunday was able to read her aunt's lips. 'Is this true, Mum?' she said anxiously, turning to Madge. '*Are* you in pain?'

'No more than millions of people all over the place,' Madge replied. 'But it's got nothing to do with – *her*!'

Louie ignored her, took out a rolled cigarette from her tobacco tin, and sat at the parlour table.

'What exactly *is* this – phlebitis?' Sunday asked.

Madge was suddenly very irritated to be cross-examined by her daughter. 'It's one of the veins in my leg – got a bit inflamed, that's all. It's absolutely nothing to worry about.'

'But you *have* been to see the doctor?' persisted Sunday.

'Yes, of course I have.'

'And what does he say?'

Madge sighed irritably. 'He rubbed some zinc ointment on my leg and wrapped it up with an elastic bandage.'

'Ha!' Louie snorted dismissively. 'Fat lot of good that's done!'

Madge immediately turned on her sister. 'Oh you know so much, don't you, Louie? You're such an expert on absolutely everything.'

'I know that if we had a Public Health Service, this sort of thing would have been cleared up long ago.'

'Politics again!' said Madge, sitting down on the sofa, and stretching out her troublesome leg. 'That's all you ever think about.'

Although Sunday had a hard time trying to work out what was being said in the angry exchange between her mum and Aunt Louie, she decided that as the conversation was reverting back to politics, she would go off to the kitchen and make a cup of tea.

Whilst she was waiting for the kettle to boil, Sunday had a lot to mull over in her mind. So this is why her mum hadn't been involved in any of her Salvation Army activities in recent weeks. This is why she had spent so much time at home with her legs stretched out on the sofa. She had clearly been in pain and was doing her best to keep it from everyone. But there was more to it than that. For instance, what had happened to her mum over these past few months? Why had she suddenly become so different from that placid little woman she had known all her life? But most curious of all was the way in which Madge was behaving towards her sister Louie. Ever since Sunday could remember, her mum had been protective of Aunt Louie, and would never allow anyone, including Sunday herself, to say one single thing that would hurt or offend her. But now, the two of them fought like cat and dog. These days, nothing Louie said or did seemed to please Madge. Every evening the two women sat at the supper table, doing their best to ignore each other's glances. It was strange, unnatural behaviour. Sunday felt uneasy. Something inside was telling her that either her mum, or her aunt, or both of them were trying to keep something from her.

A few minutes later, Sunday took a tray of tea into the parlour. Only her mum was there.

'Where's Auntie?' she asked, going across to her mum.

Madge's face was taut and strained. 'She's gone out,' her lips read. 'And as far as *I'm* concerned, she needn't bother to come back.'

That same week, the police came to tell Alf Butler that they had arrested a young Rhodesian serviceman for Bess's murder, but that after he had confessed, he had hanged himself inside his gaol cell at the police station.

When Sunday heard the news, she immediately called on Alf at number 7. She found the poor old boy very cut up, and despite the bits and pieces of food she had been bringing him each day, he was looking thinner than ever. The flat was as dark and dingy as always, and when she went to make them both a cup of tea, she was disturbed by the smell of stale food in the kitchen, and the grease-covered stove which hadn't been cleaned for weeks.

'I'm goin' away,' Alf announced quite unexpectedly. 'I always said if my Bess never come 'ome, I wouldn't stay 'ere.'

Sunday, sitting opposite him, pulled her chair closer, took hold of his hands, and held them. Despite the fact that outside it was a beautifully hot day, his hands were ice-cold.

'Got a place up the Whittin'ton. There's a geriatric ward up there. They'll keep an eye on me.'

Sunday felt quite sick. 'But you're too young to go to a place like that, Alf,' she said. 'We can take care of you here.'

Alf shook his head. 'I ain't gettin' any younger, Sun. Got arthritis in me knees, acute bronchitis, and on top of that, I've got angina. I'm much better off where they can keep an eye on me.'

Sunday knew it was no use trying to persuade Alf. She had known him since she was a little girl, and was only too well aware that once he'd made up his mind to do something, nothing in the world would change it.

'But before I go though, I got a few fings I want yer ter do for me, Sun.' The old boy eased himself up from his chair. 'Just 'ang on 'ere for a minute,' he said.

He disappeared into the kitchen for a moment, then returned clutching a small white pudding basin.

'This is fer you,' he said, handing the basin over to Sunday. 'Bess told me about it. She asked me ter give it to yer if anyfink should 'appen to 'er.'

Sunday looked at the basin. It was full of silver coins and one- and five-pound notes. 'I can't take this, Alf,' she said, and offered it back to him. 'It belongs to you.'

Alf refused to take it, and, shaking his head, said, 'She wanted yer ter 'ave it, and it's yours. I don't know 'ow much is in there, but she wanted yer ter 'ave it. Anyway, I don't need any of that stuff up where I'm goin'.'

Sunday didn't know what to say. She just sat there with the basin held between her hands on her lap.

'There's somefin' else,' said Alf. 'Yer may not like ter do this, but if yer did, it'd take a lot off me mind.' He seemed to falter a moment, before looking up at her again. 'It's 'er clothes. They're all there in the wardrobe. If yer could sort 'em out for me, take anyfin' yer want for yerself. There's one or two nice dresses there. My Bess knew 'ow ter turn 'erself out all right. Oh yes.'

The only way Sunday knew how to stop herself from crying was to squeeze the basin tight.

A few minutes later, Alf showed her into the bedroom. Sunday was surprised to see two separate single beds.

'We 'aven't slept tergevver for a long time,' said Alf, and then added quickly, 'Only 'cos I toss around too much in the night.' Then he went to the foot of what had clearly been Bess's bed, which was covered in a neat blue candlewick bedspread. 'We used to have lots er cuddles though,' he said, with a warm smile.

Alf then left Sunday alone to look through Bess's wardrobe,

where there was a row of dresses, blouses, and skirts. Some of the dresses were quite exotic, and Sunday suspected that Bess had received those as gifts from a few of her customers at Rainbow Corner.

For the first few minutes, Sunday found it difficult to take in what she had been asked to do. She felt like an intruder who had no right to be there. These were Bess's own clothes. She had admired, chosen, and worn them, and for another pair of hands even to touch them seemed sacrilegious. Sitting on the edge of Bess's bed, Sunday's eyes scanned the room, taking in the dressing-table which was still laid out with Bess's half-used perfume bottles, cheap earrings and bracelets, comb and brush, hand mirror, lipsticks and nail varnish, face-powder and cream, and a few of her personal possessions, such as a lighter and a cigarette packet with only one left. Sunday got up from the bed, and looked over the dressing-table, then moved around the room, feeling the chintz floral-patterned curtains which Bess had been so proud of, and her collection of miniature cats, which she had scattered all over the two windowsills. She stopped to look at a small framed photograph of Alf, which was propped up on Bess's bedside cabinet, and a rather crude reproduction of a Constable landscape, which was hanging on the wall between both beds. Although the room was not very big, everywhere Sunday went she could 'feel' Bess's presence, even down to the remains of her cigarette ash in a small glass ash-tray.

But the most difficult part was still to come. First, she started to sort through Bess's collection of shoes, so many of them fashionable and ideal for the dance floor. She took off her own shoes, and slipped into a pair of red patent ones, which, to her amazement, fitted perfectly. Then she tried on a few more pairs, including an expensive pair of suede shoes with a large metal buckle. Again they fitted perfectly.

The rest of the wardrobe was a treasure-chest of glamorous clothes to fit what Sunday considered to be a truly glamorous woman. Some of the stuff there was purely daytime functional, but a few of the dresses had clearly been used for 'business' purposes, and Sunday imagined what a knockout her old mate must have looked in them. As Alf had told her to take her time, she decided to try on one of the dresses hanging there. It was of emerald-green velvet, and had a large brooch in the shape of a spray of daffodils pinned to it. She was surprised how easily she fitted into it, although she couldn't reach behind to do up the back buttons. And when she stood in front of the long wardrobe mirror, she felt quite strange, for there seemed to be a genuine likeness between Bess and herself. In fact, the dress fitted so well, and looked so sensational, it could almost have been Bess herself who was standing there.

After nearly an hour of sorting through Bess's clothes and personal possessions, Sunday's emotions were draining her. So after placing on Bess's bed most of the clothes she intended to keep for herself, Sunday went back to the wardrobe to close the door. But one of the wardrobe drawers was slightly open, and as she went to close it, she noticed something protruding from beneath some of Bess's undies there. When she investigated, she discovered that it was a small photograph album. Opening it, she found lots of early snapshots of Bess and Alf on holiday at Ramsgate before the war. It was an endearing album to find, for beneath each picture, Bess had scrawled when and where it had been taken. However, when she got to the last page of the album, she was shocked by the final snapshot there which was stuck on to the blank page all on its own. The snapshot was of a small girl, aged about eight or nine, with short, strawberry-blonde hair, and wearing a bathing costume on the beach at Southend. The child looked as though she was deliriously happy, for the camera had captured her laughing her head off. The picture was of Sunday herself.

Still clutching the open album, Sunday flopped down on to the edge of Bess's bed again.

Only now did the tears really begin to flow.

When she got back to her own flat, Sunday was shocked to find a small gathering of neighbours on the landing outside. She quickly pushed past them, and went in.

'Mum! Aunt Louie!' she called, just as Louie came hurrying out of the room she shared with her sister. 'What is it?' asked Sunday, fearing something terrible had happened. 'Where's Mum?'

'I warned her!' growled Louie. 'How many times I warned her!'

Sunday pushed her out of the way, and rushed straight into the bedroom.

To her horror, she found her mum lying stretched out unconscious on her bed. The sheets were stained with blood.

# *Chapter 24*

A LABOUR LANDSLIDE
CARETAKER GOVT. LEADERS
FALL LIKE NINEPINS

The headline on the front page of the London evening newspaper, the *Star*, told it all. After a particularly acrimonious General Election campaign, on Thursday, 26 July, Winston Churchill and his caretaker Government were voted out of office. It was a result which clearly shocked the nation, including those who had voted for Clement Attlee's Labour Party.

In 'the Buildings', the residents reacted in different ways to the shock news. Doll Mooney said, 'I can't believe it, I really can't. Poor ol' Winnie. If it 'adn't been for 'im, we'd 'ave lost the war.' Joe Mooney wasn't quite so perturbed; he thought the result 'quite funny'. The most upset, however, was good old Tory stalwart, Jack Popwell. 'Disgustin'!' he proclaimed. 'It's like stabbin' yer best friend in the back!' But there were plenty of other residents who were overjoyed at the result.

'Now we can feel proud to be British!' boasted Aunt Louie, who particularly welcomed the news after having to spend the past week or so looking after her sister.

Madge's close brush with death had been averted only by the quick thinking of Jack Popwell, who had rushed downstairs to the public telephone in Camden Road and dialled 999. Luckily, the ambulance had come as soon as it was called, and within fifteen minutes, Madge was in the Emergency Wing of the Royal Northern Hospital, with a perforated varicose vein in her left leg. The whole incident had deeply upset Sunday, for the moment she had seen her mum's bed saturated with blood, she had feared that she was dying. However, after an emergency operation, in which the offending vein had been removed, Madge was eventually allowed back home. But she needed several weeks of rest, which meant that she had to sit with her feet up, and take as many walks as possible.

Although Sunday was concerned about her mum's condition, she was relieved to have her job at the Deaf and Dumb School to go to each day, for it gave her a break from the constant bickering between her mum and Aunt Louie. And as each day passed, that bickering was getting worse, invariably ending up in a blazing row over the most trivial incidents. It was at times like this that Sunday yearned to have a man around the place. The two elderly women she was saddled with were getting out of hand, and for Sunday the flat was turning into a kind of straitjacket. Luckily, Madge's friend Mr Billings was a frequent visitor, and he often brought one or two of Madge's Salvation Army friends along to see her during the afternoons, much to the disapproval of Aunt Louie. Things finally came to a head late one afternoon in early August. Sunday returned home from the Deaf and Dumb School to find her mum out, and Aunt Louie in the bedroom packing her clothes into a suitcase.

'Aunt Louie?' Sunday asked, as she entered the bedroom. 'Is anything wrong? Where's Mum?'

Louie looked up only long enough for Sunday to read her lips. 'Gone out with her boyfriend,' she said sourly, whilst continuing to pack.

Sunday approached closer. 'What are you doing?' she asked.

'What does it look like?' replied Louie, irritably. 'I'm packing my bag. I'm leaving.'

Sunday suddenly felt a surge of excitement. Many a time her aunt had threatened to do what she was doing now, but there was just a hope that this time she meant it. 'Why? What's happened this time?'

When Louie looked up at Sunday again, she realised that her aunt's face was white and drawn, and her eyes were puffed up from crying. 'I'm not welcome here,' she replied calmly. 'I haven't been welcome for a long time.'

Sunday sat on the edge of her mum's bed, kicked off her shoes, and watched her aunt whilst she continued packing. 'You mustn't take too much notice of Mum,' she said, unsure why she was being so nice to her aunt. 'She's not properly well yet.'

'She's not been well for a very long time,' sneered Louie. 'And I'm not talking about her varicose veins.' She went to the chest of drawers, took out some of her underclothes, and put them into the suitcase. 'This time she's gone too far.'

'What do you mean?'

For a moment Louie stopped what she was doing and looked

straight at Sunday. 'She resents my being here. After all these years, she can't bear me being here any more.'

Sunday was astonished to read what her aunt was saying. 'It's not true,' she said. 'You know how fond Mum is of you.'

'Used to be,' said Louie, with her lips quivering as she talked. 'That was years ago, when she needed me. If I'd known then what I know today, I'd never have set foot inside this place. What your mother said to me today, I'll never forgive.'

Sunday was absolutely intrigued, and as she looked at her aunt's heavily lined face, now crumpled up in obvious pain and anguish, she actually felt sorry for her. 'What *did* she say then?'

'She said she only ever let me come here out of pity. She said I was a sponger, that I've always been a sponger, that I outlived my welcome long ago.'

Embarrassed, Sunday lowered her head.

Louie stretched her hand towards Sunday and raised her chin. 'Oh I know that's what you think too. But it's not true. None of it's true. I've always paid my way. All the years I worked for the Civil Service, I paid over half the rent, and I did the same even after I retired. It's not fair. It's just not fair.'

Sunday wanted to say something, but Louie seemed determined to get things off her chest.

'I never came here for me,' she said, staring Sunday straight in the eye. 'I came here because after your father died, Madge couldn't cope on her own. I'm talking about your adopted father, not the real one.'

This made Sunday sit up with a start. 'Did you *know* my real father?' she asked eagerly.

Louie shook her head. 'But I knew your mother. Your real mother.'

Sunday felt her flesh turn cold. 'You *knew* her?'

Aware that she had gone too far, Louie didn't reply, and carried on packing her suitcase.

But Sunday had no intention of leaving it there. She quickly got up from the bed, stood directly in front of her aunt, and made her look at her. 'Mum has always told me that I was found in a bundle on the Salvation Army Hall's doorstep. She said they never discovered who my real mum was. What are you trying to tell me, Auntie?' she said, grabbing hold of Louie's arms and gently shaking them. 'Tell me!'

Louie looked up slowly. The pupils of her eyes were misted over. She shook her head. 'Madge is the one to ask, not me,' she replied.

Frustrated, Sunday released her grip on Louie's arms, turned away, and stared out of the window.

Louie went to her, stood at her side in silence for a moment, then gently turned her round to face her. 'Sunday,' she said, her lips moving more slowly and precisely than Sunday had ever seen before. 'There are a lot of things you don't know about me. Things that you've taken for granted, without ever knowing the truth.'

Sunday turned her face away, but, with one hand, Louie gently turned it back towards her again.

'You think I don't know anything about love,' she said, her eyes flickering as she talked. 'You think I'm just another old man-hating spinster who prefers the company of women friends.' She slowly shook her head. 'You're wrong. I *do* know how to love. I've always needed love.' Her eyes flicked down and then up again to Sunday. 'All my life I've been in love with Reg Collins.'

Sunday's face froze. Had she understood correctly? Aunt Louie in love with her adopted dad? What was she talking about? Reg Collins had been dead ever since she was a baby.

'Yes,' continued Louie, nodding her head. 'I fell in love with him before your mum even met him. But she took him away from me. He was the only man in the world I ever wanted, and she took him away from me.'

Outside, the sun was trying to put in an appearance after a rather disappointing start to the day, and for a few seconds the two women's faces were illuminated by a bright glow. Louie's light grey eyes sparkled in the light, and although to some people her short, cropped hair made her look like a man, at that moment Sunday could imagine that, as a young girl, her aunt must have been quite beautiful.

'You see, when your dad died, I never stopped loving him. I still love him, even after all these years.' She swallowed hard, and licked her dry lips with the tip of her tongue. 'After he died, and your mother asked me to move in, I said no. I just couldn't bear the thought of being in the same place where he'd been living with someone I know he didn't really love.'

Sunday felt uneasy at this remark, and tried to turn away.

'It's true, Sunday,' Louie said, taking the girl's hand and holding on to it. 'I know it's hard for you to understand, but it was me that your dad loved, not your mother. He knew he'd made a mistake going with her, but she had this hold on him.' She clenched her fist and stared hard at it. 'She had him right there, where she wanted him. Don't ask me how, but she did it.' She looked back up at

Sunday again. 'It was soon after she was told she couldn't have babies of her own that you came along.'

Sunday tried to pull away. But again, Louie held on to her.

'I should never have come here, Sunday, I know that now. But after he died, I wanted to be near him, and coming here was somehow the next best thing.'

Sunday was bewildered, and stared hard at Louie. 'Auntie,' she said, 'are you saying that all the things you told me about Dad are untrue? About being jealous of Mum, about beating her up and everything? Why did you have to lie? Why?'

Louie covered her face and dissolved into tears. For Sunday, this was the most remarkable sight she had ever seen. Throughout her entire lifetime, her aunt had been a tower of defiance and mischief. She had never once shown a moment's weakness, never once revealed any sign of vulnerability, or care or interest for anyone but herself. The woman standing before her now was like a perfect stranger. Suddenly, Sunday felt immense pity, so she took hold of Louie's hands, and as she gently prised them away from the old lady's face, tears came streaming down the lines on either side of Louie's nose.

Then Sunday did something that she had never done before. She put her arms around her aunt's waist, and hugged her. Louie immediately responded, and as her entire body heaved up and down in pain and anguish, she leaned her head on one side on Sunday's shoulders, and sobbed her heart out.

Madge Collins and Stan Billings made slow progress through Finsbury Park. Although Madge's leg was now much improved, she was still relying on a walking stick, mainly as a precaution rather than because she actually needed it, and it was also a comfort to have Stan's arm to cling on to. The weather had been a little unsettled during the morning, with just a light rain shower, so most of the benches were still quite damp. But by the time they reached the bandstand, the clouds had more or less cleared and some attendants were just setting out deckchairs for an amateur band concert that evening.

Sunday knew exactly where to find her mum, for this was the place where Madge invariably came for her afternoon walk, which was part of the recuperation ordered by her hospital surgeon after her own GP had mistakenly diagnosed phlebitis for varicose veins. Madge loved this area of the park, not only because the old bandstand was surrounded by tall oak, elm, and chestnut trees, but because it was well away from the lake. Madge was scared of the lake, scared of water, which is why she never learnt to swim, never went in a boat, and why, when Sunday was a child, she rarely brought her there.

As she hurried to catch up with her mum and Mr Billings, Sunday couldn't help feeling how odd it was that whenever Madge went out anywhere, she always seemed to wear her Salvation Army bonnet and uniform, even when she wasn't on duty. Sunday also found it hard to reconcile what her aunt had just told her about her mum with the frail old woman who was walking at a snail's pace just ahead of her.

'Mum!'

The moment they heard Sunday's voice, Madge and Stan came to a halt and turned.

'Sunday,' Madge said, taken aback. 'What a lovely surprise.'

''Allo, Sunday,' said Stan, with a welcoming smile.

'Aunt Louie's gone,' Sunday said straight away, without even acknowledging Stan's greeting. 'She's packed her suitcase and gone to stay with her friends up at Swiss Cottage.'

Madge's smile had faded. 'I'm not surprised,' she replied quite coolly. 'Don't worry. She'll be back.'

Sunday was astonished by her mum's reaction. 'Don't you care?' she asked.

'Why don't I leave you two girls ter 'ave a talk on yer own,' said Stan uneasily. 'I'll see if I can rustle up some tea in the cafeteria.' Embarrassed, he backed away, and hurried off, leaving Sunday and her mum to face each other alone.

'You shouldn't have mentioned your auntie here,' said Madge calmly but firmly. 'Not in front of Mr Billings.'

'Mum!' snapped Sunday, eyes blazing. 'How can you be so callous? What's been going on between you and Auntie?'

'Your aunt and I had a difference of opinion. She's been getting restless for quite some time now. You know how difficult she can be.'

Sunday waited for her mum to sit down in a nearby deckchair, then sat in the one next to her. 'I don't understand all this. You've always been so fond of her, so protective. You've never allowed me to say one single thing against her.'

'That's a slight exaggeration, dear.'

'It's true!' insisted Sunday. 'D'you remember the time when you said, "Whenever you have a row with Auntie, it's not her you hurt, it's me"?'

'Things are different now,' said Madge bitterly. 'Over these past months, your aunt has changed.'

'Oh Mum, so have you.'

Madge's eyes flicked up irritably. 'You have no reason to say such a thing.'

'It's got something to do with Dad, hasn't it?'

Madge was angry now. 'Whatever that woman has been telling you is a lie!' She tried to raise herself out of the deckchair again, but Sunday stretched one hand across and gently held her down by the shoulder.

'No Mum,' Sunday said. 'You can't keep putting off what you should have told me years ago. You know as well as I do, we have a lot of things to talk over.'

Two deckchair attendants passed nearby, but thinking that the two women were part of the brass band rehearsal, they ignored them.

'Aunt Louie told me you know who my real parents are.' Despite Sunday's efforts to keep her voice low, it still carried right across the empty rows of deckchairs. 'Mum. I want to know. Who are they?'

Madge's voice was firm and decisive. 'I have no idea.'

'Mum, stop playing games with me! I have a right to know. I have a right to know who they are and why they dumped me in a box on the doorstep of the Salvation Army Hall.'

Madge had her walking stick resting across her lap, and every so often she would grip it hard, as though unconsciously trying to snap it in half. 'At the time when your father and I first adopted you, we only knew that you'd been abandoned.'

'But you found out later?'

Madge inhaled and exhaled irritably.

'Who were they, Mum?'

This time, Madge practically spat out in anger and frustration. 'They were monsters! Monsters to make a child in the sight of God without His blessing. Monsters to cast a newborn baby aside as if it were a piece of rubbish in a dustbin! Why do you want to know about such monsters, Sunday? Haven't I given you everything you've ever asked for?'

'No,' answered Sunday, firmly. 'You've never given me the truth.'

Stan Billings returned with three cups of tea on a small wooden tray. But as he approached the two women, he could see they were in the middle of a tense exchange, so he decided to wait a few minutes, and sat down in a deckchair some distance away from them.

'Let me say something to you, Sunday,' Madge said, doing her best to keep her lip movements clear and precise. 'When the Lord decided that He didn't want me to have children born of my own blood, I knew that He would compensate me in another way. I found that way on the night I saw you wrapped up in a blanket in a box outside the Mission Hall. The Lord gave me a daughter of my own, and I was truly grateful.'

Although Sunday couldn't hear what was going on behind her, on the old bandstand in the background, some of the youthful members of an Air Training Corps brass band were tuning up for their rehearsal.

'For months, your dad and I fought to adopt you,' continued Madge, taking off her spectacles, and cleaning them on her handkerchief. 'But we had to wait until the court was quite satisfied that no one was going to come forward to claim you. I thank God the woman who gave birth to you never dared show her face.'

'But you do know who she was?'

Madge hesitated before answering. 'Yes,' she replied, putting on her spectacles again. 'I know.'

'Then why won't you tell me?'

'Because she was not worthy of you.'

In the background, the rehearsal began. But the first item was the ATC choir singing a rather shaky rendition of The Lost Chord. This immediately brought small groups of people wandering across to watch from behind the back row of deckchairs.

Sunday got up from her chair. 'You'll have to tell me, Mum,' she said. 'One of these days, you'll have to tell me who and where I came from. Whatever my real mum has done, I'm still a part of her. I can feel her inside me. Every time I look in the mirror, I know she's there. I must know who she is, Mum. Not because I'm not grateful for all you've ever done for me, but because I can't go through my life in someone else's shadow.'

With that, she turned and walked off.

When Madge got home from her walk in Finsbury Park, she found a letter from Louie waiting for her on the parlour table. Sunday wanted no part of it, so she went into her bedroom and closed the door.

Madge went into her own bedroom, took off her bonnet and uniform, and carefully hung them up inside her wardrobe. Most of her sister Louie's clothes had already gone, and she had also cleared out her own personal possessions from the dressing-table and bedside cabinet. Madge tried hard to ignore what she considered was yet another of her sister's impetuous moods. She'd be back, just like always. She'd made her point, and stirred up trouble, but she'd be back. There was no doubt in Madge's mind whatsoever.

Back in the parlour, Madge ripped open Louie's envelope. There was no note inside. Just Louie's front-door key, and a ten-shilling note, being her final share of the rent.

# Chapter 25

'The Punch and Judy Show' was always a very popular event at the Deaf and Dumb School in Drayton Park. The thirty-minute show was devised by Pete Hawkins, who, because he himself was both deaf and mute, knew exactly how to use the puppets for communication. The moment Sunday arrived at the school, she could see what a wonderful rapport Pete had with the kids, for he was always clowning around with them, and making them feel that he was one of them. Pete was also highly gifted, for he not only made the puppets and model theatre himself, but also operated them. Each week, Eileen Roberts and Jacqui Marks took turns to explain the action in sign language to the children, and eventually, Sunday made her own contribution by introducing a kind of audience participation. This involved her sign-talking to Punch, Judy, and a crocodile named 'Snapper', and getting them to sway in time to a beat which Sunday herself initiated. The device proved a huge success with the children, and those that were lucky enough to have vocal chords roared their approval, and those who were mute clapped their hands and showed their appreciation with broad beams lighting up their young faces.

As each day passed, Sunday was enjoying her work at the school more than she had ever dared to hope. It was the kids themselves who instilled so much confidence in her. None of them ever seemed to be feeling sorry for themselves, and they had accepted their fate as though there was absolutely nothing unusual about being deaf or mute. Amongst them, of course, were a few victims of the air-raids, with whom it was only natural that Sunday should feel a special empathy. It was odd and poignant how, when she sometimes sat with these particular children, they would draw pictures of all those deadly weapons, such as bombs, 'doodlebugs', and rockets, which had been responsible for their own disability. It took her some time to realise that these kids were teaching her a lot about life, and how to live it.

But the school also offered Sunday a great deal more: the kind of companionship and independence that she could never get at home. And being at home these days was nothing short of an ordeal. Despite her mum's assurance that Aunt Louie would 'soon know which side her bread's buttered', it had been over a week since the old lady had left the flat to go and stay with her friends at Swiss Cottage, and she hadn't been near the place since. Luckily, Madge Collins's health had improved, and she was now walking quite normally again, without her walking stick. But, no matter how hard Sunday tried, Madge was still unwilling to discuss anything to do with Sunday's real mother and father, either who they were or where they came from. It was becoming a crisis of identity for her, with a desperate feeling inside that she had to know the answer to so many questions, about herself, about the woman who had brought her into the world, and about why she had been so rejected even before the start of her life. She was completely disoriented, floundering in a sea of uncertainty. There was no one she could talk to about it all, no one to confide in. She needed advice, someone she could pour it all out to, someone who would understand what it was like to live in the shadow of their own self. And at the heart of it all was Gary. It had been almost three months since she had last heard from him, and it was getting her down. Why couldn't he have been truthful with her before he went back to America? Why couldn't he have just said that it was nice while it lasted, but that everything has to come to an end sooner or later? She felt let down, betrayed. One letter from Gary would have made all the difference, would have helped to make this mess bearable. Gary was a man, and a man was supposed to know about these things, to know what to do. In fact, from the time she got up in the morning to the time she went to bed, she yearned for a man's company, yearned to be held in his arms and be told that everything was going to be all right, yearned to feel the warmth of his body against her own. It was for all those reasons that she started to see Pete Hawkins.

At the beginning it all seemed very half-hearted, and she had only really got to know him during an evening out with Helen Gallop and Jacqui Marks at Dick's Wine Bar in the Holloway Road. Sunday had never tasted wine before, for it had always been considered a posh person's drink, but Pete seemed to be quite an expert, and knew exactly what to order. In many ways, it had been a hilarious evening, for despite the fact that he could only use sign language, Pete had a marvellous sense of humour, and consistently made all three girls laugh. He was able, seemingly effortlessly, to project his bubbly personality, despite his handicaps. Sunday was fascinated to watch the delicate way he moved his fingers and hands, which seemed to paint pictures in the air. The more she saw of Pete, the more she was attracted to him, with his mischievous eyes, and long brown hair that was always flopping over one eye, and his thin wire-like body which was always restless, always on the move.

The first time Sunday slept with Pete she felt guilty. In some ways she felt as though she had seduced him into doing it, for, after Helen and Jacqui had got their bus home, it had been Sunday herself who had suggested that he invite her back for a drink at his top-floor flat in Aberdeen Park just off Highbury Grove. At the start, Pete seemed quite nervous about what he was doing, for despite all his clowning, he was actually quite shy and nervous. It was also very evident that Pete was not very experienced, which meant that Sunday had to take the initiative. However, this was what she had wanted, what she desperately needed, and although making love with Pete Hawkins only made her think of Gary all the more, for the time being it would have to do.

During the first week in August, there were very definite signs that the war with the Japanese was coming to an end. Every newspaper carried reports of Allied successes in the Far East, with mass bombing raids taking place every day on the Japanese mainland itself. But it was not until 6 August that events took a dramatic turn, with the announcement that the United States Air Force had dropped an atomic bomb, which had completely devastated the Japanese city of Hiroshima. A few days later, Russia declared war on the Japanese Empire, and after the Americans dropped another atomic bomb, this time on the city of Nagasaki, the Government of Japan surrendered.

The VJ Day celebrations in 'the Buildings' were a further opportunity for the residents to let their hair down. Apart from a tea party for hordes of kids, there was also another knees-up for the adults, most of whom had contributed anything between five and ten shillings to help pay for the spread. The new Prime Minister, Clement Attlee, told the nation to 'go out and enjoy yourselves', and everyone in 'the Buildings' did just that. At last the war all over the world was at an end. It was now up to the new Government to build the peace.

A few days before the celebrations, Alf Butler moved out of number 7. It had been a massive undertaking, for over the years he and Bess had acquired many personal possessions, which had to be disposed of. So, with Sunday's help, he set about doing so, giving a lot of the stuff to St George's Church in Tufnell Park for sale at their next bazaar, other things to some of the more friendly neighbours in the same block, but the bulk of Bess's clothes to Sunday.

Once Alf had settled in at his new 'home', which was nothing more than an old people's block attached to the Geriatric Ward at the Whittington Hospital in Highgate, Sunday went to visit him. She hated the place on sight, for it smelt of wintergreen ointment and incontinence, and the elderly residents seemed to spend most of their day either reading newspapers or just nodding off in their armchairs. Alf, however, was in surprisingly good spirits, probably because he now had people around him to talk to, so it seemed the right moment for Sunday to ask him something that had been on her mind since the day she had sorted through Bess's clothes.

'Why did she keep a pitture of you?' replied Alf, repeating Sunday's question. ''Cos she fawt the world of yer, Sun. Yer was about the only one she could talk to in those "Buildin's". Yer was on 'er wavelengf. She reckoned yer 'ad guts,' he said, adding wistfully, 'like she 'ad all 'er life.'

Sunday covered his cold hand with her own. She had to sit directly opposite to enable them both to communicate with each other. 'What I don't understand though, Alf, is where did she get that snapshot of me? It was taken years ago, on the beach at Southend, on a day trip with my school.' She watched Alf's lips carefully, to make quite sure she could understand his reply.

Alf was a bit slow on the uptake these days, so he had to think hard for a moment. Then, after shrugging his shoulders, said, 'No idea. Yer mum must've given it to 'er.'

Sunday did a double-take. 'Mum?' she said incredulously. 'But they never met, did they?'

'Oh yes they did,' answered Alf firmly. 'Quite a few times yer mum come ter see Bess over the years. Tried ter save 'er soul wiv a bit of Bible-punchin', I reckon. I never 'ung around, oh no, not me! I just let 'em get on wiv it.'

Sunday was so astonished that when a nurse came along with the tea trolley, she accepted a cup of tea without thanking her for it.

'Alf,' said Sunday, leaning forward so that she could get a closer look at his lips when he replied. 'Are you saying that my mum came to visit Bess, in *your* flat?'

Despite his growing loss of cohesion, Alf was again able to answer quite firmly, 'Lots er times.'

'And they talked – about religion?'

'Far as I know. As I said, I always used ter push off. Din't want ter know anyfink about it.'

Sunday sat back in her seat, dumbfounded. The idea of her mum having any contact at all with a woman like Bess seemed totally incomprehensible. Ever since Sunday was a child, Madge had never done anything but condemn Bess and her sinful lifestyle. Even the very mention of Bess's name had turned the look on her mum's face from one of sweetness and heavenly light, to a kind of puritanical disdain. Over and over again she tried to imagine the two women together, and in Bess's own flat! Why had her mum never told her about these meetings? Why had she always kept it such a secret? As she watched Alf sipping his hot tea, and blowing it to cool it down, all she could think about was the strange mind of the woman who had adopted her. And that snapshot of herself, so proudly positioned on a page of Bess's photograph album. Was it really possible that her own mum had actually given it to Bess? It was an utterly intriguing thought.

'It's not all that surprisin', yer know.'

When Alf suddenly spoke, Sunday leaned forward again.

'I said, it's not all that surprisin' – about yer mum comin' over ter see Bess.'

Sunday was puzzled. 'What d'you mean, Alf?'

Alf was very deft at drinking down hot tea, so he quickly drained the cup, and his rather shaky hand put it down on to the small table beside him. 'She tried ter do too much, Sun,' he said, eyes lowered but turned towards her. 'My gel, I'm talkin' about. She let 'erself go ter look after me. That's why yer mum come ter see Bess – ter try an' change 'er ways.'

Sunday tensed. What was Alf telling her?

'Oh, it's all right – I know,' Alf continued, his elbows leaning on both arms of the chair, his chin resting on his fists. 'I fink I've always known. And yet I refused ter believe it. I refused to believe what she was up to each night, where she was goin', and why she was doin' it.' He looked up at Sunday, and shook his head. 'The fact is, Sun, I *let* 'er do it, and I'm ashamed of meself.' His eyes were watery, so he took out his handkerchief and dabbed them. ''Ow'd yer like an 'usband like me, eh? Lets 'is missus go out on the game just so's 'e can live a life of ol' Riley.'

Sunday could see that he was on the verge of tears, so she leaned forward, hugged him, then looked directly at his face. 'It wasn't like that, Alf,' she said reassuringly. 'Bess loved you. She never stopped loving you. What she did, she did because she wanted the best for you.'

The old boy's face crumpled up, and he sobbed deeply. Sunday pulled his head gently on to her shoulder, and held him tight.

'Is everything all right?' asked one of the nurses, who was on her rounds collecting empty teacups. As Sunday was not looking at her, she tapped her on the shoulder and repeated the question.

'Oh yes,' replied Sunday, holding on to Alf. 'Everything's quite all right, thank you.'

Leaving the hospital, Sunday made her way down Highgate Hill, passing by the commemorative stone to London's first Lord Mayor, Dick Whittington, as she went. But her mind was racing so much, and as it was such a clear and fine Sunday afternoon, she decided not to go straight home.

A short time later, she found her way up on to the bridge high above the busy Archway Road. Strolling idly along the narrow pedestrian path beside the bridge road made her feel just a little woozy, and if she had suffered from vertigo it would have been like a nightmare. But her mind was on other things, and a few minutes later she hadn't realised that she had already reached the middle section of the bridge. Over the years, there had been quite a number of suicides from this spot, which meant that a wire grille had now been erected to prevent any more attempts. Sunday came to a halt, and peered through the grille. She was astonished how high the bridge was, for down in the Archway Road below cars and buses streaming up towards the Great North Road looked like toys, and people walking along the pavement were nothing more than crawling insects. After a while, the scene below became transformed into a kind of still picture, and in Sunday's mind, everything came to a halt.

'*'Ow'd yer like an 'usband like me, eh? Lets 'is missus go out on the game just so's 'e can live a life of ol' Riley.*'

Alf's words seemed to bounce up from the road below, and during the few minutes that she closed her eyes, she could see his face before her. And then she remembered her own words: '*Are you saying that my mum came to visit Bess, in* your *flat?*'

And then she saw her mum's face.

Suddenly, she felt someone touching her on the shoulder. Her eyes sprang open, and when she turned around she found herself staring straight into the face of a police constable.

'We're not goin' to do anythin' silly – *are* we, miss?' he asked.

Sunday hesitated for a moment. Then she smiled. 'Oh no,' she said, shaking her head. 'Not me.' Then she walked off.

Madge was in a good mood. Not only was her leg almost fully recovered, but, apart from the odd headache, she felt fitter than she had done for a very long time. She was also back to cooking regular meals again, and by the time Sunday had got home from visiting Alf in hospital, she was just taking some fairy cakes out of the oven for tea.

'How was he?' she asked, as Sunday came into the kitchen. 'Settled in all right, has he?'

Sunday went straight to the small kitchen table, and sat down. 'He's fine,' she answered blandly.

Using a tea cloth, Madge put the tray of piping-hot cakes on to the table. Then she closed the oven door, and collected her favoured blunt kitchen knife from the drawer. 'I thought we'd have a little treat for tea,' she said, waiting a moment before removing each cake from the tin tray. 'I've made a few extra to take to the band concert this evening. Don't forget, you promised to come, and you're going to bring that nice friend of yours from the school with you. I'm so looking forward to meeting him. Don't forget though, if it rains, it'll be in the Hall, not on Highbury Fields.'

Sunday had forgotten about her promise to go to the weekly Salvation Army Band concert. She hated band concerts, and thought it was inconsiderate of her mum to expect her to sit through the ordeal of not being able to hear one single note that was being played.

'My friend Sarah Denning loves my fairy cakes. She says no one can make them as light as I do.' Madge finished removing all the cakes from the tray, and arranged them in a neat pattern on a large plate. 'Your Aunt Louie likes them too.'

Sunday was watching her mum carefully. 'Well she's not here to eat them, is she?' she said caustically.

Madge hesitated a moment before answering. 'Actually, I wanted to talk to you about that.'

She sat down opposite Sunday, and rested her hands on the table. 'I've been thinking,' she said, her eyes trying hard not to make contact with Sunday's. 'I think I should go and see Auntie. Ask her to come home.'

Sunday could say nothing. She was too shocked.

'I can't deny it,' Madge continued. 'I feel guilty about her. We've always been such good friends. It seems unkind to let this happen after all these years.' She sighed and looked straight at Sunday. 'How would you feel about that, Sunday?' she asked.

Sunday was nonplussed. It was astonishing to see her mum actually owning up to her own guilt, especially after all the harsh things she had said about her sister. All she could say was, 'It's your decision, Mum. It's up to you.'

'It hasn't been easy for me, you know,' Madge said, as she unconsciously rearranged the cakes on the plate. 'The trouble is that I don't like getting old. It's my stupid brain, you see – it gets so muddled at times.' She gently ran two fingers across her forehead, as though trying to clear it. 'Silly, isn't it?' she continued. 'Someone with my faith, my devotion, and yet I can't even face up to the passing of time. Even so, Louie shouldn't have kept getting at me.'

Sunday was curious. 'Why was she getting at you?' she asked.

'Oh, you know Auntie,' said Madge. 'She's always been a bit of a gossip.' She paused, looked down, then suddenly looked up again. 'No. That's not true. Auntie wanted me to tell you about – your parents.'

Sunday sat bolt upright.

'Sunday, I know I haven't been as honest with you about that as you want, but there were reasons. I've always intended to tell you everything, but not until you reached twenty-one. You've been through quite enough in this awful war. I didn't want to distress you even more.'

Sunday suddenly found herself warming to her mum all over again. She was like she used to be, with a sweetness that would melt the heart out of even the biggest cynic. 'I'm not a kid any more, Mum,' she said as gently as her throat chords would allow. 'No matter how painful, you must tell me everything I ought to know.'

Madge was deep in thought for a moment, then she got up from the table. 'Come into the other room,' she said.

Sunday followed her into the parlour, where the table had already been set for tea with three places. Madge immediately disappeared into her own bedroom for a moment, whilst Sunday waited for her to return, her heart thumping hard with the reality that her whole life was about to be explained. Feeling how flushed her face was, she sat down at the table in an attempt to keep calm.

It seemed an eternity before her mum returned, but when she did eventually reappear, she was carrying something in her hand. 'This is your father,' she said, giving Sunday a small photograph. 'Your flesh-and-blood father. I wasn't going to give it to you until you were twenty-one.'

Sunday looked intently at the small faded photo of a young man, probably in his early twenties. She looked hard for any sign of a resemblance between this man and herself, but the only clue was his short blond hair. 'Who is he?' she asked tremulously.

'A man,' said Madge, without emotion. 'Just a man. Someone who passes in the night.' And then she added, 'Like so many.'

Sunday looked up from the photo. 'Where did you get this?' she asked intensely. 'Did my mother give it to you?'

Madge shook her head, and sat down opposite her daughter. 'Sunday, you'll have to understand that there are some questions I just can't answer. Not because I don't want to, but because I don't know. All I can tell you is that when he knew you were on the way, he wanted no part of you. He disappeared a long time ago, Sunday. No one knows where.'

'Not even my real mother?'

Madge took a deep breath before replying. 'Not even your – real mother.'

Although Sunday couldn't hear the sound, church bells in the distance were ringing out five o'clock.

Sunday realised how difficult this moment was for her mum, but now this long-overdue discussion had got this far, she wasn't prepared to let it go. Leaning across the table to Madge, she gently took hold of her hand and asked tenderly, 'What about *her*, Mum? Where does she come from? Where is she now?'

Madge slowly shook her head. What she was doing now was clearly causing her great anguish. 'I can't tell you.'

'Why not?'

'Sunday, you have to realise that all this has caught up with me quite suddenly. I'll tell you all you want to know – yes, I promise I *will* tell you. But I know that when I do, I'll have lost you – for ever.'

Sunday shook her head.

'Oh, I know what you're saying. But believe me, no matter how hard you try to convince yourself, you'll no longer be my daughter, my little girl. You'll be someone else's.'

Sunday sighed, leaned back in her chair, head lowered.

'Look at me, Sunday – please, dear.'

Sunday didn't hear what her mum had said, but allowed Madge's hand to raise her chin.

'Sunday, there's something I want you to know. Whatever you

think of me, I can assure you that everything I've ever done has been for you – not for me or anyone else – but you. You're the child I never had, the child our Lord never allowed me to have. When you came along, my life began. Oh, I know I've made mistakes, lots of them. I know I should have told you about who you were and where you came from. But believe me, Sunday, I did it to protect you, and for no other reason. But from now on, it's going to be different, everything's going to be different. Whatever the consequences, I'll no longer hold anything back from you.'

They were suddenly interrupted by a ring on the front doorbell.

'That's Stan come for tea,' said Madge. But before she could get up from the table, Sunday took hold of her arm.

'*When* will you tell me, Mum?' she asked, a look of pleading in her eyes. 'I shan't sleep until I know.'

Madge tried smiling back at her. 'When we get back from the band concert,' she said with assurance. 'I promise you I won't let you down. Not this time. Not ever. I love you, Sunday. Don't ever forget that. Just trust me.'

A couple of hours later, Sunday met up with Pete Hawkins, and before they went on to the band concert, they stopped off for a drink at a pub. As much as she liked him, Sunday found it hard going with Pete, for their only means of communication was through sign language. That was fine for a time, but Pete was absolutely fluent with his knowledge of the alphabet and with phrasing, but Sunday had to concentrate all her powers when she was sign-talking back to him. Her greatest difficulty was the fact that Pete only used his hands to communicate, but despite her consistent sign-writing practice, reading lips was still the easiest option for her. However, at least the other customers in the pub were fascinated by the way the two young deaf people communicated, and whenever either Sunday or Pete turned in their direction, one of them always nodded with a smile.

'Pete,' Sunday said, after putting down her usual glass of shandy on the counter, and plucking up enough courage to sign-talk. 'I'm really sorry about dragging you out like this. It was a crazy idea of mine to ask you to a band concert!'

Pete understood perfectly what Sunday had signalled, and his face broke into a broad grin. 'I'm not coming to the concert to hear music,' he said, his hands and fingers darting about in a rapid reply. 'I just want the chance to sit next to you for an hour.'

Sunday laughed. 'Better not tell my mum that,' she signalled. 'She takes her music very seriously.'

'I take you seriously too,' replied Pete, gazing straight into her eyes. 'Will you come back with me tonight – *please*?'

Sunday suddenly felt herself tense. Even if she had wanted to go back home with Pete after the concert, there was no way she could do it. Not tonight. One way or another, this had been a truly traumatic day for her, and her entire body felt emotionally drained. Also, the sad fact of the matter was that she didn't want to go back with Pete. Although she felt awful about it, she had no feeling for him, no *real* feeling, and it would be very unfair to lead him on any further. But this was not the time to tell him. 'Not tonight, Pete,' she said, trying hard not to appear as though she was rejecting him. 'I've got some important things to talk over with Mum.'

When they left the pub, it was raining. Neither of them had an umbrella, so Pete pulled up his jacket collar and, hurrying along with his arm around Sunday's waist, tried to use the jacket to cover her shoulders. The evenings were now not nearly so bright as they had been for the past few months, for it was now mid-August, and lighting-up time was only a couple of hours away, at around nine thirty. But as the two of them walked as fast as they could along the glistening, wet pavements of Holloway Road, there was a lovely freshness in the early-evening air.

With only two minutes to spare to the start of the band concert, Sunday and Pete decided to run the last few yards or so. To their surprise, a small crowd was gathered around in the rain outside the entrance doors of the Salvation Army Hall. Alarmed, Sunday rushed forward to see what was going on. Some of the crowd recognised her, and called to the others to make a path for her.

The corridor inside was also jammed with people, some of them in Salvation Army uniform and carrying their own personal copies of the Bible. By this time, Sunday was getting even more concerned, and, with Pete following on close behind, she finally succeeded in pushing her way through into the Hall itself. There she was met by Captain Sarah Denning, one of Madge's closest Salvation Army friends. She was in tears.

'What is it, Mrs Denning?' asked Sunday anxiously. 'What's happened? Where's Mum?'

The poor, distressed woman shook her head, took hold of Sunday by the arm, and gently led her towards the platform, where members of the band and other uniformed officers were huddled around in a group. The moment Colonel Faraday noticed Sunday, he stepped forward to help her up on to the platform. 'My dear child,' he said, looking white and shattered. 'You've got to be very brave.' He called to the others to stand back, then did so himself.

Lying stretched out on her back on the platform floor was Madge.

'Mum!'

Sunday rushed forward, and knelt beside the motionless figure. The shock too much for her to take in, she immediately looked around for some kind of explanation from the sea of distressed faces around her. Then she looked back down at her mum again. The old lady, dressed in her much-cherished Salvation Army uniform, and who only a few hours before had looked so alive and well, had her head resting on someone's folded-up uniform jacket. There was no movement at all. Sunday leaned forward to take a close look at her. 'Mum?' she asked in a puzzled, bewildered voice which echoed around the silent hall. But the old lady's eyes were firmly closed, and she made no response at all.

'Mum!'

But Sunday's call of despair went unanswered.

At the age of seventy-four, Madge Collins was dead.

# Chapter 26

Madge Collins's sudden death was a devastating blow for Sunday. During her final few weeks, the old lady had been in such good health, recovering completely from the varicose vein operation, and looking fitter than she had done for many a year. Unfortunately, however, a post-mortem examination had revealed that, following the operation, a blood clot had been carried away in the circulation, and had become lodged in Madge's brain. Most people in 'the Buildings' were shocked and saddened by their neighbour's death, but said that at least she had died quickly and without pain. But for Sunday, the sudden loss of her mum was a disaster. The irony of losing the old lady just hours before she was due to tell Sunday everything about her natural mother had been a cruel act of fate. Sunday was convinced that now her mum had gone, she would never know the truth.

Madge's funeral had been a grand event. The service of Thanksgiving for her life was held in the Salvation Army Hall up at Highbury, which had been overflowing with the old lady's friends from what she used to call 'God's Army', and there were also many of her neighbours from 'the Buildings' there, including a tearful Doll Mooney and her husband Joe, and Jack Popwell with his lady-friend, Ivy Westcliff. But a lot of people agreed that the most poignant part of the day had been the slow procession of the cortège and mourners, moving along the busy Holloway Road, and preceded by Madge's beloved Salvation Army Band playing a selection of her favourite rousing hymns, such as 'Onward Christian Soldiers', and 'Shall We All Gather By The River?' The most noticeable absentee from the proceedings was, of course, Aunt Louie. But although she refused to attend the service at Highbury, she went to Highgate Cemetery to watch Madge's interment, but only from a distance. Sunday knew her aunt was there, but decided not to upset her even more by approaching her. Luckily, the rain held off just long enough for the graveside ceremony to come to an end, but as the crowd of mourners quickly dispersed and filed their way out towards the cemetery gates, the heavens opened, and there was a heavy downpour.

This, however, did not deter Louie. Once she was quite sure that everyone had left, she slowly approached her sister's graveside, where council diggers were about to fill in. Out of respect for the feelings of the last remaining mourner, they withdrew to the cover of a huge chestnut tree. For several minutes, Louie stood by the grave, rain pelting down on to her short cropped hair and black cotton dress. And as she stared down at the tiny oak coffin with its shining brass plate showing Madge's name, date of birth and date of death, there was so much that she wanted to say to her sister, so many misunderstandings that she wanted to put right. But now it was too late, and all she could do was to make her last conciliatory offering, a small posy of violets, which fluttered down into the grave, and came to rest alongside Sunday's solitary pink rose on top of Madge's coffin.

Her mum gone, Sunday now had to decide what to do with her life. With the help of her neighbours, she was allowed to stay in the flat, but it was a completely new experience for her, and for the first week, it scared her. At night, as she lay in bed deep in thought, she imagined all sorts of things, either that her mum was moving around in the next-door bedroom, or that there were people on the landing outside, trying to get in. But as she gradually got used to living alone in her silent world, the more she came to understand what she had to do in order to survive.

Jack Popwell turned out to be an enormous help, for his advice about how to budget out her school wages to pay for such things as the rent, food, gas and electricity taught her a great deal about housekeeping. And from the moment Madge died, Doll Mooney was convinced that Sunday was going without her meals, so, despite the continued food shortages, she was constantly bringing her titbits, and making her apple pies and scrag-end stew with dumplings. In fact, nearly all Sunday's neighbours showed how concerned they were, for when she was at home, there was hardly a moment when someone didn't call on her, just to keep her company. However, as time went by, Sunday began to stand on her own two feet. In the past, being independent was something she had only dreamt about. Now it was a reality.

For the next couple of months, Sunday learnt to take care of herself. Every day from Monday to Friday she went to the Deaf and Dumb

School, where she was becoming more and more involved in showing the kids how to express themselves through dance, and at the weekend she went through the frustrations of shopping, queuing for hours on end for everything from food to clothes. In fact, since the war had ended, endless queuing was beginning to get everyone down, and housewives were organising themselves into protest groups. However, Sunday was also learning how to cook, and she was amazed how many recipes she could find using Spam!

The best news came at the beginning of September when Jinx wrote to say that she had given birth to a baby boy weighing six pounds four ounces. Naturally enough, she had named the new arrival Erin, adding that she had wanted his middle name to be Sunday. However, after desperate pleas from the rest of her family, she had decided that as Sunday was a girl's name, perhaps David might be a more sensible choice. But she warned that as soon as young Erin Junior was strong enough to travel, she would be bringing him straight to London to meet his Auntie Sunday.

It was at this time that Sunday made up her mind that she just had to talk with her Aunt Louie. She hadn't seen the old lady since that fleeting glimpse at her mum's funeral, and there was something important that Sunday needed to say to her. Luckily, Louie had left a forwarding address, which was in Adelaide Road up at Swiss Cottage, and so one afternoon after she had left school for the day, she took a trolleybus to Camden Town, changed on to a petrol bus to Chalk Farm Underground Station, then walked a short distance up the hill towards Swiss Cottage along the main Adelaide Road.

When she found the terraced house she was looking for, Sunday was quite impressed. It was a four-storey Edwardian-style house, and although the brickwork still carried some wartime bomb-blast scars, to Sunday it seemed like quite a posh place to live in, for when she went up the steps to the street door, the smell of tobacco flowers in the small front garden was quite overpowering.

'Goodness!' gasped the rather petite elderly lady who opened the door. 'You're Sunday, aren't you? I saw you when we came down to the VE Day party – at the flats where you live. Oh, do please come in.'

'Thank you,' replied Sunday, with a smile. She rather liked the woman, for she was quite dotty, and had lovely long curls which jumped about on her head as she closed the door behind them, and led the way into the front room overlooking the road.

'You just sit down and make yourself comfortable,' said the old lady, quite breathless with excitement. 'I'll go and call your aunt. We were just playing some gin rummy upstairs. I'll make us a nice cup of tea.'

Sunday wanted to tell her not to go to any trouble, but by the time she could even open her mouth, the old lady had scurried out of the room, closing the door behind her.

Whilst she sat there, Sunday couldn't help noticing how much more interesting the room was than her own parlour back at 'the Buildings'. There was so much bric-a-brac scattered around, two lovely big leather armchairs placed either side of the fireplace, and lots of books on shelves built into the alcoves. The huge aspidistra on a small polished table in front of the window brought a smile to her face, and she loved the draped floral-patterned curtains that were pulled back to reveal delicate lace ones beneath. There were several family portraits hanging on the walls, and there was hardly an inch of room on the mantelpiece, for it was crowded with framed photographs of various middle-aged ladies.

When the door opened again, Sunday was surprised to see how different her aunt was looking. She had lost a great deal of weight, which somehow made her face look gaunt and weary.

'Why didn't you tell me you were coming?' asked Louie, remembering to keep her lips facing Sunday. 'It's quite a surprise.'

Sunday felt quite awkward. 'I hope you don't mind, Aunt Louie,' she replied weakly.

To Sunday's surprise, her aunt went straight to her, hugged her, and kissed her on the cheek. 'I don't mind at all,' she said, with even the suggestion of a smile on her face. 'Come and sit down, Sunday. Tell me how you've been getting on.'

They both sat in armchairs facing each other.

'It's strange,' said Sunday. 'I never thought I could cope, living on my own.'

'I must say, you look well on it.'

Sunday smiled. Then she looked aimlessly down at her lap for a moment, before looking up again. 'Haven't seen you since Mum's funeral.'

Now it was Louie's turn to look down. But she quickly recovered from her uneasiness, and looked up at Sunday again. 'I didn't want to be involved in all that Bible-punching,' she said. 'I wanted to say goodbye to Madge in my own way.'

'I understand.'

Louie was grateful for Sunday's response.

For a brief moment, they sat in silence.

Sunday was first to speak. 'Auntie. I had a reason for coming to see you. I've wanted to do it ever since Mum died. But, I just had to get over it all first.'

The two of them moved automatically to the edge of their seats so that they could be facing each other much closer.

'The day Mum died, she told me that she was going to come up to see you, to ask you to come back home.'

Louie froze and gripped the arms of her chair.

'She said a lot of things,' Sunday continued. 'She said she felt guilty about the way she'd treated you, that you'd always been such good friends.'

Louie leaned back in her chair again. 'We were as close as any sisters could be,' she said with a sigh.

Sunday watched her aunt as she gazed aimlessly into the fireplace. 'Anyway, I just wanted you to know. We had a long talk about it, only a few hours before – before it happened.' She leaned forward and touched her aunt on the knee. 'What I'm trying to say, Auntie, is, try and forgive Mum. She didn't mean half the things she said.'

'I'm the one who needs to be forgiven,' replied Louie, her face looking much more taut than Sunday had remembered. 'I was ungrateful. Your mum did a lot for me, and I was ungrateful. I was jealous because she had something that I wanted.' Just occasionally she forgot to keep her lips turned towards Sunday, and every time she remembered this, she had to repeat herself. 'Reg Collins didn't want *me*. I tried to convince myself that he did – but he didn't.'

'Auntie.' Sunday was now stretched forward, holding both Louie's hands. 'You told me once that you knew my mother, my real mother. Who was she?'

Louie tried to look away.

Sunday persisted. 'Please – won't you tell me?'

'There's no point, Sunday,' Louie replied. 'Your mother's dead – both of them are gone.'

Sunday was determined to coax something out of the old lady. 'What do you mean, Auntie?' she pleaded. '*Both* my mums?'

'No, Sunday,' Louie replied, pulling her hands away and resting them in her lap. 'I promised your mum, I promised Madge that I'd never be the one to tell you. That was the trouble. That's why I fell out with her. I wanted you to know. I wanted to hurt her by telling you.'

'Then tell me, Auntie!' begged Sunday. 'What's the use of keeping it from me now?'

Louie sat up straight in her chair. As she did so, Sunday thought how much she looked like her mum.

'Because that's how Madge wanted it,' Louie replied firmly. 'And that's the way it's going to be.'

It was half past nine when Sunday got back to the Nag's Head, and it was almost dark. During the war years, Sunday had always hated walking home in the dark because the streets were pitch-black, but now there were lights everywhere, not only from the streetlamps but also from some of the shop windows. It was a few yards' walk from the bus stop to the backyard of 'the Buildings', and when she got there, and was just about to disappear through the entrance to her block, someone came up from behind and touched her on the shoulder. Sunday turned with a start. It was Doll Mooney.

'Guess where I've bin?' she said perkily. 'I've bin 'round the Marlborough ter see this singin' an' dancin' pitture – *Coney Island*, wiv this great big sexpot, George Montgomery.' She was clearly reeling from seeing someone on the screen that she really fancied, for she was talking so fast, Sunday could hardly follow what she was saying. 'Ooh, Sun,' she said, practically drooling, ''ave yer ever seen 'im? Drives me wild! Can't imagine what 'e sees in bloody Betty Grable.' Then, without pausing for breath, she added, ''Ere. 'As anyone ever told yer, you look a bit like Betty Grable – only better!'

Sunday, embarrassed, laughed dismissively and shook her head. 'How come you went on your own?' she asked.

'Got Joe ter baby-sit. 'Bout bleedin' time. 'E spends most 'is nights down the boozer, so why shouldn't I 'ave me bob's werf of George Montgomery!'

They both laughed, and whilst they were standing there, it was such a pleasantly warm September evening, some of the neighbours popped their heads out of their windows to see what was going on down below.

'Wot's all the bleedin' row then?' yelled Bert Vickers from the window of his second-floor flat.

Doll looked up and yelled back. 'Go back ter bed, Bert! We're too young fer you!'

The moment Bert saw who was calling out to him, he knew there was no hope of winning an exchange with her, so he disappeared inside, and slammed the window.

'Silly old sod!' said Doll. 'Be glad ter get out of this place.'

Sunday immediately stopped laughing. 'What was that you said, Doll?' she asked.

Doll suddenly became serious, and after looking around to make sure no one else was listening, she lowered her voice, and emphasising her lip movements, drew as close to Sunday as she could. 'Look, Sun. Keep this to yerself, but – it's just possible me and Joe are goin' ter split up.'

Sunday was shocked. 'Doll!'

'Ssh!' she said, again checking all around to see that no one could hear. 'There's nuffin' definite yet, but – well, 'e's got 'is eyes on this uvver woman now. Some cow lives up Mile End way. Joe goes a bundle on the East End!'

Sunday was confused. 'But you said you'd never leave him. You said you still loved him.'

'I do. But I'm sick er bringin' up four kids all on me own. And now wiv this new one due any minute.' She sighed despondently. 'I must've bin off me chomp. Still, it's me own fault. 'E got randy one night, and just banged away. But wot can I do? If I can't stop 'im, I just have ter lie back an' imagine 'e's George Montgomery!'

Although Doll roared with laughter again, Sunday knew only too well what she was going through. Doll was such an easy-going woman, who would do anything for anyone. But the way Joe Mooney was treating her was cruel and unfair. She deserved so much better than an occasional wrestling match followed by yet another howling baby.

'Anyway,' Doll continued, 'now the war's over, 'e says 'e wants ter get out of London, and give up doin' work as a brickie. 'E reckons 'e can get a job at some car-makin' place over at Dagen'am.'

'Will you go with him?'

'That's up ter 'im now,' replied Doll. 'It's goin' ter take an awful lot for me ter give up all me friends 'round 'ere – 'specially you.'

Sunday leaned forward and hugged her.

A few minutes later, Doll went into her block, and Sunday made her way across the yard to her own entrance. Her chance meeting with Doll had made her very depressed. Although Doll wasn't all that clever in the brains department, she was very astute about everyday matters. And over the years she had been the most wonderful support to Sunday, especially during the height of the Blitz, when she, her mum, and the Mooney family often had to spend the night together in the public shelter. With bombs dropping and guns blasting away outside, Doll had always been the one to keep up everyone's morale with an endless stream of good old Cockney humour, which cunningly disguised her own fears and apprehensions. No, Doll deserved better than being treated like a sex machine. She was a worthwhile person, and it was about time someone told Joe Mooney what a shit he was.

As usual, the entrance door to Sunday's block was stuck, so she had to use her shoulder to force it open. Cursing, she asked herself how many times had the council been told about all the things in 'the Buildings' that needed to be repaired.

Once inside the ground-floor landing, Sunday had to grope her way towards the stairs in the dark, for the solitary electric light bulb wasn't working. However, she had her small pocket torch in her handbag, so she got it out, and started to make her way up the stone steps. She hated the climb, and whilst she was doing it, she couldn't help thinking about the number of times her poor mum had been absolutely breathless by the time she had reached the fourth floor. As she went, the torch beam not only picked out the harsh stone steps that she was taking one at a time, but was also casting a dim glow on some of the graffiti that had been scrawled across the walls during the war, including plenty of V-signs, a couple of 'Winnie!' slogans, and several more proclaiming, 'Labour For Peace!'

Eventually, she reached the door of her flat, and immediately cursed herself again for not removing her front-door key from her handbag at the same time that she had retrieved her torch. Before she found the key, however, she was suddenly aware that she was not alone. She turned sharply, but as she did so, someone's hand slammed across her mouth, preventing her from screaming out. Then she felt the torch being taken from her own hand, and when the beam was directed on to the face of the person who was restraining her, she saw that it was Ernie Mancroft.

'Wotcha, Sun!' he said cheekily, his lips moving stiffly in the torchlight. 'Bet you're glad ter see yer ol' mate again, ain't yer?'

Sunday struggled, but he kept his hand clasped across her mouth and held on to her.

'Tell yer what, Sun,' he said, making quite sure she could see his lips. 'If I take me 'and away, let's say yer promise ter be'ave yerself. Bargain?'

Sunday nodded.

Ernie cautiously took his hand away from Sunday's mouth. 'Yeah, that's better, mate.' He kept the torch beam directed at his face. 'Sorry ter 'ear about yer ol' woman, Sun. Rotten luck that. Goin' ter ask me in for a shandy, are yer?'

Sunday shook her head violently.

'Now, that's not a very friendly way ter treat someone who saved yer life, is it?' said Ernie, with a leer, voice low. 'Bet yer wouldn't do the same ter your Yankee pal.'

'What do you want with me, Ernie?' Sunday said, her eyes carefully looking along the row of front doors to see if there was a light on anywhere. 'Didn't you learn your lesson down at Thorpe Bay?'

Ernie refused to let this remark intimidate him. 'Don't get too smart wiv me, Sun – just 'cos yer Yankee boyfriend got lucky.'

As he spoke, a light came on in the hallway of one of the flats further along the corridor. Sunday tried to make a move, but he quickly held her arm with his hand. Then he put a finger up to his mouth, signalling her to keep quiet. After a moment or so, the light went out again.

'They should have put you away, Ernie,' Sunday said, her voice speaking louder than Ernie would have liked. 'You're the one that struck lucky.'

Ernie's fixed grin faded. 'I'm sorry to 've disappointed yer, Sun,' he said. 'But I was innocent, y'see. Not guilty.'

'You were absent without leave. They shoot people for that.'

This brought a smile to Ernie's face. 'Mitigatin' circumstances, Sun. My big bruvver, Denn – you remember 'im, don't yer? 'E was a para. Got a packet at Arnhem. The court martial got sorry for me – silly bastards!'

Sunday again tried to pull away, and again he restrained her. She tried very hard to show that she wasn't frightened, for, knowing him only too well, she was sure that it would be the one thing he wanted most of all.

At this moment, Ernie felt confident enough to release his grip on her. But he held on to her torch, and kept the beam turned towards his face. 'What is it about me that yer 'ate so much, Sun?' he asked.

'I don't hate you, Ernie,' she replied. 'I just feel sorry for you. You've got so much going for you. You should be looking for someone who'll love you, who you can settle down with.'

'I've found someone I want to settle down wiv.'

'It'll never happen, Ernie. I promise you, it'll never happen.'

Ernie leaned as close as he could towards her, so that the beam from the torch was casting a light on both their faces. 'I want ter tell yer somefin', Sun,' he said, the torch beam reflected in the pupils of his eyes, his voice softening. 'When that 'bug come down on the Bagwash, I told you that yer owed me one. Well, yer don't – see? All I'm askin' is that yer give me a chance, a chance ter show yer that I'm not nuffin' like the person yer fink I am. I love yer, Sun. Why can't yer understand that? There's no uvver person I want, no uvver person that means a sod ter me.' He blinked in the torchlight, and when he looked into Sunday's eyes again, he thought he saw the first signs of guilt. 'Y'know, I've 'eard 'ow some people *grow* ter love each uvver. It's not there at first, but after a while, there's a feelin', a feelin' that wiv a bit of work an' understandin'—'

'No, Ernie!' Sunday pushed him away. 'I don't love you. I never could love you. I'm sorry about that, Ernie, I really am. But what's happening is all one-sided.' Then she shook her head, and backing a few steps away from him, said, 'You can never make someone love you if they don't want to.'

There was a moment's pause between them, then Sunday decided to take a chance, and walk back to the steps. However, just when she thought she had succeeded in getting away from him, he leapt at her and tried to kiss her. Sunday was terrified, and as his lips pressed hard against hers, she tried desperately to pull away. She was repulsed by him, and knew that if she didn't soon get some air into her lungs, she would suffocate. She finally succeeded, but when she let out a yell, Ernie hit her across the face with the back of his hand.

'Cow!' he yelled, now oblivious to the lights that were being turned on in the front halls of all the flats along the corridor. Then he grabbed hold of her, and threw her to the ground.

Sunday fell to her knees, and as she did so, she suddenly felt a soaring pain in her left ear. She let out a piercing scream. Suddenly terrified of what he had done, Ernie started to back towards the steps.

'My ear!' Sunday screeched several times.

Some of the neighbours started to peer out from their front doors, which sent Ernie rushing down the stairs, pushing Jack Popwell out of the way as he went.

'Don't leave me!' yelled Sunday, clutching the ear that was throbbing violently. 'Don't leave me, Ernie! Don't leave me!'

And as Jack Popwell reached her, Sunday grabbed hold of him, yelling, 'Say something to me, Jack! For God's sake – say something to me!'

# Chapter 27

Mr Callow, the ear specialist, hadn't examined Sunday for quite some time, so he was intrigued by her claim that during her scuffle with Ernie Mancroft, she was positive that she had heard a faint sound in her left ear. Sunday spent nearly two hours in the ENT Clinic at the Royal Northern Hospital, and the endless impedance and audiometry tests she underwent proved very tiring. Each ear separately and then both together were subjected to rigorous sound waves, and although at times Sunday felt as though the pressure was going to split her head wide open, she was unable to recapture those extraordinary few seconds in which she was convinced she could hear *something*. However, once the sceptical Mr Callow had finally studied the tests and X-rays, he had no alternative but to conclude that the acoustic nerve in Sunday's ears had been damaged in the 'doodlebug' explosion, and, as surgery was not yet available to repair such damage, it was highly unlikely that her hearing could ever be restored.

Sunday fell into the depths of depression. It seemed so cruel that her hopes should have been raised only to be dashed again by a whole lot of hospital X-rays and tests. During the following weeks, she refused to believe Mr Callow's diagnosis, and when she was lying in bed at night there were times that she could imagine hearing the sounds of life again, a cat wailing in the backyard below, a neighbour's wireless set, or her Aunt Louie snoring in the next-door bedroom. But they were nothing more than false hopes, and she knew that she had to get on with her life as it now existed.

More than anything else, Sunday missed Gary. Since coming back from Ridgewell she was only now realising what an influence he had been on her life, how he had given her the confidence to cope with the trauma of being deaf, and the will to survive even the most challenging situations. Most of all, she missed Gary himself, his quirky sense of humour and those pale blue eyes that turned her knees to jelly. She missed the warmth of his body lying beside her, she missed his cheek resting against her own and the touch of his short, wavy blond hair as she ran her fingers through it. She couldn't bear the thought that she might never see or even hear from him again. Nothing or no one could replace him. Not even Pete Hawkins.

Sunday's relationship with Pete was getting nowhere. It wasn't his fault, and she knew it. After their solitary night of passion, Pete had asked her back to his flat several times, but Sunday had always found an excuse to decline. The fact was, of course, that she had only used Pete as an outlet for her unhappiness and frustration. In her own mind, she was telling Gary that if he didn't want to contact her any more then that was fine with her, that as far as she was concerned, there were plenty more fish in the sea, and she didn't need him. But the fact of the matter was that she *did* need him, and the way she was feeling right now, she was finding it hard to do without him. After a while, Pete began to get the message, and he gradually stopped pursuing her. Not that he didn't fancy her any more, but the competition from someone he didn't even know was too much. However, they remained good friends, and when Sunday did eventually start talking to Pete about her feelings for Gary, the young deaf and dumb teacher became an even better friend. On his advice, Sunday wrote to the Commanding Officer at Ridgewell Airbase to see if she could get some information concerning Gary's whereabouts. Needless to say, the reply she got was fairly official and vague, and all she discovered was that, at the end of June, Gary had been transferred to combat air duties in South-east Asia. Which left one big question unanswered. The war out there was now over, so why hadn't Gary written?

As summer gradually turned to autumn, the worst problem for Sunday was loneliness. With the nights drawing in again, once she had got home from school in the late afternoon, she felt that she didn't want to go out anywhere or see anyone. And when she remembered how only a year or so before she had been dancing with Pearl up at the Athenaeum every Saturday night, she again questioned what she was going to do with her life. And always at the back of her mind was the nagging feeling about who she was and where she came from. At the beginning of November, however, her life was to change dramatically.

It came after the Armistice Day Service of Remembrance at Islington Green, in which the Salvation Army joined representatives from the Armed Forces in honouring the dead of two world wars. Sunday had always tried to avoid this annual event, for she found it such a sad and sombre occasion. But, as her mum's old 'Army' band was playing at the service, she decided to go and give her support. Despite the bitterly cold morning, there was quite a crowd around the modest white stone war memorial, and amongst them were several local dignitaries, like Dr Eric Fletcher MP and the Mayor of Islington. Sunday thought it was a very poignant sight, for everyone, including herself, was wearing a red poppy in their buttonhole, which seemed to be a wonderful symbol of all those young men and women who had given their lives for their country in two horribly savage wars.

During the service, Sunday stood next to her mum's old Salvation Army friend, Captain Sarah Denning, who constantly kept her informed about the next item. Although Sunday couldn't hear any of the readings, the address, or the hymns, during the one minute's silence on the stroke of eleven o'clock, she deliberately kept her eyes open so that she could study the dignified, but war-weary faces of the young and old veterans. As soon as the service was over, and the military and civil procession had wound its way back to the Town Hall, Sunday and Captain Sarah walked together down Upper Street towards Highbury Corner. As they passed the imposing grandeur of St Mary's Church, the congregation was just swarming out on to the pavement after their own Remembrance Day Service, and the pealing of the church's bells could be heard quite clearly above the rooftops from the Angel to Canonbury and Highbury.

Once they had crossed the main road to get away from the St Mary's crowd, Sunday and Captain Sarah ambled along at a slow, comfortable pace, regardless of the fine frosty rain that was beginning to dampen their topcoats.

'You must miss your dear mum a great deal,' Captain Sarah said, adding wistfully, 'I know *we* all do.'

Sunday never found it easy trying to watch what people were saying whilst walking together. But Captain Sarah was different. She had a wonderful aptitude for summing up a situation, and doing the right thing. 'I can hardly believe it sometimes,' Sunday replied.

'Madge was such an important part of our group, you know,' said Captain Sarah, as she strolled along, clutching her Bible in both hands in front of her. 'It's taken all our strength to carry on without her. However,' she said, with a glowing smile, 'at least we've inherited you.'

Puzzled, Sunday was about to question her, when two small

snotty-nosed kids rushed by, giggling and yelling at the funny lady in the bonnet and uniform.

'What do you mean?' Sunday asked, as soon as the kids had disappeared.

'Surely you must know what your mum's dearest wish was?'

Sunday shook her head.

Captain Sarah beamed. 'For you to join us.'

Sunday came to a dead halt. '*Me*!' The look on her face told what she thought.

'Why yes,' replied Captain Sarah. 'Your mum was always telling us how much you embraced the things we do.'

Sunday stared in horror at the bright face looking straight at her. In her mind she asked how her mum could have given such an impression? Yes, it was certainly true that Sunday had always admired everything about the selfless work the men and women of the Salvation Army were always doing for the community, but the idea of her becoming a part of it all scared the life out of her. And yet, she didn't know why. They were, after all, just ordinary men and women, good Christians who were joined together in a common faith. So what was there to be afraid of?

Sunday shook her head. 'I don't think so, Mrs Denning,' she said awkwardly. 'I don't think I'm ready for anything like that – not just yet.'

Captain Sarah smiled serenely. It was an infectious smile that immediately transformed her long, droll face into that of a naughty, mischievous schoolgirl. 'We're not all doom and gloom,' she said, with a twinkle in her eyes. 'We have a lot of fun at the Hall.'

Sunday tried to smile. But although she had a great deal of time for Captain Sarah, the idea of taking over her mum's place in the Salvation Army was still too unnerving.

'Anyway,' continued the Captain, patting Sunday gently on the cheek, 'there's no rush. After all, we're not going to run away.'

They moved on, and a few minutes later they reached Highbury Corner, where a drunken old regular was just leaving the pub. But when he suddenly caught sight of the Salvation Army officer just passing by, he quickly swivelled round on his heels and beat a hasty retreat back inside.

The incident made both Sunday and Captain Sarah laugh. 'Looks like there's one sinner who's not yet ready to be redeemed!' said the Captain, with a hearty chuckle.

After crossing the road, they had soon reached the entrance door of the Mission Hall. Captain Sarah invited Sunday to come in and join some of the group for a cup of tea. At first Sunday refused. The place had so many difficult associations with her past life that she just didn't feel she could cope with it. But soon after she had taken leave of Captain Sarah, she had second thoughts. A few yards along Holloway Road, she turned and made her way back to the Salvation Army Hall.

As soon as she was inside the building, she knew that she had made a mistake. Wave upon wave of panic swept through her, and by the time she had entered the Hall itself, the sight of that same platform where she had been shown her mum's dead body filled her with a sense of guilt and despair. To make things worse, she suddenly found herself surrounded by all sorts of well-meaning friends.

'Sunday!' 'Hallo, Sunday, my dear!' 'How lovely to have you with us again!' 'Your mum would be so proud to know you were here.' In every direction she looked, there was a sea of faces, all of them with lips that seemed to be moving in grotesque shapes. It was such a strange feeling, for she knew that behind every one of those faces were kind, decent, and loving people. But she felt hemmed in by them, as though they were quite unintentionally trying to suffocate her. Then Captain Sarah eased her way through the group, and hugged her. After saying something that Sunday didn't understand, she led the way towards a table in front of the platform where one of the uniformed ladies drew a cup of tea for her from an urn. Sunday took the cup, and tried to respond to what people were saying to her from one side to the other. She tried to smile, but somehow it felt false. Then she tried to sip her tea, but it was too hot and she burnt her lips. Something was happening to her, and she didn't know what. She felt as though she had a fever, for she was now burning-hot, and her underclothes were wet with perspiration. Everyone was making such a fuss of her, everyone was so sympathetic, so over-sympathetic. They were radiating goodness, and she felt wretched for not being able to respond. But why was it that there was such a fine line between good and evil? These people were undoubtedly good, they were God's creatures, God's messengers. And yet, she was afraid of them. Why? Why? Why?

Sunday was in such a state of panic that she suddenly dropped her cup of tea, which went cascading down on to the wood-tile floor, smashing into pieces. She had no idea what was happening to her, and while she was apologising for all the trouble she had caused, she was unconsciously backing her way through the group, and heading for the entrance door. Although everyone was deeply concerned, Captain Sarah beckoned to them to give Sunday some breathing space.

As she continued to back down the corridor, Sunday could see the Captain coming after her, arms outstretched, calling to her. But Sunday was shaking her head, and just couldn't stop.

In the street outside, Sunday could at last breathe again. The ice-cold drizzle was now turning to sleet, and she turned her face upwards to cool it down. As she did so, Captain Sarah followed her out, and she could tell that the poor woman was calling her name.

'I'm sorry, Mrs Denning!' Sunday repeated over and over again. And she kept on backing away from the entrance, further and further across the pavement towards the kerb. 'I shouldn't have . . . I didn't want to . . . I'm sorry, sorry . . .'

'Sunday! Don't go any further, Sunday! The road!'

Sunday didn't understand what the woman was saying, and when some of the others came out to join her, it only made her panic even more. 'I'm sorry!' she called out again in utter confusion. 'I can't! I just can't . . . !'

She had no idea that she had stepped off the pavement and was now backing across the road. She was also unaware that a small goods van was hurrying towards her.

The moment the van hit her, Sunday seemed to be tossed into the air as if in slow motion. As she came down again, the back of her head hit the hard tarmac road with a thump.

When Sunday regained consciousness, she found herself in a hospital bed, her head swathed in bandages. It took her several minutes to recover her faculties, but when she did, a searing pain shot across the back of her head. She had a burning desire to sit up, but as she tried to do so she felt a sharp pain in her right shoulder, which was strapped up. So she flopped back on to her pillow again, and as there was no one around her bed she could turn to, she closed her eyes and just lay there.

Gradually, images started to dance across her mind. Captain Sarah and those people at the Salvation Army Hall, all stretching out towards her. Then it all came back. The cup and saucer smashing to pieces on the floor, her backing out into the street, the frantic look on Captain Sarah's face as she called out to her, and suddenly, the dark rain-swept sky whirling round and round as she spiralled out of control through the air. Only then did she remember what started it all. The humming sound. Subconsciously, her hands were gripping the blanket on top of her. She felt quite giddy, and lacked all sense of cohesion. And then she heard it again. The humming sound. A voice? No. It wasn't possible – imagining it again. There it was again! A voice! Yes – definitely. Small and distant. A voice! Her chest was heaving up and down beneath the sheets. She felt sick. She felt giddy. Humming? No – a voice!

'Sunday?'

Someone was gently stroking her face.

'Sunday?'

A voice!

'Are you awake, Sunday?'

Sunday's eyes sprang open. The smiling face of a nurse was staring down at her.

'Hallo, Sunday.' Sunday saw the girl's lips move. But as she watched her, she also heard her voice. Far and distant – but she *heard* it.

Her stomach lurched. Then she was sick all over her pillow.

Mr Callow had already spent nearly two hours peering into Sunday's ears, probing around with cotton buds and all kinds of surgical instruments, and looking at the results of the latest tests and X-rays. It had been another exhausting day in the ENT Clinic for Sunday. She had spent most of the time in a special examination room where every few minutes different specialists and therapists had come in to look at her eyes, her nose, her throat, feeling for any tenderness beneath the ears, and using all sorts of gadgets to peer down at the size, shape, and condition of her eardrums. Then there were the nurses, who took her temperature, blood tests, and pulse. She felt like a guinea-pig. The only difference from all the tests she had taken just a few weeks ago, was that whilst these ones were being carried out, she could hear the faint voices of those who were discussing her. Needless to say, there was quite a lot of scepticism as to whether she was fantasising about regaining her hearing, so that it became a wonderful game for her to play when she was able to tell people what they were saying whilst their backs were turned towards her.

Although Sunday respected Mr Callow's skills, she couldn't bear his manner, for like so many doctors and specialists, he rarely addressed a single word to her personally, and when he discussed her condition with anyone, he made her feel more like a specimen than a human being. But when she first heard him speak to her, she was amazed by how different his voice had been from what she had imagined, for it was much more high-pitched, and somehow didn't fit the rather powerful frame of his body.

'Miss Collins,' he said formally, at last looking up from the pile of examination notes he had been hunched over at his desk for more than twenty minutes. 'I want to ask you a few questions. Only this time, I want you to listen to them, without reading my lips. How do you feel about that?'

'What do you want to know?' replied Sunday, tired but confident.

Mr Callow got up from his desk, collected a chair from the corner of his consulting room, and placed it to one side of Sunday. Then he sat down, picked up a clipboard and pad, and spoke in a slightly raised voice towards her left ear. 'This humming sound. You say you first heard it in the Salvation Army Hall, *before* your road accident. Is that correct?'

Sunday nodded and replied, 'Yes.'

'Can you remember the precise moment?'

Sunday thought for an instant, and her mind went blank. For several seconds, all she could concentrate on was the strong smell of sterilising liquid in an enamel jug on Mr Callow's desk. 'I think it was when everyone started crowding in on me,' she replied. 'I couldn't breathe. I started to panic.'

Mr Callow was busily scribbling down notes. 'Did anyone bump into you, or knock against your ear?'

Sunday shook her head. 'Not that I can remember.' Then she sensed that he was making some kind of movement at the side of her.

Mr Callow tapped what looked like a tuning-fork on the desk, then held it against Sunday's left ear. 'Can you hear anything?' he asked.

'A humming sound,' Sunday replied immediately.

Although she couldn't see Mr Callow's reaction, he was certainly interested, if not entirely convinced. So he struck the tuning-fork again, but this time he held it further away from Sunday's ear, and gradually brought it closer. 'What about that?'

Sunday heard the humming sound quite clearly, but, like Mr Callow's voice, it remained at a distance. 'I hear it,' she replied.

'Loud?' asked Mr Callow.

'Not loud. Sort of – faint.'

Mr Callow scribbled some more notes, then got up from the seat and returned to his desk. 'Right then,' he said, leaning his elbows on his desk, resting his chin on his clasped hands, and staring directly at Sunday. 'So, what do you think this is all about?' he asked.

Sunday shrugged her shoulders. 'I don't know,' was all she could reply.

Mr Callow grinned. 'To be honest, Miss Collins, neither do I.' He rubbed his chin, which he had only shaved an hour before. 'But one thing I can say is that you are a very lucky young lady.'

Lucky! Sunday thought back over her last year and wondered how 'lucky' she had been to be nearly killed in a 'doodlebug' explosion, how 'lucky' she had been to lose first her hearing, and then her mum, how 'lucky' to be stalked by Ernie Mancroft, how 'lucky' to be knocked down by a van, and, most important of all, how 'lucky' to have found someone to love, and then to lose.

'You see,' continued Mr Callow, sorting through his notes, 'after your first injury from the flying bomb explosion, all our tests indicated that the labyrinth, one of the two sensitive structures of the inner ear which control your balance, was severely damaged. Now, under normal circumstances there would be no way to correct a situation like that. However . . .' He sat back in his seat, looked at her, and making sure his voice was raised just enough for her to hear, said, 'Sometimes Nature has a way of stepping in and taking over where we poor mortals quite often fail. What I think has happened in your case is that not only was the labyrinth not damaged as severely as we first thought, but the other part of your inner ear, which we call the cochlea, was not affected at all. To be perfectly honest with you, I think both these sensitive areas are simply healing up on their own.'

Sunday looked baffled by all the scientific explanation. 'So what happens now?' she asked.

Mr Callow shrugged his shoulders. 'Once your road injuries are properly healed, you can go home.'

'But will I get my full hearing back again – in both ears?'

Mr Callow leaned forward again and, for the first time, gave her a beaming smile. 'That's a question we can only ask of Mother Nature herself. Or maybe even a higher authority!'

A week later, Helen Gallop collected Sunday from the hospital, and accompanied her back home. Although it was only a short walk back to 'the Buildings', Sunday had to hold on to Helen's arm, for, as Mr Callow had warned, for the time being it was possible that her balance would be impaired. Even so, the moment she came down the hospital steps, the world seemed like a completely different place, for not only was the November sun bursting through heavy wintry clouds, but the faint sounds of the busy road she could now distantly hear all around her had transformed her silent world into a world of clanging trams, horses' hooves and cartwheels, and the *sound* of people's voices.

'You know, Helen,' said Sunday, as she held on tightly to her arm, 'you have one of the most beautiful voices I've ever heard. In fact, it's even more beautiful than I ever imagined.'

Helen laughed out loud. 'You wait 'til you get home and hear some of the kids yelling,' she said, without the need to turn and look at Sunday. 'Then you'll remember what voices are really like!'

When Sunday got back to 'the Buildings', people seemed to appear from everywhere. The news about her accident had caused great distress to all the neighbours, but when they heard that her hearing had been partially restored they couldn't wait to come out of their flats and hug her and pat her on the back.

Doll Mooney was in her curlers when she threw open the main door of her block. 'Sun!' she screeched, rushing straight at Sunday and throwing her arms around her. 'Oh Sun, is it true? Is it really true? Can yer really 'ear again?'

Sunday nodded her head. 'Just about,' she said. 'As long as you don't whisper.'

'Me – whisper!' yelled Doll, tears streaming down her cheeks. 'That'll be the day!'

A chorus of laughter echoed around the backyard and floated right up to the top-floor flats. And Sunday *heard* it! Far and distant, but she did *hear* it! She felt like she was coming through a dark tunnel and seeing light again. For the first time in over a year, she would actually be able to *hear* the sound of her old 'gang' in 'the Buildings' as they laughed and jeered and complained and coughed and sang and kept the volume of their wireless sets too high. Suddenly, life was worth living again!

It was all like music – to her ears.

# Chapter 28

There is always something quite special about autumn, and the year in which two ugly wars came to an end was no exception. All the trees in Islington were a riot of gold, brown, red, and yellow, and in both Holloway and Seven Sisters Roads the pavements were, in some places, ankle-deep in dead leaves. When she was a child, Sunday hardly ever noticed the crunching of autumn leaves beneath her feet, but now that her hearing had been partially restored, she thought it was one of the most beautiful sounds she had ever heard. However, after the late-autumn rains, the pavements soon became hazardous underfoot, as the crisp dead leaves were quickly transformed into a squelchy quagmire. It was a sure sign that winter was close at hand, for it was now cold – yes, really cold, and every chimney pot for as far as the eye could see was belching out thick black smoke.

If Sunday's initial euphoria had somewhat diminished in the week following her discharge from hospital, it was only because she had come to accept the fact that her hearing really was only partially restored, and that she had to concentrate hard on the faint sounds that were squeezing their way through what appeared to her to be a tiny hole in her eardrum. Nonetheless, it was exhilarating to hear anything at all and not to have to rely on watching the lip movements of everyone who talked to her. For a time she found it quite awkward, for it generally meant having to turn her good ear towards the sound source whenever she wanted to hear anything. But at least she was more than compensated by the fact that she could now have an opinion about a person by the sounds they made, as well as how they looked. Even so, she longed for any sign that would give her hope that her hearing would eventually be fully restored, and dreaded the thought that that day would never come, or that the sounds she could now hear, no matter how weak, would be taken away from her.

Sunday's most extraordinary experience came when she returned to her job at the Deaf and Dumb School. The children had clearly missed her, and the moment she walked through the front door they practically mobbed her. But it was the poignant little sounds they made that moved her the most, and when she brought in an old, portable wind-up gramophone for their dance lessons, she was astonished how swiftly they picked up the rhythm of a nursery children's song without being able to hear the actual music. Their total dedication convinced Sunday not to abandon her sign-language efforts, and as time went on, she learnt more from them about communication than any expert. And she also told the Principal, Eileen Roberts, that, despite the fact that part of her hearing had now been restored, she wanted to carry on with her work at the school. As far as she was concerned, the children were now an important part of her life, and she would always be one of them.

At the beginning of December, Sunday went to Jack Popwell's wedding. No one in 'the Buildings' was surprised, for he had been courting his lady-love, Ivy Westcliff, for over two years, and Doll Mooney told Sunday quite categorically that the two of them had been 'bunkin' up' in Jack's flat for most of that time. However, no one seemed to care, and there was general agreement that Ivy, who was a widow of five years and worked in a ladies' hairdresser's shop in Hornsey Road, was a wonderful match for house-proud Jack.

The wedding service itself took place in St George's Church in Tufnell Park, and apart from the happy couple's friends and relations, quite a posse of neighbours turned up. Most people agreed that December was a daft time to have a wedding, for everyone nearly froze to death in their party dresses when they were grouped together outside the church for the marriage portraits. Jack's grandmother, who looked about a hundred years old, grumbled all the way through the ceremony, and could only be consoled by being fed a continuous supply of black-market jelly babies. Sunday was very impressed with the wedding reception, which was held in the Ancient Order of Foresters Hall in Holloway Road. Following a slap-up sit-down do, Jack had hired a three-piece band through one of his mates who worked with him at the Gas, Light, and Coke Company. Sunday was in her seventh heaven, for it was the first time she had been able to hear live band music since her Saturday dance nights at the Athenaeum Ballroom. Many of the guests there asked her to dance, including both Jack and his new bride, Ivy, but it was a strange experience to dance again to a tempo that she could actually hear. No wedding reception round

Holloway would ever be complete without a knees-up, and that included a 'Hokey Cokey', a 'John Paul Jones', and the inevitable 'Knees Up Mother Brown'. It was the end of a perfect evening, a perfect day. Until, that is, Jack announced to everybody that early in the New Year, he and Ivy were leaving 'the Buildings' to move into a council house out at Epping.

A few weeks before Christmas, Sunday had a letter from Jinx to say that, as she was coming on a weekend visit to an aunt and uncle at a place called Finchley, she would like to bring young Junior along to meet his Auntie Sunday. Sunday wrote back immediately, and on the last Saturday afternoon before Christmas, a trolleybus drew to a halt outside Jones Brothers' Department Store in Holloway Road, and amongst the passengers out stepped Jinx clutching Erin Junior wrapped up in a large blue blanket.

'You don't 'ave to tell me 'ow fat I've got, 'cos I know!' These were Jinx's first words as she walked through the front door. 'You can blame it on this little bugger,' she said, immediately plonking Junior down on to the sofa. ''E's turned me into a bloody porpoise!'

Sunday roared with laughter, then threw her arms around her old mate, and hugged her. 'Oh, Jinx!' she said, shaking with excitement. 'I can't tell you how wonderful it is to see you again.'

Then all the attention was turned on Junior, who was looking very disgruntled after the long, cold, and uncomfortable journey he had been made to endure.

'He's beautiful, Jinx,' gushed Sunday, on her knees by the sofa, prodding her finger at poor, misunderstood Junior's mouth. 'He's got Erin's lips, that's for sure.'

'Ha!' spluttered Jinx, indignantly. ''E certainly knows 'ow to use them, if that's what you mean. You should 'ear 'im some nights, blowin' out raspberries to keep me awake!'

As if to confirm what his mum had said, Junior put his tongue out and made the most disgusting raspberry sound, spraying his Auntie Sunday with spittle. But this only made Sunday roar with laughter again.

Jinx kicked off her shoes, and flopped out on to a chair at the parlour table. 'D'you mind if I 'ave a fag, girl?' she asked, with a weary sigh. 'I'm gaspin' for one.'

'You shouldn't be smoking now you've got a baby,' replied Sunday.

Jinx, outraged, came straight back at her. 'Now look 'ere you, Miss Big City bloody Collins, if you think I'm goin' to—' She suddenly stopped in her tracks, and swung a startled look across to Sunday, who had her back turned towards her, still fawning over Junior. 'Sunday?'

Sunday turned, with a mischievous grin. 'Yes, Jinx?'

Jinx felt a chill run up her spine. 'You 'eard me!' she gasped, leaping up from the chair. 'You bloody '*eard* what I said!'

'Of course I did,' replied Sunday. 'And the answer's yes. Go ahead and smoke if you want.'

Jinx couldn't take her eyes off her old mate, and after no more than a few seconds' hesitation, she threw her arms around Sunday and hugged her. 'Oh, Sun!' she mumbled into Sunday's shoulder, close to tears. 'It's too won'erful for words. Just won'erful! What 'appened?' she asked excitedly, pulling away from Sunday, and holding her at arm's length. 'Tell me about it!'

And for the next hour or so, Sunday told her just about everything that had happened to her since they bid a tearful farewell to each other on that sun-drenched country railway station at Great Yeldham. For Sunday, it was a rich experience meeting up with Jinx again, and to hear for the first time that spicy, coarse voice, with its lovely Welsh twang, and the deep chesty cough which was the mark of all dedicated smokers. And as she watched Jinx breast-feeding the very hungry Erin Junior, she was so impressed to see what a good mother her old mate had become, and how she had refused to feel sorry for herself after Erin's death. For Jinx, too, it was a truly emotional reunion, meeting up with Sunday in her own environment, and actually to be able to have a conversation with her without the need to keep looking her straight in the face. However, as much as Sunday was elated to have Jinx and Junior with her for these few precious hours, the visit gave her the opportunity to ask about Gary.

''E's 'ad malaria, Sun,' Jinx said, in reply to Sunday's question, whilst trying hard to rock Junior gently to sleep in her arms. 'Really bad, by the sounds of it. I 'eard it from this buddy of Erin's. Mickey Quinn – d'you remember 'im?'

Sunday nodded. She was sitting beside Jinx on the sofa, watching Junior's eyes gradually becoming heavier and heavier.

'Got it out East or somethin',' continued Jinx, knowing only too well how concerned Sunday was. 'From what I can make out, 'is plane come down in the jungle. Took 'im an' 'is crew ages to get back to safety.'

'Does that mean – he's dead?'

Jinx found it a little disconcerting the way Sunday now turned her good ear towards her to hear what she was saying. 'Oh no,' she replied reassuringly. 'But they go into a terrible fever, you know. Touch an' go it is.'

'I thought they had drugs to prevent things like that?'

Jinx shrugged her shoulders. 'They do,' she replied, raising her voice a little so that it could be heard clearly by Sunday's good ear. 'But a nurse up at the base once told me that quinine is about as useful as a dose of Exlax!' It wasn't easy for her to make light of this news about Gary, but she was trying. 'Anyway, I'd say that's why you 'aven't 'eard from 'im.'

Sunday wasn't really convinced, so she merely nodded.

'Why don't you write off to his CO in Carolina or wherever it is? I could get the address for you from Mickey.'

Sunday shook her head, and smiled falsely. 'If Gary wants to contact me again, he'll do so. It's up to him.'

Although Sunday obviously felt despondent about this latest news, Gary's name wasn't mentioned again, and after a midday meal of roast chicken and bubble and squeak, the afternoon was spent talking about 'the good and the bad old days' at Cloy's Farm. Sunday heard all the gossip, about how Ruthie, snooty Sue, little Maureen, and Sheil had all now given up working at the farm because so many men were now coming back home to reclaim their jobs. Then they laughed about the fact that Cloy had got himself some new farm machinery, and because he really hadn't the faintest idea how any of it worked, it kept breaking down. Sunday and Jinx had the most perfect afternoon together, and at times it seemed as though they had never been apart. But just as it started to get dark, Jinx said it was time for her to get Junior back to Auntie and Uncle's at Finchley. It was only then that she decided to tell Sunday something that she knew was going to upset her.

'I'm goin' off to America, Sun. Erin's family have asked me to go. They're payin' for everythin'. If I like it over there, I'm goin' to stay.'

Sunday was sitting at the side of Jinx on the sofa when she heard the news, but in the fading light she couldn't see the wistful look on her old mate's face. 'That's wonderful, Jinx,' she replied, once she had taken it in. 'I'm so happy for you – and Junior.' She gently stroked Junior's tiny head. 'How do your folks feel about it?'

'I couldn't care less,' sniffed Jinx. 'Ever since I got 'ome, me mam's been a pain in the arse. I've 'ad so many lectures about the sins I've committed, an' it's all a load of ol' rubbish – unfortunately!' Then her usual cheeky quips gave way to a look of some apprehension. 'I'll miss me dad though. He's a good sort really.' She looked down at Junior for a moment, then quickly looked up at Sunday again. 'I'll miss you too, Sun.'

Sunday took Jinx's hand and held it. 'Don't be silly, Jinx,' she replied. 'We hardly ever see each other.'

'No,' said Jinx, gently stroking Sunday's face with the back of her hand. 'But I think about you more than you'll ever know.'

For a moment or so, both girls studied each other's faces in the rapidly fading light. Then they hugged each other.

A short while later, Sunday helped carry Junior, as she and Jinx made their way to the main bus stop outside the Marlborough Cinema in Holloway Road. Fortunately for both of them, they didn't have to wait long, for the bus came fairly quickly. Jinx climbed up on to the bus platform, then took Junior from Sunday.

'If you ever dare lose contact with me, Sunday Collins,' Jinx yelled back, 'I'll be on the first boat back 'ome!'

Sunday laughed and waved both hands at her. It was a false laugh.

The bus-conductor helped Jinx and Junior into a seat on the lower deck, then pressed the starter bell. As the bus moved off, Sunday went to the side window, where Jinx was waving madly to her. She waved back.

The trolleybus made a silent departure, and missed having to stop at the traffic lights as it made its way up Holloway Road, past the bombed-out Gaumont Cinema, and on towards the Archway. Sunday waited for it to disappear, then went home.

The moment she opened the door of the flat, Sunday could still smell from the kitchen the remains of the midday meal. She sighed, closed the door, and switched on the electric light. The flat was beautifully warm because she had had the gas fire on all day. But even though the tea things were still on the parlour table, she decided she didn't want to wash up the cups and saucers and plates that she and Jinx had been using such a little time before. Not yet anyway. So she put down her front-door key on the mantelpiece, took off her hat and coat, went into her bedroom, and switched on the light. Suddenly lacking in energy, she threw her hat and coat down on to the bed, then lay there, staring up at the ceiling, thinking of Jinx and little Junior. And when she thought of Jinx, she thought of Cloy's Farm, and the girls she had shared the barn with, and Erin, and young Ronnie, and Mario the Italian POW. And Gary. Those few months at Ridgewell had meant so much to her, much more than she had ever imagined. The whole experience was stuck in her mind, like a series of richly coloured paintings, each one of them telling a totally different story. And then she thought of Jinx again, and how she loved her, and how she had loved Pearl. It seemed so ridiculous to love a woman, *any* woman, for a woman could never be like a man, not in the same way. But companionship was different from love. Companionship meant not being lonely. Nonetheless, she did love Jinx, and she did love Pearl. And she missed them – oh God, how she missed them! And then she thought of Gary, and how she missed *him*, and wanted him, and needed him.

Her eyes opened. The first thing she saw was the small framed picture hanging on the wall facing her bed. She'd hung it there herself soon after she got back home from her time on the land at Cloy's Farm. The picture was the one drawn by Sheil, strange, disoriented Sheil.

It was her crayon sketch of a red painted house, seen in the far distance across a wild East Anglian field.

On Christmas Eve, Sunday plucked up enough courage to go to a carol concert at the Mission Hall. She had delayed her decision until the last moment for two reasons. First was that she had been busy at the Deaf and Dumb School helping out with the Christmas party and the Nativity play, which was performed by the children entirely in mime and sign language. The second reason was that she hadn't been to the Hall since the day of her road accident, and sadly, her most vivid memories of the place were all traumatic. However, on the evening of the concert, she decided that she owed it to her mum to make the effort, so, wrapping herself up warm against the biting wind, she took a tram up to Highbury Corner. As she peered out of the tram window from the top deck, she found it so uplifting to see so many shop windows lit up with coloured lights and Christmas trees, for, despite the endless shortages of practically everything from coal to food, toys, and clothing, everyone had made an effort to rise above the drab air of austerity. Someone from the local Borough Council had even shown enough heart to allow the words, 'MERRY CHRISTMAS TO ALL' to be displayed on a scrawled banner across the white façade of the Central Library, and Sunday thought that was a real sign of progress!

When she arrived at the Hall, it was, as usual, bursting with

Christmas joy and exultation. There were home-made paper chains, tinsel and cotton wool draped over framed photographs of humble Salvation Army Commissioners, a beautiful Nativity setting laid out in one corner of the Hall, and a huge Christmas tree on the platform, which formed a wonderful background for the choir of children and 'Army' singers, and the band itself. And there was a most wonderful smell of Camp coffee and chicory, which was being served from a table in the corridor, alongside a selection of cakes and sandwiches made by the delightfully enthusiastic 'Army' volunteers and helpers.

'Welcome home, Sunday!' said Captain Sarah, arms outstretched in greeting as she approached her inside the Hall.

'Thank you, Mrs Denning,' replied Sunday, hugging her mum's old 'Army' friend. Although she didn't agree with the exact intention of the greeting, she appreciated the sentiment.

After promising to have a cup of coffee with the Captain during the interval, Sunday found an aisle seat next to a chattering, excited group of young pupils from the Highbury Fields Girls' School.

The concert turned out to be more inspiring than Sunday had ever known. The band was in rousing form, rustling up every musical instrument they could muster for the occasion, including cymbals, a xylophone, and several tambourines, which gave an invigorating accompaniment to such firm favourites as 'Good King Wenceslas', 'Hark The Herald Angels Sing', and 'Christmas Is Coming'. The mixed choirs sang as though their hearts were full of glory, and despite the curious melancholy Sunday felt, the joy of being able to hear these beautiful musical sounds again after a year of silence and despair, gave her a tremendous feeling of hope for the future.

And yet, there was still a nagging feeling inside that would just not go away. As she watched the delirious happiness of performers and audience swaying, singing, and clapping in time to the music, her mind kept returning to the image of a small child who was found abandoned in a brown paper carrier-bag on the steps of this very same building. Would she never know the truth, never know anything about the woman who had left her there? By the time it came to the interval, she had a curious feeling that there was still one person who could tell her what she had a right to know.

'How long did I know your mum?' replied Captain Sarah, in answer to Sunday's unexpected question. 'My goodness, now you're asking. Long before you were born, that I do know. We joined the 'Army' at about the same time.'

'Then you must remember when I was found outside on the doorstep.'

'Indeed I do!' replied the Captain, at this point unaware of the implications of Sunday's question. 'We were having a Bible class in this very Hall. You were such a loud little thing. They must have heard you all the way up at Highbury Corner.'

Sunday smiled as she listened to Captain Sarah's affectionate reminiscence. Then, with a burning, inquisitive look in her eyes, she asked, 'Mrs Denning. Who left me there?'

The immediate disappearance of the smile on the poor woman's face told all. She replaced the half-finished cup of coffee she had been drinking back on to its saucer. 'Sunday, dear,' she said, careful not to make eye contact. 'You know the situation.'

'No, I don't, Mrs Denning,' Sunday said, shaking her head. 'But someone here does. Why won't any of you tell me?'

'You know as well as I do, Sunday, it was your mum's wish that you know nothing about the poor, unbalanced soul who was unable to take care of you.'

'What about *my* wish?' persisted Sunday. 'Mrs Denning, can't you understand, can't any of you understand how night after night I'm haunted by the image of this woman? She lives inside me every day of my life. So does the man who allowed her to do this thing. Why won't you put me out of my misery? Why?'

Captain Sarah felt a deep sense of anguish, and there was no doubt that, within her, she was struggling against a powerful sense of betrayal to both Sunday and to Madge Collins. 'I'm sorry, Sunday,' she said, slowly shaking her head, with a despairing sigh. 'There's nothing I can tell you. Not now. Not just yet.'

'Then you mean, you will eventually tell me?'

'Eventually.'

Sunday pressed her eagerly. 'When?'

'When the time comes, Sunday. And not before. That was your mum's wish.'

At that moment, Colonel Faraday came forward to greet Sunday. 'My dear child!' he said effusively. 'I can't tell you what joy it brings to my heart to see you here tonight.' He took hold of both her hands, squeezed them tight, and shook them heartily, adding, 'May the Lord be with you!'

As Sunday took her aisle seat again, band and choir resumed the concert with the poignant strains of 'Away In A Manger'.

# *Chapter 29*

On Christmas morning, Sunday was woken by a banging on the front door. She only just heard the distant sounds because she had left her bedroom door open, but by the time she had put on her old towelling robe and shuffled out barefoot into the parlour, the banging was more like thunder. The moment she opened the door, all the Mooney kids came bursting in, excitedly yelling the place down in unison, 'Merry Christmas!'

'Come on, Sun! It's gettin' late!' Alby, the eldest, was already pulling at Sunday's hand. 'We wanna show yer all the presents we've got.'

Sunday took a quick glance at the clock on the mantelpiece. It wasn't even half past seven.

'Farver Chris'mass brought me a smashin' machine-gun!' squealed a delirious Josie, the youngest.

'A machine-gun!' spluttered Sunday, astonished. 'That's not a girl's present,' she said, having in mind the child's pastry-set she had waiting for Josie under her own small Christmas tree.

'She's not a gel,' sneered Alby. 'She's a moron!'

'No I'm not! No I'm not!' Josie started pummelling her big brother.

It was too early in the morning for Sunday to have to cope with all this high excitement. But at least it took her mind off waking up in the flat alone for the first time ever on a Christmas Day.

'What about you, Barry?' Sunday asked, once she had separated Josie and her elder brother.

Barry, who was seven, was the studious one, and he held out a book he had got for Christmas.

Sunday took the book and looked at the title: *How It Works And How It's Done*. She looked baffled. 'What's it all about?' she asked.

Barry shrugged his shoulders. 'Makin' fings,' he replied.

It took her ages to get rid of the kids, for Josie and Alby kept taking crafty looks at the small parcels under Sunday's tree, just in case any of the labels had their names on them. Once she was finally left on her own again, she started to get herself organised. Although she had been invited to spend Christmas Day with the Mooney family, she had a few things she had to do first, like getting dressed, having some breakfast, and finishing writing the labels on some of those parcels which so intrigued little Josie and her big brother!

Whilst she was bustling around, she listened to the wireless. For Sunday, this was a magical treat, and one of the best Christmas presents she would ever have. To be able to hear early-morning carols, the traditional 'Postman's Knock' programme, and one record request after another of popular songs in 'Forces Favourites' was something which, only a few weeks before, she had thought she would never experience again. Sunday repaid this wonderfully restored gift by making an effort to keep the spirit of Christmas alive. Even though she was now living alone, she had decorated the flat with paper chains, written Christmas cards to Aunt Louie, Jinx and Junior, and friends and neighbours in 'the Buildings', and answered the cards she had received from her old mates at Cloy's Farm. She had also bought a small Christmas tree from Hicks the Greengrocers in Seven Sisters Road, and crammed the mantelpiece with all the Christmas cards that people had sent to her. It seemed right that she shouldn't turn her back on the important things of life just because she was living alone. Making an effort was what her mum would have wished.

The Mooneys' flat looked like a fairground. The entire place was draped with paper chains and lanterns made by the kids, Christmas cards were dangling from lines of string suspended from one wall to another, and a huge green Christmas tree bulging with pre-war coloured fairy lights was wedged into a corner of the parlour, making it difficult to get into Doll and Joe's bedroom. There were Alby's gawky, coloured pictures of Father Christmas pinned all along the mantelpiece, mistletoe and holly above every door in the flat, and a plethora of austere-looking toys scattered all over the floor.

When Sunday arrived, she couldn't believe her eyes. When she'd eventually managed to get through the parlour door, step over the second-hand train set Seamus had got for Christmas, and been dragged off by Josie into the kids' bedroom to be shot at by her machine-gun, she was grateful to be able to reach the sanity of the small kitchen, where Doll was attempting to baste a fair-sized turkey before returning it to the oven.

'Who was it said Chris'mass is a time fer rejoicin'?' she complained, face streaked with sweat, and strands of hair from her upswept hair-do dangling down into her eyes. 'This is more like slave bleedin' labour!'

Sunday offered to help, but Doll insisted that she go and get 'that lazy sod of an 'usband of mine' to get her a drink.

In the parlour, Joe was quite oblivious of all the pandemonium that was going on around him. He just sat in his usual chair by the fireplace, reading the sports pages of a three-day-old copy of the *Daily Mirror*, surrounded by his kids who were yelling their heads off in a fierce battle of 'Snakes and Ladders'. Finally, however, even he had enough. 'Seamus!' he snapped. 'Will yer stop that screechin'. You're not a bloody gel, yer know! Now be takin' you lot ter yer own room. This is the good Lord's birthday, and He needs a bit of peace an' quiet!'

Groaning and moaning, the kids were banished to their bedroom.

'Sorry about that, Sunday,' said Joe, draining the last drops of Guinness from his pint glass. 'Why in the world did we have ter have all these kids?'

Sunday wanted to tell him, but she thought better of it. 'I think you've got a lovely family, Joe,' she replied pointedly. 'I envy you.'

'Yes, well yer can have this lot any time you're passin'!' he said. 'I tell yer, if yer lived here, you'd be better off the way yer were – deaf!'

Sunday thought that a pretty unsavoury remark, but as she was perfectly aware that Joe Mooney was not the most tactful man in the world, she ignored it. And when he went back to reading his newspaper again, she knew there wasn't much chance of getting a drink, so she wandered aimlessly around the room casually looking at the Christmas cards and peering out the window at the dull grey Christmas Day weather.

'You know, we're very lucky, aren't we?' she said, without turning.

Joe looked up from his newspaper. 'What was that yer said?'

Sunday turned. 'I said, we're very lucky – to have a roof over our head. When you think of the number of people who lost their homes during the war.'

Joe shrugged his shoulders. 'It shouldn've happened,' he replied.

'That's the trouble with you British. Yer've always got a nose for a fight.'

Sunday stiffened. 'You're not blaming us for the war, are you, Joe?' she said indignantly. 'We didn't start it, you know.'

'No. But it could've been avoided.' He turned around to look over his shoulder at her. 'I ask yer – what was it all about? It was about land, the taking of land that doesn't belong to yer. Just like what happened back home in Ireland. Mark my words, that'll all flare up again one of these days.' He turned back to his newspaper again. 'No. If yer ask me people are too selfish. They want everythin' their own way.'

Sunday thought that a bit rich coming from someone who treated his wife and family with the utmost contempt. She was bursting to ask him if he thought it selfish to go off night after night to shack up with another woman whilst his own wife had to struggle to bring up five kids? And she was dying to ask him which one it was in this household who had everything their own way. 'Any news yet, Joe?' she asked, feeling it wiser to change the subject. 'About when you're all going to move?'

Joe suddenly slammed down his newspaper, and darted a glance at her. 'What's that yer say? Who told you that?'

Sunday looked surprised. 'I thought it was common knowledge.'

Joe immediately got up from his chair. 'Well, it's not. Not yet.'

'So you're not going to take this job – at the car firm in Dagenham?'

Joe went across to her. 'Look, Sunday. I don't know what that woman's been tellin' yer, but *I* make the decisions in this house, not her!' At that moment, he realised that he might be overreacting. 'So what's so special if we do decide ter move out? This is a block of flats. People come an' go all the time.' Agitated, he rubbed his cheek with the back of his hand. 'I'll tell yer this though. If I stand still, I'll turn ter stone, an' that's the God's truth. You know how much I earn as a brickie, Sunday – huh, do yer?'

Sunday shook her head.

'Three bloody quid a week! Just tell me, where's the justice, where's a man's dignity?'

Sunday felt embarrassed, and didn't know what to say.

Then Joe collected his coat and cap from a hook behind the front door and put them on. 'Will yer tell her inside I'm off ter the boozer for a snort.'

Sunday looked bewildered. 'But Doll said we'll be ready to eat in half an hour.'

'Then half an hour it'll be,' he replied, opening the door. 'Oh, and by the way,' he said, turning back briefly, 'I didn't get that job out at Dagenham. They turned me down. No skills, yer see.'

Joe kept his promise, and came back exactly half an hour later. To his kids' delight, he brought with him a vast slab of milk chocolate, which he had apparently bought on the black market from a casual customer over at the Nag's Head pub. But it was kept as a special treat until after dinner at one o'clock.

To Sunday's surprise, her day with the Mooney family turned out to be one of the best Christmases she had ever had. She hadn't expected it to be so, not after Joe's extraordinary exchange with her. In fact, he was amazingly appreciative of everything Doll had done, praising the way in which the turkey had been cooked, playing games with the kids, helping Barry to build a house with his Meccano set, and even doing the washing-up whilst Doll and Sunday had a sit-down in the afternoon. Doll, needless to say, worked like a Trojan. But, she clearly thoroughly enjoyed herself, especially during the evening when the family sat down to a game of Monopoly. To howls of protests from the kids, she appointed herself Banker, and cheated everyone in sight.

By the time she was ready to go home, Sunday was so blown-out with turkey and sausage-meat stuffing, roast potatoes, Brussels sprouts, carrots and cauliflower, Christmas pudding and mince pies, Spam and cheese-and-pickle sandwiches, and squares of milk chocolate, that she could hardly stand up.

When she got back to her own flat, she thought a great deal about the wonderful way in which the Mooneys had helped her to cope with her first Christmas on her own. Yes, she thought a lot about Doll, about Joe, and about the kids. Especially the kids.

In fact, it made her wish she had some of her own.

The day after Boxing Day, Sunday had a most peculiar and worrying letter from Jinx.

34 Ponreath Street — 19 December '45
Swansea

Dear Sun,

Bet you didn't expect to hear from me again so soon!

What's happened is that me and Junior are supposed to be

travelling on the *Queen Mary* to New York at the beginning of January. But suddenly it's all in doubt because of one BIG crisis! They won't let me go!

Apparently, this bloke at the base down at Ridgewell has had it in for me ever since I married Erin, and says that I have no right to 'be a drain on the American tax-payers', because I was married to Erin for too short a time before he died. What it all boils down to is that they won't give me a permit to travel! What a Yankee git this bloke is!

Anyway, to cut a long story short, I have to go and see this bloke and see if I can talk some sense into him. He's agreed to see me on 30 December down at the Base, which is only three days before I'm due to leave! The thing is, you know what I'm like. I go to pieces having to talk to people like this, and I desperately need someone to come along and support me. I *hate* to ask you, Sun, but could you do it? Don't worry, you won't have to get involved or anything, just sit there so's I know I've got someone I can trust. I'll pay all your fares and things, and as me mam's going to look after Junior for the night, I'm pretty sure we can put up at the King's Head or somewhere. I *hate* to ask you, Sun – but I really am *desperate*!

If you can make it, could you meet me at the 'K.H.' at about midday on the Sunday (30th)? If you can't, could you phone and leave a message at our local postie down here? The number's Swansea 53291. You're a brick!

Hope to see you.

Love from Jinx (*and* Junior!)

Sunday was alarmed by Jinx's letter, and absolutely astonished by the callousness of this pokey little snipe at the base. How could he do such a thing, she asked herself? How could he add to the suffering that Jinx had had to endure: a baby like Junior with no father, a loyal and devoted wife with no husband? That's it then. She would go down and support her old mate. And God help that brass hat if he tried it on with *her*!

The journey down to Ridgewell was bitterly cold. As usual, the initial train departure from Liverpool Street was late, and then the poor old unheated bus from Braintree to Great Yeldham seemed to take for ever. By the time Sunday got off at the Waggon and

Horses pub, she felt as though time had stood still, for everything was the same as she had remembered on that ice-cold November day when she first arrived. And as she made her way up the main road towards Ridgewell, she realised that she had never really seen this lovely, gentle countryside in the heart of summer. In some ways, it was painful to return, and she never thought she would have the courage to do so. Too many memories of such a short but amazingly eventful few months. But at least the sun was shining, and as she walked briskly along, clutching her small overnight holdall in one hand, the bare branches of the trees were sparkling with a sheen of white frost. Eventually, she reached the outskirts of the village, and it was then that she felt the first surge of excitement at the prospect of seeing Jinx again.

The moment she entered the public bar at the King's Head, Sunday was amazed at the transformation. Not that the pub itself looked any different, but that the sea of khaki uniforms, combat jackets, crushed hats and peaked caps had been replaced by no more than a few locals in Sunday best. It was puzzling, and for a few moments Sunday wished she wasn't there. Luckily, she was nearly a quarter of an hour early, so she went to the counter, and was about to buy a drink from a barmaid that she hadn't seen before when the local carpenter, whom she had only ever known as John, came up to her.

''Ow are yer then, Sunday?' he asked, speaking directly at her, not aware that for the first time she could now hear his clipped Essex drawl. 'Din't 's'pect ter see you back 'round these parts.'

'I've come back to see Jinx,' she replied, shaking hands. 'D'you remember her?'

The carpenter laughed. ''Course I know old Jinx. Always good fer a laugh, that one!'

They laughed together.

'So how are things up at the Base?' she asked. 'Winding down now, I suppose?'

The carpenter looked baffled. 'Windin' down? Closed down more like. Locked up shop coupla months ago – more or less. Not many khaki boys 'round these days.'

Sunday wasn't sure whether she was hearing right, so she turned her good ear towards him. 'Did you say closed down? The base?'

''Course. War's over, my girl. Din't no one tell yer!'

He really addressed his remark to his other local pals who were playing darts nearby, and they all joined in the joke.

Sunday was now too confused to take in what John the Carpenter had said. Surely he'd got it wrong? If the base was closed, there still had to be some brass hats left there. That's what she was here for.

After John had bought her a shandy and gone off to join his pals at the dartboard, she began to worry. It was now nearly ten past noon, and there was still no sign of Jinx. So she went to the window and peered out to the pub forecourt. Nothing and no one there except a couple of rusty old bicycles and a battered Morris Minor car. When it got to nearly twenty past the hour, she started to panic. So she went to the counter to talk to the barmaid.

'I'm sorry to trouble you,' she said, 'but I'm supposed to meet someone here. I wonder if by any chance there's a message?'

'No message, miss.'

The faint-sounding voice coming from just behind her caused her to turn with a start. At first she couldn't focus on the man who was standing there, casually dressed in a tweed jacket, roll-neck pullover, and warm raincoat. Her eyes widened, and her heart immediately went into overdrive. The face, the smile, the eyes, the nose, that cool blond hair!

'Gary!'

Sunday couldn't believe her eyes, as Gary threw his arms around her, and hugged her as tightly as he could.

At the dartboard, John the Carpenter and his pals had a field day, cheering and applauding the ecstatic couple.

Sunday was spluttering her words out. 'How? I don't understand. Oh Gary – what happened?'

Gary was beaming all over his face. 'That, babe,' he said, 'is a long story.'

And for the first time ever, she heard his voice.

The freshly painted exterior of the Hotel de la Mer glowed brilliantly in the cold, harsh light of day. No one along the terrace had taken the risk of asking Mrs Baggley any awkward questions about from where her hubbie had managed to get the white paint to cover the distinct pebbledash on the front and rear walls, and even if they had, she would have told them to mind their own business. But the tall, narrow house was certainly a striking image, for it was the only one along the entire seafront that had been decorated since before the war.

The previous evening, Mrs Baggley had been fully prepared and practically waiting on the doorstep when Sunday and Gary arrived to take up Gary's reservation. She told them that as it was a New Year's Eve booking, they were very lucky to have a room available, but, as they were regular guests, she was very happy to accommodate them. In point of fact, she only had two other guests, two elderly ladies from East Grinstead, who kept themselves to themselves, and made quite sure that they were down to breakfast and out again before Sunday and Gary had even opened their eyes.

And when Sunday did open her eyes first thing that morning, she still thought that she was in a dream. This was Gary lying at the side of her, his arms clasped around her shoulders, holding her tightly against his body, their legs and feet tangled together in a confusion of tingling, warm toes. She could feel his warm breath filtering through his nostrils and lips, straight on to one side of her face. So while he slept, she turned quietly and kissed him gently, first on the tip of his nose, then on the side of his forehead. Then she just lay there, staring in wonderment at his face, now decidedly more anaemic after his long battle against malaria in the rainforests of some obscure South Pacific island, but just as supple, just as gentle, and just as he always had been. And as she stared and admired that face nestled in the pillow, she could still hear that voice talking to her in the King's Head, the cool, deep burr from Montana: '*I've never stopped loving you, Sunday. Never.*' But she hadn't yet got over the shock of seeing him there, of knowing how he and Jinx had used some cock-and-bull story about a brass hat at the base, merely to trick her into making the journey to Ridgewell. But what if she had said no? What if she had ignored Jinx's letter and stayed at home? She shuddered even to think about it. But whatever else, Gary had kept his promise. He had come back for her.

The sea was quite wild. Gary didn't mind, in fact he liked it. But Sunday wasn't so sure. There was something intimidating about the way the swell rose up all along the shoreline, and then came crashing down on to the pebbled beach, leaving great pools of bubbling white foam. As they strolled along the shore, Gary loved to tease her, every so often pretending that he was going to push her into the swell as it approached. And he loved it when she screamed, and begged him not to, for he could hear the sound of her voice, a different voice to the one he had listened to in his months of soul-destroying high fever. Gary had dreamt about this day for so long, and there were times when he believed that it could never happen. But he was determined that it would. He was determined that this very special Limey girl wouldn't think of him as just 'any other Yank' out for a good time and a one-night stand. He was determined to let her know that he loved her.

'When you knew you were well again,' Sunday shouted, as they dodged back from every ice-cold wave that came rolling in at them, 'why didn't you write to me?'

'Because I wasn't sure you'd still want me,' he called. 'After all those months of not writing to you, I thought I'd lost you. It was Mickey who gave me hope, after he'd heard from Jinx. And when she told me that you could hear again – man! I flipped!'

It was bitterly cold all along the shoreline, with a stiff wind blowing directly at them as they walked. But they had their arms tucked firmly around each other's waist, so they pressed on determinedly, heads bending low against the wind, their coats and scarves fluttering mercilessly all around them. At the far end of the bay, the wind seemed to change direction, so their morning stroll needed less effort. They didn't mind that they were the only people on the beach; it made them feel different, strong, almost superior. But they ended up with blood-red faces and noses, and when they got back to the hotel, Mrs Baggley warned them about Thorpe Bay's notorious windburn. She suggested some Lyons' Ointment and a nice cup of tea with some toasted crumpets and home-made jam. All extras, of course.

After Mrs Baggley's evening meal, Sunday and Gary walked out again along the front, but this time they kept to the promenade. The sea had calmed down considerably, and the sky was as clear as a bell, full of trillions upon trillions of bright stars, and a moon so white that it dazzled the naked eye. They both wanted this night to last for ever, and when they spied an old sailing ketch that had been washed up on the beach during a previous gale, they made their way down to it and climbed in.

'It's hard to believe it's New Year's Eve,' said Sunday, snuggled up cosily in Gary's arms, whilst staring up at the dark night sky. 'I'm glad this year's almost gone. I want to forget it as soon as I can.'

Gary kissed her on the forehead, and then the cheek. 'No, babe,' he said, whispering close to her most precious ear. 'Once you forget a year, you forget all those who were part of it. That's somethin' we should never do.'

Despite the freezing temperature, they lay in the bow of the boat, protected from the cold, frosty air floating above them. At one time, they had remained without saying a word for so long that both thought the other had gone to sleep. But suddenly, they were snapped out of their tranquillity by the sight and sound of a flare shooting up into the sky from a ship anchored somewhere offshore in the distance.

'Quick!' yelped Gary, leaping up in the boat, and dragging Sunday with him.

Sunday was startled. 'What is it, Gary? What's happening?'

'Don't ask questions! Quick as you can!'

He leapt out on to the pebbled beach, stretched up to grab her hand, then helped her to jump down alongside him. As he did so, a whole eruption of light engulfed the sky, shoreline, and the entire town spread out behind them. Firework rockets were shooting up into the dark night, bursting with a loud crack, and cascading into a frenzy of kaleidoscopic patterns and colours.

'It's – beautiful!' squealed Sunday, who was enthralled by the spectacle. 'Oh Gary – just look at it. Happy New Year!'

'Sunday!'

Sunday turned with a start to see Gary's face lit up by the bright flickering glow of the overhead pageant. He was kneeling on the beach in front of her, gesticulating as if in a panic. 'What are you doing?' she asked anxiously. 'Gary, what's the matter?'

Repeating his gestures, slowly and deliberately, he signalled in sign language. 'Sunday Collins. Will you marry me?'

Sunday gasped. She was taken completely by surprise. 'W–what are you talking about?'

'Goddamnit!' he barked. 'Will you marry me, or won't you?'

'I – I don't know. I – don't know what to say,' she spluttered.

'Well, you'd better make up your mind, or I'll kidnap you!'

Sunday wanted to laugh at his quip, but she was shaking too much with emotion to do so. She raised her hands slowly, and, close to tears, signalled a calm and perfectly composed, 'Yes, Gary. I'd love to marry you. I'd love so much to marry you.'

With fireworks still cracking overhead, high in the sky above them, he took hold of her left hand, placed a ring on her finger, and kissed it. Then he gently eased her down on to her knees facing him. 'Happy New Year, Sunday,' he said.

'Happy New Year, Gary,' she replied.

Then he kissed her, warmly, tenderly, and whilst he did so they embraced and rolled over together in each other's arms, down on to the cold, wet beach.

In the far distance, the sound of crowds singing 'Auld Lang Syne' came echoing across the town rooftops of Thorpe Bay. It was a wistful, but truly beautiful sound.

And even Sunday could *hear* it.

# Chapter 30

At the end of the second week of January, Sunday and Gary were married by a special licence at a register office in Islington Town Hall. It wasn't exactly the kind of ceremony that Sunday had always had in mind for herself, for whenever she and Pearl used to talk about the day when either of them would get married, they would dream of walking down a church aisle in a beautiful white satin dress and long lace veil, a handsome posy of flowers in hand, a huge pipe organ playing the 'Bridal March', and a choir of at least a thousand singers!

Well, if Sunday hadn't quite achieved a wedding in the grandeur of Westminster Abbey, her 'do' was every bit as exciting. Practically half the residents of 'the Buildings' turned up to watch her come out of the Town Hall, and as the happy couple came down the white stone steps, they were absolutely covered in handfuls of confetti. And when all the guests had lined up outside for photographs, some of the firemen from the Fire Station next door came out to cheer them on, making quite sure that no one heard any of their ribald comments about the long, hard night the Yank and his new bride could look forward to.

During the ceremony, Helen Gallop had been Sunday's matron of honour, but as all of Gary's buddies were now back home in the USA, he had to make do with Jack Popwell as his best man. Jack was very snooty about a register-office wedding, having only recently been married himself at a rather select church ceremony. Doll Mooney, who was there with Joe and the kids, sobbed quietly all the way through, and by the time it was all over, her newly acquired black-market mascara had smudged all over her cheeks. Alby, Seamus, and little Josie behaved abominably throughout, digging each other in the ribs, and sniggering whenever the Registrar frowned over the top of his spectacles at them. Some of Sunday's mum's friends from the Salvation Army were also at the ceremony, and they sat in the same row of seats, resplendent in their black and red bonnets and uniforms. Pete Hawkins and

Jacqui Marks from the Deaf and Dumb School were there too, and Sunday got the distinct impression that they were getting on really rather well together. The talk of the day, however, was Sunday's two-piece yellow suit, trimmed with black cotton, and matched with a small black pill-box hat. 'Bet she didn't get that on the coupons,' sniffed an elderly bystander outside in Upper Street after the ceremony. 'Yer can say that again!' replied her equally elderly companion. 'Bleedin' Yanks,' she quipped. 'Trust them ter get anyfink they want. 'Specially us gels!'

The wedding reception was a pretty low-key affair. It was held in Sunday's flat, and food consisted mainly of sandwiches, cakes, and quite a lot of booze. As this was Sunday's last day in the flat before she left with Gary for America, there was very little furniture left, for most of it had already been disposed of, and the rest of her belongings packed up ready for shipment. Gary had made a huge hit with the neighbours, especially the Mooneys' kids, who had been showered with candy bars, cookies, and bubble-gum.

Doll Mooney, who had already helped herself to several glasses of Tequila which Gary had brought over with him from America, was very impressed with Sunday's new husband. ''As anyone ever told you that you look a bit like George Montgomery?' she said, ever so slightly slurring her words.

'Who?' replied a baffled Gary.

'George Montgomery,' she said. 'One of your most famous picture stars!'

Gary laughed. 'Sorry, Doll,' he replied. 'I never go to the movies.'

'The United States of America, huh?' said Joe, his mouth full of sausage roll as he talked to Sunday. 'So what are yer goin' ter be doin' with yer life over there, may I ask?'

'Trying to learn how to be a wife,' Sunday replied, clutching on to Gary's arm.

'An' what's that supposed ter mean?'

'It means that I've got quite a lot of catching up to do, Joe,' she replied. 'For this past year or so, I've stopped living. Now it's time to wake up again.'

Gary squeezed her arm in his, and they exchanged an affectionate look.

'No hope for this pair!' Joe called to the other guests. 'Another good man gone to his doom!'

Gales of laughter swept through the crowd of guests.

'Sunday. Can I have a quick word with you for a moment, please?'

In order to hear what Helen was saying, Sunday had to turn her good ear right around and face her.

'Why?' she answered. 'Anything wrong, Helen?'

Helen shook her head, but looked a bit concerned.

Sunday left the group she had been talking to, and made her way through the guests towards the front door.

'There's someone asking for you,' Helen said, looking a shade anxious. 'He says he won't go until he's seen you.'

'Who is it?'

Helen shrugged her shoulders. 'Be careful. I don't like the look of him.'

Helen opened the front door. Sunday went out. Standing outside on the landing was Ernie Mancroft.

Sunday felt her whole body tense. 'What are you doing here, Ernie?' she asked warily.

'Wotcha, Sun!' Ernie replied, holding his hand out for her.

Sunday refused to shake it.

Ernie smiled and withdrew his hand. He was dressed really sharply, in a dark double-breasted pin-striped suit with wide lapels and padded shoulders, a wide, flashy, multicoloured tie, and his short hair combed back and sludged with thick Brylcreem. He looked like what Sunday thought he probably was – a wide-boy spiv.

'I come ter offer yer congratulations, Sun,' he said. 'Looks like the best man's won.'

'We have nothing to say, Ernie,' Sunday said. 'I'm going away tomorrow, and I'll never see you again.'

'I know,' said Ernie forlornly, bowing his head quickly, and then raising it again. 'That's why I wanted ter say sorry – before yer go.'

Sunday looked suspicious. 'What are you talking about?' she asked.

From inside the flat there came gales of laughter as someone told a joke. Ernie waited for the row to subside before he continued. 'I've bin a number-one nut, Sun. An' I wanted yer ter know that I'm sorry for all the 'assle I've caused yer.' He pulled on the fag he had been holding in his hand, and blew smoke up into the air. 'Y'see, you've always bin a sorta release for me. When yer come from my kind of people, my kind of background – well, yer daydream – about beautiful fings, beautiful people. That's what yer've always bin ter me, Sun – a beautiful person. I couldn't get yer outa my mind. But . . .' He threw his fag to the stone landing floor, and stubbed his foot on it. 'As my ol' man used ter say – there's always a time ter move on. An' I reckon I'm about ready ter do just that,' he said, with one of his old mischievous grins. Then he turned towards the staircase, and called, 'Nick!'

Sunday strained to see who was coming up the stone steps. It was a brassy-looking girl, with frizzy black hair, a pale complexion, and a good slap of make-up. She actually had a sweet, smiling face, except that at this particular moment her head seemed to be a little too small for her body.

'Sun,' Ernie said, bringing the girl forward. 'I'd like yer ter meet Nicky. Nick, this is Sun.'

The girl stretched out her hand to Sunday. ''Allo, Sunday,' she said squeakily. 'Yer've got a lovely name. Ernie's told me all about yer.'

Sunday was puzzled, confused. She shook hands with the girl. 'Thank you,' was all she could say.

Ernie was enjoying Sunday's reaction. 'Nick an' me's gettin' spliced,' he said proudly. 'If we make it in time, that is,' he added, patting her belly.

'Ernie!' snapped the girl, immediately blushing. 'Don't embarrass me, for Gord's sake!'

'What the hell're you doin' here!'

Gary came out of the flat, and immediately put his arms protectively around Sunday. 'No, Gary!' Sunday said, quickly restraining him. 'Ernie's getting married.'

Gary froze, and did a double-take.

'This is his fiancée.'

The brassy girl held out a limp hand to Gary. ''Ow d'yer do. I'm Nicky.'

Gary was so taken aback, he shook hands with her.

Then Ernie held out his hand. 'Wotcha, mate! No 'ard feelin's, I 'ope?'

Gary was suspicious, and exchanged a questioning look with Sunday. But the look on her face told him that it was all right, so he shook hands with Ernie.

Ernie had a broad grin on his face. 'I'll tell yer somefin', mate,' he said cheekily. 'Yer got a good right-'ander there.' And to illustrate what he meant, he rubbed his chin. 'An' I should know!'

'Would you like to come in and have a drink, Ernie?' Sunday asked, rather daringly Gary thought.

Ernie shook his head, and took hold of the brassy girl's hand. 'Nah fanks, Sun,' he answered. 'Gotta get the ol' gel 'ome. She ain't gettin' any younger!'

The girl pushed him, and put her arm through his.

'So, all the best ter boaf of yer,' said Ernie. ''Ere's ter 'appy times.' Then he took one last look at Sunday, making direct eye contact with her. 'Be seein' yer then, Sun.'

Sunday looked straight into his eyes, and was shocked to recognise despair in them. 'Be seeing you, Ernie,' she replied, giving him for the very first time a warm smile.

Then Ernie and his girl turned, and made for the stairs. But the moment they had disappeared out of view, Ernie's voice came echoing up the staircase.

'Give me best ter Uncle Sam!' he called.

As expected, the last of the guests didn't leave until well into the evening, and once Sunday had drawn the curtains, she and Gary set about cleaning up, and putting all the remaining bits and pieces into packing-cases. It was past midnight before they got to bed, and Sunday thought it ironic that she should be spending her wedding night in her own flat and her own bed. But tonight was different, very different. After all, she and Gary had slept together before, and she was now wearing a sexy nightdress he had brought for her from the States, which *was* very different to the pyjamas and old towelling robe she had always been used to wearing. But by the time she turned off the light and snuggled down in Gary's arms, there was no doubt that both of them were absolutely exhausted. So, for a while, they just lay there in the dark, mesmerised by a thin shaft of wintry moonlight which was mischievous enough to peer through a gap in the thick velour curtains.

'You know something, Gary,' Sunday said, her voice barely audible. 'I'm scared.'

Gary turned to face her good ear. 'Scared? What of?' he asked softly.

'The future. What it's all going to be like. What I have to do to hold on to you.'

In the dark, Gary smiled. Then he smoothed her hair gently with his hand. 'The future's going to be just fine,' he said. 'We're together, Sun. You don't have to hold on to me, because from now on I'm never going anywhere without you.' He leant over and kissed her tenderly on her forehead.

'The thing is,' Sunday continued, 'when I said goodbye to all the children at school yesterday, I couldn't help thinking about what it's been like this past year.' She turned to face him. 'I still have nightmares. I can see me walking along Holloway Road, with my hands clutched over my ears. I can see people's faces as they yell at me, telling me to take cover. Why couldn't I hear what they were hearing? Why was everything so quiet, so silent? Those kids – I was just as helpless as those kids, running through streets with bombs falling around me, not being able to know how close I was to death, not knowing which way to run, not understanding what I was supposed to do in that horrible silent war.' She paused a moment, then added, 'Gary, I was so scared. I'm still scared.'

Gary remained quiet for a moment before answering. Then he spoke. 'You know why, Sun?' he said. 'You're scared because of the uncertainty, because somewhere inside you're convinced it's all goin' to happen again, that you're goin' to wake up one morning and find you've been plunged back into that silent world.'

'But it's possible.'

'Sure,' he replied. 'But you never thought it was possible to hear anythin' again.' He snuggled up closer. 'Look at it this way, Sun,' he said. 'You have a great advantage over so many people. You've been there. You know what it's like. Whatever happens from now on can never be the same. Just don't ever forget those kids, because they won't forget you. Remember everything you've learnt – about sign language, lip-reading, the whole works. When you meet my ma, show her what you can do. She understands British sign language. She'll help you. We owe it to ourselves to make sure that we keep in touch with any goddamn person who can't hear, can't read or write, or can't see. We owe it to those kids, to all kids, to everyone. You won't be scared, Sun, because I won't let you.'

They lay in the dark for several minutes without saying anything. All Sunday could think about now was how much she loved him.

After a few moments, Gary reached beneath the bedclothes, and removed his undershorts. Then, while he was taking off his vest, he heard the rustle of Sunday's nightdress as she slipped it over her head. He was soon kneeling over her, one leg either side of her. And in the dark, he leaned forward, found her lips again, and pressed his own against them.

And then they made love.

* * *

When Sunday woke first thing in the morning, she had butterflies in her stomach. So much was happening today, leaving the flat, leaving 'the Buildings', leaving Holloway, and leaving behind everything she had known since she was a child. Worst of all was the thought of going on an airplane for the first time in her life, all the way across the Atlantic Ocean, twenty hours in the air, with stops in Scotland, Iceland, and Newfoundland before even getting to New York. Twenty hours! And then that long train journey all the way across America to Gary's home in Montana. And meeting his parents, his sister, and all the family. Oh God! What would happen if they hated her on sight! She was beginning to think it was all a big mistake.

Gary took his time getting up. After all, it was only eight o'clock and the taxi wasn't coming to collect them until eleven. Anyway, the only reason he got up at all was because of the thought of fried eggs, and bread being toasted in the kitchen. So he quickly shaved and took a bath, and in twenty minutes he and Sunday were sitting at the only table that was left in the entire flat, sipping tea and Camp coffee, and making the most of their last breakfast on British soil for a heck of a long time.

Whilst they were in the middle of eating, Gary noticed that Sunday was looking a little despondent.

'What's on your mind, babe?' he asked.

Sunday put down her knife and fork. 'Aunt Louie,' she said, with a sigh.

'Yeah, that's right. She never came back here after the wedding.'

'I know,' Sunday said, leaving the rest of her fried egg and toast. 'I said goodbye to her outside the Town Hall.'

'So what's the problem?'

Sunday pondered for a moment. 'I'd hoped – that she might tell me something before I went. About my mother. My real mother.'

'Sunday . . .' Gary leaned across the table, held her hand, and stroked it affectionately with one finger. 'You're who you are, not where you came from. It doesn't matter who your parents were.'

'It matters to me, Gary,' she said, getting up from the table, and taking her plate to the sink. 'I can't bear going through life with this cloud hanging over me. My mum pledged Aunt Louie to secrecy. There must be a reason why.'

Gary had by now finished his breakfast, so he got up from the table, picked up his plate and put it down in the sink. 'Look, Sun,' he said, holding her round the waist, and looking into her eyes. 'If this is that important to you, we'll find out.'

'How?'

'We'll pay someone to snoop around.'

Sunday shook her head. 'No, Gary. It'll be all right once I'm away from here, away from this flat, away from all these memories. All I wish – is that Aunt Louie could have found it in her heart to – to tell me.'

They were suddenly interrupted by someone knocking on the front door. Both looked startled.

'It can't be already!' gasped Sunday, panicking.

'Don't be a dope, babe!' said Gary, rushing after her out of the kitchen. 'The taxi isn't due for two more hours!'

Sunday pulled her towelling robe tightly around her, then hurried to the front door. When she opened it, she was astonished to see who was standing there.

'Mrs Denning!' she said. 'What a surprise. Come in.'

Still in his vest and shorts, Gary quickly retreated to the bedroom.

'I'm sorry to call on you so early, Sunday,' said Captain Sarah, as she entered. 'But I wanted to catch you before you left.'

Sunday shut the door, and showed her into the parlour. 'I'm sorry I can't offer you a chair,' she said apologetically. 'We've got rid of nearly everything.'

Captain Sarah waved her hand dismissively. It was the first time Sunday had ever seen her out of uniform. 'What I have to say will only take a few minutes. I've got something for you to take with you to America.' She unclipped her handbag, brought out a small oblong-shaped packet wrapped in brown paper. 'It's a little wedding gift,' she said, handing the packet to Sunday.

'What is it?' Sunday asked. 'Can I open it now?'

The Captain smiled. 'Of course.'

Sunday opened the packet. Inside was a small framed photograph of the Highbury Salvation Army Brass Band.

'We thought you'd like a little memento,' said Captain Sarah, pointing out something in the photo. 'That's your mum – there, d'you see, second from the left? Euphonium on her lap, as always.' She looked up at Sunday. 'I hope you like it?'

Sunday was too upset to answer.

The Captain smiled comfortingly, took Sunday's free hand and held it. 'It's our parting gift, Sunday. To tell you that you will always be in our thoughts.'

'Thank you,' was all Sunday was capable of saying.
'Now, will you allow me to do one last thing?'
Her eyes fighting back tears, Sunday looked puzzled.
'May we pray together? Just a moment or so, no more.'
Sunday hadn't expected this. But after all the kindness this woman had shown her, she just couldn't say no. 'Of course,' she answered.
For the next few minutes, Sunday closed her eyes whilst her mum's old friend, eyes also tightly closed and turned skywards, prayed for the future happiness of this 'heavenly child, who will now go forth in the sight of our Lord Jesus Christ, son of God'.
Whilst this was going on, Gary made quite certain that he kept himself out of sight in the bedroom. But he listened at the door, and hoped that Sunday would be able to cope with it all.
When the Captain had finished, she took hold of both of Sunday's hands, then leaned forward, and kissed her first on one cheek and then the other. 'The Lord go with you, our dear Sunday,' she said.
Sunday hugged her. 'Goodbye, Mrs Denning,' she said. 'Please give everyone my love at the Hall. Tell them, tell them they'll always be in my thoughts.'
Captain Sarah smiled. Then, for a brief moment, she became serious again. 'There's just one more thing before I go,' she said. And once again, she dipped into her handbag. This time she brought out a buff, oblong-shaped envelope. 'Take this please, Sunday,' she said rather formally. 'It was supposed to be saved until your twenty-first birthday, but you're not a child any more, you're a married woman. And who knows, I may never see you again. It's from your dear mum.'
Sunday's heart missed a beat. She took the envelope, and immediately recognised her mum's rather shaky handwriting on the outside, which read simply, 'Miss Sunday Collins.'
'No more shadows now, Sunday,' said the older woman. 'May the Lord be with you.' She turned and made her way to the front door.
Sunday went with her and opened the door for her.
Captain Sarah stopped briefly to say only, 'Don't read it now, child,' she said. 'Wait until you've left here.' With that, she left.
Sunday closed the door, then just stood there, leaning her back against it, and clutching her mum's letter to her chest.

Gary had only just finished the packing when Jack Popwell knocked on the front door to say that the taxi had arrived. Again Sunday had butterflies in her stomach, and once Gary and Jack had taken the suitcases downstairs, she was left alone to bid her own farewell to the only home she had ever known.

She knew this was going to be the hardest part of all, standing in the middle of an empty flat which had always been so full of a lifetime's possessions that reflected those who had lived there. She could still see her mum pottering around the place, sweeping, dusting, polishing, cleaning the windows. And the all-pervading smell of carbolic – yes, that was still there, and probably always would be. And as she took a last look in at her mum's bedroom, now stripped bare of everything but the two single beds, in her mind's eye she could see Aunt Louie stretched out on her bed, smoking one of her foul-smelling rolled-up fags, whilst devouring every article and photograph in any women's magazine she could lay her hands on. And Sunday's own bedroom, small and airless, but the centre of her universe since she was a small child. Every room looked so naked, so utterly unnatural. Was she really turning her back on all this, leaving behind all those fond and bitter memories? But it had to come to an end some time. Or did it? Was it really possible that when the eye could no longer see, the heart would forget?

Back in the parlour, she collected her shoulder bag, and took one last look around the room. But something suddenly caught her eye. The mantelpiece. She went back there and rubbed her finger along the surface. It was covered in dust. Without being too conscious of what she was doing, she took a clean handkerchief out of her shoulder bag, then wiped it all along the surface of the mantelpiece.

'Is that all right, Mum?' she asked in a quiet and gentle voice that only she and Madge Collins could hear.

Then she replaced the dusty handkerchief in her shoulder bag, determined that it would never be washed again.

Gary, and Jack Popwell and his wife Ivy, were waiting for Sunday by the taxi, which had parked just outside the Camden Road entrance to 'the Buildings'. Gathered with them was a small crowd of neighbours and well-wishers, who had come to give one of their favourite girls a good send-off. The moment Sunday saw them, she had to take a deep breath to fight back the tears.

'You take care of this young ragamuffin, mate!' sniffed Jack to Gary, his nose red with the bitter cold, his voice determined not to crack under the strain. 'I've known 'er since she was pint-sized. Little perisher she was!'

Sunday bit her lip as hard as she could, then threw her arms around him. ''Bye, Jack,' was all she dared say. Then she turned to his new wife, Ivy, and hugged her too. Behind her, she could hear deep sobbing. Her face crumpled up. ''Bye, Doll,' she said with the utmost difficulty.

Doll threw her arms around Sunday, and weeping uncontrollably, blurted, 'Oh, Sun – I'm goin' ter miss yer so much! This place ain't ever goin' ter be the same wivout yer!'

'Fer God's sake, woman!' yelped Joe, who was standing right behind her, and was thoroughly embarrassed. 'She's not leavin' Paradise Corner, yer know. It's only a whole lot of ol' buildin's!'

'Mum,' moaned little Josie, taggin on to her mum's apron. 'I want ter go ter the lav.'

'Oh shut your bleedin 'ole, Josie!' Doll yelled. Then feeling guilty, she bent down and picked the child up. 'Say bye-bye to your Auntie Sunday,' she sniffed, with tears streaming down her cheeks.

Reluctantly, Josie allowed Sunday to kiss her. Then Sunday turned to the rest of the Mooney kids and kissed them too, though Alby thought it was a bit sissy, and after his turn, wiped his lips with the back of his hand. It took several minutes for Sunday to take her leave of everyone there, and by the time she was ready to get into the taxi, there were calls of 'Be'ave yerself, gel!', 'Don't do anyfink I wouldn't do!', 'Don't ferget ter send us some food parcels!', and 'We'll be finkin' of yer, Sun!' Then Gary helped her into the taxi, and, going round to the far door, climbed in beside her.

As the taxi moved off, Sunday's last view was of all her friends and neighbours waving madly. Then she swung round quickly to peer out through the back window, from where she could just see the Mooney family, hunched together on the pavement, suddenly becoming smaller and smaller as the taxi gathered more and more speed. And behind them, 'the Buildings', proud, erect, its brick-faced exterior glowing warmly in the cold January sun.

Gary knew only too well what this moment meant to Sunday, so he merely put his arm around her shoulders, and said nothing.

Sunday wiped the tears from her eyes with the tips of her fingers, then reached into her shoulder bag to take out the envelope Captain Sarah had given her earlier that morning. Her hands were shaking as she struggled with one finger to rip open the envelope, and when she finally succeeded, she discovered that the letter was several pages long.

My dearest Sunday, 6 April 1945

I'm sure you know how difficult it is for me to write this. I know I've asked myself a hundred times why I've resisted doing so for so long. But after all you've gone through during these past few months, I know that it's against your interests to keep anything more from you. That is why I am asking my dear friend Sarah Denning to give this to you at a time when I feel you are of the right age to understand. The chances are I may not be around to be with you on your twenty-first birthday, so I hope that when you read this, you will understand everything about your natural parents.

As your adopted mum, I know that in many ways I've been a bit of a failure. When your dad died, you were all I had left. I gave you everything I was capable of giving you, and that includes my love. Perhaps it was too much – only *you* can decide that. But I did try. I want you to know, Sunday, that I did try.

In the past year, you've asked me several times about your 'real' mother, who she was, where she came from. I always told you that when you were left abandoned as a tiny baby on the steps of our Mission Hall, the woman's identity had never been known, only because she could not be traced. As you so rightly guessed, that wasn't true – not *entirely* true. The fact is that soon after your dad and I had adopted you, the woman came to see me. She told me of the pain she had suffered in having to part with you, the pain in knowing that she could watch you pass by practically every day of the week. Your mother, Sunday, lived in the next block. She was Bess Butler.

Sunday felt a surge of blood rush to her head. Although the taxi was now winding through streets that she had never seen before, she was too engrossed in what her mum had revealed to notice anything. So she read on.

Your mother told me that before she gave birth to you, she had already gone through two premature miscarriages with other men. You were the third, but when the pregnancy proceeded normally, she became frightened, knowing that there was no way she could cope with bringing up a child on her own. To make matters worse, the man who was technically your own flesh-and-blood father, wanted no part of you, and apparently disappeared without trace. Your mother told me very little about this man, only that he was 'a casual acquaintance'.

What I can tell you, Sunday, is that when you were two years old, your mother and I came to an arrangement. By this time she had married Alf Butler, but he knew nothing about you, and nothing about her previous life. As you know, your dad, my Reg, died just about this time, and Mrs Butler knew the difficulties I was in. That was when she offered to give me a monthly sum to help towards your upkeep. At first I utterly refused, but during the recession it was impossible for me to find a job, and I didn't know how to make ends meet. And so I accepted. Unfortunately, I had no idea at that time how your mother was managing to provide that income. And when I did eventually know, it's to my shame that I continued to accept money from her. The Lord forgive me!

Sunday, you should also know that neither your dad, nor Alf Butler knew anything about this 'arrangement' I had with your mother, and they were never told your true identity. All these years I kept my part of the bargain, and, until the end of her life, your 'real' mother kept hers.

I know how you must feel, knowing that Bess Butler, that your own flesh and blood, was always so close at hand, and yet so far. But the life she led was something I just had to keep from you, and I beg you to understand why I could never allow you to be part of that life.

There is so much I want to say to you, Sunday. But my heart is so full, I have to end here. All I want you to know is that everything I have ever done, I have done for you. In some of the darkest days of my life, you were my one shining light. Try not to think too harshly of me.

We're only here for one short lifetime. Enjoy, love, and embrace yours to the full. As I embrace you.

God be with you.

Your loving mum.

Devastated, Sunday put down the letter. Tears were streaming down her cheeks.

Gary turned to look at her. And she turned to look at him.
'I guess your mum was quite a gal,' he said.
Sunday smiled tearfully. She was still clutching the letter in her hand. 'Oh yes,' she replied. 'They both were.'
The taxi wound its way through the traffic just entering the forecourt of Victoria Station.
It seemed such a very short journey from 'the Buildings'.